handwritten inscription:
may-
9-

Julie

GREEN GRASS
& High Times

one second after.

JULIE MCALPIN RICHMOND

Cover photo: Jon Feingersh

ISBN: 978-0-578-82038-5

Formatted & Edited by: Akapo Afeez

Published by Price Global Marketing, LLC
Naples, Florida
Printed in the United States

DEDICATION

To my husband, Craig, who has delighted me over the years
with spirited stories of his youth, and how those adventures
became the inspiration for this book. Thank you for always
making me smile.

ACKNOWLEDGEMENTS

*A*nother 'labor of love,' *Green Grasses and High Times*, was conceived on a sultry, summer evening as I sat on my back porch overlooking the marshes off Beaufort, South Carolina. With a glass of wine in hand, I listened and laughed to another one of my husband's colorful stories from his youth. If his stories could transport me to a simpler time of innocence and wonder, then I was sure others could delight in the same. I sat there and ideas began brewing as how I could use his stories to inspire another novel. With a mix of local color, Southern manners, dark humor and flawed characters, I knew I had a story to tell.

I put the idea of the book aside for a while as I continued teaching college and raised my daughters, but my mind was never far from the lives of the four boys I had created in my mind. The characters and their personalities were forming, and it was during the Covid crisis of 2020 that I turned back to the Collingsworth boys to put their lives to pen. In those isolated days of our quarantines, the words became paragraphs, and the paragraphs became pages and then chapters. In the span of three months, I had completed another novel; a contemporary, coming-of-age story in the American South when lives were still a bit slower, when honor and integrity still mattered, and when times were simple. The memories made by these boys became the precious things which so many of us now cherish and hold dear in our lives.

And, I can never write a book without thanking those special women in my life who helped me develop such a love and respect for the written word. My two grandmothers, Margaret McAlpin and Mary Richmond, who were mavericks before their time in the 1920's with their love of books, their college educations and their careers before marriage and children. And, my mother, Betty, who tirelessly exposed me to so much history, and never tired of giving me an endless supply of books. If not for these women, I doubt I could have achieved my goals, and I know they continue to smile down from Heaven on each book I write. I love and miss you all.

"In a place you only dream of
Where your soul is always free
Silver stages, golden curtains
Filled my head, plain as can be
As a rainbow grew around the sun
All my stars of love who died
Came from somewhere beyond the scene you see
These lovely people played just for me
Now if I let you see this place
Where stories all ring true
Will you let me past your face
To see what's really you
It's not for me I ask these questions
As though I were a king
For you have to love, believe and feel
Before the burst of tambourines take you there
Green grass and high tides forever
Castles of stone souls and glory
Lost faces say we adore you
As kings and queens bow and play for you
Those who don't believe me
Find your souls and set them free
Those who do, believe and love
This time will be your key
Time and time again I've thanked them
For a piece of mind
They helped me find myself
Amongst the music and the rhyme
That enchants you there
Green grass and high tides forever
Castles of stone souls and glory
Lost faces say we adore you
As kings and queens bow and play for you
Yeah, they play just for you"

Songwriter: Hughie Thomasson
Green Grass and High Tides lyrics © BMG Rights Management

PROLOGUE

*I*t's always a somber occasion when a person dies before they reach old age. If a person reaches their advanced years, then many will find solace in the fact that the deceased surely lived a long life, and most likely a life which had an impact and made a difference in the world; it somehow gives a sense of peace to the remaining family and friends. Any death brings sorrow, but there is nothing more distressing than when a life is taken before they have had a chance to fully live. It may be fate. It may be through self-induced actions, but nevertheless, it is a loss on either account as no life is free from tribulations. Trials and suffering build character and allow for growth, but it is a tragedy when those tests culminate in death rather than victory. While it seems to be a universal metaphor that depression and stress alter lives, it can certainly be said that some people emerge stronger while others experience such agony that their lives never recover from those trials.

Sadness, depression, or melancholy - there are many names attributed to overwhelming feelings of despair. There is no doubt that it is a common emotion which many people succumb whether from a tragedy or trial, or even the perception of such a malady, and it will always be a theme so prevalent in many verses of song, poetry and story. A vast majority of people can manage to weather the worst of circumstances and still move forward, but there is a percentage who cannot rise above any sort of pain, and, unfortunately, they fall victim. The easy way out comes in many accessible forms. Whether it is alcohol to dull the senses, drugs to ease the pain, or something as innocuous as food, it seems that many gravitate to whatever means will grant them the most relief – no matter how fleeting, no matter how dire, or no matter how dangerous, many seek relief in whatever form they can easily obtain, but tragically, many fall victims to the ultimate relief of their pain and leave this world.

The massive greenery of the banyan trees cast flickering shadows over the west churchyard. As the late morning sun did its best to penetrate through the twisted limbs and jungle-like canopy, the shadows appeared to mirror the desolate mood of those gathered in the intimate cemetery. Although it wasn't a large turn-out, it was pretty much common knowledge in any small-town that services are not always open to all, and not all would have even been welcomed anyway. It was a funeral which should have never been. It was a contradiction – plain and simple. The Collingsworth boy was well-known in Naples, and although his family was one of the most wealthy and well-respected, the actions of the son had not always produced stellar results; the pains he had caused clearly touched many. And, while George Collingsworth had made a name for himself in this Southwest Florida haven of the monied elite with his investment strategies and philanthropic efforts, his four sons had always paved their own paths in the world, and it wasn't always the same route as their father.

Trinity-By-the-Cove Episcopal occupied a central location in Port Royal in Naples. With its roots in the staid and formal Church of England, it seemed an unlikely choice of denominations to be the place of worship for the area named after the wild port city in Jamaica. When John Glenn Sample began planning the community in the 1950's he was fascinated by the Caribbean city dominated by buccaneers. So, while the ideas of foraging one's own way, independence and rebellion against the establishment were themes that ran deep in the original Port Royal of Jamaica, there was no doubt that the Collingsworth boys were bred with that same spirit pulsating rampantly through their veins.

Although those gathered were observing the end of a life, the spirit of the renewal was abundantly clear on that late spring morning. As the impatiens and bougainvillea erupted in their vibrant displays of pink, crimson and orange against the white stucco of the Church, it seemed a confirmation of another season of rebirth. And, with a gentle breeze originating from the Gulf, a sweet scent of jasmine mingled with the first hints of humidity when the weather starts to grow warmer along the coastal towns. While several birds answered one another in unison, no one in the group of mourners paid attention to the fowls' lively exchange as all eyes were focused on the rector as his words began the eulogy.

"My dear friends, we are gathered here today to pay tribute to a life that has departed this world far too soon," he began as he clasped his hands on either side of his worn Bible and bowed his head in a solemn moment.

George and Marion Collingsworth were stoic. The couple were closing in on their retirement years. Their hair was silver and thinning, their movements had clearly slowed considerably, but more so, their expressions were drained. It was true that their age had had an impact as they dealt with the tragedy of the premature death of their son, but it was also the level of stress associated with all their sons which had affected them over the years, and it was not something which seemed would end anytime soon.

The three remaining brothers stood side by side.

They were dressed in identical dark suits, crisp white shirts and dark ties. It was clear none of them were attempting to win any sort of fashion contest as everyone knew that the Collingsworth boys rarely wore suits except when necessary. The brothers were far more comfortable in Columbia fishing shirts, ragged khaki shorts and old Sperry topsiders. The brother who stood to the far edge of the group lifted his hand and attempted to adjust the collar on his starched white button-down shirt; it was clear that he was uncomfortable as he stood facing the final resting place of his brother's remains. To his left, the most serious looking of the brothers managed a sniffle and made an exaggerated wipe to his nose before he clasped his hands back together in front of him. And, the third brother raised his hand to push back his Ray-Ban aviators as he nervously shuffled his feet in an area that was void of grass. The third brother did not appear distressed, in fact, he had the beginnings of a smile creasing his lips while he listened to the service.

"And, yes," the rector raised his voice and lifted his hands to the sky. "Our son was a true child of the Lord, and we commend him to Heaven. He gave life, light, laughter and love to his family, his friends and our town of Naples, and we will forever remember his presence among us."

Although the clergyman continued his words, it appeared the brothers had shifted into another world apart from the scene unfolding before them. The words were being spoken, but the brothers also knew the words did not begin to describe their sibling, in fact, it was bordering on the ridiculous to raise him to a level of a saint. All three siblings began to steal glances among themselves, and the slight hints of smiles suddenly gave way to wide grins, but then those grins turned into muffled laughter. As their shoulders began to shake, a coughing fit ensued which concealed their mirth, but the exchange did not miss their mother. Marion Collingsworth looked over at her remaining offspring and raised one of her dark eyebrows in warning. It was a warning like the ones she had given her sons over the years when they were treading on shaky ground, and while it may have frightened them into submission when they were young, it did not appear to phase them at this point. They were grown men, and they were burying the earthy remains of their brother. If they wanted to laugh, then 'the hell with it,' they would laugh.

Their brother was gone, and the way they chose to remember him was not with his ashes being dedicated in this formal area by the Church he rarely ever attended, but rather with a smile on his face and the wind in his hair. As they stared off from the cemetery down the street toward the Gulf of Mexico several memories came to mind, but the most vivid one was of a Saturday afternoon in the summer as he gunned the engine of his Fountain boat and roared it through Gordons Pass south towards Keewaydin Island. With one hand on the wheel, and the other around the waist of a bikini-clad blonde, he was the epitome of a wild-eyed Southern boy. As the boat radio blasted Southern rock, the brothers felt the spirit of their brother they knew so well. There was no doubt on a day like this, he would be in his element as he would be raising his beer and calling out to them, "Hey, what the hell are you guys doin'? Get out of those monkey suits and come on down and join the party – yee-haw."

CHAPTER 1
Landon

My name is George Landon Collingsworth. It's a heck of a name, and when I entered kindergarten I had a tough time learning how to write it, but my teacher was a tyrant and by the time Thanksgiving rolled around I was able to write my parents the most eloquent card for a five-year old. Yes, I thanked them profusely for my life, and all that they had given me, but in the best print of any of my classmates; it was complete with a drawing of my mother, father and myself with my brothers. At that time, we are a family with four boys aged five years to one, and while many would have assumed it was a chaotic household, it really wasn't. My mother ran the home with the efficiency of a Marine sergeant, and as her sons, we knew our limits, but we would soon learn to test those limits as we grew older, and it would be hell for both parents and sons.

My father and mother met at the University of Alabama in Tuscaloosa. He was a senior while my mother was a freshman. It was a Sigma Chi and Tri Delta soiree – "a nut and bolt party" where the boys were given the bolts while the girls were given the nuts, and whichever ones matched then those two danced. George had the bolt that matched Marion's nut, but even before they danced, they had spied one another across the room and their eyes had lit with curious desire. They embraced during that first dance, and the rest was history, but it was a history that was a bit fast-forward.

Apparently, I was conceived a few months after they met. In fact, whenever I hear any song from 1957 whether it's Pat Boone's *Love Letters in the Sand*, Sam Cooke's *You Send Me*," or Elvis Presley's *Love Me Tender*, I have to wonder if my parents were listening to one of those songs when I was created. I suppose I will never know as my parents have never even told us of the exact date of their marriage, and we don't ask. It was a given that there are just some things you don't question to George or Marion, and as the oldest son, I knew that I was clearly conceived prior to their marriage vows, and probably in the backseat of my Daddy's old black Buick; but, it was a subject we never broached as it would not have gone well. It was not even a date remembered. Whenever I heard about my friends' parents going to dinners to celebrate their anniversaries, my parents never acknowledged any date, and as such, it would not have been a prudent thing for any of us boys to mention.

I suppose when you're the oldest child in a family, you naturally assume a role of responsibility. I was fine with it. I strove to always do my best. I walked early and spoke early, and looking back, I assume I was probably needed to help my mother as she had my second brother before my first birthday – "Irish twins," as they're called, but we're not Irish nor Catholic, but people still joked as they labeled us with that phrase. Still, I knew I was meant to adapt and mature early, and I assumed the role without hesitation. And, as much as I thought my parents were busy enough with two little ones, they were also busy themselves as in the next year, another brother was added to our brood. My young mother, who was only 20 years old, had three sons in three years, but hey, it was the late 1950's and there was a post-war 'baby boom' raging throughout America, and my parents obviously were happy to oblige to become part of those statistics.

One of my earliest memories was when we moved into our first house on Lakeshore Drive in Tuscaloosa. Prior to that we lived in a small apartment, but I remembered hearing that my father "got a promotion," and with that promotion, we got a house. It was on a tree-lined street in southeast Tuscaloosa, and while it was upper middle-class, it was still small by today's standards of the McMansions and not grand by any means. Still, it was a pleasant and typical one-story, red brick ranch with white wrought iron porch columns and railings. As we were in the deep South, it was surrounded by the typical landscape of stately pines, masses of azaleas in vibrant colors and gardenia bushes, but it clearly pleased my mother so that made everyone happy. It was a very pretty house, and at the time I thought it looked very much like ones I had seen in my Little Golden story books; I was happy we would now have a proper home instead of an apartment.

And, it was on a lake. While I was intrigued with the idea of having a lake, it was actually just a large pond, but when you're a kid everything always looks bigger. I knew Daddy had talked about getting us a little rowboat, and I could just envision myself leaving my brothers behind as I rowed out in the middle of the water. I would sit out there in the center of the lake, and my brothers would look across the water in envy that I was the oldest and the one able to take the little boat out by myself. Just as I was relishing this vision of solitude in my five-year old mind, I glanced over to the carport of our new house. My parents were busy talking to the bank man on the front porch, but I had spied something bright and shiny in the shadows.

I didn't say a word, but I wanted to yell, "it's mine." Instead, I left my brothers with our parents and made my way across the lawn and walkway to the object of my desire. It was a bright red tricycle. It wasn't one of the little ones like I had at my kindergarten school, but it was a larger tricycle and the perfect size for me at five-years old. I was sure that my little brothers would be too small to even reach the pedals, plus I remembered the adage, "finders' keepers, losers, weepers," and I had found it first. As soon as I rounded the corner of the carport, I grasped the handlebar and settled myself on the seat. It was the perfect fit. I immediately started to pedal away out onto the driveway of tiny pebbles, but I hadn't bargained on the fact that two of my brothers had followed in my wake. They came up behind me, and Boyd, who was two years younger, but much stockier and stronger than me, knocked me aside.

"Get off," he said in what I still considered a 'baby voice.

"It's mine," I remembered yelling back in protest as I tumbled off into the rocks of the drive.

"No, it's not," Boyd countered, and I had to admit he was a determined three-year old. He assumed the same position I had occupied on the seat on the tricycle, but he had to slide down until he was on the seat's edge as his shorter legs needed to reach the pedals.

"No, it's mine," I shouted loud enough, and I knew my parents could hear, but I didn't care.

We had lived in an apartment until this move to Lakeshore Drive, and we had never had any outside toys. I was the oldest. I had found the tricycle, and it was obvious that it was mine. With all the physical strength I could muster in my scrawny arms, and all the determination in my mind, I grabbed ahold of Boyd and pulled him from his seat on the tricycle. He landed with a thud on one of his knees and an elbow which immediately begin spouting bright red blood that exactly matched the red tricycle. I was pleased. I didn't care that he was bleeding, or that he began crying. I was just happy that I had my prized possession back, and I wasn't about to relinquish it to any of my little brothers. If they ever wanted to ride then they would have to ask my permission, and I may have granted it, or not. I was the oldest and I was in control, but I didn't realize at that point Mama and Daddy were walking up behind me.

With one hand, Daddy lifted me by the back of my plaid shirt collar and stood me up-right by the tricycle, and the next thing I knew, I got a swift swat to the behind. As much as Boyd sat still crying and bleeding in the driveway of our new home, I was crying much louder.

CHAPTER 2
Hollis

*Y*es, I am John Hollis Collingsworth, and I am named for the famous Confederate general, John Hollis, who was a relation on my father's side. While it isn't something that I naturally tell everyone when I first meet them, in certain circles, it still does bring a level of respect. It's true that I like the esteem the title brings me, and I get a certain level of joy out of it when I mention it to others – plus it's been good for business now that I'm an adult. When their eyes register the recognition of the famous Confederate general, I relish the look in their eyes as it elevates me. Also, it will be nice to pass along to my children as I'm sure my daughter will get as much prestige out of being a member of the UDC as

I do telling people about it; and that is, the *United Daughters of the Confederacy* for those of you up North, but then again, I do also have to be careful in the politically correct environment of today's world as some do not view the connection in the same way I do.

From the beginning, I feel I have always been Mama's favorite. I am not sure how I knew, but when you're the favored child of all your siblings, it is just an obvious fact. As son number two, I could have easily been shoved aside and forgotten, but when you're in the position, it makes you want to try harder to be noticed, and I surely did. I've always been Mama's sidekick, and I loved spending time with her more than with my Daddy. I loved to go shopping with her at the Piggly Wiggly, and she taught me how to cook simple meals. Mama never ever cooked anything fancy as she liked to go out to eat more than cook, but we would make dinners together like spaghetti, or fried pork chops, or a roast chicken.

And, if we weren't cooking, then we would exercise. Every morning before I went to the little church nursery school, Mama would turn off *Captain Kangaroo*, and move the coffee table away from the front of the television so we could exercise with Jack LaLanne on his show. Mama loved Jack LaLanne, but I couldn't see that all those leg lifts and knee bends did her much good because after she had four boys, she never regained her figure and remained slightly plump. Obviously, Daddy thought something else could help her more than Jack LaLanne as one year he gave her a special Christmas present – it was the biggest-wrapped gift under the tree, but my overriding concern was wondering how Santa and his elves had been able to get it down the chimney.

As Mama opened it, all my brothers and I "oohed" and "aahed," but she didn't seem to find as much delight in it as we did. I remember her saying, "George, I always like gifts in tiny, little packages, and ones that glitter." It wasn't until I was much older that I realized how much women preferred jewelry above all other gifts, and they always preferred that the presents be small, but with a hefty price tag. So, Mama's package was an exercise machine. It was a "shaker." It had a strap which wound around your middle and one around your bottom, and then it would apparently shake you to pieces. I guess it was supposed to shake away the fat, but I don't think it ever helped my Mama as she always looked the same, and it ended up in the basement of our house with clothes hanging over it.

I still remember the time that my brothers and I tried it. Mama and Daddy went to dinner, and, Miss Alice, our baby-sitter was watching wrestling on the television. Once we heard her snoring at regular intervals, my brothers and I quietly snuck out to the kitchen and down the stairs to the basement.

"Who's gonna do it first?" Landon said. He was the oldest, so he was always in charge.

We all stood in silence for a few minutes as we stared at the monstrosity which was three times the size of any of us. It surely looked dangerous and menacing, and I remembered how much it had jiggled Mama when I looked around the door into her bedroom one morning; I had to admit I was frightened at the time, but now with my brothers beside me, I was curious and ready to discover the mysteries of the *Queen's Aid Slimming Machine*.

"Who has the catalog?" Landon announced his second question and was referring to the *Sears and Roebuck* that he had asked one of us to grab from Mama's magazine rack. Landon had the idea that the catalog always had descriptions about their wares, and it might tell us how to work the machine.

"I got it," said Attie proudly as he lifted up the heavy load of the 4-inch-thick publication in the air with both hands.

"You can't read yet– give it here," Landon

remarked with his eight-year-old authoritative voice, and he roughly grabbed it from four-year old Attie.

He sat down on the floor beside the machine and started flipping to the back past all the yellow tissue-like papers in the middle. We watched as he moved through all the pages of shiny Kenmore appliances until he hit the sports equipment section, and then he spied the aqua-blue *Queen's Aid Slimming Machine*.

"That's not it," Boyd said as he thrust his finger forward. "Daddy got Mama the *deluxe* model 'cause look here, it has two belts and not one."

"Okay, okay," Landon said as he turned to the next page and spotted the deluxe model as he began to read aloud, "*Are you tired of trying every method to lose body weight? Would you rather be watching television or napping? Are you tired of spending hours at the gym when you'd rather be shopping, watching TV or going to the beauty shop? Would you like to feel more alive, refreshed and glowing for the man in your life, then the Queen's Aid Slimming Machine is your answer. This deluxe model boosts canvas belts of the highest quality of workmanship, but it also has the most comfortable belts on the market –.*"

"Yeah, yeah," Boyd interrupted. "So, does it tell us how to use the thing, or not?"

"No, just the 'description,'" said Landon in a dejected tone as he used one of those 'big' words he probably learned in third grade.

My mind drifted, and I guessed that Daddy thought that by buying the deluxe model then it could help Mama end up looking like a skinny queen, but all at once we looked over as we heard a commotion. Boyd was kicking aside a laundry basket full of clothes as he plugged-in the electric cord. And, before we could utter a word, he jumped on the flat rubber-matted base and put the wide belt around his upper back and the other around his lower back near his rear. It would have normally gone around his waist or hips, but Boyd wasn't tall enough.

I watched in what seemed like a slow-motion movie as Boyd reached his hand up to hit the round start button, and the machine started. He immediately started jiggling like Mama had, but he was jiggling even more because I suppose he wasn't as big as Mama; still, he wasn't scared. Boyd had the biggest smile on his face as he vibrated.

"What's it like?" Attie asked as he walked a step closer, but not too close.

"It's. . . it's like . . . I'm in . . . one of . . .Daddy's . . . martini . . .shakers," Boyd said in halted words, and he started to lift a hand to imitate Daddy shaking a drink, but quickly put his hand back on the handle so he didn't get shaken off. "It's not scary and it doesn't hurt."

"Come on let me try," Landon said as he reached toward Boyd's shirt sleeve to grab him but missed as Boyd couldn't stay still.

"Okay, okay," Boyd said as he reached down to hit the power switch. It seemed the novelty had quickly worn off as the anticipation was more exciting than actually doing it.

Landon took his turn and since he was a good bit taller than Boyd, the belts fit around him better. His face lit with a huge smile of satisfaction as he was clearly mastering it. He even turned sideways and then backwards in an attempt to show-off to the rest of us and moved his one hand like a Hawaiian dancing girl, and yes, we were impressed. Now, it was my turn, but I wasn't sure I wanted to do it. Sure, I liked exercising in front the television with Mama, but I wasn't sure I wanted to try the *Queen's Aid Slimming Machine*. I was scared, plus I was already pretty slim, and I didn't need to get skinnier.

"Nah," I said as I flipped through some pages of the Sears catalog. "I don't feel like doing it after eating dinner. I might throw up." I acted nonchalant, and glad I had thought of the idea of a full stomach to justify my reluctance.

"You're just scared. Hollis is a sissy," Boyd said in a sing-song voice, but I ignored him and turned to walk toward the basement steps where I sat down on the bottom step.

"I want to try," Attie said as he walked over and got on the flat platform.

"No, you're too little," Landon said as he went to pull the plug from the socket. "You could get hurt, and then we'd all be in trouble." And, with that comment he started piling the clothes back over the slimming machine, and Boyd pulled the clothes basket back to where it had been when we came down in the basement.

Our curiosity of the *Queen's Aid Slimming Machine* had been duly satisfied, and we never turned it on again. Still, when Mama was down in the basement a few days later to get some things out of the dryer she looked over at the slimming machine with a puzzled look. I was helping her fold some towels, but I didn't say anything, and kept my attention on the washcloths. "That's strange," she said under her breath. "I wonder what the *Sears and Roebuck* catalog is doing down here."

CHAPTER 3
Boyd

Some people say that 'three's a charm,' but I am not sure that's the way my parents saw my birth. After two sons in quick succession, I arrived without much fanfare. If you have two sons in consecutive years, then a third one in the following year is a bit of disappointment. I don't blame God that He opted to select me to be born the third son in my family, but let's just say I wasn't exactly welcomed with the same elation I would have experienced had I been a female. I never opted to go the female route, and I would have never remotely considered a gender change as seems to be in vogue in today's 21st century world. Plain and simple, I like being a male. So, as much as my parents may have hoped for a daughter, I am glad I was born a boy; still, I have one brother whom I feel obviously filled that void for my mother, but that's another story for later.

My name is Boyd. It is very short, simple, and it pretty much sums up my personality as I am a no-nonsense sort of guy. My two older brothers were given the fancy surnames from our family, Landon and Hollis, but my parents obviously ran out of available names for me, and I guess I was stuck with whatever seemed available at the time. As I said, I like the name Boyd, and it suits me. I am told that from an early age, I pretty much charted my own way in life, and if someone didn't like me then my attitude was short and simple - "lead or get the hell out my way." No, it wasn't exactly the words I could have uttered as a four-year old as my mother would have surely washed my mouth out with a bar of Ivory soap, but from the time I could get out of the house, I made my own way, and I never gave a damned what others thought – my family or my friends.

You see, I was born in an era when kids were still allowed to live the freedoms of childhood without any restrictions. In the summers, I rose at daybreak before anyone else in my home. I slipped on my cutoff jean shorts and a t-shirt I had usually worn the day before, grabbed a pop-tart from the pantry, and ran out to get my fishing pole to meet my friends. I am not sure my mother ever really wondered where I was all day, or if she ever really cared; my mother wasn't the most maternal-type, and it seemed her priorities ran in other directions, namely her tennis, bridge games or lunches with friends. Many may have assumed that I would have been traumatized by such 'neglect,' but that really wasn't the case in 1960's America. Just as Opie ran all around Mayberry, I was doing the same in Tuscaloosa, but looking back at that television show, I do believe that Aunt Bee and Andy Taylor may have been more concerned about Opie than my mother ever was about me.

Although I was born into the middle of the heat of the Civil Rights in the American South, I have never recalled any animosity towards my darker-skinned friends. Sure, I lived on the southeast side of Tuscaloosa, which was considered upper, middle-class as Coach Paul "Bear" Bryant also lived there, but I was never isolated. My best friend was Jasper, and he was the son of Mama's maid, Tilly. Every Tuesday and Friday, Mama would get in our 'woody' Ford station wagon and we would head out to the farmlands where Tilly lived.

"Mama why can't Tilly just drive to our house on her own. I don't know why we have to get up so early to go get her?" I inquired as I stood on the back seat and leaned over so my voice could be heard over the radio.

"Boyd, you know Tilly doesn't drive," she replied nonchalantly with a wave of her hand as a cigarette dangled from the fingers of that same hand.

"Then, why can't her husband drive her?" I persisted. Obviously, my five-year old mentality overruled any ideas of differences with our stations in life.

"Because, he doesn't drive either," my mother responded.

"Why don't he drive?" I questioned.

"Why 'doesn't' he drive," my mother corrected.

"That's what I said," I answered in a louder voice in case she hadn't heard me since the windows were down and the radio was playing.

"Boyd, I was correcting your grammar, and you know we don't speak like that."

"Well, Tilly speaks like that to me all the time, and I think she's fine," I stated, and then I felt compelled to add another thought. "I never hear you correctin' Tilly's grammar."

"That's enough young man," my mother raised her voice to a tone that meant I was treading in dangerous waters. I stopped and took time to look out the window as we were leaving town, crossing the railroad tracks and heading out to the farmlands where acres of cotton dotted the landscape and mirrored the fluffy clouds in the sky. Once we were outside of Tuscaloosa's city limits, there were no businesses or stores to be seen. There was the occasional small church, or a lone gas station that sold some basic grocery items, but it was mostly fields of cotton. Small, run-down, wood-framed houses dotted the edges of those fields where a cluster of trees shaded homes and its occupants from the hot summer suns. It was a lot different from where we lived on Lakeshore Drive, but I don't think I would have minded living out here west of town. I would have liked all the open areas to run, and there would surely always be someone to play with as all the houses always had so many kids running around the yards. Also, I spied young boys walking along the road with their burlap bags of lunches, and cane poles over their shoulders as they headed to their fishing spots for the day. I think it looked like a whole lot of fun. At that point, "Maybelline" came on the radio, and as Chuck Berry sang about cars, it took me back to our conversation about Tilly.

"Well, I know you have to get a license so why don't they both just go get a license? It just . . . " I paused as I leaned my head down on the back of the front seat.

"Boyd, how many times do I have to tell you that Tilly, being black folk, is different from us," she responded and sounded exasperated as she blew a puff of smoke. It floated back to engulf me, and I coughed as I waved my hand in an attempt to move the smoke away from me.

"But, Mama, I don't think Jasper is 'different' than me?" I said as I then blew back the smoke floating through the air and regained my ability to speak. "We like all the same things 'cause we fish in the pond, we catch grass snakes in our coffee cans, and we like all the same foods like those 'Lil' Debbie' oatmeal cakes with the cream inside."

"Boyd, I know that Jasper and you are friends, and I think that's wonderful. I love that he can come with Tilly when she cleans as you have a friend to play with, but their lives are always gonna be different than ours."

"But, why," I persevered, and reached out to touch one of my mother's dark curls that dangled on her shoulder just in front of me; it was too tempting not to touch.

"Stop that, Boyd, don't you be messing with my hair," she said as she swatted my hand with her hand still enclosing a cigarette between two fingers. "You know I don't like you touching my hair after I've been at the hairdressers."

"Sorry, Mama," I replied and sank back down in the back seat to play with my slinky.

Little did either of us know that on that summer morning in June across town it was not the peaceful scenes we witnessed as we drove out to Tilly's home. Those idyllic summer images were not present near downtown; a march and riot were taking place. A new courthouse had been built, and while the Blacks had been promised it would be integrated with water fountains and restrooms, it was not the case. The 'Jim Crow' laws were still clearly displayed on signs in the halls, and this did not set well with the local Reverend Rogers. With backing from Reverend Martin Luther King, Jr., a march was organized, but it barely got out of the church doors and never made it the few blocks to the Courthouse. The marchers were met with tear gas, beaten and arrested, but Mama and I had no idea as we drove out of town that day. We would later find out that Tilly's younger brother, who was home that summer from Tuskegee, was one of the protesters who would be admitted to the hospital for injuries, and I would always remember how quiet Tilly had been that summer morning when we picked her up. She got in the back seat with me, but she didn't look over and smile or talk to me as she normally did when Mama drove us home. She just stared straight ahead.

When we got back to our neighborhood, she never glanced out the car window to see the neighbor boys riding their bikes over to the baseball field, the milkmen in their white uniforms dropping off bottles on the front steps of homes, and she didn't even wave to the other black maids pushing baby carriages under the shade of the oaks.

To this day, I can still remember the scent of freshly tilled Alabama soil and the sight of those young cotton plants struggling to take hold as they reached to the sky for their sustenance to survive – all living things whether plant, animal or human, we all have a universal need and longing to not just survive, but to flourish in this world. Now, as I remembered those days, I began to hum that along the song that always brought me back to those days of my youth.

When I was a little bitty baby
My mama would rock me in the cradle
In them old cotton fields back home
It was down in Louisiana
Just about a mile from Texarkana
n them old cotton fields back home
Oh, when them cotton bolls get rotten
You can't pick very much cotton
In them old cotton fields back home

CHAPTER 4
Attie

*I*f you've ever read *To Kill a Mockingbird*, then you've heard the name of Atticus Finch. Apparently, my mother was quite taken with Gregory Peck when the movie came out in 1962. She had read the book, and when she saw the movie, it was a done deal that if her last child was a boy, the baby would be named Atticus, but at least I was able to skip the bird-associated part of the name. I was christened William Atticus, or it would be shortened to 'Attie' by my older brothers which was fine as it clearly suited me better. Although I had dark hair and eyes like Gregory Peck and his character, Atticus Finch, I never aspired with lofty goals as an actor or lawyer. Sure, I had ample opportunity to pursue any profession I studied when I went to college, but I always opted for the more carefree path in life. I always figured life was short, and it was best to have some fun along the way, but then again, I was not an enigma in my family as my three brothers also tested the limits in their day, too.

So, yes, George and Marion ended up with four sons in the span of five years, and I was the baby. I know they would have preferred if I would have been a girl, but that was not the case. Later when I was an adult, I would read in a medical journal that it stated, "men in high stress jobs tended to conceive daughters, while those in low stress jobs more likely conceived sons." I never thought much about it at the time, but I assume my Daddy must not have been too stressed in his job, so he had four boys. I have to believe my mother would have advocated for another career for my father had she known those statistics as she always wanted a daughter; still, my father provided well, so, ultimately, I think that was paramount above all things as Mama liked a comfortable lifestyle.

Yes, Mama led a charmed life. By the time I was in kindergarten, she had Tilly coming three days a week, and Tilly would have probably been there five days, but

Mama didn't like having to drive out to the country to pick her up and then take her home in the afternoon. Mama liked her bridge parties, her tennis matches, and her lunches with her lady friends at the Tuscaloosa Country Club, but also shopping downtown to get new dresses and hats. She was so excited when Daddy was made manager at the brokerage office and she made a point of telling all her friends that, "George is the youngest man to ever become a manager of any brokerage office in America." I didn't quite understand that since I was only four, but it made Mama smile more, and I suppose that was a good thing.

The only problem was that Daddy worked a lot and was always really tired. He usually fell asleep right after dinner in his easy chair each night, and then would eventually get up and go to bed. Mama never went to bed early with Daddy because she claimed she was never tired, but I also figured that was because she always "retired" to her room every afternoon for her naps with her novels. So, after Mama would put us to bed at 8:00, she would always stay up and watch her television shows. And, while she enjoyed *Peyton Place, The Ed Sullivan Show* or *The Twilight Zone*, she also loved her favorite snack, French Bon-Bons.

I don't think anyone was supposed to know that

Mama indulged in her French pleasures when everyone else was in bed because she always hid the fancy tin container with the French words on it. It was always placed on a high shelf above the refrigerator, but my brothers and I knew about it and sometimes we would sneak one of those little French chocolate bon-bons. We never took more than one a piece, and we never took them too often, or Mama was sure to find out. One time, she seemed to notice a few were missing, but I think she just blamed it on Tilly – poor Tilly.

While Mama normally ate her bon-bons on cozy, winter nights, we would get our treats with her in the summers since we didn't have to go to sleep as early. Once Daddy started his snoring from the bedroom, she would call us boys from our rooms, and she would load us in the station wagon. It didn't matter that we had on our cowboy and Indian pajamas as we never got out of the car. Mama loved to go to the Qwik-Mart to get snacks to enjoy with her evening shows. She always walked out with four little brown bags filled with a dozen of penny candies for each of us boys, and she even let us eat them all in one sitting, but of course, we had to brush our teeth before bed.

And, while this was a treat, I would always remember the one summer evening when the sun was late setting; it was an evening that scared me to death. It started out as any normal trip to the Qwik-Mart, and while Mama went into peruse the aisles for snacks, we boys remained in the car, but that one-night Mama must have been extra hungry because she hurried out of the car. Just as she had entered the store, the car started moving very slowly. Although at first, I thought it was just my imagination as my brothers were bouncing around on the seats and Landon reached over to swat at them, but it wasn't my imagination. We had definitely started moving backwards down the slight decline. Landon and Boyd were arguing so they weren't paying attention, but I had been looking out the side window and I noticed that it looked like those dang pine trees were moving, but it wasn't the trees moving, it was our car.

"Hollis," I said in a real quiet voice as he was next to me. "How come we're moving, but Mama ain't driving?"

Hollis looked up from his Etch-a-Sketch but didn't seem concerned at first. I pointed out the window, and by the time it registered with him, we had picked up speed.

"Landon," Hollis said in a shaky voice.

"I don't care what you think," Landon said as he punched Boyd in the arm in the way back of the station wagon as they continued their argument.

"Landon," Hollis uttered again in a louder voice.

"We're moving."

Landon released his grasp from Boyd's arm and looked around. He immediately reached for the door handle on the back panel, but before he could open it, we saw a man in a blur of white rush up to the back of the car. He was a big man, and I guess that was good 'cause he stopped our car right then and there before it rolled out to the street. Another man came over to help him, and then one of them came up to the driver's door and opened it.

"You kids okay?" He asked looking in at the four of us.

We all nodded our heads in unison, and he seemed like Superman in our minds, but he was really just our milkman who delivered milk to our house every other day. The two then pushed our car back up into the parking spot where Mama had left us. The larger one reached over to the steering column and placed the car back in park, and then pulled the emergency brake for extra protection. Both men gave us a military salute as they walked away, and we fumbled salutes back at them.

Mama came out shortly and handed us each our little brown paper sacks of candy, but I don't think she ever realized how closely we came to having an accident that night, and I don't think the milkman ever mentioned it

when he came by our house on the 'milk mornings.'
Sometimes things are just best left alone and unsaid.

1999

CHAPTER 5
Landon

And I was born in the back seat of a Greyhound bus
Rollin' down highway forty-one
Lord, I was born a ramblin' man
Tryin' to make a livin' and doin' the best I can
And when it's time for leavin'
I hope you'll understand
That I was born a ramblin' man

I sang along to the lyrics of Marshall Tucker's song as I drove along Highway 41, Tamiami Trail, to downtown Naples. Even though I surely would have never been a member of their band, it didn't stop me from enjoying the moment. I know that I am not the only one who feels songs are major defining parts of our lives. Whenever memorable lyrics or a melody emanates from that radio dial, we are transformed. We can remember the exact time and place we heard a particular song. We remember the event that came to define that song in our lives, and inevitably, we turn up the volume in hopes of a few minutes of 'time-travel' so we can return to that brief period in our lives. While most songs bring us back to those memorable times of joy, there are also songs that bring about feelings of indifference, or even pain; and sometimes, those memories are unfortunately intertwined.

So, while I was obviously not born in the 'backseat of a Greyhound bus,' it was a trip that would ultimately change the course of my life and my future. You see Mama and Daddy were headed down to Naples, Florida to see about Daddy starting a brokerage firm, but we didn't know it at the time. All my brothers and I knew was that we were headed up to Louisville to see our grandparents that summer. I was ten, Hollis was nine, Boyd was eight, and Attie was six, and we stood stoically by our mother's side when she paid our fares at the ticket counter. We later learned that it wasn't simply a three-week trip for us to spend time with our grandparents, but rather, the truth was that Mama had reached her limit in mothering skills that summer, and she was sending us up earlier so she could have a break before her trip to Naples.

"Here are the tickets," Mama said after she concluded the transaction with the clerk, and then turned to hand them to me. "You're gonna have to give these to the bus driver and then he'll tear them in half. He'll hand you the other side, and then just stick it in your pocket, but don't lose them."

I nodded, but I couldn't help but watch Attie dance around and hold his crotch. "Mama," I interrupted.

"What now, Landon?" She said in an exasperated tone as she looked at me after shutting her purse with 'that look' I knew so well.

"I don't need anything, but Attie does. I think he needs to go to the bathroom."

"Fine," Mama said as she pursed her mouth in a grimace, glanced at Attie, and then looked at me with one raised eyebrow. "Go on then and take him to the toilet."

While I was gone, she shuffled Hollis and Boyd to the benches to wait while she proceeded to maneuver our two duffle bags near the boarding area. When I returned, she handed me four brown paper bags. "Now, in here are some sandwiches and cookies that Tilly made y'all, and there are apples and peaches," she said as she opened one bag tHo show me and then rolled the top back down.

"Landon, you're the oldest so make sure they all get them, and don't go eating them all at once. Tilly also wrapped up some wet washcloths in case you get messy. Now, this food is supposed to last you until you get up to Louisville, you here – so don't go eating it all at once."

I took Attie's hand and proceeded to sit down beside my brothers, and then we all four nodded in unison.

"Now, your bus is gonna be leaving in just a half-hour so I want you all to just sit here and behave yourselves until it gets here," she said as she opened her pocketbook and began to rummage for her car keys.

"Mama?"

"Yes, Hollis, what is it?"

"Well . . . , well . . ." he stammered, but he stopped suddenly when he saw her look. We had all learned early-on not to push Mama too much, and he knew his stuttering irritated her.

"Now, I'm gonna head on out as I need to get to my tennis match, and I can't be holding up the other girls or they get upset." She shut her pocketbook with a click and held it in the crook of her elbow. A little maternal instinct obviously surfaced as she leaned over and gave a quick pat on the shoulders to each of us before she turned and walked away with her tennis shoes making squeaking sounds on the terrazzo floor.

To this day, every time I see those damned colorful chips in any terrazzo floor, I get that same sinking feeling. I know it's ridiculous, but while my brothers and I sat there and waited, I had nothing else to do but to look at that array of colors dancing as the sun cast shadows. A few years ago, when my medical office was being built, it was suggested that the waiting room floor have a terrazzo floor, and I nearly lost it. My partners had no idea why I was so adamantly against the choice as it fit into the Spanish design of our office, but I just couldn't do it. I just couldn't walk in the front door each morning and be greeted by those dancing specks of color.

In my family, it's pretty much an unwritten rule that we don't talk about feelings. We don't talk about childhood memories, and we don't question our parents on any issues even if it comes out as a joke. I've tried several times, and I was shut down; the same with my brothers. Yes, I would damn well like to know why our mother didn't give a flying fuck about us, or why she was such a cold-hearted bitch, but can't go there. To quote George H.W. Bush, "it wouldn't be prudent," so even as adults, we shut-up and we don't question.

So, as the last lines of *Ramblin' Man* ended on the

radio, I pulled my car off the road and drove into an empty gas station on Tamiami Trail. I didn't have to meet my first patient for another hour, so I had plenty of time. I parked over by a hedge of neatly trimmed Ficus trees, looked around, and then opened the glove box. I pulled out the baggy of white powder and proceeded to find my relief. In just a matter of a minutes, I felt calm. I felt as though all was right with the world, and that sense of longing was satisfied – at least for a little while I felt the comfort I was missing.

CHAPTER 6
Boyd

I want you to know that I am not here by my own accord," I offered in a measured voice so I would not be cast in the role of a willing participant before this damned thing even began.

"Yes, Mr. Collingsworth, I am well aware that your wife made this appointment, and I have it here in my notes," Mona, the therapist, answered, but then paused as she placed her John Lennon glasses back on her face, and flipped through her papers on the clipboard. "Let's see, your wife's exact words, 'He doesn't want to come to counseling, and he said he would rather sleep with Hillary Clinton than talk to some therapist.'" She lifted her glasses slightly off her nose as she looked at me, and I then I glanced over where I noted her Clinton/Gore 1996 sticker on the backside of her computer – guess I had majorly fucked up before we even got started, but whatever? I really didn't care.

Anyone who knew me would guess that I sure as hell did not want to be in this office reeking of cinnamon potpourri, plants hanging from macramé planters, and New-Age music flowing from the CD player. As far as I was concerned, this woman was a freaking hippie, and I had to think my wife was pretty much the same. Libby wasn't when I married her; she was a cute blonde who liked to fuck, but that quickly changed once I put the ring on her finger. Now, she claimed she was an 'artist,' a vegetarian, and she would have preferred to live on an Oregon commune than in our four-bedroom, three bath home on the water on Marco Island. In all honesty, I knew most women would have loved to have had our upscale home with a weekly Hispanic maid, and me, as a husband, who footed the bill. And, it wasn't as though I was some sort of repulsive, overweight middle-aged man. I wasn't hard on the eyes, or so I was told by other women, and enough of them had mentioned I was a dead ringer for George Clooney, so why in the hell wouldn't my own wife want to have sex with me? Now, she claimed that our 'marriage needed therapy." What the hell did that mean? She lived a great life with an

GREEN GRASS & High Times

enviable home, bills paid, healthy kids, and she basically did whatever the hell she wanted – that is, thanks to my hard work and generosity, and was it too much that I wanted a blowjob or sex on a weekly basis? Absolutely not. Maybe I should tell that to this therapist, and gage Mona's reaction to the fact that I had a frigid wife who didn't find me attractive or want to have sex anymore?

"So, Libby, please tell me what you feel are your 'wants and needs' in this marriage? What do you feel you need from Boyd in order to feel fulfilled?"

I looked at this fuckin' freak of a woman with her hair cut shorter than mine, heck it was worse than a new Marine recruit, and she sat there in her flowing African silk garb as though she were tribal queen passing judgment.

"He doesn't engage," Libby said with a heavy sigh as though it pained her to even say the words. "He is distant . . ." She hesitated, uncrossed and then crossed her legs again. "You know. . ."

Libby stopped and looked from me to the therapist as though she needed help forming the words. "Please, Libby, do go on as I sense you're delving into your inner self, and the emotions which are causing you such pain," she added with a knowing smile.

"He gets up early in the mornings and goes for a run

41

before work, then he doesn't come home until late, and usually the kids are in bed. Then, don't get me started on the weekends," she paused and rolled her eyes. "He's either off in his boat or takes that damned dog out hunting."

I turned my head to the side and rolled my eyes at the bullshit I was hearing from both women. I had nearly reached my limit, and I was ready to walk.

"So, I am the one who is left to take care of the home, the kids, drive them to school – you know, I am exhausted, and I need support. I need help. I mean, they're his kids, too."

"Yes, yes," Mona nodded as she viciously scribbled and then flipped to a second page to add even more notes about my bad behaviors. Hell, she would have a mini novel by the time we left here today.

"Well, I was watching an episode of 'Dr. Phil' last week, and it made me feel empowered," Libby began in earnest, but then stopped suddenly as her words clearly encouraged the therapist-mode in Mona, and the older lady moved forward on her chair in rapt attention.

"Please do go on," Mona urged.

"So, when Boyd came home, I met him at the door. I told him that whenever he drove home from work every day, he needed to use that time to focus on what he could do to make my life better."

"Yes, Libby, I do agree that would be a good use of time for Boyd. He could certainly turn off his stereo and use those valuable minutes for self-reflection to think about how he could be a good husband and father. Ultimately, one is always more content and satisfied if they look beyond their own wants and needs to focus on those who are closest to them."

I literally snorted, and I stifled my urge to start laughing. After all that I had done for this woman who came from nothing in her former life, and now lived like a queen, it was beyond belief. Both Libby and Mona looked at me with disapproving stares, but I wasn't about to give in and admit defeat because I knew I had done nothing wrong. I was a good husband. I worked hard and provided, and I had been faithful for 12 years even though God knew I had my opportunities to cheat more than a few times.

"So, Boyd, now I would like to concentrate a bit on your background – your childhood," Mona began, and turned to focus her beady eyes on me.

While I clearly wasn't comfortable, I'd still be damned if I would let these two feminist freaks get to me. There was nothing in my past that would show me as an uncaring or callous male, and I would show them.

"Do you have any siblings?"

"Yes, three brothers, but no sisters," I answered flatly.

"So, you basically grew up in a home filled with brothers?" She asked.

I nodded as it was an obvious fact that I had just stated, and I wasn't sure where she was going with her questioning. "Do you think that you may have difficulties identifying with the feminine agenda?"

"Feminine agenda?" I asked with raised eyebrows as I was not about to get caught up in any of her feminist hyperbole.

"Yes, I am sensing that you may have issues with women in your life due to the fact that you grew up in a home with boys, and you may not have been able to experience your feminine side."

Again, I snorted and shook my head. "No ma'am, I totally love and respect women, and all that they do in this world. I just believe there is a distinct division between males and females, and those lines are not blurred."

"Okay," Mona uttered a bit more slowly as she scribbled more words on her clipboard. "So, Boyd, you are clearly an alpha male," she stated flatly and then stopped as she looked up at me to fathom how I would accept her deduction.

I was not about to take her bait, so I acted nonchalant. If she wanted to play games then I could do it, too.

"Let's move on. Please, tell me about something that you remember from your childhood. I would love to hear about your relationship with your mother, and your brothers. Could you tell me about any episode when you felt vulnerable? Or maybe when you felt that you were able to be there for one of your brothers?"

I hesitated for a few moments as I wasn't really sure how much I wanted to share with Mona. No childhood is perfect, but I had a pretty good one compared to things I have heard from others. I wasn't one to dwell on the past and try to put some sort of psycho-babble analysis on everything. Still, it was so quiet in the room that I couldn't stop my mind from conjuring up some memories, and my thoughts went back to those of my childhood in Alabama. I went back to that one summer when Landon had his accident.

"Y'all come on down here and git in the car," our mother yelled from the driveway. She was sitting in the driver's seat of the woody station wagon, ever-present Winston cigarette in hand, and calling for us boys to join her. As usual, it was taking us a while to make our way to the car. It was one of those typical late summer mornings in Alabama. The heat was already intense even though it was not yet mid-day, the mosquitoes were biting, and the only relief to be found was by either drinking an ice-cold Coca-Cola, or swimming at the Tuscaloosa Country Club's pool. While it appeared that my mother was rounding up her boys to go on a family excursion, the truth was that it was an activity that brought relief to my mother. Our mother wasn't exactly the 'Kool-aide Mama' in the neighborhood. She didn't bake cookies and she never hosted the neighborhood children in our kitchen. No, this would have driven our mother insane. She clearly needed her time, and my brothers and I understood. We never questioned this, and we never dared push the issue as we knew it would not end up well. Although she was the mother of four boys, our mother was not the most maternal. I would never say that she neglected us, but she did the bare minimum, and we had learned to abide by her rules.

"Mama, I fed and watered the puppies," Landon announced proudly as he bounded into the front passenger seat and slammed the door. As the oldest, he always claimed the front seat with Mama while my brothers and I made our way into the backseat and sat side-by-side, although Attie preferred to stand and lean against the back of the front seat since he was still small and wanted to see what was going on with Mama and Landon.

"Thank you, Landon," Mamma muttered as she allowed the cigarette to dangle from her lips and put the car in reverse.

"Well, I made my bed," said Hollis proudly of his efforts as a seven-year-old.

"Yeah and bet ya put your Raggedy Andy doll right on your pillow," I added in a girlish voice.

"Stop it, Boyd," Hollis cried defensively, and gave a weak push against my arm.

"You even 'hit' like a sissy," I shot back.

Both Landon and Attie were taking pleasure in watching the exchange between Hollis and me, and they didn't utter a word, but I also knew if Mama weren't in the car then they would have been urging me on to get the best of Hollis.

"That's enough boys," Mama raised her voice as she started backing out of the driveway. Once she started down our winding street, she managed to flick her cigarette ashes out the window and turned up the radio volume all in one motion.

We always knew when Mama turned up music, it was her signal to us all to hush. Since we all enjoyed the popular songs, it wasn't too much of an inconvenience to stay quiet. Mama may have been married with four children, but she was still only 28-years old, and we all knew she loved her rock 'n roll, and she loved it when she could dance with Daddy at the Tuscaloosa Country Club dinners on Saturday nights.

The summer of 1968 was a hot one, and not just in temperatures, here in Alabama. Even though I was a kid, everyone knew about Dr. Martin Luther King's assassination in Memphis just before Easter, and then President Kennedy's brother was killed right after school let out for the summer, but still those two deaths didn't even compare to the many in Vietnam that were shown on the evening news Daddy watched every night. In all honesty, I knew these things were bad, but it didn't seem to impact my world as a kid. I figured I would have enough death to deal with as I got older; it was an adult-thing.

After we pulled into the Tuscaloosa Country Club and parked, Mama walked us over and handed us over to one of the teenage lifeguards who watched the kids at the pool. I looked up to give Mama a smile and a hug, but she seemed in a hurry as she carried her tennis racket and made her way to the courts. I just shrugged my shoulders and followed my brothers. As much as we wanted to start swimming, we were also hungry, so we made our way over to the hamburger hut to order our lunches.

"How's you boys doin'?" Miss Julia called to us from behind the counter. Miss Julia was our friend. With her hair covered by a colorful turban and a broad white apron smeared with black charcoal, she smiled her broadest smile as the smoke from the grill swirled around her, and I swear it looked like she was a ghost or some voodoo witch coming out of a swamp fog.

"We're just fine," piped up Hollis as usual, and he went front and center to place his order. "I want two hamburgers with cheese, Lays chips and a root beer float."

"Stop it, Hollis," Landon interrupted. "You know you can't have two hamburgers or a root beer float 'cause Mama says you're already too chubby."

Hollis frowned and slunk to the side of his younger brothers, and I knew he was hoping that no one else had heard the exchange. Still, it was true. Hollis loved to eat, and he loved to sit and watch his television shows instead of going outside to play with the rest of us, and as a result

Mama had to buy him 'husky' sized clothes at Sears & Roebuck in the past year.

Miss Julia never missed anything as her quick black eyes caught it all, and she leaned down her own ample frame and gave Hollis a reassuring pat on his shoulder. "It's okay, Master Hollis, you's gonna grow tall and strong, and you won't always be like this. I even think you's gonna win the most quarters today."

I heard Miss Julia's words to Hollis, but I was determined that he would never win any of the summer swimming competitions. I had been the 'king' of the quarters' game for the last two summers, and I wasn't about to let my winning streak slip.

Once we all had our little red plastic baskets of hamburgers and chips, we made our way over to one of the round cement tables and settled ourselves. It was the general belief of all the adults that we had to wait one-full hour after eating before we could swim as to avoid cramps, but we ate fast, and it was known to the kids that the tallest teenage boy usually made his way to the pool clock to covertly move the second hand up a bit if no one was looking. Today, looked to be a day that seemed a possibility as the other lifeguards who were on break from the University were flirting with the teenage girls. So, within 20 minutes rather than one hour after our lunches, I led the rest of the kids to the pool with a hoot and holler, and I did my famous cannon ball into the deep end of the pool.

Miss Julia was watching from the hamburger hut, and she gave an approving smile and nod to me as I emerged and shook the water from my soaked head of hair. While swimming to the side of the pool, I had to wonder how lucky Miss Julia's children had to be to have her as their mother. She always seemed to pay attention and care about children, so I was sure she was a good mother. I only wish my own mother could be sitting there on the side, and smiling at me right now, but that thought quickly evaporated when my good friend, Steve, aimed a water pistol at got me right in the face.

"Hey, Steve, cool it," I said using one of the expressions I had heard the teenagers using lately.

We were all anxiously awaiting two o'clock as that was the time of the annual "Quarters Race," and I was determined to be champion for another year. It was a tradition that toward the end of the summer all the lifeguards would gather together and throw handfuls of quarters in the pool, and while we had to wait for the coins to sink to the bottom, it was then a mad dash for all the kids to race to get as many as they could. Last year, I collected

$5.25 which was an enormous sum for an 8-year-old boy in the 1960's. Last year's winnings found me purchasing a model airplane set, a kite, a water pistol, Marvel comic books, and the rest I spent on penny candy from the Qwik-Mart.

The head lifeguard sounded his whistle for the kids to assemble. With the girls on one side of the pool and boys on the other, we patiently waited, but we all bounced up and down in anticipation. When I was younger, I wondered why they separated the girls and boys, but now I knew why they did this – it was because the girls were 'fragile.' It was a big word that I heard Mama use, but she used it when she talked about her good china dishes; still, I knew it meant 'something that could break easily,' and that surely meant girls as they always complained about hurting themselves if they got a bump or bruise – heck, I got bumps and bruises all the time, but I never complained like girls did.

All at once my thoughts were interrupted as I heard the shrill whistle of the head lifeguard – Jackson. The kids looked towards Jackson in awe as we knew he was a 'big man on campus.' but all the teenage girls were fixated on the tanned, sun-steaked blonde-haired 'Bama student for other reasons. "Are y' all ready?" Jackson's voice resonated across the pool, and we all stood at rapt attention.

While there were many summer events at the Tuscaloosa Country Club, this was the major one if you were under the age of ten. "Get ready," he paused as he looked from side to side of the pool. "Get set," he stopped yet again, and I heard groans from my fellow competitors, and then we heard the words we were waiting for, "Go!"

I was the first to hit the water and break the smooth, glassy flatness. With a flourish I took a deep breath and dove down where I made it to the bottom of the pool in record time. I began grabbing the quarters glistening on the base and stuffed them in the pockets of my swim trunks. The coins weren't hard to recognize as the mid-day sun shone down and made them appear as though they were shinning magnets drawing us in with our search. Within seconds both of my pockets were already bulging with my riches, but suddenly my attention was diverted. I looked to my right, and I saw a mass of redness coloring the pool water. At first, I was confused, but then it quickly registered. It was blood, and someone was hurt. I released my breath with bubbles of air and quickly ascended to the surface of the pool.

"Help, help!" I heard once I broke the surface and shook the water from hair.

"Oh my, he jumped in too short and hit his head on

the side of the pool," came a shrill female voice of a mother.

"Come, come quick," said another voice.

"Call the hospital," came the piercing voice of another.

"Is there a doctor or nurse here?" Jackson's voice rose above all the others.

After hearing all the commotion, I registered the severity of the situation, but I still had no idea what had actually happened. Once I reached the side of the pool, I focused on the group of people in a circle around someone lying on the pool deck.

I heaved myself up the side of the pool and padded over to see what was happening. I stood on my tiptoes to look over Jackson's shoulder where he was kneeling, and that was when I saw my brother; Landon was lying flat on his back with his eyes closed. To this day, I will always remember Miss Julia kneeling by the pool's edge with Landon's head on her lap and her charcoal-stained apron pressed tightly to his head to stop the flow of blood. I also remember her lifting her eyes heavenward and her mouth moving in a silent prayer as she held the child who wasn't her own, but clearly loved just as dearly as if she had borne him.

I heard another child crying, and I turned to find

Attie standing next to a table that nearly hid his small frame from the commotion. His salt-tinged tears mingled with the chlorine water dripping from his head, but any annoyance I usually harbored toward my youngest brother quickly dissipated as I made my way to him. I knelt and grabbed a nearby towel to wrap around him.

"What, what happen . . ." Attie sputtered between hiccups and tears as he pointed a stubby finger to Landon.

"It looks like Landon hit his head and got a boo-boo," I said using a word I never uttered now that I was older, but I knew would help Attie understand better.

He nodded his head, did an exaggerated sniffle, and leaned closer to me. There wasn't anything we could do but simply watch so I sat down on the concrete and Attie settled himself on my lap without even asking; he promptly began sucking his thumb.

Miss Julia was whispering, and I imagined she was praying as I knew she always said, "God bless," a lot to everyone so I guessed she was pretty religious. I always said my prayers at bedtime since my Sunday School teacher said I should, and now I felt I should probably say one for my brother. From the looks on everyone's face, I knew something wasn't right with Landon. Through the slight opening of the people circling him, I could see that he was

55

lying there, and Miss Julia still had her apron tightly pressed to his head.

My attention then shifted as I heard more raised voices from the pool gate, and I looked up to see Mama rushing in with her tennis friends. Mama dropped her racket on a table and the crowd parted so she could reach her son. She knelt by Miss Julia, but she just stared at Landon. She didn't reach for her son. Mama just looked at him, and Julia continued holding her apron to Landon's head and rubbing his arm with her other hand.

The next few minutes went more slowly than I could imagine, but then we heard the siren of an ambulance and I saw men in white come rushing up carrying what looked like a cot, and they carefully placed Landon on it. The men said some words to Mama, and she uttered some words in return before she looked over to Hollis, Attie and me. The men nodded and left with Landon.

Landon was being taken away by those men, and he was alone. Why didn't Mama go with him? I knew Miss Julia would watch us until Daddy came, but I didn't understand why Mama didn't go with Landon. I knew I would want Mama if I it was me on that cot, and I watched Landon being put in the back of the ambulance, but Mama just stared.

Mama drove us home in silence, and Daddy was there when we arrived. They left us with Tilly as she had been cleaning the house, but she said she would stay as long as needed, and then Daddy and Mama left for the hospital.

CHAPTER 7
Attie

I rolled over and rubbed the sleep from my eyes. It took me a moment to realize where I was, but then I focused on the clothes strewn across the floor and looked over at the sleeping figure beside me. God, she looked better last night, but clearly alcohol clouds judgment. Granted, she wasn't bad looking. She was thin as a rail which was better than being overweight, I surmised, but in the morning light her complexion showed signs of a hard life. I guessed her to be in her early twenties, but if she continued with her present lifestyle, she was going to pay dearly for it. I sat up and reached for the water bottle on the nightstand, but it was empty. I glanced over to the minibar where the refrigerator door had been left opened, but it had been emptied of its contents. With the empty bottle in hand, I made my way over the sink and filled it. I took a long swig and went to the window where I pulled back the drapes and stepped out onto the balcony.

I could glimpse Bryant-Denny Stadium in the distance. The field was quiet while only hours earlier it had been full-throttle pandemonium in the game against Ole Miss, and I had been part of it. I reached over to grab my Marlboro Lights on the small aluminum patio table and pulled a cigarette from the pack. Last night was still fuzzy. I remember going to the Sigma Chi house in the afternoon where I met up with some old friends, and then we made our way over to University Boulevard where we did the pub crawl. I did remember dancing to *Sweet Home Alabama*, with someone, and I guess it was this girl – God, what was her name? I couldn't remember. I think it was one of those double-barrel names so common in the South. Maybe if I stayed out here long enough, she would just get up and vacate the place. Heck, I had to get to the airport after lunch to make my flight back to Naples, and I didn't really want to engage with her any longer, but then I heard movement in the room, and what sounded like someone falling.

"Hey, there," called a distinctly lower-classed

Southern voice.

"Oh shit," I thought, and then I heard more stumbling.

"Hey, there, lover boy, peek-e-boo," she purred as she peered around the heavy drapes. She squinted into the early morning sun, but that only seemed to accentuate the fact she hadn't removed her thick eye makeup from the night before, and with her free hand, she reached up to push the greasy, bleached hair from her eyes, but that only made the dark roots all the more visible. When it was obvious, I wasn't responding in the manner she had hoped, she attempted an enticing smile as she pulled the drapes around her naked body and stepped out on the patio. I wasn't taking the bait. I had been stupid last night, and I wasn't going anywhere near this train wreck again, but I couldn't just ignore her either.

"Hi, there," I responded with as much enthusiasm as I could muster.

She dropped the drape in a dramatic flourish, but thankfully, she still had a sheet partially shielding her as she came out on the balcony.

"Can I have one of those, too?" She said as she pointed to my cigarette.

"Sure," I shrugged. If circumstances had been

different, I would have lit it and offered her one, but as far as I was concerned, she probably wasn't used to such gentlemanly offers.

"So, do you want to go get some breakfast? I love Waffle House, you know they have so many different kinds of waffles, I just never know which one to get."

I shook my head. "I think I'll pass on breakfast. I'm not feeling too great," I muttered and turned to glance back out toward the stadium.

"Hey, Addie," she said and grabbed my hand.

"It's Attie with two T's," I said rather too brusquely.

"Sorry, sweetie-pie," she apologized, and took a long drag and then blew a perfect smoke circle up in the air. "See how talented these lips can be, but I'm not telling you anything? You loved these lips and what they did to you last night, didn't you?" She finished as she attempted to lick her lips in a seductive manner, but she just looked ridiculous.

I inwardly cringed, and hoped my feelings weren't visible in my expression. How the hell was I going to get her out of here so I could shower and make it to the airport. No doubt she was counting on spending the day with me, but suddenly, her eyes narrowed, and she poked her finger on my chest.

"You're not acting the same as last night," she said in a snippy voice. "I bet ya don't even remember my name, do you?"

I hesitated, but then a thought came to mind. "I've always loved it when girls have two first names," and apparently that appeased her as her frown turned to a smile.

"So, what is it then– A- T- T- I- E," she said as she slowly spelled out the letters of my first name.

My first reaction was relief that she was literate and could spell which was one positive thing she had going for her, but she suddenly flipped back to a scowl. God, the girl was bi-polar. She could switch from hot to cold faster than I could blink.

"I said, what is it? What is my name?"

My first reaction was to attempt to weasel my way out of the situation, or figure out some sort of lie, but I was tired and hungover, and I just wanted to get her gone and out of my sight. "Honestly, I don't remember," I admitted.

"It's RaeLynn. I'm named after both my mama and my Daddy, and I'm proud of it. I'm RaeLynn Yoder from Duncanville," she said as she let her sheet drop to the balcony floor and placed her hands on her almost non-existent hips.

I'm guessing she wanted me to respond, but I just

stood there and stared at her pale white body adorned with a tattoo of a sunflower on her stomach while a belly button ring of a cheap metal glistened in the morning sun.

"Well, Mr. Attie, from Naples, Flor-i-dee, I appreciate your company last night, but I will not stay here and be insulted any longer."

She tossed her still lit cigarette over the balcony and whipped around the drapes blowing in the cool morning breeze. I heard her shuffling around the hotel room for a few minutes, and then heard a door slam, but as I peered through the open doorway, I saw that she had only gone into the bathroom. Shit, it was too easy to expect her to just get dressed and leave, but maybe if I gave her a little something it would accelerate her departure. I made my way over the dresser, grabbed my wallet and pulled out a fifty. It was the least I could do so she could catch a taxi to get back to wherever the hell Duncanville was. While I waited for her, I refilled my water bottle and sat down on the end of the bed. With nothing else to do, I grabbed the remote and turned on the television. The grinning faces of George W. Bush and Al Gore filled the screen, and the journalist spoke about the upcoming interviews. I sat in a stupefied gaze as I watched clips of the two hopeful presidential candidates in their candid interviews with FOX news.

RaeLynn obviously wasn't one to take too long with her morning grooming as she opened the door a few minutes later.

"Hey, RaeLynn," I said as I stood up and she turned to me with narrowed snake-eyes.

"You remember my name now," she laughed bitterly. "Guess, you didn't think it was important to remember my name when you were fucking me last night?" She said attempting to sound hard-hitting, but I could see her bottom lip quivering. "I'm leaving now, and I hope you enjoyed your little 'football weekend' back in Tuscaloosa."

"Wait, RaeLynn," I said as I reached for her arm, and when I touched her, I could see her features soften, and she suddenly resembled a scared little girl. "Look, here's a fifty, please get some breakfast – maybe go to Waffle House and get a taxi home."

She reached for the bill and stuffed it down her bra that was exposed from the low-cut opening of her blouse. She reached down to pull up her short faux leather skirt, and then glanced back up at me. I could see her eyes beginning to tear up, but she didn't utter a word. She turned to the door and quickly left. I breathed a sigh relief that she was finally gone, but I couldn't understand why I was also feeling an overwhelming feeling of both dread and gloom.

Even though I was in Coach, it felt like First Class as I leaned my head back and breathed in the stale air streaming down from the vent over my face. While it was a cool autumn afternoon, I had still been sweating like a field hand since I left the hotel, and my white oxford-cloth shirt was soaking wet. I noticed that my seat mate had looked over at me when I sat down, and it was obvious she was none too happy to be in my vicinity. I shrugged it off. When we were finally up and reaching cruising altitude, I was relieved to see the cute flight attendant approaching with the drink cart. Yep, a few vodka and cokes, and I would happily sail through the blue skies back to south Florida.

College football in the 1960's had been a stellar era. Coach 'Bear' Bryant and Alabama football set a precedence for what the sport would evolve within the next few decades. Alabama would be the crown jewel of the SEC, but back when I was a boy, I just accepted their wins as a fact of life. I never comprehended that our neighbors down the street were Paul and Mary Bryant, and he was a national hero. I still remember those cool afternoons of autumn when my brothers and their friends would gather in the empty field on our street to play football, and they would pretend to be their favorite players on the 'Bama' football team. They told me that I was too little to play so they let me sit by the 'sidelines' where I would watch in a folding lawn chair and wear my miniature black and white herringbone fedora. They told me I could pretend to be Coach Bryant so that was nearly as good as being able to play.

Tuesday afternoons were my favorite. Coach Bryant's wife, "Miss Mary" always made a point to drive by us playing football as she came home from playing bridge.

"Hey, boys, y'all are so cute" she called from her blue convertible Cadillac and waved like she was the Queen of England. She slowed the car down to a stop and reached up to adjust a loose curl that had slipped from her hair scarf, and then added, "Now, y'all remember to come on over when you're done, and I'll have cookies and Kool-Aid for you boys."

"Yes, ma'am," we all replied and waved back in unison.

We loved Miss Mary, and she loved to spoil the kids in the neighborhood after her two children had grown. We rarely ever saw the Coach, and I think it was the same with Miss Mary, and she was lonely. Those autumn afternoons at Miss Mary's house were incredible as she would feed the hungry neighborhood boys her homemade cookies, and listen to us ramble on, but in turn, we loved hearing her tell stories about Coach Bryant, and we would sit mesmerized by her gentle voice. Still, there was one time that Coach Bryant came home early and found us boys assembled around the long kitchen table in his kitchen. Rather than brushing us off as some sort of nuisance, he invited all of us boys down to see his basement filled with all his prized football memorabilia not only from Alabama, but also his time at Kentucky and Texas A & M. None of us said too much as we were in awe in the presence of the 'Great Bear Bryant,' but then to be able to glimpse his collection of trophies, framed autographed pictures of sports stars and other memorabilia was a treat; it was obvious that Coach Bryant was proud of this private haven that housed the accolades of his accomplishments. So, looking back, I have to think that Coach Bryant and Miss Mary must have enjoyed entertaining us little neighborhood boys just as much as the famous sports personalities and potential Crimson Tide recruits, and it spoke volumes of their characters.

I took another sip of my Vodka and Coke and smiled at those memories. And, while Tuscaloosa had always been a place that gave me a sense of peace and tranquility, I couldn't exactly say that it was the same after this weekend. I had a nagging feeling that what was meant to be a carefree football weekend with my frat buddies may have just turned into a nightmare.

CHAPTER 8
Hollis

"*H*appy, Birthday to you, Happy birthday dear Daddy, Happy Birthday to you," I listened as my family sang to me. I managed a weak smile, but honestly, how happy can you be when you're turning 40. Only ten years away from a half-century, and that much closer to the inevitable realization of one's death.

"Daddy, Daddy, you need to blow now," Lily urged as she leaned across the counter from the stool where she had been seated and pointed to the cake which Helen had managed to place 40 tiny, glowing candles.

I took a deep breath and complied. What else could

I do? God knew I did not want to be here now, but I was taking a breath deep enough to manage to extinguish all those flaming candles.

"Yeah, yeah for Daddy," George Jr., Geoff and Lily all clapped and yelled in unison at the top of their little lungs.

I watched in a daze as Helen removed the candles and began slicing the cake. Each of my children took a piece of the sugary confection along with a scoop of vanilla ice cream. All I could think of was that they would be so 'sugared-up' it would be a struggle to get them to sleep tonight. Helen appeared to take it all in stride, and I marveled at her patience with them.

"Daddy, Daddy," Lily's high-pitched voice broke through my thoughts, and I turned to give her a smile.

"Yes, sweetie, what is it?" I said and nodded to Helen as she handed me my plate.

"The best part . . ." she started and glanced at me in confusion as I obviously did not seem as enthused as she felt I should be. "Your present, silly Daddy."

"Oh, of course, I am silly," I responded and rolled my eyes in an exaggerated fashion which made Lily collapse in giggles.

"Here Daddy," I heard George Jr., say as he and his

brother huffed and puffed while they managed to pull an exceptionally large box along the tile floor to me.

"Open it, open it, Daddy," Lily clapped and bounced up and down on her stool.

"Okay," I said as I attempted to muster at least a portion of the passion the kids possessed, but I felt like a charlatan. It was at that moment that I saw the large box visibly move, and I swore I heard a whimper from it.

I raised my eyebrows above my wire-rimmed glasses. All three kids, as well as Helen, gave nervous laughs.

"Quick, Daddy, just open it," Lily urged.

I complied and tore at the loose bow, and then pulled the string and wrapping. There was a dead giveaway as I spied various holes not only in the wrapping paper, but the box itself, and I then heard a distinct whimper. There was no doubt another member was getting ready to be added to our family. As soon as I lifted the lid, I saw a mass of golden fur and I immediately smelled puppy breath as a Retriever pup leapt into my arms.

"Oh my, it's a puppy," I said, but obviously a little less eagerly than my family had hoped.

"Dad- dy," Geoff said in a droll voice, and hit himself in his forehead with his hand. "Of course, it's a puppy."

As much as I didn't care for the added responsibility, I found myself smiling at this little guy. He wiggled in my arms and I was the recipient of instant love and affection as he bestowed a series of wet kisses on my face.

"Okay?" Helen questioned in a small voice and raised her eyebrows as if she were wondering if she had made a major mistake by giving in to the children's demands for a dog. "I just want you to know he's already five months old, and has been fully trained," she added as though she hoped her dedicated search had turned up a dog that would make not only our family, but me, happy.

I looked back at her and gave a positive nod. She looked visibly relieved and I saw her shoulders relax.

"What do we name him?" George, Jr., chimed in."

I'm not sure?" I responded but held up the pup and looked at him from side to side. "It's a boy, and I've always heard that one-syllable names are the best for dogs -"

"One cell - a – bill?" Lily uttered with a slight lisp.

"It's syllable. It means part of a word," said George, Jr., in an exasperated voice.

"How about Mac? Or Beau? Or Jack?" I suggested.

I heard the name, "Beau" in unison from everyone.

"So, little boy, I christen you, Beau," I said as I reached over to my glass of water and poured a bit of water into the palm of my hand before I flicked it on top of the pup's head.

Beau promptly shook his head, and everyone laughed.

"Daddy, I love his name," said Lily. "And, I am going to get so many little bow tie collars so that Beau can wear bows every single day!"

Even though Helen and I had never had a dog together, Beau was hardly the first dog in my life. I looked over at the puppy, and I was suddenly transported back to one summer in Alabama.

"Landon, Hollis, y'all come here," my mother called from the porch, and we climbed down the ladder from our treehouse and ran over to the back patio.

"Yes, ma' am," we answered in unison as we stood in front of her.

"We've got a problem with the new litter of puppies," she stated very matter-of-factly, and we looked up at her with a quizzical look as the puppies appeared

73

perfect in our eyes.

Daddy's English Springer Spaniel had just delivered a prized litter of pups. "It's those rats from the lake," she said with a grimace as she looked out across the backyard to the body of water behind our house. In Alabama, as anywhere in the South, if there was fresh, or even saltwater, there was bound to be an issue with rats, and even though we lived in a nice area on Lakeshore Drive, we still battled the age-old problem.

"Those rats are trying to kill my puppies," she further informed us, and I was shocked to see such a tender side to Mama.

Landon and I nodded in agreement with her, but not entirely sure what she meant.

"Now, y'all listen here," she said, and her black eyes narrowed. "I want you to gather the other neighborhood boys over here 'cause we're gonna get rid of those rats today."

At this point, Boyd and Attie had climbed down from the treehouse and joined us, but we were all still somewhat perplexed by Mama's proposition, and as to how we were supposed to help.

"Now, y'all go on and tell your friends to come on over. I need all your help, and afterwards I'll give y'all cookies and Kool-Aid," she hesitated as though she was deep in thought for a moment or two. Then she added, "Now make sure you tell them to wear their tennis shoes, too."

"Yeah," yelled Attie as he raised his small fist in the air as he loved the idea of cookies, but honestly, I think we all wanted to raise our voices in astonishment that finally Mama would be one of those neighborhood mothers with snacks.

So, while we still didn't fully understand what Mama wanted us to do, we followed her directions and proceeded to run around the neighborhood where we bellowed to our friends to follow – which they did with the promise of cookies and Kool-Aid. It didn't take much in the South to recruit young boys. I guess it was sort of like when the Confederacy called young men to sign up to fight – many of those young men weren't exactly sure what they were fighting for, but the idea of defeating the foe and gaining a bit of glory was enough to entice.

Once we returned and assembled in our backyard, Mama came out and stood with her assorted paraphernalia. I wrinkled up my brow in confusion as I took in the various metal garbage can lids, but then I saw that Mama had a 5-gallon can of gasoline, plus she held her monogramed silver flip lighter that she used each time she lit up a cigarette.

"You boys come over here," she beckoned, and we all came closer where she stood on the back patio. "Those dang rats are gonna my puppies and I won't have it. I need y'all to help me get rid of those rats." She stopped and we all stood totally still waiting for her next words.

"Now if y'all will help me with this little problem, I've got a batch of some peanut butter cookies I just made and Kool-Aid inside -"

She didn't even finish with her enticement before we interrupted with a whoop-yell as it was summer, and we were all always game for a snack, but especially homemade and not those hard, store-bought cookies.

"Now listen here," she began slowly. Taking her lighter and held it high in the air as she walked over to the garbage can lids and the 5-gallon can of gasoline. "Now, I'm gonna pour a bit of gasoline down each of those rat holes, and then I'm gonna light a match and throw in down the hole, but once I put a garbage lid over the hole, I want a boy to come over and stand on the lid."

"I don't understand, Miss Marion," Robert Joe said, but he was always a bit slow. I knew what Mama was getting at, and she had figured out a way to rid herself of the pesky rat problem even though many others may have found it a bit unconventional.

So, we all watched as my Mama marched to the edge of lake. She nodded to us all and we followed in a uniform line like little soldiers following their sergeant. When she came to one hole, she proceeded to pour the gasoline down it, then promptly lit a match with her lighter, and quickly tossed it down the hole. In the next moment, she placed one of those metal garbage can lids over top of the hole, and asked Landon to stand on the lid. Landon didn't question, and he complied, but it was hot. He started jumping up and down as the heat was penetrating the lid, and his tennis shoes didn't exactly insulate his feet from the heat.

"Stop jumping so much," Mama cautioned to Landon. "You need to stay still," she added, and at that moment was when we started to hear the loud thumps.

Suddenly, it dawned on our young minds that the rats were being burned alive, and the "thumping" was their attempt to escape from the burning hell. I didn't exactly think of the rats as my friends, but in the same instance, I didn't really want to see them being tortured to death in such a callous manner.

Mama then proceeded to do the same to the other rat holes, and we all followed suit to stand on the garbage lids so the rats couldn't escape. Little Attie was the last one to stand on the metal garbage lid, but at only four-years old he wasn't very big. The rats under Attie's lid were a forceful bunch, and they attempted to pound their way out. Attie fell to the side and several large rats escaped the inferno. The rats were so disorientated that they didn't seek relief in the lake, but rather ran across our yard to the neighbor's. It had been a dry summer, so the parched grass immediately caught the flames from the rats' fur, and there were streaks of fire taking hold.   We all hadn't noticed, but Mama also had something else in her arsenal – a shotgun. When we saw her lift the gun, we all scattered, and then she took aim. With a succession of shots, she took out two of the four rats one-by-one as they attempted to run back to the safety of the lake. No one said anything. Heck, we lived in the Deep South where we were used to seeing guns, but it still bothered me to see those bloodied figures stagger and then drop as they attempted to escape. I looked over at Attie when I heard him sniffle, and I could see that he was attempting to stifle the tears. I reached over to put my arm around his thin little shoulders, and he leaned back against me where he hid his face against me.

"What in heavens," we heard our neighbor yell. Miss Nellie came running out the back door of her house and the screen door slammed shut behind her with a bang.

"My Lord, the whole place is gonna burn down."

Miss Nellie was older and a grandma, but I never saw an old woman turn and run as fast as she did back into her house. At this point, Mama had dropped her shotgun and was turning on the water hose in attempt to stop the flames, but it was clear her attempts were futile. Mama clearly couldn't compete. Those gasoline-drenched rodents were obviously a magnet for the parched grasses and plants. Within minutes, Miss Nellie's colorful garden that had been filled with a collection of roses, caladiums, balloon flowers, salvias and daisies was consumed, and her hopes of winning any of the Tuscaloosa Garden club honors was gone for that year.

None of us boys said anything, but as we stood back watching the scene unfold, I knew that Daddy was sure to be mad as a hornet when he heard what Mama had done. Within a few minutes, we all started hearing sirens growing louder and louder as they came near, and there was no doubt in my mind that they were coming to our house. The last time I had seen a firetruck was when it came to the elementary school last fall, and the firemen had told us about fires and how they put them out. Now, I guess I was gonna see it in person and for real. As the firetruck pulled up in the driveway, Mama joined us, and we all stood silently side-by-side and watched as the men did their job with their powerful water hoses. I was shocked that they were able to accomplish in under ten minutes what Mama had been unable to do.

"We're done, and it's out, ma'am," the fire chief said as he walked up to us, nodded and took off his helmet to wipe the sweat from his reddened face.

"Thank you, sir," my mother said in a muted voice.

He nodded, and then turned to look directly at us boys. "Now, can anyone tell me who started this fire?" He asked, and it was clear he thought it was one of us boys playing around in the backyard with matches or a lighter.

It was then that Attie pushed his way forward through the taller boys and looked up at the fire chief.

"It was her," he said pointing a stubby finger at Mama, and I had to think he was relishing the fact that Mama was the guilty party. After all the times that she had lashed out at our indiscretions, she was now the one who was going to get reprimanded, and secretly, I think we all were enjoying watching Mama squirm under the gaze from the fire chief.

80

Sure enough, Daddy was mad. We heard him yelling at Mama in their bedroom, and she was unusually quiet for a week, but then things slowly got back to normal. Mama's clothing budget was cut-short for the next three months since Daddy had to pay Miss Nellie a small fortune so the older woman wouldn't press charges against Mama. Needless to say, Miss Nellie never spoke to our family again, and no doubt, she rejoiced when the Collingsworth family left Tuscaloosa and moved to Naples.

But, to this day, I will never forget that hot summer afternoon, and as much as I had been troubled about Mama's method of making those rats suffer, I still developed another level of respect for her that she would go to such lengths to protect her baby puppies; still, I wondered why she never went to the same lengths to protect her own babies – her sons.

CHAPTER 9
Landon

Jennifer had left for a long weekend in St. Louis as she was hostess of her sister's bridal shower, and even though I was left in charge of the three girls, I was still a free man as I had secured a babysitter. I had lined up the new receptionist at my office to watch the girls, and she was more than happy to stay the entire weekend - Deena. Deena was a pretty little thing who had dropped out of college, and now sat front and center in our reception area to answer phones and greet patients. Even though she was in her early twenties, she had a mature knowledge of the realities in this world. She always smiled in the right way at the older, male patients – it was just enough to give them hope, but not enough to seem forward and shocking, or cause concern with their wives. With her long, straight auburn hair and brilliant green eyes, she was an Irish dream for any man, but there was no doubt she was well-aware of her charms. When I ventured into the office every morning with my Starbucks in hand, and honestly, still half asleep, she would greet me with the most genuine smile, but she always followed it with a long, appreciative appraisal down the full-length of me. Even in my lab coat, Deena took in my appearance with my crisp white shirt, stripped tie, fitted trousers, and she would finish with a nod of approval when she concluded with my Cole Hann loafers. God, I wish Jennifer would look at me like that, but I didn't know many wives who still looked at their husbands with any sense of longing or desire after the rings were placed on their fingers. Who knew, I might get lucky when I got back from the fishing trip on Sunday? Maybe Deena would be acceptable to staying a bit later to shake-off the stress from watching the kids all weekend and take a dip in the hot tub with me.

"So, what are you smiling about, Landon," Boyd shot out as he held up a beer in salute to my obvious good mood.

"Whatever, or whoever it is, Landon is smiling like a cat that caught the mouse," Attie chimed in from the backseat.

I looked in the rearview mirror to Attie and Hollis in the backseat, and just gave a knowing smile with a nod of my head. It was going to be a very good weekend, a very good weekend, indeed, in more than ways than I could imagine.

It was late Friday afternoon, and my brothers and I were headed to Islamorada where we had a weekend of offshore fishing lined up. Granted, I would rather be driving my two-seater Mercedes, but since we couldn't fit everyone in my car, we were driving to the Keys in Jennifer's Grand Caravan – the 'Mama van.' Yes, it would be a mess when we returned, but I could get it detailed on Monday morning and Jennifer would be none the wiser to our decadent behaviors.

After three hours of speeding across Alligator Alley along the swamplands of South Florida, and then down A1A, we sang along to Segar's *Against the Wind* and Boston's *Peace of Mind* - the songs of our youth. We made it to our first stop as it was just approaching sunset. I pulled into the parking lot of Holiday Isle, and the large sign over the Tiki Bar with its colorful lights beckoned all to come and partake. We could never drive by Holiday Isle without stopping as it had become a 'tradition' over the years.

Whenever we drove down to the Keys, we had to have their famous Rum Runners. Even though the frozen concoction tasted like the Icee's of our youth, they were far more lethal with a floater of the 151-proof Rum. We each got two plastic 'to-go' cups and jumped back in the van to go the short distance down the two-laned road to Woody's on Matecumbe Key.

Woody's was an institution in the Keys. To most tourists driving by, they would have ignored the non-descript building from the 1950's as they breezed by on their way to one of the flashy new resorts. With its cinderblock construction and turquoise blue trim, it was a relic from the past. While it was a watering hole for the natives, we always considered ourselves 'natives' as we had been coming to the Keys on holidays since we moved from Alabama as boys, and granted, we would have never entered the doors Woody's until our teens, it was the place of memories.

"Yeah - hoo," Attie's voice rose to a fevered pitch of a Rebel yell as I pulled into the parking lot. "We're finally here."

I parked the van to the side of the sandy lot, and we all stopped by the sea grape bushes to take a piss before we made our way inside.

Music pulsated throughout the establishment, and as we opened the door we were bombarded with song, smoke and the stale stench of damp that was common to most establishments in the Keys. As much as it would have assaulted many, it was a comfort to my senses.

Boyd threw his cigarette butt to the side and ground it into the crushed shells with the toe of his shoe, "Do you hear, it's 'Big Dick and the Extenders," playing tonight?"

'Big Dick' was a Seminole Indian who stood well over six feet. In his wide-brimmed hat constructed from palm fronds, he stood front and center on the small stage in a ragged fishing shirt, faded shorts and bare-foot while he strummed a guitar and his bandmates played backup. His music was a mix of Blues and Southern rock tunes, but he also was known for his raunchy humor usually at the expense of certain members of the audience.

A raucous crowd applauded as the last strains of *Flirtin' with Disaster* ended as we walked through the screen door, and then the more mellow sounds of Lynyrd Skynyrd's *Simple Man* began. It was Friday so there were wall-to-wall people packed into the small establishment. While it was primarily the locals who were getting a buzz after being out on the water all day, or letting off steam after work all week, there were also return visitors like us, and despite the crowd, we still managed to find a table off to the side near the front corner. Scantily clad waitresses, who were still in their teens, pranced around as they took orders and served the patrons.

"Hey, boys, I'm Ashley," a cute blonde with a high ponytail bounced up to our table and snapped her gum as she held out her pad. "How are y'all doin' tonight," she asked as she leaned down and placed her pad on the edge of the table. It was obviously a well-practiced move to give us all an ample view of her cleavage. We weren't stupid. It was clearly to entice patrons to get bigger tips, but we didn't mind as taking care of Ashley would be our pleasure.

Big Dick ended the song with a flourish on his guitar and took a bow to the applause. While the band took a well-deserved break from playing in the stuffy room, it was time for Big Dick's monologue. He took a slow long appraisal of the audience as he lifted his head to see beyond the brim of the hat and focused on a busty blonde who was headed to the restrooms.

"Hell, I we got us a dang celebrity in the audience tonight," he said in a boisterous Southern drawl. Everybody looked around the dimly lit room, but none of us could see anybody that looked remotely famous.

"Yes, siree," he said as he pointed to the blonde, but

she was obviously pretty wasted, and she looked up as she stumbled through the tightly packed tables. "Whew- ew, it's Dolly Parton," his baritone voice resonated through the room.

"Hey, Dolly girl, you come on up here with me, and we'll sing us a little song together for everyone," he gestured to her, and several of her friends urged her on, but she hesitated. The hesitation was eliminated when one guy picked her up and swung her over his shoulder to pass her up to the stage. Her tight cropped top had ridden up while she was being carried, and when she was set down on her feet, the entire bottom of her breasts were on view for everyone to see.

The crowd was on fire. The wolf whistles, the calls, the shouts and the cameras going off only encouraged Big Dick. Big Dick put his arm around "Dolly" to steady her, and she then noticed her shirt and pulled it down to the dismay of many of the guys, but then she flashed a huge smile before she leaned up and gave Big Dick a kiss on the cheek.

"Who-ee," he yelled, and let go of her as he swung his guitar back up and began strumming it. "Let's see, honey, why don't you tell me your real name?"

"It's Jessica," she murmured.

Big Dick just smiled, and then his fingers started strumming a few chords until he got it just right, and he launched into *Jessica* by the Allman Brothers.

All during the song, I could tell that Big Dick kept glancing over our way, but I didn't give it much thought. After two rum runners in quick succession, I was nursing my beer, but Attie and Boyd were pounding Chokoloskees, the well-known South Florida drink of vodka and coke. Hollis was his usual quiet self until he got sufficiently sloshed and then he came out of his shell, but then again this wasn't exactly his sort of place. Although Boyd, Attie and I were clad in khaki cargo shorts, fishing shirts and flipflops, Boyd was in his usual attire of plaid shorts, pink polo shirt and Sperry topsiders; he stood out in this crowd.

"Thank you, honey," Big Dick said to Dolly/Jessica with a wink, and she didn't waste any time scurrying off the stage to get to the restroom. With a pause to take a long drink from his beer, Big Dick looked pointedly over to our table. "Now, it looks like we got us a Yankee, preppy visitor tonight."

The audience turned to look in the direction where Big Dick directed his attention, and I immediately sensed that Hollis was the next victim.

"Hey, there 'Mr. Pink Shirt," the Indian looked

directly at Hollis. "So, where you from?"

Hollis nearly choked on his beer and gave a cough to clear his throat. "Naples," he replied, and I was almost afraid he was going to add, 'sir,' but he didn't.

"God, I could have sworn you were from some New England town, but Naples - just as bad," he made a gesture with his nose in the air, and the audience laughed.

"So, not only hoity-toity from Na. . ples," he said dragging out his syllables. "But glorified, gay bait," he said as he pointed at Hollis' pink polo shirt, and the audience screamed and clapped in laughter.

"I guess you got your directions messed up as in a shirt like that, I'm thinking you belong in Key West rather than here, pretty boy."

Even in the dark, I could see Hollis face redden, and he suddenly reminded me of the little boy back in Alabama who had borne the brunt many jokes. Big Dick continued with more jokes at Hollis' expense, and as much my brothers and I loved to give him a hard time, it was another thing when others did it, and I saw Boyd sensed it, too.

Standing up, Boyd waved his hand to attract Big Dick's attention, but the Indian just kept the jokes coming as the audience was loving it. Whenever Boyd had too much to drink, he was ready for a fight, and I could see it in his eyes. He made his way the short distance from our table to the small stage, and in a blink of an eye, he grabbed for Big Dick's hat, but he didn't see the bouncers coming behind him. The two men easily grabbed Boyd by each arm, lifted him in the air, and gave him a toss off the stage towards our table. Boyd was pissed, but I shook my head at him when I saw the gleam of revenge in his eyes. Our evening was finished here. I threw a hundred-dollar bill down on the table and motioned for us all to get out of there.

Once we were back in the van, I pulled out a baggie from the side pocket of the door, and took a quick sniff; I was stressed, and I needed relief quickly. We had all seen our share of bar fights, and it could have gone far worse. Boyd was still boiling for a fight, but Attie lifted the cooler and handed a beer to him and then more cans to the rest of us.

"Let's get the hell out of here," Attie said, and then paused as though he was deep in thought. "Sort of reminds me of that other time in the Keys when we had to 'make like the wind,' and vamoose," and no more words were needed as we all remembered exactly what he meant.

"Here's to Beauregard," we all said in unison as we held up our cans and I skidded the tires on the crushed shells before we headed to Cheeca Lodge for the night.

Beauregard . . . Hell, I hadn't thought about Beauregard in years. It had been Memorial Day weekend of '79 – God, was that really 20 years ago? Our friend, Dex, had managed to convince his Daddy to let us have their family's Winnebago for the weekend. We had all just finished up college classes, and even though Attie was still in high school, we had pity on him and let him come along. Besides, Attie was always ready for a party, and heck, we were planning a weekend of fishing, drinking and smoking in the Florida Keys, and not necessarily in that order.

As we cruised along Highway 41 past the Seminole Indian Chickee huts, the airboats filled with tourists, and made our way along the water mazes of sawgrass, we all relished our freedom. Even though the RV was heavy with pot smoke, we cranked up the music as we jammed along with ELO's *Don't Bring Me Down* and Deep Purple's *Smoke on the Water*. Both songs seemed to totally define the confined lives we were seeking to escape for a few days, and the beers flowed so that by the time we arrived in Islamorada we were certifiably wasted.

"We're here," Boyd turned and yelled to the rest of

us from front as he was riding shotgun to Dex. After five hours of trudging along at 50 miles per hour in the sluggish RV, we all glimpsed the battered sign with its faded pink bird which announced the entrance to the Flamingo Isle Campground. Typical of any trailer parks in the Keys, it was mix of restaurant workers and seasonal transplants who simply just wanted to escape the suffocating, confined lives of responsibility. Once you left the bottom on the State of Florida, you entered an entirely different world as you passed from one small island to the next one. Whether it was salt-tinged breezes blowing through the palms and bougainvillea, or first taste of a fresh catch, it allowed for stresses to evaporate, and the general consensus was to tell the world to 'fuck-off' while you were here.

Dex pulled the RV up along the chocolate brown, octagon-shaped house/office on stilts, and Boyd and I jumped down. We were both a bit wobbly on our feet as though we had just stepped off a boat, but the damp, salt air triggered our senses within seconds. Still, it was obvious that we were pretty high as we mounted the steps, and Boyd turned to me.

"Did I just see a monkey in a cage under this house?"

"What?" I stumbled a bit and grabbed hold of the

wooden rail of the stairs to steady myself. I shook my head, "A monkey?" I repeated.

"Yeah, just look under there," Boyd said as he pointed past the wire fence attached the silts that enclosed the entire bottom of the wooden structure.

I retreated and lowered my head. It was just after sunset and the area was dark, but I could make out a shape moving in the shadows. I peered down to get a closer look, and as my eyes refocused to the darkness, I could make out what Boyd was talking about.

"Hell, it's a fucking monkey, alright," I agreed with a laugh, and we both spied the animal sitting on an upside-down white 5-gallon bucket.

Obviously, the monkey was used to human interaction, and he rattled off some grunts and noises as he tilted his head to us.

"Hell, let's check-in, and then we'll come back with the others to pay "Mr. Monkey" a visit," Boyd suggested with a devious gleam in his eyes.

After Dex maneuvered the large, rectangular vehicle into empty spot #34, we gathered our cooler filled with beers, and Attie brought up the rear carrying the plastic sandwich baggie filled with the joints he had wrapped on our drive over. Even though we had told the others about the monkey, I still don't think they believed us, but they were more than willing to take a look, and Boyd was in the mood to have some fun.

"Sure enough, it's a dang chimpanzee," Dex roared as he neared the fence and leaned closer to see the animal.

"And, look here," Hollis said as he pointed to a rusted metal sign dangling by one nail. "His name is Beauregard." "He's a 'Southern Confederate" chimp – think he was named after General Beauregard?" Attie laughed.

As if on cue, when the monkey heard Attie use his name, Beauregard got off his bucket and came over near us. It was as though he was sizing us up as he looked from one of us to the other.

Boyd had popped the top off his beer, and after one sip, he tossed it through the fence to the monkey. Beauregard didn't hesitate and caught it without a blink. He was obviously a seasoned Conch who was used to his drink. The animal took hold of the can of Budweiser and tilted his head back as he proceeded to guzzle it down until it was empty. We all erupted in unison, and Dex spat-out his beer while Hollis laughed so hard beer came shooting-out his nose.

"What the hell," Attie nearly lost it as he doubled

over, and stumbled backwards until he hit a palm tree and slid down while he continued to hoot.

It seemed that Beauregard looked on in envy, and he clearly wanted to be part of our fun. Boyd was urged on by all our guffaws, so he popped another beer before throwing it in the cage. Again, Beauregard didn't hesitate, and he downed the second beer in a matter of seconds.

"I can't believe this fuckin' monkey is drinking beers - I'm ready to shit my pants," Boyd said with tears in eyes, and without another thought he threw his lit joint into the cage. As with the beers, Beauregard didn't hesitate, and he reached down to pick up the joint from the ground of sawdust and began to smoke it in the same fashion as we were all doing. None of us could stop laughing at our new-found friend.

Then, there was the sound of dribbling water, and we turned to find a totally wasted Hollis peeing over the fence at the back side of the cage. He was weaving from side-to-side as he tried to keep his balance while taking a leak.

As Beauregard finished the joint, he turned to follow our attention and watched Hollis in apt attention until he had finished. The monkey was taking it all in, and then without hesitancy, Beauregard grabbed ahold of his own long dick and proceeded to start peeing, but he didn't just aim it down to the ground, he turned and looked at Hollis. Beauregard then took direct aim at Hollis' chest and began spraying my brother from 10-feet away. At first, Hollis was oblivious of what was happening, but within a few seconds he registered it all, and began stumbling back from the cage.

"Help . . . help me . . . help me," Hollis cried as he fell to the ground and the monkey took aim as though he was moving a water hose from side to side and continued to douse Hollis.

Boyd, Attie, Dex totally lost it, and I was sure that the owner of the trailer park would be coming out of his house, but then again, he was probably just as wasted and had passed out. Once Beauregard finally relieved himself, he turned back to rest of us as if to say, 'how about another beer and joint,' but we knew we had to get Hollis cleaned up.

My brother still lay on the ground, but he was whimpering like a child as he curled into a fetus position on the sandy, shelled road. As much as Hollis pissed us all off on a regular basis, we couldn't let him sit in the sand covered in monkey piss, so I looked at the swimming pool and then to Hollis. The four of us nodded, and we each grabbed a limb and carried him the short distance to the swimming pool and gave him a toss.

"What the fuck," Hollis yelled as he was monetarily revived from his wasted state when he came up from air. He gave his head a shake of the water and looked at us with narrowed eyes.

"What else could we do?" Boyd shrugged. "You were covered in monkey piss, and you stink."

With that comment, we all walked back to the RV while we disregarded Hollis getting out of the pool and swearing at us.

We had planned to grab a couple of pizzas once we got settled, but none of us wanted to go anywhere at this point so we made do with what we had left from the road trip. Dex set out the couple bags of Lay's potato chips and Cheetos, and then found the box of stale Dunkin' Donuts so we cranked the music in the RV and continued through our cases of beer. It was the end of another semester down of school, so we sat, told tales, and reminisced about days gone by. None of us were sure when we finally found places to lay our heads, but in the morning, I looked out one of the windows of the RV, and saw a red, convertible Cadillac El Dorado with its top down parked next to us.

"Shit," I muttered, and I saw Dex rouse from the sofa bed.

"What's wrong?" He asked as he stood up stretching and the reached down to rearrange his crotch.

"Just come here," I motioned for him to follow me out the door.

We both stood looking at the car. It wasn't a pretty site. The candy apple red Caddy with white interior was littered with our empty beer cars. I wasn't sure what prompted us to start throwing our empty cans out the RV window last night, but once we started, it had become a game; still, neither of us could remember seeing a car when we came back from Beauregard's cage.

"This isn't good," Dex said as he looked to the rear of the car and I followed his eyes.

The car had a personalized license plate with four letters, B-E-A-U.

"Holy shit," I said, and we both turned to get back in the RV.

"We need to get out of here pronto," Dex said as he got in the driver's seat. "Grab me a beer for the road," he said as he started the ignition and accelerated out of the park.

He turned right onto A1A to head down to Marathon. The morning sun was not yet at its most intense, but it was growing warmer, and the humidity of the islands was steadily rising in preparation for the daily afternoon thunderstorms. Dex turned his baseball cap to the side in an attempt to block the sun hitting the side of his face, and I could hear him give an audible sigh of relief that there was now some distance between us and the Flamingo Isle RV Park, but the peace didn't last long. All at once we both heard a knocking sound in the RV.

Dex turned to me, "Did you hear something?"

"Yeah," and I turned around, but I saw Hollis and Attie still snoring in the back.

Again, we heard the knocking noise, and it steadily grew louder and more intense.

"What the hell," I said. "Nobody's up, but us," I said as I turned again. "Hollis and Attie are still sound asleep."

Dex was silent for a few seconds, and then he said very slowly, ". . . Where's Boyd?"

"I guess he's asleep in the back," I answered with a shrug figuring he was likely passed out somewhere in the rear of the camper.

Again, the noise reverberated through the RV, and then we both looked up at the front windshield as we saw a hand wave across the front of the glass.

"Shit," Dex muttered as he let off the accelerator

and pulled over to the emergency lane on the Seven-Mile Bridge.

Once we stopped, Dex and I both got out and turned to look at the roof of the RV. Boyd was sitting atop and staring back at us with a grin.

"Hey, I appreciate y' all stopping," he said with a wave of his hand.

"Why the hell are you up on the roof?" I squinted into the sun as I looked up at my brother.

'I don't know, I just remember I got tired last night, and the stars were out, and I decided I wanted to go up on the roof and look at them – guess I fell asleep."

"Get the fuck down here, you dumb-ass," Dex laughed.

CHAPTER 10
Attie

I looked over at my phone lighting up. It was only 8:00 in the morning, and I didn't usually get out of bed until ten o'clock, so I reached over and switched off the ringer. Even though it was a weekday, it had been a late night and I was ready to turn over and sleep a little more.

After dinner with Mama and Daddy, I had ended up on Third Street and then Fifth Avenue where I ran into my buddies. We made our rounds to Tommy Bahama's, Zoe's, Yabba's and Bistro 821. It wasn't even Thanksgiving yet, but all of Naples was ready for the Christmas season. All of downtown was aglow with festive decorations, and the streetlights were fashioned to emit soap flakes that resembled snowflakes. Yes, it was South Florida, and the temperatures were still in the 70's during the evening hours, but Neapolitans were determined to have that 'Northern' Christmas season, so those white soap flakes floated among the palm trees and gave us the ambiance of the season we so desired.

Although I had had a couple of cocktails before dinner with my parents, and then a few glasses of wine during dinner, it hadn't stopped me from continuing to indulge with my buddies. Dex, Tom and Steve were good friends all through school, and none of us had seen fit to leave Naples. True, we had left for several years with college, but we all returned. Dex took over his father's landscape company. Tom had gone to law school, but was disbarred and now gave massages to the rich, bored housewives, and Steve had married a cute little wine heiress, so he was set for life. And, I had my trust fund so none of us ever worked 'banker's hours,' but we still held our heads high and moved among the elite of Naples' society.

I lit a cigarette and inhaled deeply as I pulled my sheet higher and placed one arm behind my head. While the ceiling fan cast shadows over my bed, I watched the movements in a mesmerized amazement and fell into a trance. I thought about my 'agenda' for the day. Let's see, I would shower, have a cup of coffee, and then walk down to the 7-11 on Third Street where I would get my copy of the *Naples Daily News*. I decided I would then stop off at Tony's café and have a croissant and another coffee as I read over the paper. Once home, I needed to gather my laundry and drop it at the dry cleaner, and then I might wander over to Dex's house where we could hash over our escapades of the previous night-out. No doubt, I would be kicked-out once his wife got home from picking up their children from school, but that was fine as I had a new novel and I loved relaxing in my hammock for a few chapters and an afternoon nap. So, once I woke from my siesta, I would have a quick swim in the pool and then go to for my dinner date with Lisa. Lisa was new in town from Philadelphia, and after meeting last night at Zoe's, she was keen to get to know not only Naples better, but me, as well.

"Shit," I uttered as my phone rang again. I thought I had turned off the ringer, but obviously I hadn't in my slumbered state. Whoever was calling twice within five minutes, would likely be ringing again until I answered. So, with a heavy sigh, I sat up in bed and reached for my phone.

"Hello," I said flatly.

"Is this Attie?" A distinctly Southern-tinged voice

asked.

"Yeah, who wants to know?" I countered their question with one of my own and reached over to the ashtray to flick off the ashes from the end of my cigarette.

"It's me."

I didn't immediately respond. I wasn't sure about this person who was so presumptuous that they felt I should automatically know their identity.

"At-tie," the female voice said my name again, but this time she emphasized the two syllables very slowly. I could actually hear a hint of hesitancy and fear in the voice, and I had to admit the voice was eerily familiar.

"Sweetheart, you've got me?" I give up," I answered with a sigh. God only knew how many women had passed through my life, and she could be one of many. Still, I suddenly got a sinking feeling in my gut.

"Attie, it's me, RaeLynn," she stated flatly, and then she paused which I surmised was her way of hoping it would aid my memory, but I remained silent. "We met when you were in Tuscaloosa in October. We spent the night together in your ho-tel."

She didn't have to bother attempting to say another word to spark my memory as when she first spoke her name, it had already registered.

I stubbed out my cigarette and rubbed the wild mess of hair on my head. I suppose I was stalling, but what man wouldn't in this position? What the hell did she want, but more importantly, how the fuck had she gotten my phone number. I never remembered giving her my number, much less my last name.

"Yeah, so how are you doing?" I reluctantly asked attempting to make small talk, but I really didn't care to hear her answer.

"Well," she started in a whinny voice that irritated me. "I'm not so good. I've been sick a lot, and I'm really tired. I haven't even been able to work at my job at the Piggly Wiggly."

I rolled my eyes. Hell, she was a clerk at a grocery store, but I should have guessed as much. RaeLynn obviously hadn't gone far in school, but then again, I'm sure she didn't aspire to do much more in life than scanning people's groceries in a small Southern town.

"Sorry to hear that," I said doing my best to sound sympathetic, but again, why in the hell was she calling me. I only met her one time, and granted, I couldn't remember, but I was pretty sure we slept together when she was at the hotel; still, that didn't mean I was her doctor so why was she calling me about her aches and pains.

"Attie," she began again, but then stopped, and I wondered if we had been cut-off. If that was the case then 'thank goodness,' as I had no desire to continue any conversation, but the gods were not on my side, and I heard her intake of breath.

"Attie, as I said, I haven't been feeling none too good," she stopped again. "Well, my sister had a suspicion. So, she done took me on over to the Planned Parenthood in Tuscaloosa, and . . ."

RaeLynn didn't need to go any further as I surmised what was wrong with her. I mentally calculated in my head that it was now about six weeks since I had been up there for the 'Bama game, and she was calling to inform me of her 'news,' but I stopped for a second as everything slowly fell into place and registered - what the fuck, I thought.

"Attie, are you there?" She uttered.

"Yeah, sure I'm here," I answered more quickly than I imagined I could.

"Great," she said, and I guess she was relieved that I hadn't immediately hung up on her.

"So, you're pregnant?" I stupidly asked even though I knew the answer.

"Yeah," she giggled, and at that moment wondered how old she was as she sounded like a young teenager.

"RaeLynn -"

"Yes,' she enthusiastically interrupted.

"Just relax, honey," I said, and then took a deep breath as I had to ask. "You're pregnant, but we only knew each other that one night -have you been dating anyone else?"

I heard her start to sniffle and then some ragged cries. "I had a boyfriend, Dwayne, who works at the Auto Zone, and we dated since I was 15, but I haven't seen him since he cheated on my with my best friend."

I rolled my eyes and felt like I entered some sort of Southern White Trash reality television show.

"RaeLynn, how old are you?" I needed to know. She didn't immediately answer, and I knew this wasn't a good sign.

"I'm 16 . . . and a half," she replied sheepishly. "My birthday's in April if that's what you want to know?" Her voice suddenly took a sing-song tone of a child.

Shit, I thought to myself. She was underage, and I could potentially be charged with statutory rape. I knew this was the case in Florida, but I would have to check what the age limit was in Alabama – knowing Alabama it was probably 14, but somehow that didn't alleviate my fears.

"Listen, I'm just getting up, but I've got your

number now. You hit me with this as I'm just trying to wake-up, and I'm trying to process it."

"Okay," she responded with more enthusiasm than she had mustered during the entire conversation, but obviously whatever I said, even though it wasn't much, had given her a boost and renewed sense of life.

"I'll give you a call tomorrow. What's a good time?"

"Oh anytime, Attie," she responded without delay. "I'm always free for you."

I rolled my eyes at her response, but shit, I could be in big trouble. Would I be in an Alabama prison within a year for statutory rape of a minor?

CHAPTER 11
Boyd

I took my cup of coffee and walked out on the dock to watch the sun rise over the islands in the distance. The bright orange ball contrasted against the vivid cobalt blue sky while the twisted trunks of the mangroves resembled a mass of newly hatched snakes rising from the confinement of their watery nest. It was the Everglades, but also known as the "River of Grass." While to anyone's eye, the waving grasses in these marshy wetlands clearly appeared to echo times of the past when it was first named by journalist, Marjory Stoneman Douglas. You could look in any direction and not glimpse any sign of human existence; it was as though you were transformed back in time to another era. It was a place where you could spend the day on your boat without glimpsing another soul – no sort of any invasion of the modern world. The environmentalists loved this place for the uncorrupted purity to study nature in its most natural state, but I loved the simplicity and peace I found when I needed to escape from the world and its constant bombardment to my senses. A snow-white heron swooped so low that I could feel a rush of movement from its passing, and I turned to lift my face to reap the warmth and peace from the rising sun. Since the age of eight, I had called this home. Yes, I was born in Alabama, and raised on that red-dirt clay where I caught my first bass in the freshwater lakes and roamed the woods of pine scrub to the call of the quail, but this pristine area of wetlands, alligators and ten-thousand islands was where I transitioned from a boy to man.

All was still quiet in my home as I stood on the dock, and I treasured the tranquility of the scene. I needed the solitude. I needed peace, but I needed validation and love more. Being a husband, a father and working at a demanding job had taken its toll on me. It seemed so many men I knew took it in stride. They drank away their evenings to mask over the drudgery of this lives, or else they hit full throttle on their boats to take them farther and farther out in the Gulf on Saturday mornings, or else we scooted our golf carts around the endless array of courses in Naples as we hit those little white balls mindlessly over and over again. Yes, we had done what was expected of us. We all went to college, partied hard, and then graduated. We all married cute little blonde, sorority sweethearts who loved to give the best blowjobs, but had gained 30 pounds from giving birth to several children, and now only gave us looks of disgust in bed at night as though we were some lecherous stranger on the street rather than their husbands. Clearly, our wives preferred to read about others making love in their book-club novels, but when it came to their own husbands, it seemed we were the last thoughts on their minds after car-pools, ballet lessons, or picking up pre-made dinners from Costco.

I lit a cigarette and inhaled deeply. Immediately, a sense of calmness transformed my senses, but I knew it wouldn't last. Once the kids woke, Libby would be up, and it would be non-stop chaos for the rest of the long weekend – this was Thanksgiving. With her ever-present need to control things, Libby had organized the next four days with the precision of someone with OCD on overdrive. The lists for the kids and me were front and center on the kitchen bulletin board, and God knew we would all have hell to pay if we deviated from her plans.

"Go on then," I heard Libby's exasperated voice as she slid open the French door to let the dog out. Finn instinctively knew where I was and bounded down the dock to my side.

"Hey, boy," I leaned down and rubbed his flopping ears. God, it was nice to know that at least one living soul in this home appreciated me – if only my wife could love me as much this old dog. When I saw Libby still waiting at the door, I took a deep drag and then sent my cigarette flying into the water even though I hadn't finished it.

"Do you need something?" I called.

"What do you think?" She countered my question with one of her own and continued to stand there in the doorway with her arms crossed. Shit, I thought. I really didn't want to engage in one of her verbal challenges so early in the day. Hell, my coffee hadn't even kicked in yet.

I just shrugged my shoulders and looked down as Finn sat obediently at my side. His sad Spaniel eyes looked up at me in empathy to my misery. We shared a common bond; he also bore the brunt of Libby's words as often as I did.

"You did it again," she spat. "I told you that I can't stand to wake-up and smell pork. You fried that bacon, and it makes me nauseous, plus I said I made a vegan breakfast casserole for this morning," she paused, but only apparently to catch her breath to continue her tirade. "I . . . told . . . you . . . last . . . night," she uttered each world very slowly as though I was some sort of imbecile who couldn't understand her.

I turned away to look back out at the water.

"Boyd, you're not following Mona's instructions. Remember you are supposed to be listening to my needs, or else how are we ever going to get our issues resolved? You know it's a two-way street, and I will not assume all the work in this relationship," she stopped. "Boyd, do you hear me?"

I heard her voice just fine, but the words weren't registering; they blurred together as though she was speaking another language I didn't understand – sort of like how the teacher spoke to the kids on the Charlie Brown shows. It may have been Thanksgiving, but I wasn't sure I was 'thankful' for having a wife at this moment.

Without giving it another thought, I looked down at Finn, and went over the storage closet on the dock where I grabbed my tackle box, two fishing poles, and proceeded to my boat. "Come on, boy," I said, and he didn't hesitate to jump on the Fountain. With one leg over the side, I turned to look back up at Libby, and gave her a salute that I knew would royally piss her off. She raised her middle finger in return before she turned and slammed the door.

The Port Royal Club was a glimmering jewel on this overcast evening. With the palm tree trunks swathed in tiny white lights, the light rain allowed the luminous display to resemble that of diamonds glistening on a black velvet backdrop.

"Oh, Daddy," my three-year old daughter, Carly, called from the backseat. "Look, Daddy, the lights are hugging the palm trees." She said as she pointed a stubby finger on the glass window of the car.

"Carly, you're right," I said with a laugh as I inched my way up the tree-lined drive to the portico.

Our drive had been in total silence, so I was glad for the respite with Carly's observation. Libby had been giving me the cold shoulder since our encounter this morning, and it didn't seem like she was going to let it go. At least, I hoped she would be civil with my parents and not lapse into one of her silent, pouting moods. As the valet opened her door, Libby exited with a flourish and swung the fringe of her wrap over her shoulder, but in the process, she hit the young man in the face.

"Libby," I cautioned, but she just turned and glared at me.

While my eight-year-old son, Perry, took the lead, I held Carly's hand and led her up the steps trimmed in crushed shells, but I paused to bend over to whisper in Libby's ear. "You need to reign it in with your attitude, or it's not going to go well for you tonight," I warned.

"Whatever?" She sneered and proceeded to advance to the host's stand. I was really beginning to believe that Libby suffered from either bi-polar disorder, or else she was simply just cunning and malicious, but either way, I was growing weary of her roller coaster of emotions.

Although it was Thanksgiving and a reminder of America's most humble of holidays, it was not the case here in this private club.   Excess was in abundance and overflowing.   With the elaborate floral arrangements artfully staged, the dining room was filled with the normal holiday fare of turkey, dressing, potatoes and assorted vegetables, but was contrasted with the intricate turkey ice sculpture which dominated the center of the elegant salad and seafood buffet. And, a colorful display of desserts in a separate room was something more akin to a European gourmet bakery rather than a few simple pies most people had on Thanksgiving.

It was then that I looked over and saw Libby pause at a table to do a double-cheek air kiss to one of her friends, but once we made our way to my parents' table her scowl had returned. Oh shit, I thought, it was going to be hell tonight as I knew my mother would somehow find a way to cast the blame on me for Libby's attitude.

Daddy stood and buttoned his sports jacket as we approached the head of the table. I greeted him with a pat on the shoulder and watched as Libby and the kids gave my father and then my mother the obligatory hugs and kisses on the cheek. I bent down to continue the ritual with my mother, but I nearly gagged as she had heavily doused herself with Opium. She spied my revulsion, and she knew I always had an allergic reaction, but I swear she wore that stupid scent just to spite me. She narrowed her eyes and nodded her head as our eyes met, and I knew my 'dear' mother had obviously considered me when she applied her scent this evening.

The long table was nearly filled as we were the last to arrive. Landon and Jennifer were seated on either side of Daddy with their three daughters, Poppy, Missy and Lucy in succession. The three little girls were giggling as usual, and their overly large hair bows bounced atop their little blonde heads as they bobbed up and down in their chairs. I still couldn't get over the fact that Landon had acquiesced to his wife to allow her to bestow their daughters with names that brought to mind little French poodles, but I guess Landon picked his battles. Hollis was seated next to Mama, as usual, and beside him was his rather unfeminine wife, Helen. Helen had at least two inches in height on Hollis, and I swore she could likely take down my weak brother on any level. Their little hellions were the worst of the bunch in my opinion as they kissed up to my parents to the point of revulsion. Hollis' kids, George, Jr., and Geoff, and Lily all smiled so sweetly as we approached, but then his little girl looked up at me with an evil gleam in her narrowed eyes.

Her head turned, but her little shoulders never moved, and she reminded me of the girl from *The Exorcist*. "You're a butthead, Uncle Boyd," Lily uttered in a whisper as I leaned down to kiss the top of her little strawberry blonde head of curls.

I recoiled in shock, but I knew better than to say anything. Hollis' children were Mama's favorites, and I was already treading on fragile ground tonight with Libby's mood. Shit, I just wanted to leave the dining room and make my way over to the bar, but needs must when the Devil drives.

Libby pulled out an empty chair next to Mama and started to sit down.

"No, Libby, you go on - sit down there. I want Attie to sit next to me tonight," my mother advised.

"Marion," Libby cooed in the sing-song voice she always used when speaking to my mother. "I'd just wanted . . ." she started, but my mother had already dismissed her and was looking the other way across the dining room, so Libby gave a slight shrug and made her way down the length of the table to the center where she had been banished among the children.

Attie was late as usual. Of all of us boys, he was the only one who never married or had any children, but even without those obligations, he still couldn't get his act together to ever arrive on time. I guess it also had a lot to do with why he never had a job as punctuality is a pretty major factor in moving up the corporate ladder. I had surmised long ago that it wasn't simply a matter of time-management in Attie's case, but rather an attitude. And, in the case tonight, it was obvious he would rather have been anywhere else than to spend an evening with his family. I watched as he sauntered in across the dining room, and I noticed many turned to look at his entrance. Attie never did anything without a flourish, and tonight was no exception. He had on burnt orange trousers, I suppose in honor of the autumn colors associated with Thanksgiving, but he had also donned a black velvet dinner jacket and sported a white ascot. He was wearing some sort of velvet black slippers that looked gay as shit, but each to their own.

"Hello, hello everyone," he said as he held one limp hand in the air and flipped the other around the table as though he were a king bestowing favors on his subjects. "So sorry I'm late, but got held up at the condo."

At the condo, my ass, I thought. He pulled out the chair between our mother and me, and he reeked of alcohol. I knew he had more than likely been at the bars along Fifth Avenue since this afternoon and getting totally wasted before venturing to the family affair.

"No, problem, sweetheart," my mother said patting his arm after he had settled himself beside her for the evening. "We only ordered drinks," and she held up her Kir Royale before she looked down the length of the table to George. As always, it continued to amaze me how cordial and maternal our Mama could be in public.

We all knew a toast was forthcoming and followed suit as we held up our drinks. We had all been as well-trained as Daddy's hunting dogs and we knew the routine well. He stood, held up his glass and looked length of the table at the family he had produced. I wanted to think he was proud of his prodigy, but I wasn't sure from his expression. I assume it was supposed to be something akin to 'gratefulness' for this family, but it came across more as a look of pained obligation. In truth, we were about as dysfunctional as any family featured on some sort of daytime talk show, but we cleaned up well, and appearances were everything at the Port Royal Club. The four of us boys were neatly groomed, the wives were adorned in their diamonds and pearls, while the grandchildren were in their requisite little preppy clothes. Yes, our mother was delighted as she could present the image of a picture-perfect family to the rest of the members of the Club, but of course, there was not one single family present here tonight who didn't have secrets and skeletons in their closets; still, we all hid it well behind the mask of wealth and privilege.

"There are 17 of us now, and when your mother and I started back in Tuscaloosa, who would have ever thought we would end up here in Naples," he began, and I knew Daddy was going to launch into another story about their humble beginnings which led them to this day. We had heard the stories multiple times before at every holiday or birthday dinner, but we listened again, nevertheless, to the speech and then we all proceeded to break bread.

An hour later, Attie turned to me and mouthed the word 'smoke' as he nodded to the outdoor terrace. I looked around the table to see if I could dare escape. Mama had excused herself to the restroom, so we were pretty clear on our end of the table, and the grandkids were keeping things lively and animated, which was a good thing, since the adults never spoke about anything other than the weather or the variety of the foods presented. We learned early-on that certain subjects were forbidden topics by our mother as it could lead to unsavory memories she had chosen to bury in the past. I did one quick glance over toward Libby, but she was looking down at her lap and likely engaged with her phone, so I was good to go.

I nodded to Attie, placed my linen napkin along-side my plate and we made a quick exit. The minute I opened the door to the terrace, I felt the breeze on my face, and it was as though the stresses of the evening evaporated away into the humid Florida evening.

"Here," Attie said as he held out a packet of Marlboro Lights,' and I took one.

"What's up?" I said as I grabbed my lighter from my pocket to light up.

"Just a bunch of crap," he said as he inhaled deeply

and looked out at the stars glittering in the dark skies over the waters of the Gulf of Mexico.

"So, what's new?" I laughed. "That's just life. It's been hell for me as Libby's on some sort of warpath lately. She's become a disciple of 'Dr. Phil,' and now she's got us going to some hippie lesbian for therapy."

Attie laughed and kicked at a circle of small shells that some child had obviously placed in the sand by the terrace.

"It's not funny," I protested and gave him a push on the shoulder. "Heck, I'm sitting in some incense-filled room once a week, no windows, and it's either that or I say 'good-bye' to my marriage, and my money."

"Hey, I don't think you'd have any problem saying 'good-bye' to the marriage, but the money – that's where you're gonna feel the real pain."

"No doubt," I agreed with a sad laugh, but I suddenly mellowed. "You know, I wouldn't give up my kids. Carly and Perry are the greatest, but Libby became a different person the day we married. You should have hit me in the head before I walked down that aisle."

"Daddy always told you not to marry a Jew," Attie said as he walked off the terrace onto the sand and threw his cigarette off into the sea grape bushes.

"She isn't Jewish."

Attie didn't respond, but raised an eyebrow.

"You know they say someone's Jewish if their mother is a Jew, and it was Libby's father."

"Whatever, but Hell, Boyd, her name was Gershkovich. It's about as Jewish as it comes. Don't you remember that Mama nearly had a heart attack when you said you were gonna marry Libby," he paused as he pulled another cigarette out of the pack, and I knew at that point something was bothering him as he was smoking one after another. "You know the Port Royal Club didn't even let Jews or Blacks in until the late 70's until after that Jewish doctor sued them when they denied his membership."

"Well, her Daddy was a Russian Jew if that makes any difference, but I guess it doesn't," I surmised and admitted defeat.

"Your call." Attie said, and then suddenly went silent.

"So, what's up?" I said as I knew Attie, and I was sure something wasn't right. It wasn't the norm for him to ever offer up that anything was bothering him, but I sensed he had something going earlier when he had uttered the words 'just a bunch of crap.'

He hesitated and looked back up at the Club which

was aglow with lights from the dining rooms. He walked a bit farther out onto the sandy beach and looked over at me with a pained expression.

"What is it, Attie?"

"Well, you know I went up to Tuscaloosa for that 'Bama and Tennessee game last month?"

"Yeah, so what? Great game, and they won 24 to 20 wasn't it?"

"God, Boyd, it's not the game I'm talking about," he swore as he looked over at me and stared me straight in the eyes. "I met this girl there."

"Someone you went to school with?" I asked optimistically as I always hoped that Attie would finally settle down as it might help him get his life in order, find a job and move forward with some semblance of responsibility.

"No, she's no one I knew when I was a 'Bama, and she's not someone I would ever marry, but . . ."

"But?" I countered as I walked closer to him.

"She was some girl I met at the bar before the game. I bought her some drinks. We had some laughs. She didn't have a ticket, but I got her in. We watched the game, then went out to celebrate the win afterwards, and she ended up back in my hotel room."

I shrugged. "So, you got laid – hope she was cute, and it was a good fuck."

"Apparently, it was a 'good fuck,'" he said sarcastically, and he paused for a moment. "She's just contacted me that she's pregnant."

"Shit, Attie," I said, but hesitated as it fully registered, and then I bombarded him with questions. "What are you going to do? Do you want it? Do you care about her? Are you gonna marry her?"

"Slow down, Boyd," he said as he finished a last drag on his cigarette. "She's not someone I could ever bring home. She's white trash. She's a coke addict – God, she's as skinny as a 12-year-old, and who knows how the kid would turn out."

"So, what are you gonna do?"

"No idea," he responded and grabbed for the glass of whiskey he had sneaked off the table. "That's why I was late tonight, I was on the phone with her. She was crying, yelling, and telling me that she was with her family all day for Thanksgiving, and she just wanted to tell them she was pregnant and was getting married."

"So, she's definitely not someone you could marry?" I countered.

"Hell, if Mama was pissed about Libby being a Jew,

how do you think she'd feel about me marrying some white trash girl from Alabama? Can you imagine her family coming down her for a wedding? Mama would have a hissy fit. I could just see the wedding announcement in the *Naples Daily News*, and how would she explain to her bridge club that her newest daughter-in-law hailed from a double-wide outside of Tuscaloosa in Duncanville – wherever the hell Duncanville is?"

"Attie, Attie, just calm down," I said as I went over to him and grabbed his shoulders in some semblance of comfort. "How the hell do you even know it's your baby, or even if the girl is pregnant? She could be lying about both accounts."

"I know. You're right. I'm sure I look like a better catch than any guy from Duncanville."

I was silent as I didn't want to say that Attie wasn't exactly employed himself. Yes, he lived a charmed life in Naples, but it was due to our parents' generosity and his trust fund.

"Attie, I hope you didn't tell her you're from Naples. God knows that whenever you mention 'Naples,' most everyone sees dollar signs."

"Hell, I don't know if I told her or not?" He stopped and began rubbing his head as if it pained him. "I was so wasted that I don't remember what happened, but I know she was in my bed when I woke up the next morning."

"But she contacted you?"

"Yeah, I don't get that either. I didn't give her my number that night – that I remember, or the next morning when she left. The only thing I gave her was a fifty for breakfast and a cab."

"So, there," I said sounding hopeful. "Look at it logistically. You were only with the girl one night. You don't recall giving her your phone number, but obviously she found out you were from Naples. My guess is that after you fell asleep, she looked at your wallet to see your driver's license with your name and address, and then probably used your phone to call herself so she would have your phone number." I stopped so he could process the information. "Attie, it's an obvious set-up, and I have no doubt it's not a marriage this girl wants, but a pay-out. I honestly don't think there is a baby, and if there even is one, then I doubt it's yours. She sounds like she's one to probably sleep around. So, rest easy. I'm sure it will work itself out, and God knows you can get an attorney to sort it all out if you have to."

And, with that comment, I saw Libby walking out on the terrace from the dining room.

"You both need to get back inside. Your mother isn't happy that you just disappeared," she sneered as though she somehow had the upper hand and turned on her heel to go back into the dining room.

I looked at Attie. He gave a forced smile, and we walked back inside side by side.

CHAPTER 12
Boyd

*L*ibby screeched, "Boyd, I'm talking to you."

I looked over at her, but I ignored her. Yes, we had gotten to that point of total and utter disrespect for one another. I had seen other couples in this state of disengagement, but I swore I would never be one of them. Maybe I wasn't being fair, but no matter what she said or did, I found myself finding fault with her, and I voiced it. If she said 'black,' I said 'white,' and then a huge row would ensue. It wasn't good. After my neighbor told me he heard us yelling one night, I made sure that the windows were closed after dinner each night as that was when things escalated. Sure, I was drinking more, but who wouldn't when you had a 'bitch' of a wife, and she was going through her bottles of Chardonnay like water. Although it was a simplistic analogy, we were like oil and water, and if we stayed together, I had no doubt we would destroy each other, and likely our children, as well.

She wouldn't cook for me any longer, and only made her vegan dishes for her and the kids. She wouldn't do my laundry, and if there were any negative issues with the kids, then she told me it was my fault. As far as sex, I couldn't even recall the last time we did it? I couldn't even stay hard that time six months earlier when she had agreed to give me a blow job as I kept thinking she was likely to bite me, or else pull a 'Lorena Bobbitt.' Clearly, the only reason I got any attention that night was because she wanted money to go shopping with her friends, which I guessed equated her to the position of a prostitute. In all honestly, if you're married, you shouldn't resort to pleasuring your husband for financial gain; it should be because you want to give him love and satisfaction, but that was a foreign idea in Libby's mind. So, as a result, my stress had reached its limit, and I lashed at her with a vengeance.

"I heard you," I finally answered, but in truth, I felt more like a dog on a lead getting reprimanded for bad behavior. Still, I didn't bend to her warning, and I remained solidly fixed in my position on the dock smoking my cigarette.

"No, you didn't," Libby screamed from the house and came walking out on the dock. With her hands on her hips, she stood facing me and her eyes flashed in anger.

It was the first Sunday of December, and she had planned on taking the kids to get a Christmas tree and then spend the rest of the day decorating it – it was on Libby's 'list of things to do' today, and God knew we couldn't deviate. Even though it was December, it was a gorgeous day, and while she was in the shower, I had casually suggested to the kids that maybe we could all go out on the boat and have a picnic on Keewaydin Island instead. The kids had been in favor of it, and I said we could go get a tree after school the following day.

"We already had plans today, and you can't just go changing them," she demanded as she sought to make her point, and she met face to face as though we were about to engage in a duel.

"Libby, just calm down," I began, but she sneered at me.

"Don't you tell me what to do," she countered as she came within inches of me and raised one hand to point a finger in my face.

"The world isn't going to end if we don't get the tree today, and plus I think after this long Thanksgiving weekend, it would be nice to get out to get some fresh air-"

"No, no, no," she screeched, and literally jumped up and down on the dock.

"Libby, you've got to stop this. It's Sunday morning, and the whole neighborhood will hear you."

"Boyd," she said my name barely above a whisper, but it was through gritted teeth. "I have done everything that you wanted this weekend, and now it's time to think about what I want for a change."

"What are you talking about?" I took off my baseball cap and rubbed the sweat off my brow. Even though it was morning, and a cool breeze blew off the water, I was still working up a sweat.

"Honestly, Libby, I haven't asked you to do a thing this entire weekend," I countered.

"What the hell do you call that fiasco of a dinner on Thanksgiving? Do you think it was something I wanted to do? Absolutely not. I go to those things with your family because I have to, and I do it for you." She stopped to catch her breath, and I could tell she was gearing up for another tirade. "It was so insulting. Your mother barely spoke to me, and then she basically 'ordered' me down the table to sit with the children."

"And, so you think that it's my fault, and that I somehow 'owe you' now?" I shot back.

"I most certainly do," she replied in a voice now eerily cool and collected, and I could tell she was more than ready to push the issue. "Remember our last session with Mona?"

How could I forget. I smelled like incense for the rest of the day, and all the guys at the office kept ragging on me that I must be secretly sneaking off to go to yoga sessions.

"Well, you're supposed to be thinking of me, and thinking how you can make my life better," she ended with a curt nod of her head and stared straight at me.

Literally, it felt like I was at a show-down from the Old West. Libby had retreated and we now stood eight-foot apart, but we stared at one another with looks of disgust, determination, and disappointment. No, we weren't two cowboys on some dirt street ready to pull our guns to put an end to our misery; still, I couldn't help but think how the analogy totally summed up our marriage. We were at our limit. Either she had to go, or I was ready to 'get the hell out of Dodge.' If we didn't, it would be the psychological demise of the both of us, and our children.

"Libby, I'll tell you what," I said as I walked the few feet until I was within inches of her face. "I can sure as hell make your life a whole lot better beginning today."

I saw a momentary flicker of hope that she had been victorious in reigning me in, but it was short-lived. She saw the revulsion in my eyes, and a look of fear came over her as she could tell I had had enough of her self-serving attitude.

"Now, you listen here," I said, and lifted my hand to point a finger at her face, but she flinched as she must have thought I was going to strike her. "Oh, come on, don't act like that. In all our years together, I've never laid a hand on you, and you damn well know it."

She turned away briefly as we both heard the kids sliding open the glass door.

"I'm making the plans today, and I am taking the kids out on the boat for a few hours. When I get back, I am packing my things, and I'll be gone before dinner," I paused, and in the couple of seconds I had left, I added. "So, yes, I can make your life a whole lot better," I finished with a sneer, and then turned to grab hold of the kids as they ran down the dock and they threw their arms around my legs. Without another thought of Libby, I buckled the kids into their life jackets, and I turned on the motors. I wanted to get the hell out of here, and I was ready to roll so I reached down and turned on the radio. At that moment I heard the strains of *Bad Moon Rising* coming out of my speakers, so I cranked it up. The words truly echoed my life at that moment, and when I looked down at the kids, they were sitting on the seat beside me pumping their fists in the air to the music.

> *I hear hurricanes a-blowing*
> *I know the end is coming soon*
> *I fear rivers overflowing*
> *I hear the voice of rage and ruin*
> *Don't go 'round tonight*
> *It's bound to take your life*
> *There's a bad moon on the rise*

"So, you just packed up and left this afternoon – shit, I still don't believe it?" Attie took another sip of his beer.

It seemed fitting that it was a full moon this evening as we both gazed into the fire pit on Mama and Daddy's patio overlooking Cutlass Cove. After packing, I had been headed to Attie's condo to crash for the night, but when I called, he told he was already down at the house in Port Royal. With everything that had happened today, I had forgotten that our parents always went over to Palm Beach after Thanksgiving to see her sister for a few days, and so Mama could do her Christmas shopping. As the one free of obligations, Attie was always commissioned to stay and care for the dogs, Rory and Luc, when Mama and Daddy left town.

"No, I knew it wasn't good when we talked at dinner on Thursday, but I had no idea you were planning on doing something so soon."

"I wasn't," I said as I reached over to put another log on the fire. "In fact, today Libby had us all planned to go get a tree and decorate it, but the kids and I wanted to go out on the boat."

"Damn," he said, and shook his head.

"It's not like I woke up this morning, and looked over at her, and thought this is it. This is the day that I'm leaving my wife, but I guess the whole argument this morning was just the final nail in the coffin."

"So, there's no one else?" Attie casually asked as he lit a joint.

"No, but it doesn't mean I didn't have my chances over the years," I said, but then added. "There have been a few receptionists at the office over the years that have flirted and let me know they were willing, and then I met a stewardess on a flight to Chicago one time – we talked and flirted at an airport bar, but I've never been unfaithful, if that's what you're asking."

Attie lifted his eyebrows and nodded as though he wasn't sure he had really believed me.

"I mean it," I countered. "Libby may think I'm a bastard, but I've never crossed the line. God, I'm human, and believe me I've thought about it because she stopped having sex once the kids arrived so I'm lucky if I get it once a year, and then I have to beg for it."

"Yeah," he agreed, and inhaled deeply. "I always liked Libby, but I could tell she was likely to be high maintenance from the beginning."

"I really didn't see it at first." I countered. "But, guess I should have realized when Dex told me what his sister said." "What do ya mean? Something about Libby?"

"Yeah, remember Libby was a college roommate of Dex's sister, Anna, and she came to visit. The girls were biking around Aqualane Shores one day, and Libby mentioned she wouldn't mind living there someday. Then that night, I met up with Dex down on Fifth Avenue, and Anna and Libby showed up, and they introduced me to Libby. I never knew until years later that Anna had told her, 'if you really want a house in Aqualane or Port Royal, then that's the guy you should go after,' and she had pointed to me," I ended, and started to take another sip of beer, but it was empty, so I gave it a toss toward the firepit.

"Shit, women can sure as hell, manipulate," Attie said flatly, and I could tell the pot was mellowing him out, but there was no doubt he was thinking about the girl in Tuscaloosa.

I nodded in agreement and stood up to stretch. "Hey, I'm gonna go raid Daddy's wine cellar. I think we deserve it tonight, and we need to toast to the fact that we're free men."

Attie laughingly agreed, but his eyes were half-mast as he had been pounding them hard all afternoon. I was ready for a good red wine to toast in my new-found freedom, and hell, if I had a hangover tomorrow, I would just call in sick.

Just as I had predicted, Attie was had been close to calling it an evening as he was snoring loudly when I returned. So, I settled myself comfortably and placed another log on the fire. With the stars sparkling over the Gulf, I drank glass after glass of the French wine until the bottle was empty. With each sip, I contemplated my marriage, my kids, my future, and how I was going to manage to break-free with as little collateral damage as possible. Still, it wasn't until the following morning that I realized my first damage had already been done. After I cleaned up the mess we had made in the kitchen with bags of chips, cheeses, and a box of cold pizza, I gathered up the last of the liquor bottles to throw in the trash bag I was taking out. It was then that I saw it. It hadn't registered last night, but now that I was fully conscious, I spied the empty bottle on the kitchen counter, and comprehended that I made my first 'fuck-up.' I drank one of Daddy's most expensive bottles of wine - a 1957 *Chateau Lafite Rothschild*. I guessed he had bought as future anniversary celebration to the year he had met my mother. The price tag was around $12,000.

CHAPTER 13
Landon

Jennifer and the girls were waiting at the kitchen table with breakfast, so I hesitated. Should I, or shouldn't I? It was Christmas Eve, and I wasn't sure I could make it through another family dinner. I stood in the bathroom and ruminated over it all. God, who was I? I looked physically fine, but I was struggling. It had all started so simply, but I had let it get out of control. I was sloppy. What the hell, I wasn't perfect. I wasn't a saint, and I was in genuine pain so who could blame me. The headaches had become a part of my life since the accident at the Tuscaloosa pool, but I had learned how to handle them. The weekly shots that dulled the pain had helped when I was younger, but then in high school, I had discovered pot which worked wonders; still, it seemed I had gradually built up a resistance and that eventually failed to ease the pain of the throbbing ache. So, when conventional medicine had proven futile, I had attempted every other alternative therapy out there from acupuncture to hypnosis to no avail. Finally, in the last year, I had happened on a miracle drug – OxyContin. My associate said it would help, and he hadn't lied. My pain seemed to subside within minutes of every pill I swallowed, and it allowed me to move into a place of ecstasy totally free of the agony I had known since childhood. Sure, I knew about the addiction warnings, but I followed my doctor's guidelines – at first, and hell, I was a doctor, too, so I knew what I was doing.

I continued to stand at the vanity and stared at my reflection in the mirror, but I suddenly threw open the medicine cabinet. I took out the bottle. I had four yesterday, and I had been fine, but I intended on limiting my intake today as I knew I would be drinking. God only knew it would be a trying day. I had spent the better part of last night sitting on the living room floor assembling one *Barbie* thing after another. It seemed that damned doll must have multiple personalities as she couldn't decide what she wanted to be? A pilot, a vet, a beautician or retail mogul. I had looked at the mass of pink plastic pieces scattered about the room and knew that as the 'man of the house,' I had been bestowed the job of assembling an airplane, a beauty shop, a veterinarian's office, and a mini-shopping mall.   So, my first pill had been with coffee that morning, then I had popped another after lunch, but when I came home and faced the "Barbie" construction projects, I had my third, and then after dinner I had popped the fourth pill so I could get a good night's sleep. There was no doubt I was higher than a kite after dinner as I sat crossed legged on the living room floor. I vaguely remembered that I had crooned along with Andy Williams and Bing Crosby, but after rising this morning I spied my construction efforts, and I knew Jennifer would be pissed. Undoubtedly, she would barricade me in the garage for most of the day so I could attempt to rectify my efforts before she placed all the gifts under the tree.

With the small glass, I filled it halfway with water and then quickly downed a pill. I shook my head, splashed some water on my face and then ran the brush through my hair. I looked presentable enough even though I still felt like hell.

"Merry Christmas, to me," I said sarcastically as I slammed the cabinet door.

I don't consider myself an addict. It's not as though I ever intended on continuing any drug use past high school and college, but when you grow-up in South Florida in the 1970's, it just seems to become an integral part of your life. Beginning in the Carter era, the drug trade found a niche in the remote waterways of the Everglades. Planes could fly under the radar from Central America, drop their cargo, and it was readily picked up by the local fishermen in their ramshackle boats, or else by Redneck farmers in their rusted Ford pickup trucks on the backroads. Despite it being an era before mobile phones, everyone coordinated their efforts with the efficiency of cogs in a well-oiled machine. This continued into the 1980's until the DEA swooped into the sleepy fishing village of Everglades City on that humid July morning just after the Fourth of July celebrations. "Operation Everglades" ensued with most of the adult male population were arrested, and the drug trade forever changed in Southwest Florida.

So, while in high school most of the drug transactions took place in East Naples, Marco Island or down in Everglades City, there were many times my brothers and I didn't have to venture too far from Port

Royal. It wasn't often, but on our morning drive to school we would always tune into Classic Rock 93.7, and the morning DJ, Rick, was always ready with the news in between songs. Sure, Rick told us the daily weather report and local politics, but he was also efficient with news from law enforcement. Rick would inform his listeners if there had been an early morning drug run. While the boat drivers would push forward on the throttle to outrun law enforcement as they headed back to the intricate maze of waterways of the Everglades, others would start throwing bales of pot overboard to lighten their loads. So, when we all heard DJ Rick telling us there had been a sighting of 'square groupers,' we would say, "the hell with classes," and turn our cars around to head to our boats. Most of our teachers also tuned into Rick's morning show so had learned that on the days when those 'groupers' were in abundance then their classes would be a bit lighter.

And, while we never really seemed to have any issues finding sources for our needs, we also concluded that it wouldn't hurt to have our own stash. It was originally intended for our own consumption, but we found it could be a quite lucrative side job that paid better than cutting the neighbor's grass or being lifeguard in the summer. I smiled as another memory flooded my senses.

"George, this is Sheriff Rogers," the top law enforcement officer in Collier County opened the conversation in his 'good ole boy' Southern accent.

"Hey, Aubrey," George replied as the two were on first name basis since they moved in the same social circles in Naples. "What can I do for you?"

"Well, we've got ourselves an issue here." The sheriff stated flatly.

"Yes," George answered slowly not sure where his friend was going with the comment.

"Well, one of my boys was doing some flyovers with one of the mosquito pilots, and . . ."

"Yeah, we appreciate y'all spraying it as it's been a mess for us down on the water."

"George, afraid that's not why I'm calling." The sheriff stopped and took a deep breath. "George, I'm not accusing you, but I think those boys of yours have been up to some tricks lately."

"Not following you, Aubrey."

"Well, I'm sitting here looking at some photos that my pilot took, and it looks like your house down on Gin Lane is a pot house."

"What the hell?" George was caught off guard.

"George, you've got yourself a roof filled with pot

plants," his tone softened, and he gave a hearty laugh. "Hell, some on them dang things must be three or four feet high, and they're all growing on top of your roof –"

"Aubrey, sorry to interrupt, but I had no idea, and I've never seen anything."

"George, I believe you," he empathized as he had teenage sons, too. "But, you got yourself some healthy-looking plants on the back roof of your patio. It's flat, I'm guessing the banyan trees on the sides and back hid it pretty well from view so there's no way you could have seen anything. Those boys of yours are pretty dang smart, and if my pilot wasn't flying so low, I doubt he would have seen them."

"Well, thanks Aubrey," George said with a heavy exhale of his breath. "I'm gonna head out now and take care of things. And, mark my words, those boys will be taken care of when they come in from school this afternoon."

"Appreciate it, George," the sheriff replied. "No problem on my end. You just get those things gone 'cause I have DEA on my butt with all the crap going on down in Everglades City. I won't make any waves for your boys "cause they're good boys, but just get those things off your roof."

An hour later, Landon pulled up our Jeep Wagoneer

in the driveway, and we were surprised to see Daddy's Mercedes sitting in the circle. He didn't usually get home until around six every day so all four of us boys exchanged looks and shrugged our shoulders. After slamming the Jeep's doors, we heard a thud, and it was followed by another thud of something hitting the ground.

We started walking up the walkway from the circle drive, and glanced over to the Banyan trees where we heard the next thud reverberate on the ground.

"Oh, shit," Boyd whispered under his breath as he turned to look at rest of us, and we all stared at the pile of pot plants we had so carefully tended to over the past few months.

I looked up and Daddy was up on our roof. He was in swim trunks and a t-shirt, and we could all hear him swearing as he ripped up one plant after another. The four of us continued to stand frozen in place, and didn't utter a word, but apparently Daddy sensed us watching him. He was pissed, and turned to look down at us with an expression we grew to know well over the years. His face was red not only from the exertion in the heat, but he was raging mad.

"Who the hell did this?" Daddy roared as he pulled back his baseball cap and wiped the sweat from his brow.

None of said a word, and we all looked from one to another, but finally Attie stepped forward and spoke up.

"It had to be Boyd," Attie announced in a sing-song voice, and pointed directly at our brother.

CHAPTER 14
Hollis

Christmas Eve, known to many as one of the most festive times of the year for family and friends to gather and celebrate, is normally an evening filled with memories and a time to make new. Most families are able to function well-enough to put aside differences, and the Collingsworth family was no exception – well, most of the time.

"No, no," squealed Landon's three girls as they hid their face behind Jennifer, but she pushed them aside. "Stop it girls, you can't always be afraid of the dogs. They may be large, but you know full well that they won't hurt you. Plus, you're musing my skirt," she concluded as she pushed them aside and walked on ahead through the foyer leaving

Landon to resolve the issue.

Landon didn't say a word. He just stared at the scene before him as though he was in a daze, but who was I to judge. I often fell into a detached mode when it came to the holidays, but Landon was clearly higher than a kite due to some pharmaceutical intervention to get him through the evening. Helen was behind her nieces, but then Rory, the white lab, saw the others standing down the walkway and bounded out of the front doors to greet them with his slobbering pink tongue. After knocking over one of the giant Neiman Marcus Nutcracker men, I watched as George Jr., and Geoff turned in fascination of the chaos, and proceeded to drop the presents and boxes they were carrying.

Luc, the other dog, spied the dropped items, but obviously smelled the rum cake Helen made. The dog stopped in front of the carefully wrapped cake, and then suddenly began ripping into it.

"Oh, my Lord, Hollis, do something - my poor rum cake," Helen turned to me as though I could magically stop the dog as it tore through the tissue paper, and began eagerly consuming the cake sopping with rum.

At this point, Boyd was walking up behind us with Carly and Perry, minus Libby, and his two started squealing and clapping in unison as they watched the drama unfold before them.

This was not starting out well. Mama liked her holidays to run along without any mishaps, mayhem, or the wails of children's voices. Even though she had eight grandchildren all under the age of nine, she still expected the evening to proceed along the lines of one of her adult cocktail parties. Yes, it was Christmas Eve, and we had all assembled as instructed at the specific time – no earlier and no later. And, as always, the Port Royal house was decorated to the hilt thanks to Roger's efforts. Roger was co-owner of the well-known florist on 5th Avenue, and he made sure that my parents' home was always adorned with fresh flowers and decorations on every holiday. With the twinkling lights interspersed with pine garland flown in from North Carolina which wrapped the brick columns and iron balcony over the front doors, the house always looked like it belonged in a spread from an upscale South Florida magazine.

"Y'all just go on into the living room, and I'll keep the dogs here," I said as I grabbed hold of Rory's festive plaid collar.

"Here, let me give you a hand," Stu offered despite the fact he was likely to be covered in buttered rum glaze as he reached out to Luc whose muzzle was dripping with the sugary concoction.

Helen looked at me, rolled her eyes and proceeded to follow Jennifer into the house.

Boyd closed the short distance between us, and his two ran inside after their cousins. He grabbed Luc's collar to relieve Stu of the burden, and our guest appeared visibly relieved. It was obvious Stu was used to the diminutive Princess Di, but these canines were a different breed.

"Here let me take hold of that monster," Boyd said as he held firm to Luc's collar, and with his free hand, he reached out. "Hey, nice to meet you. I'm Boyd."

"Nice to meet you," Stu returned in his cool Southern drawl.

Stu turned around to proceed inside as we guided the dogs behind him, but Boyd gave me an inquisitive look as he raised one eyebrow. "Gay?" he mouthed, but I ignored him.

As always, Daddy was in a cordial mood, but this evening he was unusually mellow. I guessed he had probably started out with a Bloody Mary in the morning to cope with Mama and the houseful of workers, and then had likely kept a steady pace all afternoon. With his flushed face, he motioned us boys to the bar and to join him for a drink. He looked around to see if Mama was in view, but she was still giving orders to the staff, so he pulled out the bottle of Jägermeister, and proceeded to pour each of us a shot.

"We're gonna need a bit of 'Dutch Courage' to make it through this one," he added with a laugh as he handed out the glasses. "Your Mama is on the warpath today so just givin' y'all a warning."

We all nodded, but thought better than to broach the subject on Christmas Eve, and especially with a guest in our presence; still, there was no doubt we all could use a little stress relief.

"To Christmas Eve," Daddy held up his glass, and we all lifted ours and joined together.

"To Christmas Eve," we all chimed in and repeated as we downed a healthy draught.

"Sir," Stu spoke up, but hesitated as he gave his head a slight shake in an attempt to deal with the fire in his throat. "Thank y'all for having me this evening."

"No, problem, I loved Ned and Lillian, and any of their family is always welcome here," Daddy gave a loud guffaw, but then stifled it as Mama walked up.

"Hello, boys," she announced in a gracious voice and a nonchalant wave of her hand. I noticed Daddy lifted his eyebrows in question as this was surely the most genteel Mama had been the entire day. "The girls and the children are already assembled in the living room, and the hors d'oeuvres are ready to be served." She stopped and looked Stu up-and-down taking in his MacIntosh plaid pants, crimson bow tie, and green velvet dinner jacket, and then added, "Oh, yes, Stu, isn't it? Hollis said you would be coming along tonight – welcome to our home," she smiled; however, the sincerity of her words rang hollow when she abruptly turned to walk away.

Roger's tree was aglow with lights and over-weighted with garish decorations, but still we all gushed over his efforts, and Mama took in the compliments. While Mama and Daddy found their respective winged-back chairs, the rest of us assembled on the remaining sofas, chairs, and a few children opted to plop themselves on the carpet. Donna and her staff made their way around with trays filled with a vast array of pre-dinner snacks, and while the adults enjoyed Mama's selections, the truth was that she never got the hint that the kids hated caviar on toast points, stuffed mushrooms, toasted brie and quail eggs. Still, it had been drilled into them that they should politely decline if they didn't care to partake, and never make a fuss about Mama Mar's foods.

"Everything looks lovely," Jennifer broke the ice, and I noticed she had a very full glass of chardonnay in hand.

"Yes, Roger worked his wonders again this year," Mama said as she took several mushrooms being offered.

"And, the food looks so delicious," Helen chimed in.

"Let's not forget the weather – I don't think we could ask for a more stupendous night to celebrate the birth of Christ in the bosom of our family," Attie suggested with an arched eyebrow as he raised his glass of scotch, but Mama was oblivious to the patronizing comment as she was thoroughly enjoying her mushrooms.

God, we were a polite bunch. Every year, it was the same. We talked about the decorations, the food, our attire, and if those topics wore thin then it was onto the weather – the weather was always a safe subject.

I glanced over at Stu, but he remained silent. He was obviously a quick learner in the Collingsworth home; still, I had an idea that his Charleston Christmases were possibly a bit more cozy, relaxed and pleasurable from what he had told me about his family at our recent lunches.

"Oh, Mama Mar, we must get a picture of you with all the grandchildren," Jennifer cooed as she pulled out her camera, and started to herd the children over to surround their grandmother. After a few flashes, the requisite photos were finished, but Jennifer wasn't done. "Boyd, your tie just matches your Mama's blouse, please go on over and let me get a picture of y'all together."

Without any hesitations, Mama abruptly rose and walked away to her bedroom. Boyd had halfway stood up, but then sat back down, and Jennifer stood front and center of the room with her mouth open. The conversation went silent, but the festive music continued to fill the void while the staff circulated with their fare which helped to distract from the awkwardness of the situation. As we all enjoyed our 'moment of silence' and chewed on our assorted finger foods both Stu and I glanced over at the kids. The kids were being quiet and patient as usual, but I could tell that they were growing weary – what kids wouldn't.

"Just curious, why can't the kids have a few board games, puzzles, maybe some popcorn, or roast some marshmallows on the fire," Stu leaned over and whispered to me.

I shrugged my shoulders, and shook my head ever

so slightly, and mouthed, 'not now.'

It was at that moment we saw Mama returning to the living room, and she had completely changed into another blouse over her palazzo pants.

Attie looked over to Boyd, and whispered, "Guess, there'll be no photo shoot for you tonight, bro."

"Like I give a shit," Boyd mouthed back.

Mama twirled her hand in the air like she was Queen Elizabeth II doing a wave to her subjects, but we were well-trained and knew the signal that it was time to move onto dinner. The children appeared relieved to quickly retreat to their table off the kitchen in the breakfast room as the adults made their way to the formal dining room. While the massive floral arrangement was aglow with candles in the center of the table, the side buffet was filled with holiday fare – prime rib, duck in a black cherry sauce, Brussel sprouts, French green beans, roasted cauliflower with a Gruyere white wine sauce, sautéed new potatoes in garlic butter sauce and a sweet she-crab soup, as well as assorted breads.

After filling our plates from the sideboard, we found our place cards and sat in our assigned spots. I think Stu was relieved that he was seated next to me, but Helen was on the other side of the table. Helen hadn't uttered two words to Stu, but this wasn't much of a problem. I sensed Stu hadn't warmed to her either, but then I couldn't really call him out on it as not many 'warmed' to Helen. Still, Stu was the epitome of a 'Southern gentleman,' and even if my family was one of the most dysfunctional ones he had ever encountered, I was sure Stu would continue to exhibit the most genteel manners, so dinner proceeded with our normal conversation centering either on the food or the weather.

"Was that the doorbell?" Daddy said as he looked up past the table.

"Who in the world would be ringing our doorbell tonight?" Mama said as she sat her glass of wine back on the table and reached for her dinner roll.

"Maybe Carolers," Attie offered nonchalantly in between bites.

"Possibly," Mama appeared nonplused, but I could tell she was maneuvering her foot to the little buzzer on the floor under the table to ring for the staff.

The buzzer rang through to the kitchen, and Donna appeared momentarily through the swinging door.

"Yes ma'am."

"Donna, please see who's at the front door, and if it's carolers please just given them a plate of cookies and send them on their way," Mama said, and then casually dismissed her with a wave of her hand that held the dinner roll.

"Ah, Mama, don't you want to bring them in and let them serenade us at dinner," Attie made the comment, and then winked back at Boyd and me.

"Attie, stop being fresh. We're having our family dinner, and we don't want any interruptions," Mama cautioned, and turned back with a forced smile at everyone although I could see her dark eyes narrow as though she dared anyone to add a comment.

"It is a wonderful Christmas Eve, Mama Mar – you totally outdid yourself this year," Jennifer offered in an obvious attempt to regain favor from the photo debacle, but I thought she was also trying to keep attention diverted from Landon.

Landon was usually the quiet one, but there was no doubt he was totally wasted tonight. He had a shot of Jägermeister with the rest of us, but I think it had likely sent him over the edge. He watched his hand in a mystified gaze as it moved the fork about on his plate, and I could tell Jennifer was growing more and more nervous.

Mama needn't worry as there wasn't bound to be a scene. Mama never liked scenes. If there was ever a possibility of something disturbing her carefully laid-out plans, then she would simply ignore the problem. Mama was very, very good at disregarding things she didn't find pleasant. There was no doubt she knew Landon was doped up, but it was preferable to overlook Landon's zombie state tonight; still, I was sure she would be addressing it with him tomorrow in a private phone call.

"Mrs. Collingsworth, I'm sorry to interrupt, but you have a guest."

A guest?" Mama tilted her head to the side and raised her napkin to dab at her mouth.

"Yes, ma'am."

Mama raised her eyebrows and looked directly down the table to Boyd. "Boyd, are you expecting anyone?"

Although Boyd had left Libby three weeks ago, Mama and Daddy made no mention of her. Hell, it was like Libby had simply disappeared off the face of the earth. No questions were asked after Boyd had said he was moving forward with a divorce. It had baffled me that both our parents could just so casually dismiss Libby from their lives after 12 years. She was still Boyd's wife, the mother of two of their grandchildren, but we all knew they had never been in favor of his marriage to her. Libby had one-strike against her going into the marriage because of being Jewish, but I know Mama ever really cared for Libby's hippy, vegetarian ways. If Libby had been a cute little blonde WASP, who dressed in her Lilly Pulitzer dresses and kissed Mama's ass then it may have been a different story, but she wasn't, and Mama was clearly happy to be done with the girl.

"No, ma'am," Boyd coughed and attempted to clear his throat from the bite of duck he had just taken, but it wasn't going down well.

Donna looked noticeably disturbed as she clearly didn't know what to do. "Shall I show her in?"

"Her?" Mama questioned and looked for a second time at Boyd. If Libby was going to interrupt Christmas Eve and make a scene, then Boyd would pay dearly for the price of her disrespect to our family.

"Yes, ma'am," Donna was now ringing her hands and then pulled at the front of her white apron skirt, but she remained silent.

"Well, go on Donna, who in the world is it?"

"Ma'am,' she said her name is RaeLynn Yoder."

CHAPTER 15
Attie

"Who the hell is Ray Lynn Yoder?" Daddy raised his voice above the total silence that had taken over the dining room.

Save Landon, we all looked from one to the other, and finally Attie stood up, "I'll take care of this. Excuse me," he said as he rose from his chair and tossed his napkin on the seat.

"Again, I said, who the hell is this Ray Lynn person?" Daddy reiterated in a louder voice. "It's two damn names not a single person, who is Ray and who is Lynn – hell, I don't know any Ray or Lynn – do you Marion?"

"Shit, shit, shit," I muttered as I walked from the dining room through the hall and down to the foyer. As my heels clicked along the marble tile, the rhythm of my footsteps seemed more like a death knell than a simple walk through the house I had known for years. The front doors were still ajar from Donna opening them, and there stood RaeLynn plain as day holding Donna's plate of cookies.

"Hey, Attie," she said as she shyly smiled.

"RaeLynn, what the fuck?" I said as I stepped outside and partially closed the doors behind me.

"Attie, don't swear at me," she said in her whinny voice. "I've been trying to call you since we talked on Thanksgiving, but you never called me back. Why not?" She finished with a noticeable pout of her lips.

I looked around to make sure no one had followed me, and I was in the clear, but still lowered my voice. "RaeLynn, we aren't boyfriend/girlfriend," I said using simple words that I hoped would help her understand. "We don't have any sort of relationship. We met and had some fun one night when I was in Tuscaloosa -"

"But, Attie, we made a baby so now we have to be a family."

"RaeLynn, you already told me you had a boyfriend – Darryl something – "

"Dwayne . . . his name is Dwayne, but I stopped seeing him before I met you. Don't you remember, I told you he cheated on me, and I just don't stand for my man cheatin' on me," she stated with a firm nod of her head.

"Whatever," I said under my breath, but all I was thinking was how in the hell I was going to get rid of her tonight. It was one thing if she showed up at my condo, but to show up at my parents' home on Christmas Eve. Okay, I closed my eyes, and sought to take a deep breath to calm down, but she seemed more than patient to wait for my reply. "So, why are you here, and what do you want?"

"Oh, you're a silly boy," she said, and then reached out to hand the plate of cookies to me which I accepted without protest. "Attie, I'm really tired. I traveled from Tuscaloosa on the Greyhound for the past two days, and I really couldn't sleep on those nasty seats. Can I please come in and sit down?"

It was at that moment when she handed me Donna's plate of cookies that I noticed the rounded stomach bulge in her tight, red polyester dress.

I stood holding the damned plate of cookies as my mind raced to what I was going to do with her, but at that moment I turned to see the front doors crack open – it was Boyd.

I was sent to scout out what's goin' on," he said, and then focused on RaeLynn with a charming smile that I could have knocked off his face. "And, I'm guessing you must be a friend of Attie's?"

"Yes, sir, but I'm more than a friend, I'm Attie's girlfriend, and we're gonna be parents," she offered, placing both hands on the belly bump in case Boyd had any doubts.

Boyd turned to look at me and raised an eyebrow with that same look of self-satisfaction I knew from childhood whenever I got in trouble.

"Well, I guess congratulations are in order, Attie?" Boyd said in a patronizing tone, but I only rolled my eyes, and now I really wanted to show him my fist.

"Attie," RaeLynn whined again. "I told you that I'm really tired - I need to sit down. Can I come inside?"

I hesitated, but Boyd was enjoying this way too much.

"Sure thing, honey," Boyd put his hand out on RaeLynn's shoulder to guide her through the front doors, and with his other hand he picked up her blue vinyl suitcase. I had no choice, but to follow down the corridor with the plate of cookies.

"Y'all, this here is RaeLynn, and she's a friend of Attie's," Boyd announced as we entered the candlelit dining room.

"Oh, wow," I heard RaeLynn mutter as she took in the opulence of the decorated room, but also the table filled with all Attie's family and that of her soon-to-be-child.

Through to my dying day, I don't think I will ever forget the look on Mama's face. It was mixture of emotions as those dark eyes bore into me. Annoyance, irritation, and outright rage that I would have the audacity to allow someone to destroy the ambiance of her family's holiday. As much as we knew we would have to keep this little intrusion quiet from the rest of Naples society, there was no doubt Mama knew the staff would talk, and if your staff talked then it was a given that it would circulate to others. Mama was sure to be royally pissed. Again, silence permeated the room, but still we could continue to hear all the distant sounds from the children in the breakfast room off the kitchen, and those sounds only reinforced the whole drama of the reason for RaeLynn's appearance.

Finally, my airhead sister-in-law, Jennifer, stood up, and I could tell she was tipsy as she attempted to stand straight, but had to catch hold of the table so as to not topple into Landon's lap. "It's so nice to meet you, RaeLynn, I'm

Jennifer and this is my husband, Landon, he's Attie's oldest brother."

I guessed Jennifer was only attempting to utilize the etiquette skills acquired from her debutante days, but Mama only sent a glare in her direction to stop it and sit back down. Jennifer ducked her head down like a reprimanded child, and readily complied, but she made a noticeable hiccup before sitting back down.

"Where are you from, girl?" Daddy broke the silence.

RaeLynn beamed at the attention, "I'm from Tuscaloosa, sir, well, actually Duncanville just south of there. My family's been there since before the War of Northern Aggression," she added proudly.

At that moment. Boyd had obviously remembered Raelynn's pleas for a seat, so he walked over to his place that had been beside Mama, and he pulled out the chair. "Here, RaeLynn, I insist that you take my seat. I know you have had a long trip," he added with all the chivalry of a Southern gentleman, and now I wanted to hit him upside the head for the third time tonight.

"Why, thank you, Boyd, you're so sweet," she said, and settled her skinny bottom on the chair, but then without any hesitation, she reached out to touch Mama's hand that was holding steady to the table.

Without a word, Mama looked at the girl, and lifted her hand away as though it had been touched by a leper.

"So, how do you know Attie?' Daddy asked after he wiped his mouth on the napkin.

"Oh, we met at a bar in Tuscaloosa before a football game this fall, and since I had never been to a 'Bama football game, Attie offered to get me a ticket and take me, and then we just had the most amazin' night," she finished beaming for all to see her crooked front teeth, and I cringed.

I turned as the door to the kitchen opened and Donna appeared. Without a sound, she reached and quietly removed the cumbersome accoutrement from my grasp, but I wished that she hadn't as now I just stood there without a clue what to do. I didn't want to go over to take the seat beside RaeLynn, but I also didn't want to get any closer to Mama as I knew she was madder than a hornet.

"So, why did you decide to come on down here to Naples – on Christmas," Daddy persisted.

"Well . . . well," she hesitated, and looked around the table, but paused again. "I'd thought Attie would have told y'all," and then she looked across the table to where I was standing. "You didn't tell them, Attie?"

This was it. The shit was ready to hit the fan now.

Of course, everyone turned to look at me, so I just shoved my hands in my pants' pocket, and waited for my execution.

"Yeah, we met in Tuscaloosa, and we hung out with some of the guys from Sigma Chi."

"There, you go," Daddy interrupted. "It was a fraternity party, so I'm guessing you must now be down here in Naples visiting some of your relation?" He ended on a hopeful note, but we were all well-aware that RaeLynn wasn't exactly some little fraternity sweetheart.

"No sir," RaeLynn promptly answered Daddy.

"Oh, were you a Tri-Delt," Jennifer interrupted as she must have forgotten the earlier warning glance from Mama, and in her inebriated state she was only catching bits and pieces of the exchange. "I was a Tri-Delt at Ole' Miss – maybe we've met before," Jennifer gave a short laugh not even registering the fact she was likely 20 years older than the girl.

RaeLynn politely smiled at Jennifer as she waited for her to finish laughing. "No, ma'am, I'm still in high school," she answered directly. "I ain't never been in any sorority. Attie and I just met at a bar, and then we had the most wonderful time – I think it was destiny."

This really was not going well from the look on Mama's face, but as I looked over at Hollis' friend, Stu, it was apparent that our guest was thoroughly enjoying the exchange from the expression on his face. There was no doubt that Stu thought he was in for an evening of some sort of staid holiday dinner, but he was thrilled it was turning into a memorable Christmas Eve after all.

"Attie, tell them?" RaeLynn persisted.

"Well," I began, but stopped as I literally felt as though I was going to throw-up right there in the middle of the dining room.

"Attie, if you don't tell them, then I will," she reiterated with more gumption that I imagined from a 16-year-old girl.

I hesitated again, but then as everyone continued to stare at me, I knew I couldn't avoid the inevitable much longer – I had to own up. "RaeLynn is pregnant," I stated flatly.

"Yes, we are," Raelynn added proudly. "Me and Attie are gonna be a mama and daddy come July of next year."

It took several seconds for the words to register with Mama, but when it did, she threw her napkin on the table and got up from her seat. Without any word, she left the dining room, and I supposed she retreated to her bedroom for the second time that evening. I looked over at

Daddy, but he was downing his glass of wine like it was water. Hollis was white as a sheep, while Stu had a smile like the cat who ate the canary. Helen was totally concentrating on her dinner as she attempted to cut threw her thick slice of prime rib. Jennifer was pouring herself yet another glass of wine from the bottle at her end of the table, and Landon looked at me blankly before his head fell on chest and he began snoring. Boyd and I both stood on either side of the table looking at one another without a clue what to do.

RaeLynn was oblivious as she grabbed a dinner roll from the breadbasket, and then with a shrug of her shoulders, attacked the remnants of Boyd's plate. There was no doubt, she was hungry after being on the Greyhound for two days, plus she was now eating for two.

CHAPTER 16
Boyd

*I*t was a new year. It was a new decade, and it was a new Millennium. A time for putting away the old, and ushering in the new. It had been over a month since I had walked out on Libby, and I had to say we had been cordial considering the fact that we were ending a 12-year marriage. Very few words had been exchanged when we were forced to meet to make exchanges with the kids, but at least she wasn't spouting venom so that was a relief. She had retained a high-powered female divorce attorney from Boca Raton within two weeks after I left, but I figured her silence indicated that she was formulating a game plan. Libby may have appeared to be the free-spirit, vegan, yoga enthusiast who espoused riches, but in reality, she wasn't far away from that young girl right out of college who bicycled through Naples and set her sights on a home in one of the most exclusive areas in the United States. While she may want others to see her as the ultra-Liberal feminist, Libby still wanted to be able to proclaim her views from the comforts of a million-dollar home and not some run-down duplex in East Naples.

Once I had got settled in a small studio apartment on Fifth Avenue, I contacted Jack Monroe. He was touted as one of the best divorce attorneys in Naples, and a tennis buddy of my Daddy's so I knew he wouldn't screw me. And, although he had no problem taking me on as a client, he was honest that it wasn't going to be cheap. Just having the last name of Collingsworth appeared to raise the stakes in my settlement.

"Boyd, I've got to tell you that the fact that your wife has retained Sarah Rosenstein isn't going to be good," Jack reared back in his chair and smacked his chewing gum as he looked straight at me awaiting an answer.

"She's a major bitch, and I can tell you she will be out for war if you don't settle the case to her standards. I've had two other cases with her over the years, and both times I represented the husbands. For some reason, Sarah hates men, and she takes every case personally. I'm just telling you this so you can be prepared. Many people think I'm all about the money here in Naples, but being dragged through a nasty divorce is about as bad as major surgery – hell, maybe worse. From the way I see it, we can hunker down for the long haul which could last a couple of years and run into the hundreds of thousands in legal fees -"

"What?" I interrupted. "How in the fucking world?"

"Oh, easy my friend, it's very easy, and not uncommon in Naples with high net-worth divorces," he paused and popped another stick of chewing gum in his mouth. "It's Nicorette, I'm trying to quit smoking," he added as though I needed an explanation, which I didn't. "You see if you get one side that sees the divorce proceedings as a game then it becomes an all-out battle to see which side will win, and they will drag it out until Kingdom comes."

"But, what about the kids, doesn't this affect them?"

"Hell, yes, it does, and it affects the husband and wife, but if you get one attorney with a stick up their butt, they will fight without any regard to the how it affects the family. They will start with motion after motion to request a parenting advisor, a parent evaluation, a custody evaluation, a psychological evaluation, and all these experts have to be paid for their services, and their testimony during court proceedings," he paused to take a breath and looked down at some papers on his desk. "And, I'm not even considering the fact that your soon-to-be ex may very well play the domestic abuse card -"

"Sorry to keep interrupting you, but 'the abuse card,' what do you mean?"

"I mean many women, especially those with vicious female attorneys will try to coerce their clients into making accusations of spousal or child abuse from their husbands."

"But that's never happened? I've never laid a hand on Libby, and I've never touched the children even with a spanking on the butt."

"Good, and I'm glad to hear that as it will make our position all the more solid and sound, if it should come to it, but what I'm saying is that you need to be prepared for the worst, and hopefully it won't come to that," Jack ended on a note which I imagined was his attempt to reassure me.

"Well, is there any way to prevent it?" I asked as I leaned forward in my chair. There was no doubt, I was starting to become very, very uncomfortable.

"We could offer up a settlement. It probably sounds like a lot of money in the beginning, but if we can negotiate a settlement early-on, it would likely be less than stringing out your case for a couple of years, and believe me, I have seen some Naples' divorces last several years. If that happens, it only serves to make the attorneys and court cronies rich while draining the clients."

I nodded my head in an attempt to understand, but all the words about money, settlements, and negotiations were beginning to make my head hurt. "So, what exactly do we do to get this settlement 'early-on' as you say?"

"Well, I can draft up a Marital Settlement Agreement in the next week, and if we're generous with alimony, child support, and custody of the kids, I think there might be a chance. Of course, I can always tell Sarah that if her client doesn't accept the settlement, then we will have to fight it out in court, and there's the possibility of her getting a far less generous resolution."

"Okay, let's go for it," I said.

"I will have my paralegal email you a detailed settlement plan, and I need you to put in the numbers," he stopped and leaned forward in his chair to place his elbows on his desk. "I'll get it together, and I think we may have a settlement to present before the judge by Easter."

I nodded my head, but suddenly felt sick at my stomach. When I married Libby, I never intended to be seeking a divorce 12 years down the road, and it was sad. Granted, I loved the idea of marriage, and I loved my kids, but I knew I couldn't live with myself if I stayed in a marriage to her any longer. I knew I would have steadily lost myself and I would cease to function. I needed love. I needed confirmation of my worth from someone I loved, and I wanted to share my life with someone I could respect, but a woman who would also respect and love me in return.

While Jack may have been small and scrappy in stature, his tactics in the courtroom were regarded as vicious and cut-throat, and I didn't doubt it as I looked around his office. On the floor in the center of the room lay a zebra skin rug, and the mahogany-lined walls were amassed with shelves of law books, but also hunting trophies. From the look of the animal heads adorned with horns or antlers, Jacks was clearly a first-rate hunter, and I had no doubt his prowess likely also extended to the courtrooms of Southwest Florida.

"Yeah," I mumbled looking back at him from the walls.

"Pretty damn impressive, huh?" He boasted as he abruptly changed the subject. "Started out here as a boy in the Everglades killing 'gators, bears and even a bob cat or two, but the real thrill is over in Africa. Been over there now eight times."

"Yes, sir," I admitted flatly.

"Listen hear, son," he said as he leaned forward in his swivel chair and placed both hands on his desk. "I know you don't want to be here. None of my clients want to be here. Hell, you're ending a marriage, it's gonna cost you a small fortune, and sometimes you're gonna be physically sick from the hoops we have to jump through to get this thing resolved, but you're gonna make it."

I nodded, and looked down at the paperwork the secretary had given me.

"Boyd, I guarantee you that a year from right now, you're gonna be a different man. Hell, you're a good-lookin' guy, with a great job, and you're from a good family. I'm sure you're gonna meet a sweet little gal, and I know you'll be coming back to thank me."

"Yes, sir," I agreed, but also looked at the blank check I was ready to fill out. Attie had been right about the money part hurting far more than Libby's absence.

I watched her dance and sway, and I was mesmerized. She was gorgeous.

Well, I've never been to heaven, but I've been to Oklahoma
Oh, they tell me I was born there, but I really don't remember
In Oklahoma, not Arizona, what does it matter?
What does it matter?"

After leaving Jack's office, I made my way over to the Naples Beach Club. It was late afternoon, but the New Year with the new Millennium was only hours away, and I wasn't about to go back to my little studio apartment to ring in the new year alone. I had just written a check for a $25,000 retainer to Jack's delight, so I needed some liquid therapy.

While I sat at the bar of the outdoor cabana nursing a cocktail, I watched as the band played and the people danced, but I kept focusing in on one dancer. She was dancing by herself with her eyes closed. God, she was sexy as she slowly swayed her hips, closed her eyes while lifting arms and moved instinctively to the rhythm. She wasn't looking to call attention to herself as she never interacted with the others around her, and she appeared content to simply exist in a world of her own. She seemed at one with the music. She was the epitome of innocence and sincerity.

Still, how could a woman be so incredibly sexy, and still exude such inexperience in this world? She was an enigma. She looked as though she couldn't have been more than her mid-twenties, but I sensed she was likely in her early 30's. Even though I hadn't spoken a word to her, I was certain I could sit down with her and have a deep conversation.

I nearly hit myself in the head. What was I thinking? I had only been separated from Libby for a month, but did it give me the freedom to pursue a relationship? Sure, I had a couple of one-night stands since I left Libby – I wasn't a saint, but it didn't mean I was looking for a serious relationship. God knew I took a beating after being with Libby. My self-esteem had been shot to hell, but still, I knew I wasn't a bad looking guy, and when I went out to the bars on Fifth Avenue, I was approached. To be honest, it was a boost to my ego that women still thought I was attractive. There was no doubt that all those years with Libby had greatly affected my self-worth, and I suffered. Still, I wasn't a man who wanted a lifetime of 'one-night stands.' I wanted a relationship with someone who not only cared about me, but someone who loved me. I wanted to find someone and make her feel as though she was the most special woman in the world. One-night stands were a release, a brief confirmation that I was still a man, but it wasn't something I considered a long-term plan. Hell, I wanted to be married – did I actually still think that after all the hell I'd been through with Libby?   As much as my marriage had been a daily agony with Libby, I still wanted what the union of two people represented. I wanted the commitment, the shared history, the security, the desire, and I wanted the love; I wanted to be cared for and someone to love me. Call me old-fashioned, but I didn't want to be like those men I saw across the bar from me. They were in their early sixties and they looked like leeches ready to pounce on any young woman who walked by them; still, it was a given in Naples that it didn't matter what a man looked like, or even if he had the personality of a conceited jerk, if he possessed enough wealth then there were plenty of young females who were ready and willing to fill his void. It was sad. I didn't want to end up being one of those men who had a woman with him because of his wallet. As corny as it sounded, I wanted her to love me for my heart and not my bank account.

I took another sip and looked back up at the girl I had been watching, but she had stopped dancing and turned to the band to clap as the song ended. I had no idea who she was, but I was determined I was going to find out. Without even talking to her, I wondered if she could be the person I envisioned.

She sipped her sparkling water and looked up at me with the most remarkable green eyes. Her name was Tess, and while she had accepted my invitation to have a drink, she refused anything alcoholic. She already had two drinks, and she said that was her limit. I respected that, and actually thought more highly of her because of that position.

With her honey-colored blonde hair that just fell past her shoulders, she looked like an angel, but when her green eyes lit up, they literally looked like they were smiling. I had never seen anything like it. There was no doubt those eyes had the power to not only pull me into her soul, but could transform me.

"Isn't a gorgeous sunset," she mused as she looked out beyond the beach, and we both watched the big orange ball disappearing over the horizon. "I wish I had brought my camera to capture the last sunset of the Millennium."

"You like to take pictures?" I asked and leaned a bit closer so I could hear her answer as the band had struck up a pulsating tune that was rocking the entire place.

"Yes," she turned and flashed that smile directly at

me. "I'm a photographer. I work for the *Naples Daily News*, and don't get me wrong, it's a great job, but taking pictures of car accidents, crime scenes or weather-related tragedies isn't exactly a load of fun. I'm grateful to have a steady job to pay the bills, but my passion is taking in nature, landscapes, animals, children - I also do weddings, which are great as everyone is so happy."

So, we went on talking for another hour about various impersonal subjects – the town of Naples, restaurants, music, boating and just all the usual neutral topics you broach when talking with a stranger, but my curiosity was getting the better of me, and I wanted to know. I took a deep breath, and finally came out with it. I just had to know.

"It's New Year's Eve, and I can't imagine that you don't have someone waiting to spend it with you?"

She raised up her left hand for me to see and then shook her head.

"I can't believe it! You are absolutely gorgeous. You're intelligent, you've got a great sense of humor – I mean you've got it all."

Tess shrugged her shoulders nonchalantly at my compliments, but then begrudgingly smiled before replying. "It's not to say I wasn't attached. I was until two months ago, but it wasn't a healthy relationship." She stopped for another moment, and I could sense that she was contemplating how much she should disclose. "He was even talking about marriage, but I broke it off. He's an arrogant attorney here in town, and one night he got a little too rough."

I raised my eyebrows, but didn't inquire as I figured she would tell me if she felt comfortable enough; still, the image of someone harming her was difficult to process, and it brought out my protective mode.

"In my profession, I've seen too many crimes scenes to know what happens to women in abusive relationships. Either they end up dead, or physically and emotionally scarred for the rest of their lives. I just wasn't going to go down that path." She paused, and then turned to look me directly in the eyes. "So, how about you, Boyd, are you married?" Tess questioned me point-blank.

I knew she was a woman who would accept nothing but the truth. She had been in a relationship with someone who cared nothing for her feelings, and I wanted her to know that there were still honorable men in this world. Sure, I could feed her a line as I had done recently with a few other girls I'd met down on Fifth Avenue, but Tess was different.

"I know this isn't going to sound good, but I'm going to be straight-up honest with you," I stopped in an attempt to decipher her reaction, but she only looked on patiently for me to continue. "Yes, I am still married, but I am legally separated."

I was ready for her to roll her eyes in response to my answer as it was a typical line most guys would offer a woman in their first meeting, but she didn't. She continued staring at me, and said nothing, but from the purse of her lips, I could tell she would only accept the complete and total truth.

"Honestly, I have been separated for over a month, and I just came from my attorney's office – heck, I just wrote him a hefty check if you want me to prove it."

She shook her head and continued to twirl her finger around the rim of her glass.

"Do you have children?" She asked.

"Two, a boy and a girl, and while I'm no longer a husband, I'll never stop being their father."

She nodded her head, and then took the last sip from her glass.

I wasn't sure if I had screwed up by telling her the truth, but I intended to be upfront with this woman. And, if she was going to walk away because I had been married and had kids, then so be it.

Tess waited a few more minutes as she looked over at the band playing, but then took her glass and pushed it away. She turned to me and smiled. With her hand, she reached out and pulled me up from my stool. "Let's go dance, Boyd," and I followed her as the band had started playing *Caught Up in You* by .38 Special:

> . . . *So caught up in you, little girl*
> *And I never did suspect a thing*
> *So caught up in you, little girl*
> *That I never want to get myself free*
> *And baby it's true*
> *You're the one*
> *Who caught me baby you taught me*
> *How good it could be* . . .

CHAPTER 17
Hollis

*N*ew Year's Eve was upon us, and Helen had worked herself up into her usual agitated state as she prepared for our annual celebration. As much as she loved it once all the guests arrived, it was pure hell for the week leading up to the event as she agonized over every detail. You would think after hosting the party for eight years in a row, she would have resigned herself to the idea that routine bred the ability to find balance, but continued to strive for perfection.

Our closest friends, four couples, were due at 6 'clock, but I still hadn't mentioned to Helen that I had also invited Stu. How could I not invite Stu? In the five weeks since we had met, Stu and I had regular lunch dates, walked our dogs together and spent countless hours talking on the phone. Helen hadn't come out and directly said it, but I know she wasn't thrilled about my friendship with him.

Helen had her usual fare spread out on the dining room table for everyone to partake in their leisure. With a floral arrangement in the middle festooned with sparkers, garland and pop-ups that said '2000,' Helen had elegantly arranged the foods. Chilled shrimp on ice, stuffed mushrooms with crabmeat, Russian caviar on toast points, oysters in the half-shell, warmed French breads with a rich cheese fondue, gourmet deviled eggs and assorted fresh fruits completed the colorful and tasty display, plus there was also side assortment of mini gelatos and sorbets.

"It looks wonderful, dear," I said as I walked over to her, and gave her a quick kiss on the cheek while she reached over to light the candles amassed in the floral centerpiece. "I think you may have outdone yourself this year," I complimented, and she turned to give me a nervous smile.

She had a half glass of wine sitting on the table, but I offered to top it off as I knew if she had a glass or two of wine in her system then she would be far more relaxed, and if Helen was relaxed, then we all were at peace.

Howard and his wife, Gloria, were the first to

arrive, and there followed the other three couples, who were all our closest friends. All of them lived in Park Shore as our neighbors, so it made for a relaxing evening that they could all drive their golf carts back to their homes, rather than be out on the roads after an indulgent evening.

After the last couple arrived, I lingered in the foyer for a bit, and peered out the long side windows on either side of the door.

"Is something wrong?" Helen questioned. "Everyone's here, let's go get our drinks and make our way to the patio."

I hesitated and didn't move.

"Hollis, you're being rude. Our guests are waiting – let's go," she said with the insistence of a mother chastising her child for not following directions.

There was no way around it, and I just blurted it out, "Helen, we have another guest. I invited Stu-"

"Oh, for heaven's sakes, Hollis. He's going to stand out like an odd duck, we have all couples, and they're old friends. How could you do this to me?"

I shrugged my shoulders, but I knew she wouldn't protest too much with the others within earshot – it had proved to be my salvation that I waited to tell her until now.

She turned back to me and narrowed her eyes.

"Whatever?" She said and turned on her kitten heels and clicked her way down the marble hall to our guests.

George Jr., and Geoff came walking out dressed in their *Toy Story* pajamas. Everyone turned, and while the pair elicited many levels of 'oh's' and 'awes of cuteness from the women, Helen was having none of it as she jumped up.

"Why aren't you boys upstairs with Miss LaWanda?" She said as she made her way over to where they stood by the patio doors.

"But, Mama," George Jr., protested. "It's New Year's Eve, and it's not just a normal New Year's Eve, it's a special one 'cause it's a New Millennium . . . and, Miss LaWanda scared us?"

"For heaven's sake, how did she scare you?" Helen protested, and the rest of us all listened in apt attention.

"Well, she said that spirits come out . . . you know, when there's a big change happening . . . in the world, and, and she said this New Mill – line- ne- um," Geoff, who stuttered was having a difficult time so George, Jr., pushed him aside and came to stand front and center before Helen.

"Miss LaWanda, told us that there would be strange things happening tonight, and that people should be careful 'cause there will be spirits out making people do things they don't normally do."

"That's total nonsense, boys, and you know it," Helen countered, and turned to look at the rest of us with a shrug of her shoulders. "If you will excuse me, I'm going to take these two back upstairs, but I'll be right back."

We all shared a laugh at the preposterous ideas of 'spirts controlling people,' but then Stu interrupted.

"Y'all know I come from Charleston, and I will say that the Black people, the Gullahs, have held tight to the superstitions from their African culture. It was brought over with the slaves' years ago, and many of them in South Carolina have passed down those traditions and beliefs."

"Sounds similar to the voodoo you hear about down in Jamaica," someone said, and we all nodded.

"Exactly," Stu agreed. "Hell, my Mama had a maid that every time someone in her family died, she'd turn the mirrors around in our house, and it used to drive my Mama crazy seeing all her beautiful gilt-framed mirrors turned backwards. Also, they believe the color blue will ward off evil spirits, and many people, even those with brand new houses, will paint the underneath roofs of their front porches light blue so spirts don't enter the house."

"That's unbelievable in this day and age," one of the women offered.

"Not uncommon with the Gullah people as they honor their ancestors, and those traditions have been handed-down and remain strong to this day, but I will say that those beliefs have become intermingled with their Christian beliefs – you will see Christian burials, but then as with their African traditions, there will be wooden carvings, broken dishes and other items on top of the graves to ward off bad spirits," Stu added.

Tom, one of my tennis buddies, stood up, and added, "No, Stu's right," and then continued as he walked over the bar to refresh his drink. "My mother's family is from Savannah, and I remember hearing stories about a 'Root Doctor' or a 'Doctor Buzzard,' and these men would provide protection against witchcraft, or else perform ceremonies to take away the effects of a curse. Many of them still believe dangerous spirits are capable of enslaving a person by controlling his will and make them into a puppet."

"Oh, I don't like this talk, boys, it's giving me the willies," uttered one of Helen's bunco chums.

"I agree," replied the youngest woman in the group.

"I was reading the horoscope predictions for 2000, and it says there are some strange things going to happen. Unusual things happening in the world, politics, and even in personal relationships -"

"Like all us husbands are gonna find out how much you women have been hiding your shopping and personal grooming, and then our relationships will change real quick," Tom said with a loud guffaw as he came back and settled on the lounge chair where he promptly received a playful jab in the ribs from his wife.

At that moment, Helen walked back in, "I'm so sorry. I gave LaWanda a talking to about scaring the boys. She should know better."

"Helen, it's fine now, so let's just let it go," I said, trying to get the evening back to normal. I looked around to everyone else, and raised my glass, and said, "To kids."

Everyone laughed. "To the kids," they responded unison, and we toasted our children.

"Just wait for another 15 years, and you'll be free," Howard boasted as he raised his glass again and placed his arm around his wife's waist. "We've been officially-free since August, and it's been heaven. Since our last left for college, it's like we're newlyweds again. Hell, we even go skinny dipping," and he ended with a snicker.

I smiled back and nodded to Howard's remark, but I have to say I wasn't exactly relishing the idea of 'skinny dipping' with Helen now in the present, much less in another 15 or 20 years.

I stood up, and looked around, "On that note, I'm going to take Beau out for a short walk before the fireworks start at midnight . . . I'll be back in 15."

Everyone nodded as the drinks were having their intended effect on relaxing them, so they just waved me away and returned to their conversations.

"Hey, I want to try-out my new Cuban cigar, so I'll go with you," said Stu as he rose and followed me to the door.

I glanced around, and Helen had tilted her head to the side. Even though she was listening to another story by Tom, she was looking directly at me, and she narrowed her eyes at me again. Obviously, I would pay later for allowing Stu to accompany me on Beau's walk, but I really didn't give a damn at this point.

"Hey, Beau, boy," Stu reached down and roughed up the dog's head and ears in an affectionate gesture.

"Sorry, I don't have Lady Di with me tonight, but we'll get you two together soon, boy."

We walked along in companionable silence for a few more minutes until we were out of hearing distance from the house, and I knew Stu could sense I was unusually quiet this evening. In years past, our New Year's Eve parties were riotous affairs with our friends, but this year it had taken a turn. I'm not sure when it exactly happened, and it wasn't just Helen's reaction tonight to Stu' presence; things had been becoming strained between Helen and me for a while now. It wasn't that there was downright animosity, or overt nastiness, but just an underlying tension simmering, and I had to wonder if Stu's appearance tonight was going to send it to the boiling point.

"Everything okay?" Stu asked, and blew the smoke to the side.

"Yeah, just things with Helen-"

"I'm guessing you neglected to tell her I was coming tonight?"

"Yup," I said flatly, and stopped as Beau found an interesting smell in the grass.

"Do you want to talk about it?" Stu pushed, and a part of me was glad that he cared, but another part of me was conflicted as my relationship with Helen was none of his business.

I hesitated, but the more I thought about Helen waiting for me at home, and the encounter we were likely to have after everyone left wasn't something I was looking forward to. "You know, Stu, I would like to talk to you, but we can't tonight. We need to get back to the others in a few minutes so maybe we can meet up at Starbucks on Sunday."

"Sounds like a date!" He smiled, and lifted his cigar to take a long, deep drag.

I inhaled the smoke that drifting my way, and the sweet-smelling tobacco filled me with a sense of peace.

"You know, Hollis, I think it was fate that we met that weekend after Thanksgiving. As much as I hate that my Aunt Lillian died, and I cussed the thought about having to come to Naples to settle everything up, now I think she may be looking down with a smile on her face."

"What do you mean?" I questioned as I gave Beau a pull on his leash.

"I think you know what I mean?" Stu returned my question with one of his own and stopped to turn and look at me.

I couldn't return his gaze, so I looked over at the dog.

"Are you?" He asked.

"Am I what?" I shook my head in confusion.

Stu threw the rest of his cigar down on the sidewalk and put of the toe of his Italian loafer over it and twisted it three times before he kicked down the water gutter.

I watched his actions, and then lifted my head to look at him. He leaned over and put his hand on my shoulder to pull me closer. We were both pretty much the same height, and that, in itself, alleviated some of the awkwardness. Stu leaned in and kissed me on the lips. I pulled back and shook my head.

"What did you just do?" I was suddenly filled with feelings and emotions of shame, dread and being unclean.

"I think I just did something that you and I have been wanting to do for a while now – am I not right?"

"Do you think I'm gay? I'm married. I have three children – I'm not gay," I protested a little too much, and Stu only gave a half smile at my words.

"Okay, okay, I hear you," he answered. "But, you must have realized I'm gay?"

I shrugged my shoulders. "Well, I wondered?"

"Does that bother you, Hollis?"

"No, why should it? You're my friend-"

"Well, I'm hoping that it can develop into more than just a friendship . . ."

"Stu, I'm married. I have children, I have obligations. I made vow to Helen."

Stu was silent, but we both turned around and started to make our way back to my house.

"Did you make that vow to Helen because you felt an obligation?" Stu pressed.

"I do feel affection for Helen," I admitted.

"But did you marry her because she's your 'soulmate,' and you couldn't imagine your life without her, or did you do it because that was what was expected of you from your family?"

I looked at him with my brows in a crease, and I wondered how he had guessed.

"Hollis, we're not that much different. When I was 22, right out of Clemson, I married a cute little Charleston girl from an old family, hell, I think we're something like third cousins, but I could only put up the charade for a year. She soon realized it when I had no desire to make love with her, but she would have been fine to just go along with it as she only wanted my name, a house south of Broad, and would have been satisfied if I gave her a couple of children and then left her alone."

"What did your family say?"

"Oh, I just admitted to an affair with my secretary,

so my wife became the victim, and I was the cad," he said with a casual shrug. "But, my Aunt Lillian knew the truth – she was the only one. She accepted me for who I was, and she never questioned it. She just wanted me to be happy. She never had any children, so I became the son she never had – even if I was gay. As you know, Lillian was an artist, so she was much more accepting of the gay community than the rest of my family in Charleston," he paused. "My family got over my divorce, but they still hold out hoped that I'll finally find the right woman, and remarry."

"But . . ."

"I won't," and he gave me the most genuine smile of acceptance of anyone I had known in my life.

"We're almost back, and we need to cut this conversation," I warned.

"I get it," Stu nodded with a wink that nearly made me melt.

We opened the front door, and I unclipped Beau's leash to place it on the hall table, and then I turned to Stu.

"So, it was hilarious – the look on your Mama's face," Stu was having a difficult time controlling his laughter and I could see tears forming in his eyes. "That poor girl in her Walmart dress walking into your Mama's Christmas dinner."

Although I cringed at Stu's words, his words did the trick to dramatically change the recent dynamics between us, and I felt myself joining in with his vivid description of the recent event on Christmas Eve, and we joined the others as we continued the conversation at Raelynn's expense.

I never told anyone. No one ever knew it happened. I was only eight-years old, and I wasn't even sure if somehow it wasn't my fault. Maybe I was to blame? All I knew was that it was not something I could mention, and at the time, I was almost positive it was wrong.

It was early spring Saturday afternoon, and I had just finished my tennis lesson at the Tuscaloosa Country Club, but Mama was late picking me up. Landon was supposed to come with me as we always had lessons together, but he was working on his science fair project so Mama said he could skip that day. Looking back, I will always wonder if it would have happened if Landon had been with me? It's not that I think Landon would have protected me, but just him being there might have prevented it from happening.

Miss Betty was my tennis coach, and I loved her. I

remembered hearing that she had taught tennis at the Club since World War II which seemed like ages ago. She loved the kids, and she took good care of us. After my lesson, she said she had to leave to go for her hair dressing appointment, but I should just sit tight and wait for my Mama. Mama wasn't normally late, but there were times when she got caught up at one of her stores, and we just had to wait, but Miss Betty had always stayed with us until Mama arrived.

Miss Betty bid me 'good-bye' and told me I had a good lesson, so I was okay. I looked in my pocket and saw that I still had a nickel left so I went over the to the Coca-Cola machine to get a bottle of Coke. I went back and sat on the bench by the fence to finish the drink. Nothing much was going on, and it was a quiet afternoon, but then again, the tennis courts were far busier in the mornings or late afternoons as to avoid the direct sun. I kicked and dragged my feet in the green clay on the court and watched as my shoes gradually became more and more covered with the green dust. I knew Mama would likely yell at me, but I didn't really care. I was just hot and tired, and wanted her to hurry and pick me up.

A half-hour later, she still hadn't shown up, and I had to pee, so I left my racket on the bench, and made my way into the restroom. It was dark, but my eyes soon adjusted. I walked over to the urinals, and proceeded to lower my tennis shorts, but after a few seconds, I turned as I heard a shuffling sound of someone coming nearer and nearer.

They say that smells and sounds never leave your consciousness. The part of your brain where your memories are stored can instantly bring back a time, a place, or a feeling when you breath-in a certain scent. Whenever I catch a whiff of damp cement, I remember. Whenever I smell that cologne, I remember. At the time, I had no idea it was called, *English Leather*, but later one day in college when I smelled it on someone as they passed me on the sidewalk, I promptly went over to some nearby bushes and threw up. And, when it was happening to me that afternoon, all I remember seeing was the green dust rising from my white tennis shoes, and thinking I wished I hadn't messed up my tennis shoes.

CHAPTER 18

Landon

I sat staring at the official memo. Although I was an equal partner in the medical group, I was being treated like an outsider. An outsider in this practice that I had helped to establish from the ground up 12 years earlier, but now my four partners penned this letter and signed their names with a flourish. Where was the loyalty? Hell, I would have stood by any of them if they were in a crisis, but as I reread the memo, it was a slap in the face. There was no doubt I had done something wrong. I had gotten sloppy, but I was a good doctor. I had never made a mistake in all of my years of practice before now, and didn't they realize we are all human – we're all capable of messing up.

Without thinking, I automatically reached in the top drawer of my desk and pulled out the bottle of pills. I had been good all day. I hadn't had a single pill, so that proved I didn't have a problem. My head was pounding. I had a genuine need for relief so why was I hesitating. I was a trained in internal medicine, so I knew how to properly diagnose a malady, and what was the problem that I diagnosed myself? I unscrewed the bottle, shook out a pill, and grabbed my can of Diet Coke to swallow it.

Sure, I had passed out at dinner on Christmas Eve, and I had missed a few days of work over the past few months, but my big mistake had been with a long-standing patient. I had treated Mrs. Hamilton for nearly a decade. She was an elderly, diabetic with a heart condition. It was late in the day when she had her visit, and I had already endured back-to-back patients without a break. I had been going on an adrenaline rush, but my head had started throbbing again, so I had popped not one, but two pills. When I tried to remember her appointment, it remains a blur to me. In the confusion, I had handed Mrs. Hamilton what I though was a sample packet of a new hypertension medicine, but my nurse and front office hadn't followed up as they normally did. That night, Mrs. Hamilton took all her pills, went to bed, but never woke-up. At 88-years old, it was first chalked up to old-age, but Mrs. Hamilton had a granddaughter who was a personal injury attorney, and she had delved deeper by requesting an autopsy. It was found that Mrs. Hamilton died from consuming methylphenidate. I had inadvertently given her a package of 54 mg. of Concerta which had been the sample I intended to give a teenage patient the following morning.

Now, I was looking at the Complaint filed by the law firm representing Mrs. Hamilton's heirs, as well as the memo from my partners. I shuffled the papers around on my desk, but no amount of rearranging the papers would change my life right now. Sure, I had malpractice insurance, and the practice had been set-up to deal with the possibility of one of us screwing up, but we hadn't. We were well-respected in the Naples community, but it wasn't going to look good for one of us to have messed up as it reflected badly on the entire group. In the memo, I was informed that there would be a story in the *Naples Daily News* tomorrow, and I had been politely 'urged' by my partners to take a leave-of-absence. Not only had my partners been adamant that I leave for three-months, they also had been insistent that I go into a residential treatment facility. They had graciously offered to pay for the first month of treatment – God, how bad did they think I was that I should be there for more than a month?

I pulled into the driveway, but I didn't immediately hit the garage door opener. I wanted to just sit there a few more minutes to take in my home, and the life I had built. From all appearances, Jennifer and I led a charmed life. We had a beautiful home on Gordon Drive, we had three healthy daughters, and I had a successful medical practice, but the latter was now 'past tense'.

How was I going to explain to Jennifer? I would have to couch it delicately. She wasn't exactly the brightest girl, but I loved her simplicity. Her goals in life had been to work towards an elementary education degree at Ole Miss, but she got sidetracked and only ended up achieving her MRS degree. She had no aspirations beyond being a wife and mother. Sure, she did her volunteer work with the hospital service league, junior league, the garden club, and did her share of fundraising for the girls' private school, but that was the extent of any work outside of the home. I didn't complain as she did a great job with the home, and I had stepped back to let her handle the girls as they were her little 'dolls.' I had long ago come to the conclusion there was nothing I could do about her spoiling them. The girls were always dressed to the hilt in their designer clothes, bows in their hair, and were little versions of Jennifer. There was no doubt they were going to be entitled little hellions as teenagers, but I guess I picked my battles. Jennifer was compliant, she never complained about my long hours at the office or hospital, and she was more than happy to let me have weekends away for fishing, golfing or at sports games. Still, I was going to have to frame the situation in words that she could comprehend, and trust that she would be able to survive the next three months without me around. I couldn't delay the conversation any longer as I was leaving tomorrow, but the newspaper articles were also coming out in the morning. Jennifer never read the newspaper, but there was no doubt her phone would be ringing off the hook before she even got the girls off to school. So, with a heavy sigh, I reached for my visor and pushed the button for the garage door, and I watched as it slowly lifted.

"Hey there," Jennifer called to me in her rich Southern drawl, and I smiled at the site of her still dressed in her tennis whites. As usual, she was rushing around the kitchen, and the girls were all seated in a row at the kitchen island doing their homework.

"Hey, Daddy," the three girls greeted me in unison

in that same Southern drawl they had learned from their mother.

I followed my normal routine when I came home and went to deposit kisses on top of each of their little heads, and then went over to Jennifer. I pulled her into a hug and gave her a deep kiss.

"Ew, yuck, Daddy," Poppy, the oldest, declared as she twirled her pencil, and rolled her eyes.

"My goodness, Landon, what's prompted this?" Jennifer giggled as she pulled out of my embrace. "You must have had a good day," she said with a smile as she patted my chest.

I shrugged and knew my conversation about the recent developments would have to be delayed until later.

Jennifer turned to me and flashed one of her glamorous smiles, "Sweetheart, I made one of your favorites – chicken marsala, mashed potatoes and French green beans."

"Sounds great," I responded, and then looked around the kitchen taking in everything that so defined our home – the girls' pictures and handprints that were matted and framed on the wall, her grandmother's old Singer sewing machine that now served as a serving board in our breakfast area, and Jennifer's mother's dishes displayed on the hutch. All these things would surely be handed out to our three daughters in hopes that they would proudly display them in their homes one day.

Still, I had to wonder had I truly screwed it all up? Would my family be able to continue this charmed life without any thoughts of worry about their futures, or had I totally messed it all up? I looked over it all once more and took in the idyllic scene of my wife and daughters before I walked out of the kitchen. Most people would kill for my life, but I had ruined it. I had taken it all and threw it into the wind, and now I was set to leave it. Would I be able to return in three months, and would we be able to resume life as we had known it, or would Jennifer blame me? I knew the girls were too young now to comprehend the severity of my actions, but at some point, when they grew older, they would know and grasp the truth of what happened to their father when they were young.

I walked back over to Jennifer and pulled her close again to whisper in her ear. "Let's take a bottle of wine out of on the patio after the girls have gone to bed. I just want to have some time alone with you."

Jennifer looked at me, and slowly nodded her head. It was a Monday evening, and we never usually had a bottle of wine and patio time unless it was the weekend or a special holiday. No more words were needed now, and I kissed her again before I made my way to our bedroom to change, but she only continued to stare at me with a confused expression.

It was a cool evening for Naples. Most of the tourists from up North would have considered it a time for shorts and t-shirts, and walking on the beaches, but after being a Neapolitan for much of my life, we were conditioned to feel that any temperature under 60 degrees was worthy of a jacket/sweater, or a fire. Before Jennifer joined me, I had piled up the wood on the firepit by the pool, and I had a nice blaze going by the time she had finished putting the girls to bed. Although we weren't on the beach-side of Gordon Drive, we still reaped the benefits of feeling a nightly breeze off the Gulf, and it always made for a pleasant evening whether summer or winter. I turned as Jennifer approached, and saw that she had changed into a long, flowing silk dress, and she walked close I could smell her signature scent of *Giorgio*, which meant she had taken time to freshen up from her afternoon tennis game. Although I never had been able to have deep intellectual conversations with her about politics or world events, I still appreciated the efforts she put forth to make me happy, and care for our home and children. A lot of my friends' wives were far more equal in intellect, but with that came a price; it was the fact that many wives wanted more power in the marriage. I guess we all have to make a choice with our mates, and Jennifer and I had made ours. I busted my butt to make a nice living, and she lived up to her role as a wife and mother without question or struggle; but, now I was wondering if that would always be the case when I broached the subject of our change in circumstances.

"Here, sweetheart," I said as I handed her a glass of red wine, and she reached up to place a soft kiss on my lips.

She accepted, and I lifted my glass to hers. "Here's to us, our marriage and our daughters."

She took a sip, and then turned her blue eyes on me. "Landon, what's going on? We normally never do anything like this without an occasion, and we never come out here on a weeknight."

"Can't a man just want to have a relaxing evening with his wife without a reason?" I countered, but immediately wondered if she would see through my lie.

Jennifer raised one of her eyebrows in a questionable arch, and I had to wonder if I had underestimated her in the past. She may have been complacent without any desire to have a career, but it didn't mean that she hadn't become intuitive to me and the dynamics of our relationship over the years.

"Landon, I can sense something isn't right." She sat her glass of wine down on the table and walked closer to me so she could place her hands on my chest.

I had only allowed myself one pill this afternoon, and I was so tempted to have another right now as I would welcome the relief to the anxiety, but there was no escaping the inevitable. Jennifer was already suspicious, and I had to come clean.

"Do you remember me telling you about my patient, Mrs. Hamilton, who passed away?"

She nodded, but there was a question in her eyes as to why in the world I would want to talk about a dead patient when we were having a romantic evening.

"Well, it so happened that she didn't die from complications with her diabetes or heart, but I gave her the wrong medication . . ." There I said it, and it was out in the open whatever the consequences would be now that Jennifer knew.

"Oh, Landon, that's terrible," she cried. "You're always so cautious and careful, I can't even imagine how you could have made a mistake – are they sure?"

"Yes, they did an autopsy," I stated flatly.

She was silent, but still stayed close to me, and kept her hands on my chest. There was no doubt she could feel the thundering of my heart beneath her hands, and I just hoped I wouldn't have a heart attack myself right here and now from the level of stress I was feeling.

"So, exactly what does this mean?"

"Jennifer, come here and sit down," I said as I motioned and pulled her over to one of the chairs by the firepit. It was a large chair, so she climbed up on my lap, and placed one hand on my shoulder. "I've got to be honest with you. I have a problem, and I've had a problem for quite a while. You know the accident I had when I was younger at the pool in Tuscaloosa, well, you know that I still have issues and pain from it."

She nodded and declined to respond, but began to gently massage my shoulder.

"Well, I've been taking oxycodone for a few years now, but there are times that I have taken more than I should. I've been prescribing them to myself, so no one knew how much I have been taking."

"Is that why you fall asleep so often, and why you don't always remember things," she asked as I could tell she was racking her brain to rationalize everything. "Heavens, you fell asleep on Christmas Eve – had you taken too many pills that day?"

I nodded as I looked down and intertwined my fingers with hers. As much as I had been dreading this talk to her all afternoon, I was shocked at how she wasn't being irrational or judgmental, but still, I hadn't given her the full picture so there was still the possibility she might not be as understanding.

"Yes, I took too many pills on Christmas Eve, and I took too many pills the day I saw Mrs. Hamilton. The end result is that my partners have asked me to take a leave of absence for a few months, and they have insisted I go to a rehab facility up in Atlanta."

"Do you want the girls and me to go with you?" She said in a confused tone.

"No, it's an in-patient facility meaning that I will go there and stay for three months, and the hope is that at the end of my treatment I will have been able to knock my addiction," I answered as I hoped by laying it all out there she could better understand.

Again, Jennifer nodded, but no words of repercussion or anger at my actions.

"So, the girls and you will stay here while I'm gone,

and once I've completed the treatment, then I'll come home," I hesitated, but knew how much most women needed security. "You will have money put into your bank account twice a month which should cover your expenses, and I've given Daddy's secretary access to my bank account, so she'll make sure the mortgage, tuition and all the other bills are taken care of, and you don't have to worry about anything."

"So, once you're done in three months – let's see that would be around the first of May," she stopped and counted on her fingers. "Then, everything will go back to normal."

"Well, not exactly, honey," I said as I reached down and lifted my glass of wine to my mouth where I emptied it. "There's another issue."

"What's that?"

"Well, Mrs. Hamilton's granddaughter is an attorney, and they have filed a wrongful death action not only against me, but the entire medical practice."

Again, Jennifer nodded, but I knew she did not fully grasp the concept of litigation.

"We have medical malpractice insurance, and it's a high limit, but in the Complaint, they are also suing me personally."

"Oh, goodness, Landon, that can't be good," she suddenly understood the severity of it when I mentioned the word, 'sue.'

"It won't be easy, but we got a good team of attorneys from Tampa who deal with this sort of thing all the time. Florida is filled with so many senior citizens, and there are many cases when relatives want to sue the doctors when a relative dies. The good news is our house is in an LLC, so it can't be touched."

Jennifer stayed on my lap, but sat up now and looked me in the eyes. "Landon, if we're being sued could we lose everything?"

"No, sweetheart, we have good attorneys, and this happens all the time to doctors."

"But, it's never happened to you," she protested.

"No, it hasn't, but I'm confident that with the insurance and the attorneys, we will be fine. I don't want you to worry. Your life with the girls will continue as it has been, but I'll just be gone for a few months."

Jennifer seemed pacified for the moment and leaned her head down on my shoulder, and it seemed that she had weathered the worst, but I still had to tell her about the publicity tomorrow in the newspaper and the local television news programs.

"Jennifer, there's one last thing," I added, and I didn't waste any time. "Tomorrow it's going to be in the newspapers here in Southwest Florida and on the local news programs, so I don't want you to be alarmed. I know that some of your girlfriends who are gossip hounds will be circulating it like crazy, but please just ignore them. I want you to make sure the girls don't turn on the television as they don't need to hear it and get any wrong information – please promise me this?"

"Yes, of course," she said. "But, Landon, you'll be here with me, too, so we can watch over the girls together when they get home from school."

"Jennifer, no I won't," I responded and saw the disappoint in her eyes.

"It was agreed with the partners that I have to leave tomorrow to fly to Atlanta. With the fallout from the press, the best thing to counter the negative press is if I'm seen to be heading to a rehab facility – at least that makes me look like I'm trying to do something about my problem, and hopefully, it will go a long way towards make amends with the court case."

At that moment, we saw little Lucy come out through the French doors onto the patio, and she rubbed her eyes in a sleepy fashion.

"I had bad dream," she uttered to us with words of a three-year old.

"Oh my," Jennifer said, but I shook my head to her.

"Listen, let me put her back to bed, I want to have a little more time with the girls before I leave – I just want to go and watch each of them sleep for a bit. I need the memories," I said, as I lifted her from my lap and placed her back on my chair. "You just stay here and finish your wine, and I'll be back shortly to put out the fire."

She nodded, and I said I silent prayer as I walked to the house. It wasn't perfect, but my wife was still with me and supporting me, and I still had my family. Even if I lost everything, I still had them, and that was priceless.

CHAPTER 19
Attie

I walked out on the balcony of my condo and looked down at the pool. There was RaeLynn sprawled out on a lounge chair. She had on a hot pink bikini with her little round ball of a belly protruding, and the sunflower tattoo surrounding her navel was literally enlarging and growing right along with the baby. With her headphones attached to her Walkman, she was moving her head from side to side and wiggling her red-polished toes as she obviously kept time with the music. There was no doubt she was enjoying Naples far more than Duncanville. She had been here almost two weeks, but to me, it has seemed more like two months. Even though I had delicately broached the subject of her going back to

Alabama several times, she would always change the subject. I had been as polite as could be, but this wasn't going to be a permanent thing. There was no way she was going to continue living here in Naples with me, and there was no way in hell I was ever going to marry her.

I had been putting it off for the last several days, but it was down to the wire. Mama and Daddy weren't happy with me. Mama's silence spoke volumes. She hadn't spoken a word to me since she left the table at dinner on Christmas Eve, and the only thing Daddy had said was to ask, "when's that girl leaving Naples?' I was due to go by Daddy's office tomorrow morning to get my monthly check, and I knew I could be jeopardizing my comfortable lifestyle if Daddy was inclined to get hardnose about this whole thing.

I looked at my watch, and it was near 4 o'clock so RaeLynn would be coming in soon from her afternoon of sunbathing. It was now or never. With a quick glance at the notepad by the phone, I tore off the top sheet and shoved it in the pocket of my shorts. As I waited for her arrival, I paced back and forth across the narrow living room as I contemplated what I was going to say her. I wasn't naturally a mean person, but there was no way around it with RaeLynn. Every time I tried to be nice to her, she just twisted it into an idea everything was 'fine and dandy' in her words, and that she was moving forward with a life with me. Shit, this wasn't going to be pleasant, but it had to be done.

"Hey, there Attie," she said with a flourish as she came in the door and promptly dropped her beach bag and towels on the floor. "Whew, I don't like lugging all that dang stuff up to the ninth floor."

"RaeLynn, there's an elevator."

"I know, but I was reading in my pregnancy magazine that it says it's healthy for the mama and baby to get a little exercise every day." She said and flashed that smile that always made me inwardly cringe. "So, now every day when I go out, I'm gonna take the stairs so I'll get my exercise."

"RaeLynn, why don't you come on in and sit down, and I'll get you a glass of iced tea," I said, and then chastised myself for being too nice again, but heck, I couldn't always be a cold bastard as she was pregnant. I went to the kitchen and poured her a large glass of tea, and when I returned, I saw that she had settled herself comfortably by pulling her legs up under her. How could I tell her that I didn't want her coconut-smelling tanning oils seeping into my leather sofa? I guess I had to pick my battles as getting her out of here was far more paramount than worrying about any damage to my sofa at the moment.

"Thank you, Attie, you're a sweetheart," she said and blew me a kiss.

This was it, and I wasn't about to back down as I had to get to the point. "RaeLynn, you're only 16. You just can't sit around the swimming pool all day listening to music and reading magazines. You have to think about your future. You need to finish school – you still have another year and half left."

"Oh, you silly boy," she said and shook her head at my comment. "I was never gonna stay in high school until graduation. I already had me a plan. You see I had talked to them over at the technical college, and I was set to go study in the beauty school. I could start early and found out that I could be cuttin' and stylin' hair even before I would normally graduate from high school," she ended with a smile, but then tilted her head. "But, now all that's changed."

"Why has that changed?"

"I'm preggers," she removed her sunglasses that were still atop her head and used them to point at her belly, and then rolled her eyes at me. "I can't be goin' to school and workin' if I have a baby to care for."

"Lots of women have children and work outside the

home," I said, hoping that my answer would suffice.

"Attie, I know that none of the women in your family work once they have children," she countered, and I had to admit she was quick with her responses.

"But . . . but RaeLynn, you're only 16, and we're not married."

"No, but we will be soon," she answered without delay as she tucked a small pillow behind her back and settled more comfortably on the sofa.

"RaeLynn," I began in a firm voice as I walked back over to stand in front of her. "You know that we met before a football game. We had some fun, a few laughs, and yes, we ended up back in my hotel room, but we don't have a relationship. We aren't planning a future together," I stopped to take a breath before I continued. "And, we aren't planning to get married."

"What?" She screamed at the top of her lungs and pulled the pillow from behind her back and threw it directly at my face. "How could you? How could you lead me to believe we're getting married, and we're gonna raise this baby together?"

"RaeLynn, I never proposed marriage to you, and you damn well know it?"

"But, but," she stammered, and her bottom lip

began quivering. "How could you not want to marry me when I'm having your child?" She continued in an almost child-like voice.

"I don't love you, and I won't marry someone I don't love," I responded flatly.

RaeLynn looked up at me from the sofa, and she almost looked like a little girl sitting there, but then I glanced down and saw her swelling belly with the exploding sunflower tattoo. I had to admit I was totally repulsed, but I was also ashamed I ever allowed myself to be so wasted that I would have had sex with her. I know she woke up in my bed of the hotel room that morning, but I still wasn't sure I was being a fed a line that she thought I was the father of her child. Even at her age, there was no doubt this girl had been around the block a few times.

She sat there looking down at her hands and began picking at her chipped fingernail polish in a habit I had learned she resorted to when she was anxious. "So, what are we going to do?" She added with a sniffle and lifted a hand to wipe the snot coming out of her nose.

I gave a heavy sigh and proceeded to walk over to the sliding glass doors to look back out over the pool. As much as I disliked her, I didn't hate her. I couldn't be mean, but God knew if I gave her an inch, the girl would take a mile, so I had to pace myself.

"RaeLynn," I began in a measured tone. "You need to go back home to Alabama. We aren't married, and it isn't right that you're staying here -"

"Well, it's not exactly like we're sleeping together," she interrupted in a droll tone.

I heard her words, but I wasn't even going there.

"You don't know anyone here in Naples, and the best place for you is to be back home with your family."

"But, Attie, we're family now. We made a baby, and we have to be the baby's mama and daddy – nothing can change that."

"RaeLynn," I said in an exasperated tone and let out a heavy sigh as I rubbed the back of my neck. There was no way to get any understanding into this girl's brain. "Listen to me," I turned around, and finally looked her straight in the eye. "Listen, I don't love you. I don't want to marry you, and even if the baby is mine, we're not getting married. If the baby is mine, and I repeat if the baby is mine, then I will do right by you, and I will support it, but you and I don't have a future as a couple. Can you please understand me?"

RaeLynn continued to sit there and picked at the red bits of chipped nail polish. I didn't say anything about the littered bits that were all over and sticking to my leather sofa; I didn't like it, but it was the least of my worries right now.

"Can I have some more iced tea, please," she said and reached over to hand me her glass.

With an exasperated sigh, I grabbed the glass and went to the kitchen to refill it.

"Here," I said a bit brusquely as I handed it back to her.

"Okay, I'll leave, but I don't want to ride home in no Greyhound bus again," she said with a pout.

"No, problem," I said as I reached into my pocket for the paper I had shoved in earlier. "I got you a plane ticket back to Birmingham. I'm guessing your folks can drive over there to get you as there were no flights into Tuscaloosa."

She looked up at me and wrinkled her forehead in confusion. "You already got me a ticket without even knowing if I would agree to leave?"

"Well," I stammered, and then went over to sit down in a chair opposite of her. "RaeLynn, we've already been through this again and again. We don't have a relationship, and it wasn't right that you remain staying here – it's just not right." I stopped, stalled and ran my hand through my hair in an attempt to find the right words. "Yes, I made the reservations this morning, and you have a flight tomorrow afternoon."

"Wow, that was quick," she said and rolled her eyes. "Guess you really do want to get rid of me."

"Well, it's not exactly like I invited you down here, RaeLynn. You just took it upon yourself and showed up," I replied, and there was no doubt she heard the rancor in my tone.

So much for the meek RaeLynn and her tears as I could see the look of 'piss and vinegar' rising in her eyes. She narrowed her eyes to slits and stared directly at me.

"Okay, you're a high and mighty, little rich boy from Naples," she began as she sneered her words. "I'll leave on that dang aeroplane tomorrow, but it's gonna cost you, or rather it's gonna cost your Daddy 'cause I already figured out you're a lazy bastard who doesn't even have a job. You just live this life," she paused as she waved her hand around in the air. "Yes, you just live in this life of luxury because your Daddy pays for it."

"RaeLynn, that's uncalled for," I interrupted.

"No, don't you go interruptin' me, At – tie," she said as she stood up and placed her arms akimbo. "As I said, if you're wantin' me to leave tomorrow, I want a settlement. I heard you talking to Boyd on the phone last week about him payin' his wife a settlement, so I want one, too."

"RaeLynn, you don't have any idea what you're talking about? Boyd and Libby were married for over 12 years and they have two children together. They're getting a divorce so, of course, there's going to be a settlement – that's just the way it works."

"Really?" She raised one thinly plucked eyebrow in question as she remained in her same position. Obviously, she felt it gave her some sort of dominance over me as I still sat in the chair. "Excuse me, but I think you're wrong, Attie."

I looked at her, but I wasn't going to give into her scare tactics.

She removed her hands from her hips and placed both of them around her expanding stomach. "Right here, we got a baby so that does make a difference. I want a settlement, and I want it tomorrow before I leave."

At nine o'clock the following morning, I walked into Daddy's office down on 5th Avenue. I had debated on whether or not to call him last night, but he was at home, and there was no way I wanted to get in a conversation with him about RaeLynn's demands with Mama around. She still hadn't spoken to me since Christmas Eve, and I knew it wouldn't be prudent to have her privy to the conversation. At this point, all Daddy knew was that I was coming in for my monthly check, but I had already called ahead to ask his secretary if he was going to be with anyone this morning, and she had assured me he was alone in his office for the entire morning. Whew, that was a relief, but I still had to make a case for asking for RaeLynn's 'baby settlement,' as she so coyly referred to it all evening and this morning.

"Hey, Daddy," I said as I gave a quick knock and peered around the half-way open door.

"What do you need? I already gave Margaret your check, it should be on her desk as it always is," he said, but looked back down to the papers on his desk.

"Well, if you're not too busy, could I have a few minutes?" I said as I still stood by the door and was praying, he wouldn't turn me away.

"No," he said with a heavy sigh, and reclined back in his chair as he motioned for me to come on in and shut the door. "What do you need, son?"

"Well, the good news is that I'm taking RaeLynn to the airport this afternoon so that's done and over."

He nodded, but grimaced. "Yeah, but there's no doubt you're gonna have to go up there this summer and take a DNA test just to be sure, but I'm hoping that old boyfriend of hers will step up and marry her before the baby gets here."

"Yes, sir, that's what I'm hoping for, too."

"Okay, so sounds like you have this whole situation worked out, son. I'm just glad that girl is getting out of Naples and headed back up there. She had no business coming down here uninvited, and then barging in on our family's Christmas Eve dinner. Your Mama was livid."

"Yes, sir, I know, she still hasn't talked to me."

"Well, just get that girl gone out of here, and your Mama will manage to get over it. It may take her a little time, but she'll be fine."

I nodded in agreement, but still didn't get up from my seat in front of his desk.

"Is there something else you're needing because I need to get these spread sheets up to corporate."

"Well, she's making a demand -"

"What the hell sort of demand is that little shit making on you now?" Daddy's voice rose, but then he caught himself and quieted down so the rest of the office wouldn't hear.

"Well, she claims she overhead me talking to Boyd about the divorce settlement made with Libby, and now

RaeLynn thinks it entitles her to some sort of settlement if I send her back up to Alabama."

"But, you two aren't married, and we damn well don't even know if the kid is yours?"

"That's exactly what I told her, but she's adamant she won't leave the condo unless she gets some money."

"I'm guessing she had a figure in mind?" Daddy moved forward and put both elbows on top on his desk and tapped his fingers.

"Yes, sir, she said $25,000."

"Twenty-five thousand dollars," his voice rose again, and we could see Margaret looking up from her desk through the glass wall of Daddy's office. He waved her away, and she resumed her work.

"Well, you sure as hell don't have that kind of money, do you?"

"No, sir, you know I don't," I answered meekly.

"Well, I'll give you a check, but I'll call over to Jack Monroe and have him write up some short of settlement agreement that I want her to sign. It's got to be notarized so come back by here and I'll send Margaret out to your car to notarize it."

I nodded and breathed a sigh of relief.

"Now this girl is obviously not very sophisticated

about legal issues, but with her notarized signature and her acceptance of the check, I think we should be in the clear. If I have to, I can always pay-off whatever small-town lawyer she gets up there in Alabama, but I doubt it will come to it. To someone like her, $25,000 is a small fortune."

"You go on now, and I'll have it ready when you come back by here," Daddy said, and smacked his hands together. "But, whatever you do, I don't want you bringing that white trash girl in this office, and don't let her get out of your car – as I said, I will send Margaret out with agreement and a check."

"Do you remember her full name?" I asked as I rose from the chair.

"Hell, yes, RaeLynn Yoder," Daddy answered directly. "How could I forget."

CHAPTER 20
Boyd

"Are you sure this is a good idea . . . it may be too soon," Tess grimaced as she glanced over to me.

I turned down the music on the radio and glanced across the seat in my truck. "Honey, it's gonna be okay," I attempted to reassure her, but in my heart, I wasn't so sure it would be as easy as I hoped; I just prayed we weren't heading for disaster when we confronted Libby.

Jack Monroe had secured Libby's signature on the Marital Settlement Agreement earlier this week, and now it had been given to the judge in our case. At Jack's original suggestion, I had made a generous offer to Libby in hopes that she would forego a long-drawn out litigation process. It certainly hadn't been cheap, but when I considered the time it involved with emotional warfare, and attorney's fees on both sides, as I was also paying Libby's attorney, it made sense. Libby was given the house on Marco Island, and I would pay the mortgage until it was free and clear. I agreed to pay her alimony for ten years, or until she remarried. I also agreed to pay her tuition so she could get her master's degree in psychology – I still cringed at the idea of Libby giving others counseling advice, but so be it. It wasn't my problem, and if it got her off my back, then it was worth it. I also agreed to a generous amount of monthly child support above the guidelines, and to pay the kids' private school tuition until they graduated high school. While it still hadn't been 'signed-off' by the judge, or recorded as final, it did mean that the litigation was over, and so my marriage to Libby was just days from being officially over.

With that in mind, I had suggested to Tess that she meet Perry and Carly for the first time. I felt that going out on the boat for the day would be the least awkward way to make the introduction. Both kids were comfortable on the boat as it was like a 'second home,' so that was the easy part. The hard part would be stopping by my old home to pick up the kids and having to encounter Libby.

We pulled up to the house on South Barfield Drive, and I looked around. It was so familiar as I glimpsed the walkway I knew so well and had made my way down hundreds of times over the years. I glanced around the yard where I had thrown balls to Perry, hid Easter eggs for the kids, and recently watched as Carly pedaled her tricycle for the first time. I shook the thoughts from my head and turned to look over at Tess. Just seeing her, my heart lightened from the tension, and I turned off the ignition.

"Boyd, this is so awkward - I think it's best I just sit here and wait for you and the kids," she offered.

As much as she was now an integral part of my life, and Libby would have to come to grips with it, I knew that it was still likely too soon for the two of them to meet. Seeing one another from a distance was one thing, but having to meet in person and exchange pleasantries was not something I was looking forward to observing.

"I'm sorry," I said, and reached over to grab her hand to squeeze it. "Give me a few minutes to get them, and then we'll head off to the boat."

She nodded and smiled. God, I was so happy. This girl was one in a million, and I loved that she was so easy-going without any animosity towards anyone or anything. After over a decade with Libby, I had fallen into the habit of always being on guard, and ready for the next verbal assault for even the slightest thing she had considered to be a major issue. I was loving this new life, and my stress level had decreased considerably. I had been for my annual check-up at the doctor for my hypertension, and he had happily reported that my blood pressure readings were low once again for the first time in years. It was amazing what stress did to the body, but more amazing what a healthy relationship could also do to heal the body.

I jumped down from my truck, and made my way down the crushed shell path to the door. I could do this, and I vowed it was going to be quick and painless – or, at least I was hoping it would be.

I rang my doorbell – wait, it was Libby's doorbell now. I listened as the sound echoed through the house, and then I heard the voices of my kids as they came to the front door.

Perry opened it, and it still amazed me that he could now reach my shoulder – God, he was going to be taller than me.

"Hey, Dad," he said in a lowered voice to make it sound deeper. I could tell he was attempting to be mature, and I imagined he had now assumed the role of 'man of the house' since I was gone.

"Hey, son," I said, and I grabbed him in a bear hug as I still saw him as my little boy no matter how big he thought he was getting.

He wiggled out of my grasp with an embarrassed shrug, but that was alright as my little Carly came running up to me.

"Daddy, Daddy, I missed you so much," she said, and I picked up her slight frame and twirled her around a couple of times. She giggled and buried her face in my neck, and I relished the fresh smell of her Johnson's Baby Shampoo. God, I missed these two, and I had to knock back the tears that were about to emerge.

"Boyd," Libby rounded the corner and made her way to the front door. She had lost a considerable amount of weight since I had left, but I never considered how noticeable it was until now as she was in a sundress and the bones across her chest visibly protruded while her arms were as thin as Perry's.

I nodded to her, and she lifted up a couple of bags for the kids. "This is Carly's diaper bag. She was potty-trained before you left, but she regressed when you weren't here," she said it in an accusatory tone.

I shrugged as it was no big deal. Perry had taken a while to be potty-trained, but I was here the entire time, so she had no basis to place any blame on me. I had to wonder if she was ignoring the kids, and spending more time with her girlfriends as I had heard that she had been going out quite a bit at night to the bars with her friends. I wasn't sure if she was letting off steam, or she was trolling for a new husband. Heck, great if she found a new husband as that would let me off the hook for the alimony if she decided to remarry, and I smiled at the thought.

"What the hell are you smiling about?" Libby sneered.

"Am I not allowed to smile? Heck, I'm getting ready to spend the day with my kids so I'm happy, and as far as your language, please don't swear in front of the kids."

"Yeah, Mom," Perry said, and turned to his mother. "You heard Dad, it's not good, and none of my friends' moms swear in front of their kids."

Libby rolled her eyes at me and crossed her arms in front of her. "When will you be back?"

I glanced at my watch; it was ten o'clock. "We're going to head over to the Snook Inn for lunch, and then we're planning on spending the day on Keewaydin. How does six sound?"

"Fine," she said. "I may not be here, but the

babysitter will be?"

"Big date?" I asked.

"Whatever?" she said with a flip of her hand, and then looked out across the driveway to my truck. "I'm not the one who started this, this, – just go have the day with your little," and she stopped to mouth out the letters of the word, 'w- h- o- r- e-.'

"Fine," I said when I flashed the most genuine smile I could muster. I knew I had her when her eyes narrowed and then turned to shut the door in the faces of the kids and me.

"Hey, Perry, look what I brought you?" Tess said as she reached in her beach bag. She hadn't mentioned to me about bringing anything to the kids, but I had to admit it was a great idea to break the ice as kids always liked surprises. She handed him a small, blue-stripped bag, and Perry wasted no time pulling out the small box.

I was behind the wheel of the boat, but watched as Tess sat on the seat on the bow of the boat with Perry and Carly on either side of her.

"Cool," he exclaimed as he held up a box that held

a small digital camera.

"I'm a photographer for my job with the newspaper, but I also love just taking pictures for fun. I thought you might enjoy having a camera, too."

"Yeah, I've never had one, I love it. Thank you," Perry added, and I was so glad he hadn't forgotten his manners.

"Look here, she leaned closer. "It's a digital camera which means you can look right here and preview the shot you've just taken. If you like it, then you can keep it, but if it's something you don't like, then you can just delete it."

"Wow," he said, and began opening the box so he could see the real thing.

While Perry was engrossed his new gift, Tess turned to Carly. At three-years old, Carly could be very open to strangers, or outright distant, depending on her mood.

"Carly, I have a surprise for you, too." Tess said in a softer voice and leaned down to Carly's level.

Hesitantly, Carly looked up and smiled at Tess.

"I like your hat," my daughter said in a timid voice.

"Oh, Carly, I'm so glad you do because look what I have for you," and Tess pulled another bag from behind her beach bag.

Carly was curious and came closer. She put her little hand on Tess' leg and leaned over to peer in the gift bag. Her eyes lit up when she saw a miniature version of the same straw hat that Tess was wearing except that Carly's had a pink flower and ribbon on it. Without any hesitation, Carly crawled up onto Tess' lap, and I smiled as Tess placed the hat on Carly's head.

"But there's one more thing," Tess said as she pulled a bottle of soft pink nail polish from the bag and held it up before Carly. "I thought while your Daddy and brother fish today, we could do our nails? Would you like that, Carly?"

Carly didn't utter a word, but judging from the smile lighting up her face and the nodding of her head, no words were needed.

I had wondered how Tess would do with kids as she wasn't a mother, but it appeared she was off to a great start.

I maneuvered the boat up to a slip in front of the Snook Inn, and I waved to many of my friends who sat in the tables under the palm fronds or at the bar. While I tied up the boat, Tess and the kids walked up and secured a table. Jim, one of my favorite guitar players, was already front and center by the small dance floor, and I gave a wave to him, too.

I went up to the bar to say hello to everyone while Tess settled herself at a table with the kids and they all started coloring on the paper placemats.

"Hey there, Boyd," Kathy said as she leaned on the bar. "What can I get for you?"

"We're gonna order lunch, but I wanted to come up to say, 'hi,' and order two rum runners as you're the only one who makes them the way I like."

Kathy smiled, and I followed her glance as she nodded over to the table.

I shrugged my shoulders.

"I heard, Boyd – no need to explain," as she started mixing the frozen concoctions.

"Yeah, Libby and I finalized everything this week," I said. Kathy was well aware of the dynamics of my marriage as Libby and I had been here off and on over years, and we lived only a few miles away.

"Boyd, it's none of my business, but you're a good guy. You deserve to be happy, and I watched you over the years. Yes, I'm a bartender, but I get to know people, and I can see through them. I may not have had any formal schooling, but standing here behind a bar can help you learn more about human nature than any degree."

I looked at Kathy and pulled out a twenty-dollar bill for her.

"Boyd, this one's a jewel. I watched you with her when you were here last week, and now I'm seeing her with your kids. She adores you, and she's the real deal," Kathy quickly slipped the bill into one hand, and continued to wipe down the counter with her other. "Don't' mess this up, Boyd."

I gave her wink before I took both of the plastic cups and made my way over to the table.

"Daddy," I heard both of my kids say in unison, and I sat down between the two of them. Tess had politely moved to the other side of the table so I could sit on the bench between Perry and Carly, and I gave her a gratifying smile.

I don't think I ever remembered a time that I enjoyed being Snook Inn as much as I did now. Granted, I had been there so many times over the years with my parents, my brothers and buddies, Libby and the kids, but this time, I finally felt as though I was seeing and living it as a new person.

CHAPTER 21

Landon

I walked across the lawn with my book to the Adirondack chairs. New Horizons Rehabilitative Retreat was renowned across America as a premier abuse recovery facility. Several Hollywood celebrities touted its remarkable feats in turning their lives around from alcohol and drug addictions, but I wasn't sure I was totally buying into the hype.

It was nearly March, and I had been here for five weeks. Believe me, I knew it down to the day and hour, and I was counting until my sentence would come to an end. Every morning, I woke at dawn for the mandatory prayer breakfast, then we had to go on our 'reflection walk,' and that was followed by our morning group therapy session.

Lunch was more health food, and I was literally dying for a Big Mac and some greasy fries, but they felt food fed the mind. Their motto was 'if your mind is healthy, it is free, and a free person has the will to choose their destiny.' Yes, I knew the motto well as we were all instructed to repeat the mantra multiple times a day just like we were little robotic slaves. Still, I was the dutiful patient just as I had always been the dutiful son. I did what was asked without question, but in my head, I was pissed, and I resented every single person here who felt I was defective and in need of change.

I settled myself in the chair and leaned my head back to catch a few rays on my face. I was missing the South Florida sun as it was still was cool here in Georgia. Today, was a 'warm one' according to the staff as the temperatures were registering in the low 60's, but I still wore a heavy sweater over my t-shirt. At least there was no breeze, and if I sat directly in the sun then it was bearable. I pulled my sunglass from my pocket and placed them on my face. I had found out that if I feigned sleep then other patients wouldn't seek to engage me in conversation. I had already heard their addiction stories in our mandatory therapy sessions, and when I had some free time, the last thing I needed was to hear their stories yet again. No one was in my immediate vicinity, but it was always good to take precautions.

Suddenly, I heard someone clearing their throat, and I realized I must have drifted off to sleep when my arm involuntarily jerked.

"Oh, you're awake." I heard a male voice, and assumed it was likely directed to me, but I remained in my semi-reclined position with my sunglasses still covering my eyes.

I didn't reply, and I wasn't intending to engage. Despite the fact that we were all here for one sort of addiction or the other, I still didn't feel any affinity for the other patients. Sure, there were a couple of other doctors, but they were weak-minded souls, and I had proven that I was not addicted as I was functioning just fine – in fact, I didn't have any withdrawal symptoms as many of the rest of them so that proved I wasn't too bad. I likely could have tapered off and quit on my own in Naples, but I had never been given the opportunity. No, they took my one mistake, and continued to insist I was a ruined human being in need of intervention and cleansing of the poisons that had somehow 'overtaken my body.'

A bit of pine pollen must have drifted over, and my nose itched. I lifted a hand to rub it, and then I sneezed. I sat up as the sneezing fit continued. I took off my sunglasses, and then glimpsed a figure who had taken a seat in the semicircle of chairs.

"In need of this?" The older man held out a small packet of tissues.

"Guess so," I said, and reached for the packet to pull out a couple. "Thank you."

"No problem," he answered with a smile. "Don't go anywhere this time of year without a few of these as the pine pollen and everything else in bloom can get aggravating."

I nodded, but then lifted my book that had slipped off my lap to the ground. I held it up and nodded to him in hopes that he would get the hint and let me read in peace. I opened the book, but then realized I had forgotten to turn down the page where I had stopped reading, so I was forced to flip and skim a few pages to find my place.

"I hate when that happens," he added, but I only nodded. If I avoided looking over to him, I was hoping 'Tissue Man' would get the hint and go back to where he came from.

Finally, I felt sure I had found the place where I had left off reading last night, and I stretched out my legs and leaned back to start.

"It's Dr. Collingsworth, isn't it?" The man interrupted.

I nodded, but didn't look up from my book. It

wasn't that I had a burning desire to read right now, but it was a ploy to get this guy to just leave me alone. Granted, he looked like a nice enough older gentleman, but I didn't plan on getting close to anyone at this place; it was just the matter of counting my days until departure, and putting in my time.

"My name is Lester Smalls . . . "

I slammed my book shut – that was it. What was wrong with this man that he couldn't just leave me alone. "I don't mean to be rude, but I would really like a bit of quiet to read my book."

"I understand, son, but I was hoping at some point we could sit down and talk," he concluded, and I swear he sounded like a Southern Baptist preacher who had a message for someone in his flock.

I nodded, "Maybe another time, Mr. Smalls. I'm just not in the mood today."

He stood up "Perfectly understandable, and we'll make time to conversate on another day – Good day, Dr. Collingsworth," and he lifted his hat from his head in polite gesture before he departed.

I watched as he walked away back across the lawn to the main building, and had a nagging feeling I hadn't heard the last from him.

I sat uncomfortably on the cold metal chair in the circle with the rest of everyone in my daily therapy-sharing session. It was Friday, and it was our last session of the week as a group. On Saturdays, we met individually with our sponsors, but on Sundays we were given a day of rest.

"So, Shannon can you share your thoughts for this week? Did you bring your journal to jolt your memory?"

Shannon was a gung-ho convert of New Horizons. Truly, there was no doubt she had partaken of the grape Kool-aide.

"Yes," she said enthusiastically. "Monday was really difficult for a variety of reasons. First of all, it was my two-month anniversary here, and it was my mother's birthday – a lot of emotions going on," she finished in flurry and finally took a breath.

We were all supposed to clap, and it still puzzled me how the clapping promoted recovery, but so be it. It made the staff and patients smile, and while I begrudgingly went along with it, there was no doubt that many suspected I was simply going through the motions. Although Shannon had just a month left in her program, I had an idea she would

251

probably willingly stay-on with her recovery as she continually doubted her ability to stay on the straight and narrow once she left.

"So, let's move onto Landon – our last contributor for today," said our leader, Chad, who leaned forward towards me and placed his hands in a prayer position. "Landon, how has your week gone? You've completed Week #5 so you're well into your routine here at New Horizons, and I imagine you're beginning to feel a great sense of accomplishment. I'm sure you have some encouraging things to share with some of our new friends?"

Nothing like 'leading the witness,' I thought, and I stared back at Chad. I rubbed my hands down the thighs of my jeans, and then crossed one leg over the other. I absolutely hated this 'sharing crap,' but I was getting good at telling them what they wanted to hear.

"Well, Chad, I've enjoyed all my group meetings, my 'reflection walks,' and just hanging around a lot outside catching some rays as I've been missing South Florida-"

"Landon is from sunny Naples," Chad interrupted and offered to the group which elicited yet another round of applause, and for what I wasn't exactly sure. "So, please go on."

"Well, been reading a lot while I'm outside, in fact,

been through two books this week," I replied, but this was a lie. I checked out the books from the library, and turned down a few pages to make it look as though I was reading them, but it was all for show. I had never been much of a reader, and it wasn't like I was going to suddenly develop a literary streak just because I was here, but at least it allowed me some quiet, uninterrupted time from the others.

"It's great to be able to read and lose yourself in a book," Chad exclaimed. "I highly recommend it as it's a great help when you're feeling vulnerable – pick up a 'self-help' or even a novel . . . and it truly can help ease and distract from feelings of hopelessness."

I nodded. Chad was happy, so it looked like I was off the hook until next Friday.

"Hey, guys, just one more thing of housekeeping on my agenda," Chad said as he laughed at himself; Chad had this habit as he must have thought himself a comedian. "This Sunday, we will have a special guest speaking at our religious service. As you know, the service is always non-denominational, but the Reverend Doctor Lester Smalls will be our special guest speaker. It starts promptly at 10 o'clock so I'll be looking forward to seeing all your smiling faces at the service," Chad concluded with a passionate fist pump in the air as we all stood, and I concluded Chad must take a fucking happy pill every morning.

Still, it didn't totally register until I started to walk away. The Reverend Doctor Lester Smalls, it sounded familiar, but then it hit me. Hell, that was the guy who wouldn't leave me alone when I was trying to 'read' my book. Oh great, so much for a relaxing Sunday.

I felt like I had been in a Southern tent revival meeting, and I was welcoming the end of the service. It was a gorgeous spring morning, and several dozen folding white, wood chairs were assembled before a make-shift podium. I knew coming into the program at New Horizons, it would focus on faith and religion to help overcome addictions, and while it was touted as a non-denominational base open to all faiths, Reverend Smalls apparently leaned very heavily to the Southern Evangelical agenda. Having been raised in the Episcopal church, I was used to tradition, form and repetition rather than this overly emotional message of hell, fire and brimstone. I had watched as many became caught up in the message, and throughout the sermon many were uttering loud '*Amens*' in agreement with Reverend Smalls' proclamations, as well as raising their arms and waving in time with his gospel music. This was all fine and well as it was a person's individual choice, but I resented having this service foisted on me as a requirement for my sobriety program.

"Did you enjoy the service?" Reverend Smalls personally asked me after the service concluded, and the others were leaving their chairs to make their way back to their apartments.

What in the world are you supposed to say when someone, basically corrals you, asks for a compliment, and you know you cannot express your true thoughts? Would I somehow 'fail' in my progress here if I spoke the truth? The truth was that I felt he was an overbearing man. A man who felt that his beliefs were the only true ones to commune with God, and that you had to redeem yourself through the exact manner he set-forth in his sermon, or else you weren't going to make it Heaven? I just didn't buy it.

My brothers and I were baptized and confirmed in the Episcopal Church, and I never questioned it. It suited me just fine. We went to church on Sundays, well, most of the time, and Mama held a few volunteer positions over the years so I guess you could have called us 'dedicated Episcopalians.' Daddy didn't much care, but I had an idea he just followed along with Mama taking us all to church as it was a great way for him to get clients for his brokerage business. We went to Trinity Episcopal in Tuscaloosa, and then Trinity-By-the-Cove Episcopal in Naples. Granted, Jennifer and I didn't attend regularly, but we were members, and the girls did the little Wednesday afternoon programs.

Yes, I believed in God, Heaven, and that we should do good and help others in this life, but that was about the extent of it. I wasn't a perfect person, but who was? I had slept around a few times on Jennifer, and most recently with my receptionist, Deana, but what guys didn't? We all kept it quiet, and as along as our wives were happy, then it seemed we could have a little fun on the side. And, yeah, when out-of-town, I liked to hit the strip clubs, but that was just letting off steam – I never considered any of this cheating. Cheating was when you let emotions get involved, and if you got emotional over a girl then that could screw up your marriage – it was purely physical. I liked to think of it as a physical release - sort of comparable to how I felt when I exercised and got that endorphin release.

As far as the drugs, sure the Oxycodone had become a crutch in the last few years, but I wasn't a druggie.

I never considered drugs to be an issue. Hell, I was a teenager and in college in the 70's, so what guy didn't partake regularly. Like the Jimmy Buffet song crooned, "I've done my share of grass," and I guess a whole lot more, but did that make a bad person? Still, I had never told Jennifer about my arrest for cocaine in college, but did it really matter now? It was over twenty years ago, and I had pushed it to the back of my head as just another stupid indiscretion of youth. Yeah, compared to most of my friends, I have to think I was a saint, or at least that's what I told myself.

I had an 8-track of Bob's Seger's newest album *Against the Wind* album in the stereo, and I leaned back in the driver's seat as we cruised north along I-75 back up to Gainesville. Granted, this green '74 Chevrolet Caprice wasn't my ideal car, but it was what Daddy gave me after I wrecked my Triumph TR-6 so I dealt with it. On the upside, I could take more buddies along than in the two-seater Triumph. So, there were the four of us. While I drove, Dex rode shotgun, and Boyd was in the backseat with Hollis.

We had all come down to Naples from UF for a

long weekend as we had been missing the water, and while we told Daddy we needed the boat to get a little fishing in, it wasn't all we needed – we had heard there were some shipments of coke and pot coming in from South America, and we didn't want to miss a prime opportunity for some 'square grouper.' Our sources hadn't been wrong. Early that Sunday morning, while everyone else was sleeping-in or headed to church, we were skimming across the flat waters south of Naples toward Marco Island, and we heard the three planes flying low under the radar. We weren't the only ones out that morning as a lot of our buddies were out, too, plus the usual crowd from Everglades City who were the distributors. As long as we didn't get greedy those good 'ole boys didn't mind us picking up a bit here or there. They laughed us off, but we knew if they ever needed a favor from us Naples boys then we had to pay up. Most of our fathers were friends, or somehow connected, with the local law enforcement, attorneys and the judges so if we put in a good word for them, the Everglades crew felt our few 'takes' were just fine.

"Hey, Landon, can you either turn down the A/C or let's crank the windows 'cause it's getting damn hot back here," Boyd called from the back seat.

"Shut-up, you pussy," I laughed. "I got the air

down, and it's fine up here," but still I reached over and adjusted a front vent towards the back seat as I knew Boyd couldn't roll down those back windows.

Granted, it was September and still pretty damn hot in Florida, but even I had to admit it was getting warmer in the car. We all had lit joints so it was a smokey mess, but that didn't necessarily mean the temperatures should be rising so I cranked the A/C as low as it could go, and gunned the engine to sail around a slower moving semi-truck. Just as I shot back over in the right lane, Boyd started kicking at the back of my seat and swearing.

"What the hell's wrong with you, Boyd," I asked looking in my rearview mirror.

"There's smoke in here-"

"No shit, asshole, we're smoking," Dex added as he turned halfway around to look at the backseat, but then he hit my arm.

"He's not shittin' - there's God-damned flames coming up from the floorboard -"

Hollis had been asleep, but he suddenly woke-up and was squealing like a baby as he stamped his foot in an effort to help put out the flames.

"Pull the car over, Landon – now!" Boyd demanded and kicked the back of my seat again causing me to slam up against the steering wheel.

"I am, I am," I said as I slowed down and pulled into the emergency lane.

Within seconds of Landon pulling to a stop, we all jumped out of the car. Sure, enough there were flames coming up from the bottom of the car and a blaze soon shot up from where we had just been sitting in the back seat.

"What the hell's wrong with the damn car?" Dex said, and then realized he was still holding a joint, so he tossed it over into the nearby drainage ditch.

"I don't know," Landon said as he ran his hand through his hair and shook his head. "On Saturday, Daddy took it get an oil change and I'm sure they changed all the other fluids so I can't imagine that if something was wrong, they would have found it."

"Is it gonna explode?" Hollis whined and started stepping farther away into the grass.

At that moment, I remembered what was in the glove box and I started back toward the car.

"What are you doing?" Dex called out in a loud voice.

"Just getting' something," I said, and I pulled open the front passenger door, and reached in. In a matter of seconds, I pulled out the two small bags, shoved them under my shirt, and ran back to the others in a safe distance on the grass.

The fire continued, and then the car was consumed in a fireball. Most of the cars had stopped, or else a few were cautiously going around us in the median before they continued on their way, but in a day and age before cell phones no one was able to call the fire department; still, within five minutes, I head the sirens and we saw two firetrucks barreling towards us, as well as a couple of state troopers.

I knew that Dex and I had both tossed our joints when we raced away from the car, but still looked over to make sure that Boyd and Hollis were in the clear. I mouthed my question to them, and they nodded they were okay.

"So, who's the owner of this car?" One of the Highway Patrol officers walked over to us and pulled his pad and pen from his shirt pocket.

"I am, sir," I responded and walked over to him.

"Obviously, you probably don't have your registration and insurance information, but I was able to just make out the plate number so I can trace it," he said and jotted down a few words on his pad.

"Your name, address, son," he asked without looking up at me.

"Landon Collingsworth, my home address is 23 Gin Lane, Naples, 34102, but I'm a college student up at UF. My buddies and I were headed back up there when the car caught fire."

"Do you know why your car would have caught fire?"

"No, sir."

"Well, I detect the smell from an electrical fire, but there's no doubt I smell pot, too."

I didn't respond, but just remained silent and raised my eyebrows as though in question.

"Obviously, we can search you boys, but I imagine if y'all had any pot on you, it's long gone by now." He didn't look up, but kept writing, and I turned to look at the other three who were just listening, but not offering anything – thank goodness.

"Well, once the firetrucks put out the fire, we'll call a tow truck, and they'll haul your car away, but there will be an investigation as to the cause," he paused as another officer came over to join him. "Now, you boys can't stay here, and we need to see about getting you a ride. Do you want us to call one of your fathers?"

"Actually, three of us are brothers, so we have the same father," Hollis piped up, and I just turned to look at him like he was an idiot.

"Fine," the officer replied. "I can give him a call, and we'll take you boys back to headquarters. Venice isn't that far from Naples so I'm guessing your father will come up here and get y'all."

"You know, you boys are lucky," the second officer said as he came closer to us, and he reached over to pat me on the shoulder, but I wasn't expecting him to touch me and I suddenly twisted around. When I did, I suddenly felt something move under my shirt, and all at once the two baggies of coke fell from under my shirt to the ground in front of all of us.

Shit, shit, shit, I had it now, and I inwardly cringed.

The two officers looked down at the ground, and they were silent for several seconds, but it seemed like a lifetime to me. Would they let me go with a warning? Would they ignore it, confiscate it and let us go? Or, would I pay big time for my blunder. I berated myself for going back to the car to retrieve it from the glove compartment – hell, I should have just let it all go up in flames.

"Listen, son," the first officer's tone had changed from treating me like a victim of this accident to one of an outright drug dealer. He nudged one the baggies with the toe of his boot and turned to look up at me. Even though I couldn't see his eyes through his aviator sunglasses, I knew they were boring into me. "Listen here, boy, I think you know that things have changed with these little here packages."

"Yes, sir," I answered directly. "They're mine, sir. The others had no idea I had them so they're innocent." It was the least I could do as it didn't make any sense to get them involved. Dex was my best friend, and I didn't want to see my little brothers have their lives ruined. Boyd would have been able to handle it fine, but I knew it would be the demise of Hollis as he would likely have a mental breakdown if he was arrested.

"Okay, we'll take that as the truth," he said, but I knew he doubted my answer.

"We're gonna take y'all back to headquarters," he stopped and reached to pull out some handcuffs which he, in turn, reached over and placed around my wrists. "You all will be free to go on with your father, but your brother here is going to have to stay with us," and he proceeded to read me my Miranda Rights.

And, so that was my first and only arrest. Yes, I was arrested on a 3rd degree felony charge of possession of cocaine, and while I was in Sarasota county, Daddy still pulled some strings with his judge buddies in Collier who managed we get me a plea deal. I know in today's world, I would have certainly served some time, but with Daddy's influence and money, it tipped the scales in my favor. It also factored in that I had no previous convictions, plus I was a pre-med student at UF with a 4.0 GPA – I guess they thought I would eventually amount to something even if I had a propensity to dabble in illegal drugs. Heck, it was the late 1970's, and in South Florida it had become a way of life; it was rare to find any young man who hadn't imbibed, and the law enforcement knew it. And, while Jennifer had lived a sheltered life growing up in Mississippi and her time at Ole Miss, I never thought it would serve any redeeming value to tell her. Number one, she wouldn't really understand, and number two, I like having her think I was a good guy.

CHAPTER 22
Hollis

I think it's all finalized and wrapped up," Stu said as he sat in the booth across from me and looked down as he swirled the ice cubes in his tea.

"So, does that mean – that you'll be going back to Charleston soon?" I questioned, and suddenly had a sinking feeling in the pit of my stomach. Although I was eating some grilled fish, I suddenly had no appetite.

"Actually, I'm starting back this weekend," Stu said glumly. He had driven down in November so he would have his car during his time here.

"How long is the trip?" I said, and I had to admit I was making small talk of inconsequential topics, but I wasn't sure what else to do. There was no way I could broach the words I wanted to utter.

"It's about nine hours," he replied in a bored voice, and it was obvious we were both dancing around the things we really wanted to talk about.

We had our 'usual' table at Zoe's. It was a small, discreet restaurant on Fifth Avenue, but it was also one that offered privacy with its private dining alcoves, and the staff was unobtrusive. I knew many of my friends met their mistresses here for a quick lunch, but now it had become a favorite haunt for Stu and me.

Ever since Stu had kissed me on New Year's Eve, our relationship had changed. As far as outward appearances, we still looked like old friends, but I found my feelings had changed. I thought about him constantly whether at home, work, playing with the kids, or talking to Helen. Hell, one time, I nearly said, 'Stu,' instead of 'Helen' when I was calling out to her in the house. And, it wasn't just in my waking hours, I was being bombarded by the most vivid dreams night after night. So, maybe it was a good idea that Stu was returning to Charleston. There was no doubt that Stu wanted a relationship, and he had even hinted that I should come up to Charleston for a long weekend. I seriously considered it. I could easily tell everyone that Stu needed me up to finalize some more business with his Aunt Lillian's estate, and there wouldn't be any questions. Also, no one knew me there so Stu and I could be more open, and I had to admit, I had fantasized about what it would be like to be open with my feelings and not fear being judged.

Still, on the other hand, I felt guilt. I felt tremendous shame. So, with him out of sight, maybe I could shake this pull he had over me. I had even thought about going to counseling to try to sort out what was happening to me, but I hesitated. Naples was still a small town, and I knew if any sort of gossip got out it could set-off a domino effect that would reach Helen, my parents, my friends, and my clients, and then all hell would break loose.

"Tell me what you're thinking," Stu urged as he leaned across the table and patted my hand. "You're so deep in thought."

"Honestly, just a lot of conflicting thoughts going through my mind right now," I admitted, but sheepishly pulled my hand away as I didn't want anyone to see the exchange.

"Hollis, as I said, I've been in your place. I tried the marriage thing, but I knew I couldn't be true to myself, and I would never be happy. Sure, I could have gone through the motions to please my family, my clients, and present this all-American image of the perfect husband and wife, but I knew I would slowly be dying inside. I couldn't be my authentic, true self, and I always wondered what would happen when I was old and on my death bed. Would I regret it? Sure, I would have a wife there and children, probably grandchildren, but it would all be a lie. I would have been a charlatan, and did they deserve it? No, my ex-wife was a lovely young lady who deserved more, and heavens, if we would have had children, then they deserved a father that was present emotionally, as well as physically. How could I have taken my son hunting when I would have rather been down on King Street shopping for new clothes for him instead?"

I managed a droll laugh, but I knew the feelings. I knew the same emotions well as they had been present with me most of my life, but I didn't dare utter a word. Hell, when you're born into a Conservative Southern family, it would be just about the worse thing in the world to disclose to them that you're gay. They would probably have an easier time accepting if I had committed a crime then announcing my sexual orientation. But, then again, Stu and I had both been through such similar circumstances growing up with many of the same expectations from our families.

The difference was that Stu had had the courage when he was young to change it – granted, he still had not told his family the truth for his divorce, but he was discreetly living the life of his choosing rather than theirs.

"But, I did it. I married, and now I have the wife, kids, home, and the whole shebang," I countered. "You got out after a year of marriage with no kids, but my situation is messy."

"It doesn't have to be?" Stu said as he raised one eyebrow.

"What do you mean?"

"You forget that I'm an attorney, silly boy," he said stating the obvious. "I could be your attorney, and since I'm licensed both in South Carolina and Florida there would not be any issues with me representing you."

I had to admit that Stu was laying it all out there; it sounded so simplistic, but I knew there was no way around it as there was bound to be hurt all the way around if I chose that path. I cared deeply for Helen, but I don't think I was ever passionately in love with her. At least, I know that my intensity of feelings for Helen certainly didn't match the intensity of emotions I felt for Stu after only three months.

"I have to wonder if you're more afraid of breaking this to your parents than you are to Helen?" Stu pressed.

I shrugged my shoulders in a silent response, and continued to be amazed at how tuned-in he was to my feelings. It was as though he could see straight through to my soul, and I had to wonder if that's what the term 'soulmate' meant because I certainly never had it with Helen.

"Stu, I have to admit I am afraid. I'm scared shitless having to break this to not only my Daddy, but Mama, too. I have no doubt that Daddy will be both embarrassed and disappointed to find out he has a gay son, but Mama will be royally pissed. You know, Mama is all about her image in the community, and this just won't sit well with her when she talks about her family with her bridge pals. Mama likes everything to have a nice, presentable image that's tied up with a little bow on top."

Stu laughed, and pushed his plate away from him and leaned on the table to look me straight in the eyes, "So just don't tell them."

"Don't tell them?" I repeated his words with a question.

"Sure, just do what I did? I took the blame for a nonexistent affair, and looked like a cad to everyone, but I knew deep down it was better to be a cheater than gay in my Daddy's eyes."

271

"And, he's never found out to this day?"

"Nope, not that I can tell. As I told you, I am very, very discreet, and if I ever need to go to some charity benefit with a date, I just call up on my female friends, and they're always ready to help out."

"Interesting."

"You know, the other thing is that I have to wonder how much more your Daddy and Mama can endure? In the last few months, they have been hit with quite a bit. Let's see Boyd filed for divorce and now he's found a new girlfriend, Attie got some redneck girl pregnant, and Landon caused some old woman's death and now he's in an Atlanta rehab due to a drug addiction," he paused to let it all sink in. "And, now if you come out that you're gay, it may be the breaking point for them. Yes, sir, I think it's best that you just take the easy way out and tell Helen you're having an affair. You'll also look like a cad to many, but at least your parents won't be the wiser."

I nodded and smiled as I had to admit it seemed like a plan.

"Okay, my boy, I'm sure you need to get back to work, and I need to get over to Aunt Lillian's house as I'm meeting the realtor to go over some last-minute details before I leave."

I pulled out my credit card, but Stu shook his head and pulled out his Black American Express. "Today is on me. It's my treat to celebrate your impending freedom."

Once the check was paid, we walked down the long corridor by the restrooms and out the rear door. It had become a habit to enter and exit via the back door as there was far less traffic than out front on the sidewalk. The back entrance overlooked the staff parking, and in the distance was Cambier Park, which this time of day was only filled with mothers, strollers and an occasional artist set-up doing a watercolor. Still, as we made our way out the door, we were cautious and looked around. Stu's Jaguar was only a few feet away, and I walked over to it with him. Once he unlocked it, he turned to me and his eyes softened.

"Hollis, you know, I've fallen totally and completely in love with you – body, mind and soul."

"Ditto," I said using the line from the Demi Moore and Patrick Swayze movie.

We both leaned towards one another and embraced with a kiss, and while we were both lost in the moment, we separated when we heard a distinct clearing of someone's throat.

Stu looked over my shoulder, and I saw the look of shock in his eyes. I turned to follow his gaze and stared straight into the eyes of my father standing not more than 50 feet away.

I purposely took the long way back to the office. If I continued down Fifth Avenue from Zoe's, it was only two blocks, but I decided to wind around through the park as I needed to do some fast thinking. Shit, shit, shit, I said as I walked along under the shade of the tress. Stu had offered to return to the office with me for moral support, but I knew that would only make matters worse. After an hour, I made my way back to the office, but I felt like I was five-years old again, and I was getting ready to face punishment from Daddy.

"Hollis," the receptionist smiled brightly as I walked through the front doors. "Your father would like to see you in his office."

No doubt, I thought to myself, and proceeded to walk down the hall to Daddy's corner office.

"Hollis," Daddy said as I hesitantly knocked on his partially open door. "Come in and sit down."

"Yes, sir."

"And, shut the door," he demanded brusquely.

Again, "Yes, sir."

"So, do you have anything to say for yourself?"

What the hell did he think? Obviously, he saw everything so what more did I need to say. Did he want me to grovel for repentance for my sins?

"No, sir, I believe what you saw surely speaks for itself," I replied, and it sounded far more formal than I normally spoke.

"So, you're queer?" I shrugged my shoulders and looked down at his desk. "Speak up, boy."

"Yes, sir, I believe I am," I muttered.

"Well, why in the world did you marry Helen – did you, or do you love her."

"Of course, I care about Helen . . . and the children . . . but," I added.

"But, you like boys," Daddy said with a sneer. "I wish to hell that fucking pansy from Charleston had never come to Naples," he said under his breath and shook his head.

Daddy took out a cigarette from his top desk drawer. He rarely smoked after he quit when we were kids, but I knew that whenever he was stressed, he reached for one. He lit up without any regard to the fact that he knew I hated cigarette smoke. I watched out of the corner of my eye as he lit up, and he inhaled deeply.

"You know you have to go home, and talk to Helen," he said. "And, if you don't, you can sure as hell know that I will tell her myself. Do you understand?"

"Yes, sir," I said, and truly felt like I was a kid again.

"For now, I'm not gonna tell your Mama as I think it would probably kill her. She has already had about as much as she can take the last few months with your brothers, and this would really do her in."

"I agree."

"So, you listen here. I don't care if you have any clients this afternoon, you're gonna cancel them, and you get yourself to your house, and get this all straight with Helen. I'm not sure what you intend to do, but you need to think about Helen, your kids and your mother. You're not Stu Pinckney who's footloose and fancy free – you got obligations . . . you hear that boy."

I nodded, and then he lifted his hand to indicate that I was dismissed. I didn't question but retreated and left the office for home.

I was still reeling from the twist of events as I walked to my car. Just an hour ago, I had a plan. A plan that would have worked, and saved a lot of headache, but now because Stu and I hadn't been careful, I was going to pay dearly. I hit the steering wheel with the palm of my hand, and then swore because I hit my wrist instead. I stopped at the light, picked up my phone to call Stu, and he picked up on the first ring.

"How did it go with your father?"

"How do you think? Horrible," I replied. "I'm headed home to tell Helen now because he threatened me if I didn't tell her . . . then he would."

"Great," he responded sarcastically.

"Listen, I'm not sure what is going to happen, but I will try to give you a call after it's over."

"Okay, hang in there, and stay strong."

Within minutes, I pulled up in the driveway, and saw Helen out watering her geraniums on the front porch. The scene of her with her little water can, straw hat and garden gloves looked so idyllic, but within minutes this life we had made was going to come crashing down. She obviously heard me pull up because she sat down her watering can and lifted one hand to shield her eyes so she could see in the distance. Once she recognized it was me, she gave a wave and slight smile.

"What are you doing home so early – are you sick?" She called as I shut the car door and started to walk towards her.

Yes, I was literally sick, but not in the way she thought. This wasn't going to be easy, but I guessed the best way was to just be short and to the point.

"Helen, we need to sit down and talk," I said as I motioned over to the cement bench.

"Well, I don't have a lot of time. I have to head over and pick up the kids from school in a little bit."

"I really don't think this will take long," I replied, and later I would think back on how cold and callous that sounded to tell your spouse you're ending a 10-year marriage in a matter of minutes.

She sat down on the bench and reached over to grab her water bottle for a drink. "The flowers are doing so well this year – it's going to be a beautiful spring," she ended as she took a long sip of her water.

We didn't have time for pleasantries, and I was racking my brain in an attempt to find an opening line, but the more my mind raced, the more befuddled I became, so it was probably just best to blurt it out.

"Helen, things aren't working?"

"What isn't working?"

"Us. Our marriage," I retorted flatly.

Helen was smart. She was on the ball. She had been an accountant before we met so there was no reason to mince words with her. There was silence for what seemed like an eternity, but it was likely only a few minutes. She wouldn't look at me, but simply continued to stare at her fucking red geraniums, and then she looked down at her hands. Very carefully, she began to pull off one glove, finger by finger, and then the other.

"It's him, isn't it? It's Stu," she said very matter-of-factly as she stared at the gardening gloves now on her lap.

"Yes," I replied. She nodded and appeared to be analyzing my answer.

"So, you want to end our marriage, destroy the only lives that our children have always known simply because you have become infatuated with some gay man – that you've just met. You want to leave our marriage, our children, me . . . our lives because of this guy you've barely known for a few months?"

When she set-out the facts so eloquently and simplistic, it made me even wonder if I was unbalanced and self-serving. Was I just infatuated with Stu? Was I simply enamored with the idea that it was unfamiliar, provocative and perhaps even dangerous? I had always been the cautious one. I had done what was expected without question to my own desires. Sure, it makes you seem like you're the sensible one who always contemplates words before speaking and actions before proceeding, but it also makes for a staid and conventional existence. Truth be told, I liked knowing that my life was predictable, and taking that path had proven a secure one, but did it always equate happiness? Sure, I laughed here and there, and I had to admit there were good times, but was I truly content? When I reached the end of my life would I look back and question myself and my decisions? Unfulfilled passions can leave a legacy of emotional pain that surely haunts the soul as much as a physical ache. Sure, I still had time to curtail this self-serving quest with Stu – I could stop right here and now. The script had yet to be written. I could just as easily turn it around right now and stay with Helen. There was no doubt there would-be collateral damage to the others, but if I prevented their pain, I would only be burying mine, and I knew it would only be a matter of time before I needed to come up for air.

"It's not like that, Helen," I offered with a heavy sigh after a long pause.

"It's not like what?" Helen countered, but she still

never raised her voice above a normal conversational level. Helen had always been the most balanced, unemotional female I had ever met. She was never prone to outbursts or emotional tantrums as many other women, and I suppose that was one of the things that attracted me to her. "Please explain, Hollis. I'm so anxious to hear," she finished, but I could tell she wasn't pleased with me with her curt, crisp tone.

"I have to wonder if I have always been gay, but I have repressed it as I knew it would disappoint my parents."

"Always the dutiful son," she interrupted, and I could see a tic beginning under her eye.

"As I was saying, I had feelings, urges, emotions, but I never acted on them – not once. I really did want a family. I've always wanted children, and I love them."

"Hollis, I have no doubt you wanted children and you love them, but I guess the problem is that I was only temporary, and a means for you to get those children, and now that you have them you are ready to move on with the true love of your life. You're finished with me – I'm disposable in this whole scenario."

"Helen don't say that," I said, and reached over to take hold of her hand, but she pulled it away as though I was contagious. "Okay, I'm sorry, but I never went into our marriage with the intention of anything but a lifetime commitment."

She shook her head, "I really don't want to hear about your excuses. You've made your point, and it's clear. You're done with our marriage."

"You know, we're going to have to think about how we're going to resolve this."

"Honestly, Hollis," she said as she twisted her garden gloves. "Do you really think we're going to be able to settle up and end our marriage sitting here on this bench this afternoon?"

"No, I didn't mean it like that," I said apologetically.

"Well, I have to leave soon to pick up our children," she said as she emphasized the last word 'children.' "But I will give you some food for thought. This was not my fault, and I will not disrupt my life, or the children's lives. You can go on your merry way with Stu, but I will have this house to continue raising our children here. And, Hollis, I want it solely in my name, plus free and clear of any mortgage. In light of everything, I will have to go back to work as a CPA, but I don't want to have to worry about finding another home or having to pay for it. At the very the least, the children and I deserve that much." She stopped and stood up and brushed off some potting soil from her arms. "You know I've never been a bitch, and I've never been one of the typical Naples' wives who blow their husbands' money on frivolous things. I will be civil in this divorce, but I expect the same in return from you. I went into this marriage because I not only cared for you, but I loved you," she finished, and I could hear her voice cracking.

"Helen, please," I stood up and finally looked at her in the eyes. I reached for her, but she moved away. Helen was a strong woman, and I knew she wouldn't stand for any sort of groveling.

"Hollis, you stated your position. I don't like it, but I accept it," she said. "Now, I need to get our children, and I won't be home until six as the boys have tennis lessons and Lily has ballet. I'm not sure what your immediate plans are, but I will accommodate you."

"Helen, I would like to be here tonight . . . when you get home with the kids?" I asked.

She took a few steps toward the garage. "Tonight, is fine Hollis, but you will not sleep in our bed ever again – do you understand?"

I nodded. "Listen, I will bring in dinner, so you don't have to worry about it, and we'll eat together as a family." I stopped as she rolled her eyes. "I'll be here and help you put the kids to bed, but then I'll leave."

"Yes, that's probably for the best, and you can make arrangements to come back and get your things, but only when the children are in school. I don't want them privy to our problems. Somehow, someway we'll explain why you're leaving, but not right now. For the moment, I will say that you're on a business trip, and we go from there."

Again, Helen was sensible and without emotion. When the need arose, Helen was able to handle any situation without issue, and apparently this was one of them. I was still mystified. I watched as she walked away down our front walkway that connected to the driveway and our garage. I watched as she got in her Lexus SUV and pulled out of the driveway. She never looked back, and I actually breathed a sigh of relief. My marriage had just ended in a matter of minutes, and my wife was accepting of the fact that I was moving on with another life. It wasn't ideal, but it could have been a hell of a lot worse. I pulled out my cell phone from my pocket and called Stu.

CHAPTER 23
Boyd

*T*he storm raged. Twisted ropes of lightening appeared to wrap around anything in sight while monstrous sounds of thunder echoed across the flat lands and waters. South Florida storms were legendary for their ability to move in without any warning, wreck their havoc on nature and man, and then they simply disappear as swiftly as they arrived. It mystified many newcomers to the area. While many assumed that the waters of the Gulf of Mexico would be more tranquil than the Atlantic, it was only an illusion. Whether it was a summer thunderstorm that rolled in from the wetlands of the Everglades, or the mighty winds of a tropical storms hailing from the South Caribbean. These outbursts could be wicked as they bent coconut palms to submission and leveled thatches of tall sand pines in seconds, but still, they were a kaleidoscope of nature's wonder to behold.

"Boyd," Tess she screamed as woke and reached for me in the darkness.

"Honey, it's just the storm," I said as I held her close to reassure as another streak of lightening flashed outside the porthole and a thunderous explosion rocked the boat.

Although we were securely anchored inland among the Ten Thousand Islands southeast off Marco Island, it still wasn't a pleasant experience for Tess. As anyone, who has lived in South Florida for any amount of time comes to know, it is a way of life. We accept that the storms roll in about mid-May and continue to last until the heat subsides around October, but can even last into November in some years. When we had first moved to Naples from Alabama, Attie had asked me to climb down from my top bunk to sit with him in the dark during a particularly wicked storm. I had ended up telling him stories about cowboys and Indians to get his mind off the lightening streaks and bursts of thunder, and even though it bothered me, I soldiered up to be the big, protective brother.

"It was so close, I thought it was going to strike the

boat," she murmured after we had both woken to the light and noise.

"We'll be fine, it's only the storm," I replied and brushed some strands of hair off her forehead and continued to run my fingers through it in an effort to soothe her.

"Only a storm," she said in a pouting voice. "I don't ever recall storms like this in Ohio -"

"But," I interrupted. "You have your share of tornadoes in the summer and blizzards in the winter so let's see, how do we balance that out?"

I heard her voice utter a minor sound of protest, but she wasn't one to ever argue. Instead, she just pulled the sheet and blanket closer in around us as though the flimsy weight of the fabric could somehow protect from the wrath of the storm. I didn't say a word. I smiled as I thought it was cute, and if it gave her some sense of protection, then so be it.

"Well, I have to say we do have some pretty vicious blizzards which can cut off electricity for days, and in the summer, there were tornadoes that leveled towns. We had a particularly bad one near us in Xenia when I was a little girl, and I always remember we stayed in the cellar when it came through. I was wearing flipflops and a little mouse ran across my foot – it was dark down there as we only had a couple of candles and I screamed so loudly as I had no idea what it was."

I laughed and then made little squeaking noises as I let me fingers inch down her arm.

"Stop that, Boyd," she said as she playfully shooed my hand away.

While the storm raged outside, I took comfort in the fact that we were secure in this little inlet among the brackish waters of the mangroves. We weren't terribly far from Goodland if we needed to get back in an emergency, but it would be subsiding by dawn. I knew it was likely we would have storms when we planned the weekend trip, but while I brushed off their intrusions, Tess was still getting used to them, and I silently berated myself that I hadn't thought how they might affect her. Still, she was game for spending the entire weekend camped out on the boat, fishing, sunning, and capturing every glorious moment with her camera, but still, I didn't want to do anything that would hamper her enthusiasm for future trips.

Suddenly, a loud boom of thunder shook our boat and the noise echoed throughout the cabin.

"Oh, my goodness, that was so loud, I think my heart skipped a beat," Tess cried, and hid her face in my shoulder. "When I was little and that tornado came through,

I heard a noise that sounded like a train, and I thought I was going to die – I was so scared."

"Honey, you're safe," I said and reached over to kiss her. "But you know, you don't have to worry about dying. It's not a bad thing."

Tess lifted her head and looked at me in disbelief. "Of course, it is . . . you're leaving behind all your family and friends. I can't think of anything worse."

I was silent for a few seconds as I wasn't sure I should move forward or not? "You know, I died once," I responded.

Tess then moved up on her elbow and looked me straight in the eyes. "Boyd, what are you saying?"

"I was clinically dead for five minutes, but I survived."

It was the summer of 1982. I was home in Naples from the University of Florida, and it had been a wild weekend. Daddy and Mama were away in Europe on another business trip, so my brothers and I had the Port Royal house to ourselves, and we partied hard. There was an unlimited amount of beer, weed, and girls, but all I could remember was waking up before dawn in the most excoriating pain.

"Landon," I screamed from Daddy and Mama's bathroom. I was lying on the cold marble floor, but I was still shaking from cold sweats, and I couldn't stop throwing up. Over the years I had been sick, but this time it was different. I writhed around the floor as I clutched my stomach and continued throwing up blood that was mixed with some sort of green tissue – something was really wrong.

"Landon," I wailed again even louder, and reached over to grab one of Mama's little blue and white Herend animal figurines that she had displayed on a low shelf. I threw it up against the door. It was small and obviously not loud enough, so I grabbed a vase and threw it. No doubt, Mama would be mad, but I was dying. Apparently, the vase did the trick, and in a few minutes, Landon appeared in the doorway in his boxer shorts.

"What's wrong?" He asked as he scratched his chest and yawned.

"Get me to the damn hospital, I'm dying," I literally cried as tears streamed down my checks from the pain.

"Boyd, for God's sake, you've got a hangover, you'll get over it," he said. "Just drink some water and go back to bed . . . sleep it off."

He didn't wait for me to reply but turned and went back to his room. He was a pre-med student, and I suppose I should have believed his diagnosis, but I knew differently. I may not have been a doctor, but something wasn't right. It was instinctive.

There was no way I could walk, much less make it to the bed. As I lay there, I pulled over one of Mama's fluffy throw rugs to put under my head. With my other hand, I held my stomach and continued to shake. I was shivering in a cold sweat, but also burning up with a fever. If only I could make it to the bedroom, there was a phone on the nightstand and I could call an ambulance, but every time I tried to lift myself from a horizontal position, I threw-up again from the pain. Still, I must have passed-out at some point because when I regained consciousness, I found that the darkness had given way to the early morning sun as it streamed through the bathroom window. The light shone right in my face, and I came awake with a jerk. The pain was even more intense now, and I couldn't stand it any longer.

"Help me," I yelled loudly as I could with what strength I had left in my body. If someone didn't come soon, I knew I would just close my eyes and never wake-up again.

Obviously, Attie heard me. I glimpsed him through

dazed eyes as he lifted me from a puddle of blood and vomit, and dragged me out the front door to his car. I had no recollection of the drive to Naples Community Hospital, but I remembered a nurse coming out with a wheelchair and being helped into it; still, it seemed like a dream. I thought Attie was with me, but later he told me that he didn't stay. He was not well himself, and just wanted to go back home to sleep off his hangover.

"I need some help, anyone, please," the nurse screamed as I fell off to the side of the wheelchair, and she stooped down in an attempt to keep me from toppling over.

I heard a rush of voices coming near to me, but again, it only felt like a dream. At that moment, I felt a rush of wind. Suddenly, the agony was inconsequential. Nothing seemed to matter anymore, and an overwhelming sense of peace came over me. I didn't fight it. Actually, I embraced it. I welcomed it as I had been wracked with pain for the last few hours, and I had been desperate to find any sort of relief no matter how I found it. The hurt was gradually subsiding, and if it meant I could find relief by following the warm, glowing white light then so be it. If it meant I had to leave, then I was okay with it. Still, it was strange – a very strange sensation. I knew I was in the hospital, but I wasn't in my body; I was watching everything from afar. It was almost as though I was a spectator observing the chaotic scene before me. I watched as the nurse screamed, motioned the others to come towards me, and then started she started rambling as they came to help. Suddenly, there were a lot of people all around me, and then they pulled me from the wheelchair. A large, black man effortlessly lifted me on a gurney that two other men had wheeled up to his side. Another guy came rushing out with some sort of bag attached to a metal pole he was pushing on little wheels, and I was mesmerized as I watched the bag of liquid slosh around as he jerked it toward the gurney in an attempt to get it connected to my arm. My arm. I can't believe I said it like that, but it seemed like a limp doll's arm as I watched him frantically stick a needle into a vein on it. He didn't even hesitate. Then, I saw two doctors push through the swinging doors. I was still in the ER waiting room, but they were talking and motioning in rapid succession, and I had to wonder why everyone was panicking - it was like I had pressed fast-forward on a movie. I wanted to tell them that there was nothing to panic about any longer. I was feeling just fine, in fact, I don't remember that I had ever felt so carefree and relaxed in my life. It was the best high I had ever had, and I was enjoying it.

All at once, I heard one of the doctors utter

something as he placed his stethoscope on the open part of my shirt and listened to my chest. As he leaned closer, his faced lost all its color and turned pale. Actually, it was Dr. Benson, and I knew him. Heck, I had escorted his daughter to the Senior Prom at Naples High. "It's Boyd Collingsworth," he yelled to the rest of them. "I know this boy," he said as he ripped at my shirt and the buttons went flying. I heard those buttons bounce and bing as they hit the floor and wall, but no one seemed to notice. At that point, the swinging doors opened again, and they started wheeling me back to the operating room. I still didn't understand why everything was so urgent, and why they were all rushing around. Hey, I was feeling just fine, and the pain had completely subsided by now.

"Wait, there's no time for the OR," Dr. Benson said.

"Anesthesia?" The other doctor questioned.

"We don't have time," Dr. Benson shook his head. "He's clinically dead, and I want to try to get his heart started – I'm doing it right here in the hall."

At that moment, Dr. Benson took the scalpel from the nurse, and he proceeded to make an incision beginning in the middle of my chest down my abdomen. Now, this didn't make any sense. I didn't like the fact that he was slicing open my body, but yet, I couldn't feel anything. It was a strange sensation. Still, I looked down at my face. My eyes were closed as I lay on the gurney, but it was strange. I was crying. I was crying as I watched my body attempted to cling to life, and I saw tears coming out of my body's eyes, too. Wait a minute, this couldn't be happening, but it was. I was watching as Dr. Benson removed my heart and he was massaging it to get it beating again. He was frantic, and he kept yelling my name.

"Boyd, Boyd, damn it, you're not going to die. You have a lot to live for. You're gonna live – I mean it . . . and I'll be so damned mad at you if you don't." He continued to yell at me, but it was clearly more fear than anger.

Suddenly, I felt another rush of wind, but this was a cool breeze like the A/C, and not the warm, gentle calming one I had felt earlier. Also, I felt the pain return, and I didn't want it. I didn't want that pain again. Hell, I had endured it all night, and I just wanted some peace, but Dr. Benson wasn't giving up. For some reason, he was pulling me back to that pain, and he was adamant that I needed to come back and endure that agony. He really was a nice guy, and as much as I didn't want that excruciating pain to return, I felt that I would be a disappointment to him if I didn't do what he wanted because he was really upset. Slowly, very slowly

I felt I was being pulled, and even though I resisted a little bit, I knew I had to let go of this peace and return.

I was in a coma for two weeks. I don't remember a thing about being unconscious, but I distinctly remember when I returned to this world. Before I ever opened my eyes, my senses were assaulted with touch and smell. It was a warm summer morning, and there was a tickling sensation. Not just a tickling sensation, but also a warm touch of water on my skin, and the smell. Yes, it was a clean, fresh smell of soap, but it also one mixed with a scent that was so familiar. Yes, it was a perfume I had smelled on girls many times – it was *Youth Dew*.

Suddenly, my eyes opened, and there she stood. This adorable blonde in a candy-stripped uniform was standing next to my bed. There was a bed pan on the table next to my bed, and she was giving me a sponge bath. She had turned around, so she didn't see my eyes open, so I shut them to a sliver and continued to watch as she took the washcloth and held out my arm and gingerly washed the length of it and then moved to my hands. As much as I'm sure everyone wanted to know I was awake, this was too enjoyable to curtail the moment. I was a 22-year-old guy getting a sponge-bath by a cute blonde, and I wanted to relish the attention for just a little while longer.

Later, I was told I had been in a coma for 14 days. Apparently, it never had been alcohol- related, but rather I had a ruptured hernia. My doctors had told me I had a hernia several years earlier, but it was nothing to be concerned about, so I had forgotten about it. Still, with our partying over the weekend, I had volunteered to push the boat off a sandbar, and when I exerted myself, it had ruptured. Later, Dr. Benson had explained that when it had ruptured, I developed gangrene. I was literally being poisoned by the fluids in my own body, and I would have surely died that early morning had Attie not taken me to the hospital.

"I always wondered about this?" Tess asked as she carefully traced a finger along the scar that ran from my chest down my abdomen to my navel and then sideways.

I nodded. "Why didn't you just ask?"

"I didn't want to be nosy . . . I figured that you would tell me when you were ready."

"Honey, I want you to be comfortable. Please don't ever think that you can't talk to me. I love you so much, and I want to share everything with you. I promise you that I will never keep anything from you," I paused and pushed back the fringe that had fallen over her forehead. "You've become my life, and I can honestly say I've never loved anyone in my life like you."

"But," Tess began with her brows crinkled. "Are you okay now, do you still have pain?"

"Oh no, honey," I laughed. "You've seen me the past few months, I'm just fine . . . nothing stops me now." And, with that comment, I pulled Tess to me and rolled her over until I was on top and looking down into her eyes. "

God truly took care of me. I may not be perfect, but I know He watched over me. Honestly, it was a wake-up call that I turn my life around, and it did. I stopped the drugs – cold turkey, and while I do still have a drink, I've never indulged like I did before."

"Sweetheart, you don't need to explain anything else, I know you," she said as she looked up at me.

I took her in my arms. My body was filled with a passion I couldn't explain. Never in my life, had I met a woman who had cared about me in the way that Tess did. My mother did the bare minimum as that was what was required and nothing more. Yes, she surely loved me, but I later learned, it was not in the manner that most mothers cared for their children. To my mother, I felt as though I had been a burden, an obligation, and one that she didn't necessarily enjoy. There was no doubt it had affected my relationships with women going forward. I felt deficient. I felt that I was not worthy, and I sought out ways to compensate. Yes, I was surely a psychiatrist's dream patient as they could analyze the hell out of me, but I had held it together despite the fact I could have lost it.

"Are you okay?" Tess questioned, and lifted her hand to touch my cheek to pull me back to reality. At that moment, another bolt of lightning flashed through our small cabin on the boat, and she flinched.

"I'm just fine," I said as I lowered my face and nuzzled her neck.

Tess laughed and reached her arms around my neck, "I love you so much, Boyd Collingsworth."

Our lips met, we kissed, we touched, and we moved with the rhythm of the music made by the beats of the thunder as the storm raged.

CHAPTER 24
Landon

*I*t was only 12 days. In less than two weeks, I would no longer be a captive of New Horizons; I could leave, and I would finally be back home. It had been hell, but I had served my sentence. I played the role to perfection, and everyone believed I had been transformed. God, I should get an Academy Award for my performance, I thought with a wry smile. I walked the walk, spoke the words, and I had learned to do exactly what they wanted so they could add me as another statistic of a successfully, recovered addict. I knew I could have probably done it all on my own, and remained in Naples, but it was a part of the negotiated deal with the courts, and I still had to deal with the malpractice case when

I returned. Still, my lawyers said my remorseful attitude and compliance in the program would help my position immensely.

As usual Daddy and Mama left me to fiend for myself – not one phone call, not one letter, and not one visit from them, but I really didn't expect it. It was a fact of life in our family that unpleasant subjects were avoided like the plague. Why? I'm not sure I will ever know. Hell, when Boyd was in a coma for two weeks, they didn't even cut their trip short to come home from Europe so why should I have expected a visit from them now? Once in my life, I would love to sit down with my parents and have an open conversation about their indifference and distance over the years.

As a child growing up in the 1960's, it looked like we had a picture-perfect life. From outside appearances, we had a typical upper-middle class upbringing right out of a sit-com. Daddy went to the office every day in his suit and tie with the briefcase and hat, while Mama stayed home. Granted, Mama didn't vacuum or do laundry, but she portrayed the image of the all-American housewife even though she had a daily housekeeper who managed everything in the house. Still, I knew my friends' mothers, and there was a difference. I noticed it early-on when I would visit my friends' homes. We would see smiles when mothers made snacks, they would place drawings and school papers on the refrigerator with a magnet, they would give hugs when their sons made a homerun, and they would laugh and sing along with us to the radio when we would pile in their station wagons, but this was never the case with Marion Collingsworth. Even now that I'm a husband and father, it haunts me, and I would love to ask Mama why? Why she was always so aloof? Why did she never sit down and read us books at night before we went to sleep? Why did my brothers and I never have birthday parties like our friends? Why as a child, we would wake-up on our birthdays and only find an envelope atop our dressers with cash instead of a wrapped gift? As an adult, I admit that I've pushed those memories aside for the most part, but as a child, I would lay awake at night. I wished for Mama to come and tuck me in, I wished for those birthday parties where she would come walking out with a cake and all my friends would sing to me. I wished to open-up colorfully wrapped gifts rather than biking to Fifth Avenue to buy my own birthday present at the toy store with the money from my check.

Once, at a cocktail party, I overheard a psychologist acquaintance state that 'men usually pick wives just like their mothers, or else the exact opposite." Thinking back on that logic, I can't really say that Jennifer is the same, or the opposite. In fact, I'm not too keen on the whole psychoanalysis when they attempt to make thoughts and actions dependent on the roles played by your parents. Granted, I was never physically abused, nor was I ever neglected, so I shouldn't complain. So, what, if my mother was emotionally detached – not everyone is blessed. Still, I grew up secure in a beautiful home, never any financial issues, and I suppose it could have been a hell of a lot worse. Who was I to complain because my mama wasn't a warm and fuzzy type? She just hadn't been born with the maternal gene to be instinctively love and nurture.

On the other hand, my wife didn't seem much better as she hadn't come to visit me either. Jennifer told me she had a flight scheduled to come up and see me for one weekend, but then canceled it at the last minute as she claimed the girls were sick, but visiting a husband in rehab wasn't exactly something Jennifer relished as she even hated going to the doctor, and for some reason, she equated rehab with medical issues which she didn't wish to be exposed. So, it was Attie. In all honestly, I think Attie was the only family member who had the desire, time or compassion to visit me.

Although I was due to go home in less than two weeks, I was pumped about Attie's visit. It was nearly 2 o'clock in the afternoon, and he was due at any time. I had told the front desk that I would be in the garden, and to send my brother out when he arrived. The garden with the gazebo, oak trees, azaleas and Adirondack chairs had become my refuge. With the heat of the sun high overhead, I leaned my head back and was drinking in the sun when I heard a familiar voice and opened my eyes.

"Hey there, you big druggie," Attie called out as he came up and gave a shove to my shoulder to wake me up and I nearly fell off the chair.

"Hey, hey there," I'm awake, cool it," I countered as I picked up my book that had fallen on the grass. God, it was good to see my baby brother. I stood up and we gave each other a hug. Even though we had grown up without any physical expressions of affection, it seemed we had learned how to acquire it on some level as adults, and as such, it was still baffling that we had found an ability to connect with others despite our deficiencies from childhood.

"So, what's going on with you?" I asked as I sat back down and took a long drink from my water bottle. "Anything new in the situation with the girl in Alabama?"

"Hell, I don't know," he sighed and leaned back as he stretched out his legs in front of him. "She called to let me know that it's due in July – just after the Fourth of July."

"Congratulations - How about that?"

"Landon, I have no idea if I'm even the father. I told y'all she had some boyfriend who could also be the father. I'm not even thinking about it too much until I take a damn DNA test."

"I understand, but boy was that a mess when she showed up at Christmas Eve, I thought Mama was gonna have a shit fit right there at the table."

"No, you've got to remember – Mama never has a fit in public, she just ignores whatever it is, and it gets taken out on us later in some subtle way."

Attie started laughing at his own words, but then grew somber as he leaned closer. "So, seriously, how are you doing with all this?" He asked and motioned his hand in a circular motion.

I hesitated to answer. I was uncertain if I should tell the truth. I wanted to avoid the fact of why I was here, and what had happened. I just wanted to talk about neutral subjects, and not delve into history. Attie looked good, and I had to admit I missed him. I missed all three of my crazy brothers. In all honestly, I had to wonder if I longed for my brothers more than my wife, children or parents. Although we had been competitive with one another growing up, and we had been wicked in our attempts to gain the upper hand and the advantage against each other, we still were the first ones to defend each other if the world was against us.

"Come on, what have you been doing?" Attie urged.

"Oh, I'm a model patient. I go to my individual counseling sessions, I go to my group therapy, I do my physical exercise, my yoga sessions, and I say exactly what they want to hear. They love it because they think they've cured me of all my ills. I'm just another success story to them," I ended with a sardonic laugh.

"So, I take it you're feeling better with all this therapy . . . you know. . . exercise shit?" Attie said as he reclined back in one of the chairs and twisted the top from the water bottle he had been given when he checked in. It was amazing how this place shoved water at all of us like we were in the desert dying of thirst.

"No, I'm feeling like crap, if you really want to know?" I answered with a grimace. "My headaches have returned, and I'm in pain all the time. I can't remember the last time I've had a good night's sleep. All they do is hand me a Tylenol or Advil, but that doesn't even phase me."

"Yeah, you need the good stuff?" Attie suggested as he winked at me with a knowing smile.

"You have no idea what I would give for a hit of pot, or a couple of oxycodone - I just want some relief from this pain."

"I figured as much," and he reached in his jeans' pocket, but looked around cautiously before he drew out a handful of those little white pills I craved so much.

"I brough you a little present," he said in his sneaky voice.

"How did you get in here with those? Didn't they search you?"

"Nope, you know I can play a good game and sweet talk anyone – there were a couple of cute little nurses at the check-in, and I flattered them like crazy, so they forgot all about searching me," he finished with a knowing laugh.

"Well, give them here," I said, but before I reached out a hand, I simply handed him my book. "Just open it like you're reading it, and then slip them in between some pages."

"No problemo, brother," he said as he took the book from me, and held it up before him in an exaggerated manner as though the was analyzing the title. After a few seconds, he lowered it in a studious fashion as he flipped a few pages, and then sat it on his lap where he indiscreetly slipped the pills inside between several pages.

"Hello, Landon," Reverend Smalls greeted me in a mellow voice as he leaned closer. I opened eyes, but I had no idea where I was. I wasn't in my normal room here at New Horizons, and hell, it looked as though I was in a hospital. I even had an IV connected to my arm, and there was a tube up my nose.

"What?" I questioned as I attempted to turn my head from side-to-side, and pulled at the tube. "Where am I?"

"You're in the medical/detox center of the facility," he said gently.

"I don't understand?"

"Oh, yes, I'm sure you do, Landon," the pastor replied, and I could tell he was urging me to remember events.

"My brother, Attie, came to visit me, and we were sitting out in the garden. "Did something happen to me?"

"What do you think, Landon?" He continued with the damned questions, and I just wanted some peace. I wished he would just go away and leave me alone. I didn't answer and turned my head away from the side of the bed where he sat to look out the window. Maybe if I ignored him, he would leave.

"I'm guessing your brother brought you the pills – am I right?"

I refused to answer, and kept my eyes focused on the tree outside; the dogwood was in full bloom.

"How do you expect to get better, son, if you aren't honest?"

I turned around in an instant, and I was so damned tired of this guy trying to ingratiate himself into my life. I didn't want his opinion, his lectures, or his God, and I wish he would just try to find some other willing soul to save.

"Listen, Smalls," I began not even caring if I didn't use a title of respect to address him. "I'm not sure what you're after, but I don't want it. I can walk out of here anytime I like, but I will not have you following around after me as though I'm a little kid whose done something bad, and you're a parent ready to punish me."

"Is that the issue, Landon?" Reverend Smalls suggested in his soothing voice. "I know that your parents haven't called, or they even haven't come to visit you. I also know that your wife hasn't either-"

"Stop it, it's none of your business. How are you privy to that information – that should be private . . . confidential," I said, and now I was pissed. How dare he barge into my personal history with my family.

"Landon, I want to help," he said, and my threats were not discouraging him. "It's difficult when you have family – parents and a spouse, who refuse to acknowledge your pain. If your own family won't come forward to help you through your low times . . . your days of trials and temptations . . . it can be difficult to trust anyone."

"Who said I had any issues of trust?" I countered.

"No one, but I'm a keen observer of human relationships, plus I've studied the Bible, and whether you wish to believe it or not, our Lord gave us examples of nearly every situation we encounter in lives if we just open our hearts and listen to His word-"

"Don't go getting all religious on me," I stopped him.

"I'm not getting 'all religious on you,' Landon, I am just attempting to help you. I want you to know that even though you may not feel you have support with your own parents, or your wife, you have a heavenly father who is there for you. There are many of us in this world who have parents – ones who choose not to parent their children. It may be a personal decision to distant themselves, or one based on circumstances, but no matter what it is, it is a terrible disservice to their children. Children deserve to be loved, nurtured and to know that they have a safe place to find refuge, and I'm not just talking about the physical aspect. Children need emotional fulfillment just as much as they need the physical. They need to know they have an advocate for them whether it's a biological parent here in this world, or our Father in heaven," he stopped to catch his breath and then continued. "Landon, what I am trying to tell you is that I feel you have been searching your entire life for validation, for love, and to know that you have someone who is caring and watching over you. I'm not saying that your parents were wrong, or deficient, but in my opinion, they did not give you the emotional support you needed growing up, and when you didn't get that validation, you turned to other things to fill that void."

I rolled my eyes at him and of his 'observations' of my life, but he only gave a slight laugh. "Landon, why? Why are you so headstrong to refuse help? You were ordered by the courts to come here to get help, but I know what you've been doing?"

I turned away from him again to look back out at the white blossoms on the dogwood.

"You're very good at what you do. You're a smart man. You had a lot of people fooled here, and many believed that you've made progress, but now with this latest stunt, you're back to square one."

"I'm not staying here beyond the time that I agreed to," I spat the words at him. "So, I took a few pills. I've been clean for well over two months. I'm still getting my headaches, and those damn Tylenol and Advil don't even phase me. I'm a doctor, and I know how to manage medication – I just got busy and messed up that one time. I've never had any another issues over the years," I argued in my defense.

Reverend Smalls was silent for a few moments, but then ventured, "Landon, did you know there are animals who have no maternal instincts?"

Now, he was back to the issue of parents again, and even though I didn't care to further engage, I had to admit he had my attention, so I looked back over at him.

"In the reptilian world, snakes have no maternal instincts-"

"So, you're saying my mother is a snake?" I asked sarcastically and gave a stilted laugh.

"No, but just to let you know that not all humans or animals have that innate maternal longing. Snake mothers abandon their eggs soon after laying them and never return again. Nature has allowed for infant snakes to have the ability to fend for themselves."

"I can relate."

"Also, with mammals you will see if a mother panda bear has twins, she will favor one over the other."

"So, nice analogy, but where is this going?"

"Landon, sometimes when we don't get fulfillment of our emotional needs, we reach out for things to make up for that which is lacking from our lives."

"So."

"In short, I'm saying that if you found fulfillment in your life then you might not have sought out substitutes for what's missing. The drugs, the alcohol, the women -"

"Whoa," I interrupted. "Sure, I've taken a few liberties over the years with my ability to secure the medication, but I have no issues with alcohol or women – what do you know?"

Reverend Small raised his eyebrows at me. "Honestly, I don't know, Landon, but I suspect? Suppose you tell me?"

Hell, I was lying here in the hospital due to a recent overdose. I had an IV attached to my arm, a tube up my nose, and this man was attempting to engage me in some sort of psychological game to analyze me through examining my childhood and my choices as an adult.

"What's the big deal," I argued. "I grew up in the 70's, and sure we all dappled in things. We drank like fish, and sure we did drugs, but who didn't? We lived in Southwest Florida, and it was the drug import center of America. We had pot and coke flowing in from South America every day either by boat or plane, and it was ours for the taking. Was that so bad?"

"Was it? Smalls disputed my claims without any hesitancy.

"Listen, I graduated from high school top in my class, went onto UF where again I graduated top of my class, and onto medical school where I got an internship at Duke, and if I had any issues with drugs or alcohol, then tell me how could I have done it?" There, I had showed him and dared him to debate.

"Landon, there's no doubt that you were able to handle yourself very well. You functioned amazingly well despite indulging in choices that could have easily curtailed your progress."

I rolled my eyes at him.

"No, I didn't know about the women, but it's a rational deduction. If someone engages in risky behaviors with alcohol and drugs, then it is very likely that they will view promiscuous behaviors as an extension. It is simply another high to reach – am I wrong?"

"What in the hell do you want?" I finally lashed out in exasperation.

"Landon, you have so much potential, but you're limiting yourself."

I didn't understand him. To anyone looking at me, I was a shining example of success. I had a successful medical practice, I had more money than I needed, I had a beautiful wife, three healthy daughters, and a gorgeous home, a boat, and a car of my dreams. What more did I need?

Reverend Smalls hesitated as he obviously hoped I would analyze what he was saying, but now continued. "All the material successes in the world don't necessarily have the ability to ensure true and fulfilling happiness. Many wealthy and successful people in this world are some of the most unhappy ones. There are other ways to find personal fulfillment, Landon."

"And, what are you suggesting?" I asked still hesitant as Smalls reminded me of a salesperson trying to market a product.

"First of all, I think you need to have a personal

relationship with Jesus Christ, accept Him as your Savior, and then use the gifts you have been given to make a difference in this world."

"So, you're trying tell me that if I just do what you suggest then I will have a life of fulfillment, I won't want drugs, alcohol or other women, and I will magically be able to have a decent relationship with my parents," I answered him in a bored voice.

"Landon, I'm not saying that it will be instantaneous, but I do honestly believe that the Holy Spirit will fill you with a sense of purpose to find God's will, and in doing so, you will find a peace in your heart with what has been missing."

At that moment, the nurse came in with my chart, and she began checking my vitals. Reverend Smalls stood up and walked over to the door. "Landon, I will be by to visit you tomorrow, and I trust that you think of what we spoke about. Have a good night."

Despite being a man of the cloth, I had to wonder if Reverend Smalls may have placed a curse on me. I had one of the worst nights of my life – not in the physical sense from any pain, but I was emotionally wrung out when I woke. Dreams had disoriented me with visions that made no sense. In one, I was running from some unseen figures in a forest or jungle, but I kept getting trapped by the vegetation and then vines wrapped themselves around me. In another, I was some homeless bum on a street, and people kept walking by laughing at me and kicking me out of their way, and one of those people was my mother. And, the last dream was the most disturbing as I was dying, and I kept getting asked by my patients if I was going to end up in heaven or hell, but I told them I was only a doctor and not a minister.

I reached over to grab the Styrofoam cup that kept rolling on the table and lifted the straw to my mouth where I drained the entire cup of water in a few seconds. I was still parched so I refilled my cup from the plastic pitcher. God, I was dry, and it didn't seem as though there was enough water to quench my thirst. Maybe it was something they were giving me in the IV that was causing my dry mouth, but whatever it was, I hadn't felt this way yesterday. I would have to ask the nurses to show me my chart, and I would go over every medication I was being given. They couldn't deny me. I was a patient, but I was also a doctor so I knew just as well as anyone here on staff what the medications

317

and side effects would be. So, while I could get to the bottom of what my physical symptoms were, I wasn't so sure I was going to find the cause for this wretchedness I was feeling. It wasn't exactly depression, but I felt an overwhelming sense of melancholy that I couldn't shake. It was a feeling of impending doom, and disaster. Of course, it was probably due to the medications. I had cautioned many of my patients over the years to be aware and ready for side effects with their prescriptions, and sometimes it affected certain people in different ways. Confident that I would get some answers to my physical and mental symptoms when I examined my charts, I turned over in the narrow bed, and did my best to get comfortable and go back to sleep for a few hours.

It was mid-morning when I heard the distinct sound of someone clearing their voice, and I turned over to see none other than the good Reverend Smalls standing by my bed.

"Good morning, Landon."

"Hello," I said, and wondered if this man had a life other than coming to see me. Surely, he had a family, friends, work, and other things to occupy his time, but it seemed I had become his pet project.

"I was on my way to visit another patient, but

thought I would stop in to see how you're doing? Did you have a good night's sleep?"

"Honestly, no I didn't," I replied as I maneuvered myself up to a sitting position. "I've had a hell of a night – nightmares, and now I felt horrible, but it was likely due to the medications they're giving me . . . I've been dying of thirst this morning, and just an overwhelming sense of dread."

"Interesting . . ."

"Why do you say that?"

"Because I distinctly heard the nurse talking to your doctor yesterday, and you aren't on any medications – not even an aspirin."

"But the IV?"

"Intravenous feeding. You were in a coma for three days."

"I didn't know that."

"You only woke-up yesterday so hopefully you'll start eating soon."

I nodded and adjusted the sheet and blanket around my middle.

"So, you were having nightmares . . . would you care to talk?" He said and pulled up his chair closer to my bed.

"Just normal nightmares – running in jungle, I was a homeless man, but the worst was I was dying, and I kept being asked if I was going to heaven or hell."

"Well?"

"Well, what?" I countered.

"Are you going to heaven or hell?"

"Well, I should hope to heaven, wouldn't anyone?"

"You know you can be certain?"

"Yeah, yeah, I know you said as much yesterday. I told you I grew up in the Episcopal church, and I've done everything – baptism, confirmation, communion, and I give regularly to the church even though we don't go very often.

"So, do you feel that will allow you to enter the pearly gates?"

"I'm not a bad person."

"Landon, I didn't say that you were a bad person. We all are sinners, but God forgives us, and loves us. What makes the difference is that after you decide to have a personal relationship with the Lord then you will turn from your old ways in favor of new ones – I guarantee you."

I didn't say anything but reached over and grabbed my cup again to take a drink.

"Metaphorically speaking . . . perhaps your dreams are trying to tell you something. You were searching for something in the jungle, but you kept getting caught up by the vines, and the undeniable thirst. Do you know the parable about the rich man in hell?"

I rolled my eyes as I knew he was getting ready to launch into another mini sermon, but it wasn't as if I could avoid it; I was his captive.

"In the book of Luke there is a story, a rich man was in hell and he cried out to Father Abraham to have mercy on him by sending Lazarus down that he could dip the tip of his finger in water and cool his tongue as the fires of hell were not only tormenting physically but mentally." The minister stopped and looked at me directly in the eyes. "Landon, I feel God has been working on your soul, He's reaching out to you, and He has sent you a message."

"I'm a doctor, I'm not changing professions and going into the ministry."

"Who said anything about changing professions. I think you can do God's work in many ways with the medical field, but first you have to commit yourself to Him."

I looked over at Reverend Smalls for the first time in several weeks, and suddenly, I felt different. The resentment towards him was no longer a festering wound, but I felt awash with a newfound respect for him, and I simply said, "Yes."

CHAPTER 25
Hollis

Mama would be pea green with envy if she could see the Pinckney's home on Legare Street. Although it had been built prior to the American Revolution, it never fell into ruin, and it was a sparkling jewel south of Broad in Charleston. It was literally four stories. Constructed of brick that had been painted white, it boasted a double front veranda that ran the length of the front of the home, and also boasted a smaller porch on the south side. White rockers adorned the porches, and blue hydrangeas with cascading ivy greeted visitors on either side of the grand double front doors. To the right of the house, behind a black wrought-iron fence, those passing by could glimpse the English-styled garden complete with an intricate design of boxwood shrubs in which a colorful array of roses splashed color around an elaborate fountain of cascading water. The Pinckney house was the stuff of dreams for many. I had no doubt it was front and center on the historic buggy tours, and the tourists looked on in avid envy and interest as the guide told the history behind this one and other mansions.

Thaddeus and Lyla Pinckney were the epitome of all things that described a genteel Southern couple. Just like many others of the prominent Charleston families, they could both trace their lineage back to the 18th century, and they were also related through several different lines, but Stu had assured me they were distant enough that he didn't have to worry about being an inbred, crazy person. Thaddeus was a Citadel graduate, studied law at the University of South Carolina Law School, and went into his family's law practice that had been housed in a prominent landmark on King Street for several generations. Miss Lyla was a sweet Ashley Hall graduate who never aspired to be any more than the wife of a prominent Charlestonian and produce little heirs to their line.

So, I met Stu's two grandmothers who had been born before the First World War and were now revered family matriarchs who sat and contentedly watched scenes of their children, grandchildren and great-grandchildren through rummy eyes. I met Stu's three sisters, Alice, Mary, and Annabelle, and their husbands, but I couldn't remember the names of any of the children who ran around the garden in wild abandon where an inflatable waterslide had been set up next to the gazebo. It was a loud household, but it was one of relaxed chaos. Shoes were kicked off by the front door and the foyer was overflowing with assorted pairs, but Lyla didn't mind. She loved her family, and she relished the pandemonium as it meant her family was a happy one. The back-patio tables were filled with a half-finished jigsaw puzzles, while assorted boardgames vied for attention on the nearby coffee tables. The staff of three black women, who had been with the family from before the time Stu was born, circulated around the family without any hesitancies. I loved how the staff smiled, interacted, and even joked with the Pinckney's. I had to admit I was falling in love with this family as this was what I had always imagined a holiday could be.

"Mrs. Pinckney, I must admit that I feel a bit awkward just barging in on your family's Easter celebration," I said as I stood in the kitchen and watched as she garnished her deviled eggs. Stu had told me that his Mama's deviled eggs were infamous, and she never allowed anyone else to make them.

"You listen, here, Hollis," she said without looking up as she sprinkled paprika on her eggs. "You're a friend of Stu's, and your family were friends of Ned and Lillian, so you are always welcome in this home – you hear me now," she said as she looked up and licked a bit of the red spice off her finger.

"Yes, ma'am," I nodded. "I do appreciate you opening your lovely home to include me."

"You just hush now, but I'm sure you're missing your own family, and your little children – you know, Stu confided in me -"

"Confided?" I interrupted her, and then felt ashamed that I had forgotten my manners.

"Yes, that you're going through a divorce," she said and then proceeded with the minced fresh parsley atop the eggs. "God bless you and your family – it's never easy."

"Yes, ma'am, it's not what I ever thought would happen," I began, but then stopped as I wasn't sure that I should add anything further.

"It's not pleasant when you have children involved, I can say that for sure. It confuses the little ones just about as much as it confuses the big ones," she added with a laugh and paused for few moments.

"You know, Stu had a divorce when he was younger, and as much as I love my grandbabies, it would have been difficult had babies been involved. Stu's daddy is still holding out hope for Stu to find that special girl as he wants the Pinckney line to continue with a grandson to carry on the name, but -"

I saw a bowl of mixed nuts, so I picked up a handful, and proceeded to eat them as it precluded me from having to answer.

"Oh, sweet boy, you must realize that I'm a mama who knows her children," Mrs. Pinckney said in her sweet as could be 'iced tea' Southern voice. "Lillian was not only my twin, but my dearest friend in the world. Do you really think we didn't tell one another our secrets?"

Innocently, I shrugged my shoulders and selected a few more cashews from the assortment in my hand to wait as I wasn't exactly sure where this might be leading. Stu might still believe that his parents were in the dark as to his sexual orientation, but I had an idea that his Mama knew her son very well.

"Stu is my baby, but I've known for a long time," she said with some sadness in her voice. "God doesn't make all of us the same so we can't be expectin' everyone to want to follow and conform to what our family, or what society wants. Stu is a good boy, and I love him. He is a gentle man who cares about everyone and would never hurt a soul. His daddy may not ever fully understand, but if Stu never marries again, we'll survive. Goodness, with our daughters, we already have 12 grandbabies so it's not as though our genes aren't gonna continue."

I laughed, and then ventured. "So, Mr. Pinckney knows?"

"Heavens sakes, no. I've never breathed a word, but I'm sure he's got his suspicions. He's of that generation where you don't talk about things like that, and I believe he'll never acknowledge it even when he breathes his last breath."

I nodded, and then wiped my hands together to shake the salt from them.

"And, dear boy, you need to call me 'Miss Lyla' as that's what everybody here in Charleston calls me," she finished with a wink as she wiped her hands on the nearby hand towel, and came over to give me a hug.

Stu and I strolled along the Charleston Battery in the late afternoon sun. We had volunteered to walk Miss Lyla's corgis, Windsor and Kensington, and now I knew why Stu had chosen 'Lady Di,' for his dog's name. Although a true born and bred Southern lady, Miss Lyla absolutely adored anything to do with the British Royal Family, and that had obviously rubbed off on Stu. I didn't mind. Actually, I thought it was adorable. So, now we walked Windsor and Kensi down the sidewalk toward White Point garden along the Battery. Easter was in mid-April this year, so spring was in full display as the dogwood, crepe myrtle and azaleas blossoms framed the elegant mansions with their vibrant mix of colors. As we walked, I inhaled with relish the fresh floral scents that mingled with the breeze tinged in salty seawater. It was all an intoxicating assault to the senses as you didn't know what to indulge in first from sight to sense to touch. I was greedy as I wanted it all.

This peninsula on the south point of downtown Charleston overlooked the harbor where the Ashley and Cooper rivers met, and while all of Charleston was a history lover's dream, this area is especially poignant. Originally known as Oyster Point from the masses of oysters that could be found on the water's edge, it evolved as a seawall and was built to become the most exclusive area of Charleston with its promenade. Just directly across the Harbor sat Fort Sumter which became famous as the catalyst for the Civil

War when the Confederates fired on the Union soldiers occupying the Fort. And, from the historic homes and churches dating back to the 18th century to the defense artillery cannons of Civil War, I could certainly have understood why Stu and his family were so proud to be a part of the history of this glorious city.

"Stu, you live in paradise," I said as we strolled along a row of palm trees lining the sidewalk.

"Excuse me," Stu begged. "This is coming from a boy who grew up and lives in Naples, Florida."

"Well, we've both been very fortunate, but this . . . this," I said as I took my free hand and swept it out to indicate the view of the park, the harbor, and the sailboats in the distance. "This is different. Naples is 'new money,' and everything is so artificial. It's made to look the part, but there's no depth . . . no history as there is here. Sure, Naples has a history, too, but it was a sleepy fishing village a hundred years ago filled with renegades, Seminole Indians, and those who basically wanted to escape from the world – now's it the mecca for those who want to build mega-mansions and flash their money around with their Italian sports cars and their wives permanently altered thanks to the plastic surgeons. Those in Naples want to see and be heard . . . there is no understated elegance in Naples like there is here in Charleston."

Stu laughed at my description, "But, it could be a lot worse."

"Sure, you're right, but I always felt out of place in Naples. You know how much I love books, reading, history . . . honestly, I feel so alive here as there is so much culture to drink up that I feel I could be drunk on it every day."

He laughed and stopped as Windsor was inspecting a particular interesting statue. "Well, you know if you're serious, we could arrange it. I have a townhouse, and we could just tell everyone we're roommates. I don't see any reason why you couldn't work here and manage money in Charleston as well as you do in Naples – hell, maybe you could have an office in each city?"

"I'm tempted," I said as I watched Kensi now go over to her companion to see what was so interesting. "But, Helen, the kids? I'd move in a minute, but how would I ever explain it to them. I love those kids, and I can't imagine not seeing them regularly. Sure, they could come visit, and we could go down there, but it just wouldn't be the same. I want to be able to pick them up at school, I want to take them out to dinner, and not just be there for holidays, or see them in the summer months."

"Do you think Helen would ever consider moving

here?"

I laughed at his remark. "Absolutely not. She loves Naples. She was adamant when we talked about the separation that she wasn't leaving. In fact, she wants me to sign the house over to her, and she wants the mortgage paid off, free and clear. She's not moving an inch," I stopped as I gave a tug to Kensi and we all started walking again.

We continued along in silence for several minutes, and we watched as the bicyclists, joggers, and other dog walkers passed us in both directions.

"It's also Mama?" I ventured once we were out of earshot of others.

"I don't understand?"

"Something isn't right," I began. "I mean, Mama's has always used food as a crutch, but now it's not just her sweets, but literally everything in sight. I've noticed, hell everyone has noticed, and even Daddy says she's been overindulging."

"What a pleasant way to say that 'she's eating too much.'"

"I'm sure it's stress. Just look at all her sons. Landon's in rehab for a drug addiction and a nasty malpractice suit, Boyd is divorced and suddenly took up with another girl, Mama just found out that I'm gay and divorcing Helen, and Attie may have knocked- up some redneck girl in Alabama. These aren't exactly topics Mama wants to brag about to her friends at the Port Royal Club."

Stu was laughing now. "I'm sorry, but I'm still picturing the expression your Mama's had on her face on Christmas Eve when that girl walked into the dining room. It was something right out of a William Faulkner play – a wounded family, passions high with money and ambition."

"Great, thanks for bringing that memory back," I said sarcastically. "But, in all seriousness, she's not in great health to begin with, and I don't want it on my conscience that I may have exasperated it by leaving Naples. As much as I want to move here, I just don't know how I could do it."

"Hollis, it isn't something that has to be decided today," he said as he reached out and placed a hand on my shoulder. "And, there's always room for compromise."

"What do you mean?"

"I mean that I am licensed to practice law in both South Carolina and Florida – I don't have an ex-wife with children so there are no issues of me needing to be in Charleston all the time. Hell, we could get a house down in Naples for most of the year – maybe spend some Christmas holidays up here, and the summers. I think the kids would love it."

"It's an idea," I said as thoughts converged in my mind with scenes of the children playing with Stu's nephews and nieces during the Pinckney's holiday celebrations, and of the children playing on the sands at the beach house out on Sullivan's Island. How could Helen complain? She would have everything she wanted with her home, but I would still be there during the school year to help with the kids, and then we would have the ultimate get-a-way to Charleston when Naples' summers became unbearable with the intense heat and humidity.

"I've got the townhouse here, and it has four bedrooms so there's more than enough space, and we could get a house down in Olde Naples. When I was staying at Aunt Lillian's house, I always thought those Key West styled homes with the little white picket fences were adorable."

I nodded my head, and I suddenly felt as though a huge weight had been lifted. It wasn't all set-in stone, but it was a plan, and it was a plan that could work. It had the possibility of giving everyone what they wanted, and most of all, it might allow Helen and me to move on with the least amount of damage to the well-being of our family. Suddenly, my cell phone rang, and I looked down to see it was Helen's number.

"This may be a sign," I said and held up the phone so Stu could see Helen's name flashing on the screen. "Let me take this – hopefully, it's not something dire."

Stu nodded and took Kensi's leash from my hand, so he now had a hold of both dogs.

"Hey, Daddy," came the enthusiastic voices of all three of my children. "Happy Easter."

"Happy Easter," I chimed in return.

I turned to point to the phone and mouthed 'the kids' as Stu nodded again and proceeded to walk further along the Battery.

"Mama said we could call you, but we had to wait until after church, and then after lunch at Mama Mar and Pop-pop's."

"Did you have a good day?"

"Yes – sort of," George, Jr., took command of the conversation as the eldest. "We set our baskets out by the fireplace, and this morning they were all filled with candy and toys from the Easter Bunny," he ended on a droll note.

I appreciated that he didn't mention in front of the younger ones that his mother had filled the baskets with loot, but was cognizant that his younger brother and sister still believed in the Easter Bunny and the annual visit.

"Church was the usual," he said in a bored tone.

"Then we went to Pop-pop and Mama Mar's house . . . we swam, played some croquet and Uncle Boyd even helped us boys do a little fishing off Pop-pop's dock, but then Mama Mar got upset as she said we shouldn't be fishing on Easter as it wasn't what she had planned."

"Oh my," I said. Stu heard my response and came back towards me with the dogs. There was no doubt Stu relished any sort of drama with my family.

"Then, Uncle Attie told her that 'Jesus was a fisher of men,' so it was right and fine on Easter,' but that just made Mama Mar upset and she stayed inside for the rest of the time. She didn't even eat lunch with us . . . but guess she was sad we didn't have ham to eat 'cause Luc and Rory ate it after the accident, and then she didn't even say 'good-bye' to us when we left."

I gave a heavy sigh, and George, Jr. paused.

"Pop-pop said she had a headache," he added, but I could tell he didn't believe his grandfather. "Mama Mar sure does get a lot of headaches on the holidays."

"That she does, son," I commiserated, but I didn't want to dare tell him that I had just had one of the most enjoyable Easter celebrations in memory.

"When are you coming home?" I heard Lily pipe up, and then some commotion, so I assumed George, Jr., was handing the phone to his sister.

"I'm flying home tomorrow, sweetheart," I said, and my heart melted a little bit as I heard her angelic voice, and it was at that moment that I knew Stu and I had made the right decision about being based in Naples, but having a second, summer home here in Charleston. It just made complete sense.

"Yippee," she said with her soft voice growing a bit louder than normal. "Could we, could we have a 'Daddy and Daughter' date to the Dairy Queen and then the *American Doll* store. My doll, Felicity, needs a new dress." I laughed, and my heart swelled as I knew my children would never forget about me even though I was leaving their mother. Thank goodness, I prayed that this continued, and that Helen and I could have an amiable relationship.

CHAPTER 26
Attie

*A*s usual, Mama had transformed the area by her rose garden into a scene of Easter splendor. Two white tents had been erected on the lawn. Several round dining tables sported floral arrangements that nearly encompassed the entire tabletops under one canopy, while the other had food stations set up. An authentic English croquet set had been installed on the lawn down by the dock, while a net had been set-up for an impromptu volleyball game, and a well-stocked bar was front and center on the pool patio for the delight, and relief, of the adults. Roger had worked his magic for yet another holiday, so Mama was pleased. Mama never did anything without her usual flair, and of course, we were all well-trained to lavish praise on her of how wonderful it was each year.

While the image could have been a spread in *Southern Living* or *Town and Country,* it was an illusion; still, Mama always loved to imagine her life was picture perfect, and who were we to destroy her fantasies. I had to admit this year was a stretch, and I had no doubt the staff was secretly gossiping about the recent scandals plaguing the Collingsworth family. As I sipped my Bloody Mary, I walked over to the one tent and looked down at the elegant calligraphy on the place cards. Let's see, there was no card for Landon as he was still in rehab in Atlanta, not one for Libby as she was removed via the divorce, and no Hollis as he was up in Charleston with his new beau getting to know Stu's family.

Still, Helen would always be considered part of the family, and I assumed would always be welcomed as she was the unknowing victim in Hollis' caper to 'find his true self.' Of course, Jennifer was present with the girls as a representative of Landon, but it had become an unspoken rule that no one mentioned Landon being away at rehab. We also knew better than to mention anything about RaeLynn and her impending baby. It was as though we just ignored any mention of disturbing subjects, and rather only spoke of pleasant topics – namely the food or weather.

"Looking good there, Attie," Boyd said as he walked up to me and patted me on the shoulder. "Got your seersucker suit out, I see," Boyd laughed, and I had long ago resigned to the fact that he got a kick out of making fun of my fashion choices, but I didn't care. Yes, I liked to be a bit flamboyant, but it made life fun.

"As always," I said and raised my glass to him as he turned to the bar and asked for the same from the bartender. I saw Tess walking towards us, and it was obvious she had been sidetracked with Boyd's kids as she handed them beach towels and waved to them as they ran from her to the pool.

"Tess," I said, and reached over to give her a kiss on the cheek.

"Attie, how are you – love the seersucker and the Lily Pulitzer bow tie," she said with a genuine smile, but Boyd just rolled his eyes at the compliment to me.

"Why thank you, Tess, glad to see you appreciate good fashion sense, but you're lucky you managed get my brother out of an old fishing shirt and boat shoes for today," I accepted her praise and saluted her as I lifted my Bloody Mary up.

"Whoa," Boyd countered. "I got the boat shoes on

today," he said as he lifted his khaki trousers to show a new pair of Sperry's, and with his blue and white striped Oxford cloth shirt, he passed Mama's inspection, but just barely. She liked us all to dress up for the holidays, but Boyd always pushed the limits with the bare minimum.

"Do you want a mimosa, honey?" Boyd asked as he turned to her.

"No, I think water is just fine," she said, and wiped at her brow.

"Are you okay?" Boyd asked with genuine concern in his voice.

"Just a bit warm," Tess said as she attempted to fan her face with her hand, but it was useless. "I think I'm going to just go over and sit in the shade of the patio. Jennifer and Helen are there," she smiled as she accepted the glass of ice water from the bartender.

Boyd and I watched as she walked away, and the two sisters-in-law stood up and embraced Tess with a 'girl kiss' to each cheek.

"Is she okay?" I asked. "She looks pale."

"I think so – I mean we were on the boat yesterday, so she got some sun, but I was thinking the same thing that she looked pale this morning. She didn't even want to eat breakfast this morning, and then she slept until nearly eleven – she's usually out for a run early on Sunday mornings."

Attie raised an eyebrow and then drained his drink before placing it back on the bar for a refill. "Might our little Tess be preggers?"

"Hardly," I coughed as the vodka went down the wrong way and burnt my throat.

"Why do you say that? Are your buddies not swimming?"

"No, I'm fine in that department," I responded defensively.

"Well, it does happen when you least expect it – I should know?"

I laughed, but it wasn't funny. If Attie turned out to be the father of RaeLynn's child, then he was somehow going to be saddled to her for the rest of his life in some manner. He had concluded that if the test confirmed him as the father, he was not going to marry her. Sure, he would provide, and I'm sure he would see the child from time to time, but marriage was definitely not in the picture.

"So, any news from Alabama since she left in January?"

"I think the $25,000 did a lot to quiet her down for a while, but I have my suspicions that the money won't last her long. She doesn't exactly seem like a thrifty sort of person. I'm sure she likely blew a wad of it in a major Walmart shopping spree, and then probably went out to eat at every greasy spoon she could find."

"Gosh, Attie, she really wasn't that bad," Boyd suggested, but I shook my head.

"No, worse, Boyd, you forget that she lived with me for two weeks, and it nearly drove me nuts . . . there's no way I could ever survive with someone like her. She's never going to amount to anything in life – no goals, no ambition."

"Well . . . " Boyd began, but I held up a hand to stop him.

"Don't go there," I knew it was always a sore subject with my brothers that I didn't work, but it was my choice, and it was Daddy's choice that he supported me. It was none of their business.

"Well, I think it's time for a little fishing," Boyd said as he looked at the flat waters of the Cove and we both could spy some Red Fish. "I'm headed around to the garage to get some poles, if you want to round up and tell the kids."

In less than a half an hour, Boyd was the ringleader as he had George, Jr., Geoff, and Perry down on the dock with poles in hand, and it appeared they were reeling them in as fast as they could remove a fish from the hook and throw another line in water. The little girls were all playing at croquet without much success, but they were more like cheerleaders as they jumped and squealed every time one of their brothers or cousins caught another one.

I was sitting on the patio with Daddy, and we were each enjoying our third Bloody Mary. I had to say it had been a pleasant afternoon, but then again, Mama hadn't been outside much. She didn't care for the heat, but she was more than likely ordering the staff around in the kitchen.

"Everything okay with Mama?" I asked Daddy as I stretched out my legs and put them up on the wicker ottoman.

He shrugged his shoulders and continued staring out to the dock as he watched the fishing party.

"Oh, she's been having her moments lately," Daddy sighed as though it pained him to even talk about it.

"Isn't she done with her 'change of life' mess?"

He laughed a bit. "Hell, if I know? She's always been moody. It just got worse during her 50's, and now she's moved onto to just being a major pain in the ass – what do they call them, 'a cranky old bitty?"

"I just know that she complains about everything and everyone, and nothing seems to be right – so, I've just been keeping my distance."

"Probably a good idea," he surmised and took a bite out of his celery stalk.

"Look, Pop-pop," George, Jr., called from the dock as he held up the biggest one yet.

"Good job, boy," Daddy said, and raised his hand with a wave.

Boyd looked around nodded to the two of us, and then I could see he was looking for Tess. He looked worried, but once he spied her looking at the rose bushes, he looked visibly relieved. God, he was smitten. I had never seen him like this with any girl in high school or college, much less Libby. I was glad for him, but in my heart, I was envious. I wanted to find someone whom I could share a love like he had found with Tess. Granted, he deserved it as Libby had been a royal bitch for years, but I was still jealous now. All I had was some red-neck girl up in Alabama, who may or may not be having my child, but I just wasn't meeting anyone that was right even here in Naples. I wasn't bad looking, and I had my share of dates. And, sex wasn't an issue as I could walk down Fifth Avenue any night of the week, and I could always hook up with some random girl at one of the bars. I never complained as it was fun, and physical release, but I was in my late thirties, and I was getting older. Hell, some of my friends had even ended their first marriages and were onto a new one with more kids. I guess I should have counted my blessings as they complained about being torn between the ex-wife and current one, as well as kids from two marriages, but still, I wanted a part of that life. I looked at Boyd and Tess, and I wanted someone I could share a past and future; I couldn't believe that I admitted it, I was wanting a commitment for the first time in my life.

Daddy held up his glass and called the bartender over for a refill. At this rate, Daddy was going to be toasty by the time we sat down for the late lunch at two, but what the hell, Daddy worked hard, and he obviously had been having a difficult time with Mama lately. With that thought, we heard some commotion, and we both turned to look at the French doors. The staff was in the process of bringing out the warmers and platters to place on the buffet table, but Mama was in a state, and was shoving them aside as she attempted to come through the doors at the same time. She wasn't having any regard for the fact that they were carrying hot foods, but rather just pushed her way through and walked directly out on the patio where she stared straight ahead at the dock.

"What are they doing, George?" She asked in a condescending voice as she placed her hands on her ample hips and pursed her mouth in a pissed expression.

"I believe they're fishing, dear," Daddy said, and attempted to stifle a laugh at her absurd question, which only set Mama off, and there was no doubt she would launch into some sort of tangent.

"Boyd," she called across the lawn, and stood like a colorful statue in her Lily Pulitzer Mumu dress.

"Yes, ma'am," he answered directly and adjusted his baseball cap so he could see her in the sun.

"What are you boys doing out there?"

"Just a little fishing until lunch is served – the boys are loving it, and I'll clean them for you later so you can have some fresh filets," Boyd added with a devilish grin.

Mama didn't respond, but only frowned.

"What's wrong, you don't like fish, Mama Mar?" George, Jr., innocently questioned.

"Well, not on Easter day when we're getting ready to have our luncheon," she said in an annoyed tone.

"Oh, come on, Mama, Jesus was a 'fisher of men,' so it's right and fine on Easter," Attie said with a cheeky grin, and Daddy joined right in with a roar.

"No, no, no," Mama shook her head, and stamped her foot so hard that one of her Jack Roger sandals flipped off and sailed backwards where it hit one of the staff in the arm causing the woman to drop the baked ham. It was a chain reaction as though a line of dominoes had been started. The maid looked in horror as the ham fell to the first step and then bounced down one to the next one, and then rolled until it landed only a few feet from the pool. Pineapples and cloves flew off the ham and littered the deck of the patio. All at once the labs, Rory and Luc, raced across the lawn, and began savagely tearing at the ham as though it was a prize they had found on a hunt. The two dogs growled as they pulled and tugged at the meat, and Daddy and I couldn't contain ourselves. He didn't give a damn that the Easter ham wouldn't be front and center on the buffet table as this sight was worth seeing.

At that moment, the little girls came running from the croquet court with their mallets and began swinging wildly at the dogs to no avail. Rory and Luc were delighted with their Easter gift of the ham, and they weren't about to let anyone, or anything deter them from finishing their prey.

"Shoo, shoo, you nasty doggies," Poppy and Missy twirled their mallets around like majorettes with batons. There was no doubt they were attempting to help Mama Mar, but she just looked at her granddaughters with distain.

"Girls, you go on now," Mama yelled, and looked around at the chaotic scene that had unfolded in a matter of seconds and displaced her picture-perfect Easter. Rather than a page from the society pages, the Collingsworth's backyard resembled a mini war zone from any Southern Alabama family's Easter; one that Mama had sought so desperately to escape from when she moved from Tuscaloosa to Naples.

I looked over at Jessica, Helen and Tess, but they were smart enough to stay in the background and keep their distance. I mentally applauded Tess. She may have only known our family for a few months, but she was adept at knowing when and where to make her presence known, and Helen and Jennifer followed her lead.

"For heaven's sakes," Mama looked as though she would faint from the drama unfolding before her, and I glanced over to Daddy to see if he was going to help, but he just looked on in delight at his Bloody Mary and ignored her.

Mama turned and limped back up the steps with her one sandal still on her foot, but was careful to side-step the pineapple rings and cloves. When she reached the French doors, she turned around for one last look, but that apparently did her in as when she wiped at a loose strand of her elegant chignon, it fell into a mass down over her eyes. With a huff, she pushed the hair from her face and retreated into the house slamming the French door behind her.

Total silence emanated all around the patio area. No one knew what to do, so we just stared at one another. Boyd and the boys looked up at Daddy and me, while the little girls stood in stone silence with their croquet mallets flung over their little shoulders, and the women stayed in the safety of the rose garden. The staff had momentarily stopped, but then realized the situation, and began to eagerly clean up the mess. It took a half-hour to put things aright, and without a word, they proceeded to set up the buffet table. From anyone's standards, it appeared perfect with the glorious centerpieces of lilies, hydrangeas and ivy with tiny nests interspersed with pastel eggs. The fresh spring foods were displayed in an attractive fashion from the broccoli salad, potato salad, deviled eggs, a fresh fruit and cheese platter, baked beans, chilled steamed shrimp and crab claws, quiche slices, cheese grits, and Parker House rolls. Yes, the main center piece of the ham was missing, but I glanced over at Rory and Luc; those two licking their lips as they lounged contentedly by the pool side.

Just as I was ready to take my plate and fill it with the fare, my cell phone rang. I looked down as I pulled it from my blazer pocket. Shit, it was RaeLynn. How in the hell did she always time her appearance with our family's holiday meals? I glanced at it a second time, but then decided I should take it. I said a polite, "excuse me" to the rest of them, and retreated to Daddy's study where I could be assured of privacy.

"What do you want?" I hit the answer button and replied before she had a chance to utter a word.

"Well, Attie, I just wanted to wish y'all a 'Happy Easter,'" RaeLynn said in an exasperated voice.

"Happy Easter," I offered back, but I hoped she understood from my tone that I didn't wish to talk or engage in any sort of conversation.

"Are you with your family today?"

"Yeah, why?"

"Well, I'm just imagining all your family there. Don't you remember that I was there at Christmas?"

"Yes, RaeLynn, I remember," I said bluntly, and I was thinking how I could end this conversation as quickly and politely as possible.

"Well, I was just thinkin' about you, Attie," she paused. "And, I have some news . . ."

"RaeLynn," I said in exasperation. "You interrupted our family dinner and I need to get back to everyone."

"So, they matter more to you than me, the mother

of your child?"

"RaeLynn, it's not like that, and you know it? We don't even know if I'm the father of your baby. I know you were dating that other guy, so until the DNA tests tell us the answer, I wish you would stop insisting that I'm the father. You know, we were together only one night so the chances are slim."

"Attie, I'm a woman, and women know when things are happening with their bodies."

"Listen, RaeLynn, we can talk another time, but I need to get back to my family right now."

"Wait, wait, Attie," she said, and I could sense the desperation in her voice. "I went to the doctor on Friday, and they did an ultrasound. I know what the baby is – do you want to know, too?"

I hesitated. I wanted to know, but then again, I didn't want to know. If I knew, it somehow connected me more to this baby, and I didn't want any connections. As I told her earlier, the chances were slim that I was the father as we had only been together one time, and the child was more than likely to be her boyfriend's.

Still, I relented. "Fine, tell me," I said.

"It's going to be a baby girl."

CHAPTER 27

Boyd

*M*ama invited me to lunch at the Port Royal Club. It was baffling as Mama never invited me to lunch. I accepted and met her, but I was curious as to the intent of the invitation. Maybe there was an ulterior motive? Maybe she just wanted to berate me for some sin I had committed, or maybe she was just lonely and wanted someone to have lunch with her? I had no idea, but I accepted the invitation, and as I walked into the Club, I was shown to her table on the patio.

"Afternoon, Mama," I greeted her as I bent down to place a kiss on her cheek but held my breath as I knew I would be bombarded by her normally heavy saturation of

Opium. Even without breathing it in, I was still assaulted as I backed away, and I just prayed that the breeze would be blowing away from me to send her perfume in the other direction.

"So, what do I owe this pleasure, Mama?" I asked as I settled myself in the metal chair. "I can't say I ever recall a lunch invitation from you in the middle of the week?"

"Can't a mother have lunch with her sons on occasion?" She countered back with a question of her own and looked around the patio to the other tables. It was then that I noticed some of her bridge friends, and she gave a little wave at them.

Honestly, I had to wonder if I was just here on display so her friends would lavish her with praise on the fact that she had such a wonderful and close relationships with her sons that they took time out their busy work week to meet her for lunches.

As usual, we talked about the weather, what we would order, and how things were at the office, but I knew to avoid any mention of the Easter debacle as it would become just another memory for Mama to avoid. So, I racked my brain for neutral subjects, and did my best to muster the wherewithal to endure the next hour. As much as politics could be a difficult subject for many, it seemed that the current election year and candidates were safe enough subjects for us, so we briefly engaged in a brief exchange of the merits of Bush or Gore until we both grew bored.

"Aren't you glad Landon will be home on Sunday?" I said as I leaned back and put my arm across the back of the empty chair beside in an attempt to relax.

"Yes, yes," she muttered in a low voice, and then grew louder as she added. "I think it was good for him to be on that business trip for his practice."

I frowned at her, but then I saw the challenge in her eyes if I would contradict her in the presence of her friends at the nearby tables. So, I simply shrugged a shoulder, and grabbed my glass of iced tea.

"Have you seen Hollis since he returned from Charleston?" I attempted this subject as this seemed like a harmless question, but I guessed wrong.

"Let's not talk about Hollis and his Charleston excursion," she said as she reached for a roll and the butter plate.

"Did y'all get to eat the fish we caught on Easter?" I ventured, and I knew this would piss her off as it brought her ruined day to mind, but I didn't care at this point.

She narrowed her eyes at me as she chewed her

buttered roll. "No, we didn't. I just gave it to the staff – you know 'those kind of people' like fish like that – wasn't it catfish?"

"No, Mama it wasn't catfish, and what sort of comment is that?"

"Boyd, let's not have a scene," she said with a sardonic smile and then looked to a neighboring table.

"I bent lower near her ear and whispered, "Well, Mama, why don't you just tell me what I'm supposed to talk about as nothing seems to be pleasing you?"

"Don't be fresh, Boyd," she said and gave my hand a rap on the table as though I was five years old again.

Both of us remained silent as the server came to the table and placed her chicken salad plate in front of her and my club sandwich in front of me.

"Bon appetite," I said with a smirk before I took a large bite.

The food was a good diversion as our mouths were filled so talk was unnecessary, and I glanced at my watch – only 20 more minutes of hell to endure and then I was out of here. Still, I was pissed. I would rather have been at J.P's with the guys having a double cheeseburger for lunch, and watching golf on the television, but here I was, and I wasn't sure if I going to let it slide. My wild side was itching to push the limits, and I really didn't give a damn about the repercussions I was likely to face, so I decided to go for it.

"Tess is pregnant," I blurted it out. I knew I was going to have to tell Mama at some point, and I figured I may as well get it over with rather than agonizing when would be the best time to broach it; I was already on the shit list today so one more thing wasn't likely to make any difference.

"My, that was fast," Mama uttered in a condescending tone as she took another bite of her chicken salad and continued to chew in utter pleasure. She looked out in the distance toward the Gulf and appeared to be ignoring me.

"Well, it isn't like we exactly planned it," I countered.

"I should hope not as the ink is barely dry on your divorce papers," she said barely above a whisper, but still turned to glance around the patio to make sure no one was listening to our conversation.

"I'm not sure why it's a problem as you never liked Libby in the first place," I replied, and I even surprised myself that I was standing up in defense of my ex-wife.

"Boyd," she said lowering her voice so the staff clearing the next table wouldn't hear. "You know, she wasn't one of us, and your marriage was doomed from the start. Jewish people are so different from us," she stopped and dabbed her napkin on her mouth. "Heaven's sake, every Christmas or Easter, she was just going through the motions – she hated being with our family, and she made it uncomfortable for all of us . . . I simply couldn't stand it."

"Mama," I began, but stopped myself. What was the sense in attempting to reason with her when no matter what I said, she would find fault with it in one way or the other?

"So that makes two this year," Mama offered with a tisk, tisk and diverted her eyes to her plate. "I will have to say Attie and you have been busy boys this year," she added before she stuffed another large bite in her mouth, and I had to wonder if her continued shoveling of food to her mouth was a ploy to stymie the conversation.

I honestly still couldn't figure out why she called me to go to lunch with her anyway. It was torture for me, and I could just imagine she was equally miserable. Who knew? I rolled my eyes and attacked my club sandwich.

"So, are the two of you getting married?" She said after she swallowed and reached for her iced tea.

"Of course," I said without hesitancy.

"I hope you're not planning another elaborate

ceremony. You know a second wedding, and one that the bride is expecting – heavens . . . It's the epitome of tackiness."

"Guess, we won't be front and center in *Town and Country*," I replied sarcastically.

"That was uncalled for, Boyd."

Still, I knew that she relished the idea that her four sons would have married little debutantes from grand families, and we all would have been featured in the wedding section of the magazine. It was Mama's dream, and all four of our us were a disappoint as our choices of brides had not met her standards.

"So, where is this one from? I hope she comes from a decent family, and not like the one Attie found." She was a little more talkative now that the adjacent tables had been cleared of guests and staff, and I was actually enjoying it as we were finally engaged in a real conversation, albeit, one that was still a bit rocky.

I took a deep breath and then a sip of my iced tea before I answered. "Tess is a wonderful girl. She comes from Ohio where her family has a dairy farm. She graduated with a degree in journalism from Miami University, Oxford, and went into photojournalism. She works for the *Naples Daily News*, and she's never been married." I stopped as I watched her continue to eat and wondered if she was even really listening to me. "And, she's a protestant."

Mama listened, and actually nodded her head.

"I think we're just going to go away and have a simple ceremony – just the two of us. Somewhere in the Caribbean – maybe St. Kitts and Nevis. Tess has never been to the Islands, and she loves photography so I thought it would be a perfect destination."

"Well, good for her," Mama said, and I had to wonder if it was a backhanded compliment, or an insult.

"Yeah, and then we'll look for a house."

"Boyd, you make this sound all nice and well, but I will have you know that your Daddy won't be too happy about this . . . "

"What do you mean? Honestly, I don't think Daddy gives a damn."

"It just doesn't look good – a man in your position at the firm getting a girl pregnant out of wedlock," she said before moving on to her fruit and cottage cheese.

"Mama, it's the year 2000, and it's not as though Tess is going to be wearing a Scarlet "A" on her chest."

"Well, she might as well. As I said, it just doesn't look good in families in our position in the community. We're already dealing with Attie's accident, but thank goodness that girl is tucked away up in Alabama and not here."

"For God's sake, Mama, don't play coy with me," I said a bit louder than I knew she would approve, and then threw my linen napkin on the table.

"What's that supposed to mean?"

"We all know . . . ."

"Y'all know what?" She feigned innocence, but Mama wasn't stupid, and she clearly knew where I was headed with this line of thought. If she wanted to play the part of being 'holier than thou,' then I was prepared to shove it right back at her.

"I know Daddy and you conceived Landon before you were married. We all have known for years."

Now it was Mama's turn to toss her napkin on the tabletop, and she looked at me with narrowed eyes. "What did you just say to me – your Mama?"

"In simple terms, Daddy knocked you up when y'all were in college, and you had to get married. There, I said it," I stated flatly. "Don't you know that we realized it pretty early on that you never celebrated an anniversary, and there's not one wedding picture of the two of you in your house. It didn't take a lot of thought – all of us know the truth."

"This lunch is over right now," she leaned close to me and spat the words. "Now, I want you to leave and get back to the office – do you hear me?"

CHAPTER 28
B o y d

"*It*'s called Missions and Medicine, or M&M for short," I said to Jennifer. She looked at me across the table in the booth where we both sat, and a confused expression came over her face.

We had dropped the girls off at school, and then ventured over to *First Watch* by Lowdermilk Park for breakfast. I had only been home a day, but I knew I couldn't put off the inevitable any longer; I had to tell Jennifer of my plans.

"The charity, it's called Missions and Medicine. It's a group of missionaries and doctors who go to remote areas around the world to preach the word of God and care for those in need of medical care."

"But, your practice. Our lives here in Naples . . . I just don't understand."

"There's not much to understand, honey," I said as I reached over with both of my hands to grasp hers. "I explained to you that during my time in Atlanta, I met the Reverend Smalls, and he helped me find the Lord."

"Yes, yes," she nodded. "I know all that you said when you told me last night, but I just thought it meant we would go to church more often and say a blessing when we had dinner every night. I didn't think it meant you were going to stop working at your practice and go off around the world." She pulled her hand back out of my grasp. "I am not leaving Naples, and taking the girls to some remote area," she said in a forceful voice.

I had noticed a change in Jennifer when I returned. It seemed that the three months apart we had each grown in different ways, and it was now having a bearing on how we communicated with one another. Jennifer had taken a part time job at the children's shop, Beth Mone, in Olde Naples, and worked while the girls were in school. It appeared that this newfound independence had given her a voice that I had never known was possible. She was no longer the complacent wife who went along with everything, but I noticed right away when I returned home yesterday that she seemed like a different person. She was confident, more in charge of the girls, and honestly, I found her far more attractive.

"I never said you, or the girls, have to leave Naples and go with me. We will still keep the house, and everything will go along as it always has been."

"Everything except having you here . . . I suppose it will be just like the last three months while you were in Atlanta."

"Well, you're right about that. They ask that we go over for eight weeks, and then we return home for eight weeks – it's an alternating schedule."

She was silent, and I suppose she was allowing it all to set in, but I could tell it bothered her as a tic had developed under one eye, and she kept attempting to brush it aside to no avail.

"When I'm home, I will go into the office just as I've always done."

"Is this some sort of agreement you made with your attorneys because of the malpractice case? Will this help your case?"

"Well, it won't harm it, I can say that," I added and pushed back my plate with a half-eaten omelet on it.

"This whole conversion thing . . . is this why you wouldn't drink any wine at dinner last night?"

I looked at her and hesitated because I wasn't sure how much I wanted to reveal, and to be honest, I wasn't sure how she would handle my revelations. "Yes. After everything that has happened, I am turning my life over to Jesus completely, and this means that I want my body to be a temple in His honor. No more drinking, no more drugs, no more risky behaviors," and there now, I had said it.

"I don't understand what's wrong with having wine at dinner every night. I know Jesus drank wine . . . we even drink it when we have Communion at church."

"Well, that's the other thing. I am not going back to Trinity-By-the-Cove Church -"

"But, we're Episcopal. You've always been an Episcopalian. Your parents and your brothers go to the church. I don't understand if you're suddenly more connected to God then why aren't you going to stay in church."

"I never said I wasn't staying in the church, I just said that I'm not staying in the Episcopal church. I find that my beliefs now are more evangelical, and I identify with their beliefs. When I'm here in Naples, I will be going to North Naples Baptist Church, and I am hoping that the girls and you will be there with me, and that y'all can become more involved in the church groups."

"Wait, wait, wait," Jennifer held up her hand. "I understand that this has been an epiphany of sorts for you," she paused as I raised my eyebrow at the use of a word not normally in Jennifer's daily vocabulary. "But, I never agreed to it. The girls and I love the church down in Port Royal, and I'm comfortable there. I don't want to go to a new church, and I don't know anything about Baptists except they're narrow-minded. There's one woman in Junior League, and she's always trying to 'witness' to everyone and win us over to the Lord – sorry, Landon, but this just doesn't appeal to me."

"Is this going to be an issue with us?" I asked simply.

"No, but you have to respect my position," she answered. "The time that you've been away has given me the opportunity to think about things, and honestly, I feel that I am a stronger person now than I was."

"I can see that, and I love it," I admitted. "But, Jennifer, I needed to do this for me."

Again, she seemed confused by my new perspective on life and commitment to God.

"Jennifer, as you know I was in my 30's when we

married, and I had a life before we met. It was a life that you know a little about, but not everything," I paused as I wondered if I should venture into territory that may threaten my relationship with her. "Yes, I was in college and medical school, and I did well with my grades and residency, but I also partied hard. I did a lot of drugs, and I mean a lot of everything from pot, to coke, even some LSD, and well, you know about my addiction to Oxycodone. I also had a lot of relationships with girls, and I wasn't always the most respectful . . ."

"Stop it, Landon, I don't want to hear about this," she shook her head and shut her eyes as though by not seeing me, it would allow her to shut it all out.

"No, Jennifer, when I made my commitment and asked Jesus to be my Lord and Savior, I vowed that I was going to turn my life around from the way I used to live, and one of those vows was honesty. If you know my past, I think it will help me heal and move forward, but it will also allow you to understand why I engaged in such risky behaviors. Yes, I knew better, but I was hurting . . . I was reaching out for anything and everything that could make me feel whole. I wanted to feel loved, valued, needed, and I sought validation in any way I could find it. My whole life, I wanted that from my parents, and especially my mother, but

I never got it. You know, Mama, and I don't have to explain her. She's good in many ways, but she's distant. I have often wondered if she ever really wanted to be a mother, but it was something she was expected to do at that time. In the late 1950's and 60's, it was the only goal of most women – it was to simply be a wife and mother, but I think Mama resented it."

"I'm not sure about her resenting it," Jennifer countered. "I think she's just generally an unhappy woman, and she would have been no matter what course she took in life. If it's not Marion Collingsworth's way, then it's no way."

"Very intuitive, Jennifer, and I believe you're right," I agreed, and again, I was amazed by the change and maturity in my wife. "But, honey, I want to get back to why I needed the change . . . why I needed to repent."

"Go on, I'm sorry for interrupting," she apologized.

"Jennifer, as I said, I did drugs, I had a lot of women before I met you, and I'm not saying this to hurt you, but I need to confess, move on, and by doing so, I hope to make amends. I had so many demons in my life – I was searching for some sort of validation in all the wrong places. I wasn't a good husband to you."

This got her attention. She looked at me with a

mixture of fear, anticipation, worry and finally, dread.

"We've been married nine years, but in that time, I haven't always been faithful to you, and I know most men would never utter a word if they're not caught, but as I said, I want to be honest, open and move forward."

"What are you trying to say?" Jennifer's voice now changed to a lower octave, and she began to mutilate the straw she was twisting over and over in her hands.

"Do you remember when I used to go to football games in Tampa?"

She nodded.

"Well, I also hit the strip clubs, and when my brothers and I went to the Keys we used to go to the strip clubs there, and yes, we had hookers. And, when you went to your sister's shower in St. Louis, I slept with Deena from the office."

"What," she screeched, and several in nearby tables looked in our direction, but she shook her head in an apology to them. I guess my reasonings for coming to a public place to open-up about everything hadn't been a good choice."

"A good choice," she spat the phrase. "God Lord, Landon, it's not as though you were choosing to go golfing or fishing . . . you, you cheated on me, and apparently from what you're saying, you cheated on me a lot."

"I'm sorry," I muttered sheepishly.

"I can't believe it . . . the receptionist who we had stay with the girls?" She looked at me in disbelief. "That was only a few months ago," she paused for a moment as though she was in thought. "But, wait, you're wrong because she was here alone with the girls as you told me you went to the Keys on a fishing trip with your brothers. Did you not go to the Keys?"

"Yes, we went to the Keys, but we came back on Sunday, and, and . . ."

"Landon, if you don't mind, I really don't care to hear any lurid details about how you screwed your receptionist. I don't care to imagine it in my mind." She slid over to the edge of the seat and looked at me with an expression of total disbelief.

"Jennifer, I'm sorry, but I had to get it out for me to move on. I must atone for my sins by now giving back and doing good in this world, but in doing so, I have to repent to those I've wronged before I can move on."

"Landon, instead of thinking about your fucking self and how you're attempting to redeem your soul from all the sins of your past . . . maybe you should consider what your 'unburdening' would do to me . . . your wife. Honestly, do you think I really needed to know details about your drugs and affairs – are you an idiot?"

She grabbed her purse and stood up. "Listen, we came in one car, but I really don't want to go home with you. I'm going for a walk in the park, and I'll call a taxi when I'm ready to come home."

"Jennifer, please, I'm sorry," I said and reached for her arm, but she shook her head and I saw tears forming in her eyes as she turned to leave.

CHAPTER 29

Hollis

"You Collingsworth boys and your love lives – hell, I'm gonna be able to buy a new boat just off the legal fees y'all are brining me in this year."

Jack reared back in his chair and gave a loud guffaw. I had nothing to add to Jack's appraisal. It was true. With Boyd who got the ball rolling, then Attie with his settlement with RaeLynn, and now my divorce with Helen, we were a pathetic bunch, and I couldn't even look the receptionist and secretaries in the eye when I came in because I was sure they had amusing things to say during their coffee breaks about the Collingsworth crew. And, Jack was right that there was no doubt among just the three of us,

373

we were certainly keeping his law firm afloat this year.

"Well, it looks like Helen has been talking to her former sister-in-law and comparing notes as I just got a Notice of Appearance that Sarah Rosenstein from Boca will be representing your soon-to-be ex-wife, and if you aren't aware, she also represented Boyd's ex-wife."

"Well, I'm guessing that went alright as Boyd's divorce was finalized in just a few months?"

Again, Jack gave a huge laugh. "Yeah, it's because Boyd wanted out of it so badly that he basically gave her everything in the settlement agreement to just get it over with quickly."

"So, is that what you propose?"

"Hollis, I never tell my clients what to do? I advise them, but it's ultimately their decision. But, you do need to know it's not uncommon for divorces in Naples to rage on for several years, and run into the six figures. Many attorneys love it as it keeps them in business, but it's hell on the clients and their kids."

"Well, when Helen and I talked, she said she wants the house, and wants it free and clear, which I'm fine with. She is going to go back to work as CPA so I'm not sure how that would affect alimony, but I'm willing to be generous with child support and tuition."

"You sound like your brother, and I applaud you boys that you don't begrudge your wives or children to have decent lives," he said, and then leaned forward across his desk. "Our only problem is that we have a piranha on the other side. Rosenstein is a bitter woman, and she goes for the juggler when she's representing wives against husbands. Again, like with Boyd, we can make a generous offer, and hope that she doesn't sway her client to continue fighting."

I nodded and rolled my thumbs together as I was thinking.

"Tell, me how are things with the two of you . . . are you on speaking terms. Can you make it through an exchange with the kids without a mini-war erupting?"

I shrugged. "I'm sure you know that I came out as gay, and my partner is dividing his time between Naples and Charleston, but we're intending on living here most of the year – the school year so I can see the children. Helen isn't happy, and she will not allow the kids to be around him, so yeah, it's been difficult."

"I'm assuming he's a decent fellow," Jack said as he popped some Nicorette in his mouth.

"Totally, he's an attorney in Charleston, and he's also a member of the Florida bar so he will open or join a practice here. He comes from a well-respected family that has lived in Charleston for over 200 years so there are no issues regarding his character."

"Good, good, so I don't see why that should be a problem. You haven't done anything wrong other than seeking a divorce from your wife, and the fact that you're willing to make a generous settlement should go a long way. I can use your brother's example to Rosenstein, and keep your fingers crossed she's having a good day when I talk to her."

I left Jack's office feeling much better than when I had walked through the door. It wasn't perfect, but it seemed if level heads could prevail then we could end things with the least amount of damage to all. I walked over to my vintage MG, and started to get in, but then I looked around. Even though it was a late summer afternoon, the humidity was moderate in Florida terms, and the normal afternoon thunderstorm had not materialized. It was a perfect occasion to put the convertible top down; I went through the motions and settled myself in the low bucket seat. As I pulled my Ray Bans from atop my head to cover my eyes, I put the car in first gear and then quickly shifted up as I maneuvered through Olde Naples. It was a short drive to the condo Stu and I were renting until the closing of our new house, but I needed this time alone to analyze everything I had just gone over with Jack. With the wind in my face, I suddenly felt a great weight had been lifted. There was no doubt the past few months had been trying. I still had a deep affection for Helen although it wasn't the way a husband should care about a wife, and there was no doubt I would always be there for the children, but now I felt as though I could come out from a shadow of the life I had been living in. Although both my parents now knew, I really wasn't sure of their thoughts. While Daddy hadn't openly chastised me, Mama was giving me the cold shoulder and hadn't spoken a word – no phone calls and no visits. And, as much as I would have thought this would have bothered me, I was surprised at how carefree I felt about it. For the first time in my life, I didn't care what my parents thought about me or my actions, and I was living life completely on my own terms and not what they expected from me. So, with a smile on my face, I turned on the radio dial, and was assaulted with the steady beat of the music. At first, I didn't catch the song, but then the chorus came on, and I felt it was a sign.

I can see clearly now the rain is gone

> *I can see all obstacles in my way*
> *Gone are the dark clouds that had me blind*
> *It's gonna be a bright (bright)*
> *Bright (bright) sunshiny day*
> *It's gonna be a bright (bright)*
> *Bright (bright) sunshiny day*

While the music foretold of my good fortune, it didn't forestall the regular pattern of the summer rains. In South Florida it was not uncommon to have the sun shining one minute, and then suddenly a torrential rain would begin to pour. No sooner than the song ended, I pulled to the side of the road and began to put up the convertible top. I was drenched within seconds, but I didn't care. I was elated. I was happy, and I was moving forward. I got back in the car, and turned the ignition, but nothing. I tried again several times, but it wasn't turning over. Typical British Leyland motors and their electrical system. As much as I loved my MG, it had been a headache over the years, but it was a trade-off as I adored my little green British roadster. I turned off the lights and the radio in hopes that if I waited several minutes, I would be able to start her back up and make it home. So, I sat there a little longer as I listened to the raindrops beat a gentle tattoo on the soft canvas top, and then tried the ignition another time, but still nothing.

I looked around. I was on Third Street South and I only had a few blocks to walk to make it back to our condo on 7th Avenue North. It wasn't a long walk, and it would be pleasant if it weren't for this torrential downpour, but I really didn't have any choice other than to sit here and wait, or venture out in it. The choice wasn't difficult. I decided I would walk it and enjoy the rain on my face along with my newfound freedom. So, I locked the car, and began my walk home; I'd just call the tow service to take it to the mechanic once I got back to the condo.

I set off walking the few blocks, and even though I was saturated within minutes, it didn't faze me. Several cars passed by, but they were courteous and pulled to the middle of the street so I would be deluged by the waters swiftly running to the gutter. Then, I looked up and saw a silver Mercedes slowly making its way down the street and avoiding the low areas where deep pockets of water collected. I looked closer and recognized the car. It was Mama. Thank goodness, what luck that she was coming along right now. I would be able to get a ride home and avoid having to continue walking through the downpour. She was going slow, so I reached up my hand to wave. Mama looked over at me, briefly focused and made eye contact with me, but then she abruptly turned to stare back over her wheel as she moved on without stopping. I stood there stock-still with the rain continuing to beat down on me as I watched my own mother drive away down the street.

"So, you're telling me that she saw you, but didn't even stop." Stu said as he handed me a second towel after I had soaked the first one he had given me.

"No," I answered as I gave my head a shake like a dog.

"Thanks a lot," Stu joked as he backed away from me to avoid getting wet.

"She looked directly at me, so I know she saw me, but then just turned her head and looked straight ahead as though I was a stranger."

"What a bitch," Stu uttered. "Wait, I'm sorry, I should never say that about anyone's mother, but that woman doesn't have a maternal bone in her body."

I just shrugged as I was used to it, but after getting to know Miss Lyla over Easter, I had a feeling that in her I would finally find the mother-figure I had been longing for my entire life, and I knew Stu was more than happy to share his Mama.

"Listen, I know you want to get out of those wet clothes, but then I want to hear all about the visit with Jack. I'm not a divorce attorney, but I always enjoy hearing details as those cases are they're so much juicier than my probate ones," he said as he flipped a dish towel over this shoulder and turned back to the chopping board on the kitchen counter.

"Give me a minute as I'm going to get out of these clothes," I called as I left the kitchen, but Stu didn't give me the time of day as he was immersed in a conversation with the two dogs. Both Beau and Princess Di stood on either side of him as they were ready and waiting for any bit of food that Stu would bestow on them.

After a quick change, I stopped and placed several CD's in the player and made a cocktail.

"What's for dinner, it's smells good," I asked as I walked into the kitchen and was intoxicated by the mix of delicious smells.

"I marinated a pork tenderloin in a teriyaki sauce, plus doing an angel hair pasta with fresh vegetables, and some French bread with a garlic butter."

"Sounds good, and no wonder the dogs are salivating."

"So, how did it go with Jack?"

"Well, I signed the contract, and the first step is a financial disclosure, and then he's going to ask for a mediation so we can try to make some headway and settle things. I'm thinking I'm just going to go the route of Boyd and make a generous offer so it can be resolved. The last I want is litigation wearing me down and taking its toll on the kids . . . with Helen being a former CPA, she's good with numbers, and she's a no-nonsense woman. I'm just hoping that she will want to get resolution as much as I do."

Stu nodded and tossed a couple pieces of cheese to each dog.

"Well, it's not my place to get in the middle of things, but just know I'm here to support you, and if you need a sounding board."

"Thanks," I murmured, but my attention was focused on my cell phone as I saw messages waiting on the screen. I looked down, and realized I had missed several calls, but I didn't remember hearing anything.

"Did my phone ring while I was changing?"

"Not that I know of . . . I didn't hear anything," Stu said as he reached over to taste a bite of his pasta sauce.

I picked up my phone only to realize that I had neglected to turn the ringer back on after I left Jack's office. I hit my voicemail and proceeded to listen to the three messages I had missed. George, Jr., was telling me about a swim meet that he wanted me to attend, a call from my assistant that my meeting first thing tomorrow morning had been canceled, and then one from Attie. I listened to Attie's long message, and I looked up at Stu as I did.

"What's wrong?" He mouthed as he could tell by my expression something had happened. I held up my finger to my lip to silence him until the message was complete, but then I turned my back so I could hit the repeat button to listen again.

Once I turned the phone off, I sat down, and Beau came up next to me where his eyes met mine in consolation.

"Attie's on his way to Alabama. He got a call earlier this afternoon that RaeLynn went into premature labor. She's a tiny thing, and she's only 16 so it sounds as though there could be complications with the baby coming early."

"Oh, no," Stu responded.

"He's at a layover in Atlanta so he wanted to let us know."

I reached over to pick up my cocktail and quickly drained the contents in one gulp.

"Hollis, I'm sure the girl will be fine. She strikes me as one who's a firecracker and nothing will stop her.

Mark my words, she'll make it through and be just fine."

I was silent, but nodded in response to Stu, and continued to rub Beau's head.

"So, here's to the possibility of a new nephew or niece for you," Stu said on a positive note as he held up his cocktail and gave an air toast to me.

"Maybe," I corrected him. "We won't know if the baby is actually Attie's until the DNA results."

CHAPTER 30
Attie

"She' still in labor," one the nurses answered after I inquired at the station on the maternity ward of Druid City Hospital.

It was just after seven in the evening, and it took me a little less than an hour to drive from the Birmingham airport. I had no idea about women giving birth, but since it was going to be a premature delivery, I guess I naturally assumed it would be quick.

"Sir, are you the father?" A very smiley, plump nurse asked in her high-pitched voice.

"No," I hesitated. "Just a friend."

She nodded and looked back down at the clipboard she held, "Miss Yoder is in Room 232 if you would like to visit? I believe her Mama is in with her right now."

"No, I'll just wait. Can you tell me where the waiting room is?"

"Oh, of course, silly me, I should have told you right away," she giggled like a schoolgirl, and I had to wonder if she was flirting with me. "It's down the hall," she said pointing her stubby finger. "It opens up off the hall so you can't miss it."

I muttered a simple 'thank you,' but I don't think she heard me as she started humming some country song.

I considered just getting back in my rental car and heading over to the hotel, but I needed to be here. I already made arrangements after the baby's birth to have a DNA test done. If I wasn't the father, I was getting on the next flight back to Florida, and if it was the worst scenario, well, I hadn't really considered what I intended to do, but I was nearly certain, I couldn't be the father.

Hell, I don't even remember having sex with RaeLynn, and then it was only one time so what were the odds – everything was in my favor.

I glanced in the waiting room. While I hadn't been in too many hospital waiting rooms, it looked like what I imagined was typical with about a dozen lime-colored vinyl covered chairs, a television mounted on the wall, a small area of some blocks and assorted toys for kids, plus a few side tables with magazines. Two men were seated on one side of the room, and they were staring blankly at the television. I noticed a vending machine, so I went over to grab a Coke and some chips. The older of the two men nodded in my direction, and I nodded back. Not caring to watch some stupid cartoon about a yellow sponge with arms and legs, I opted to sit off to the side, and read some magazine. There wasn't much of a selection – well-worn issues of *Family Circle, Parenting* and a *Cosmopolitan* dominated the side table, but on closer inspection, I spied a *National Geographic*. I flipped through it for the pictures, but then started reading an article on Belize. It really didn't hold my interest, and I suppose I must have drifted off to sleep, but then I woke when I heard several people in an animated conversation.

"Is she doin' okay?"

"Oh, she's doin' jest fine, and the nurse said it won't be much longer until she can start pushin'," the woman said as though she was out of breath.

I kept my head down as though to look like I was still sleeping, but I cracked one eye and looked over at the scene. No doubt it was RaeLynn's mother who had joined the two men. She was an older version of RaeLynn with the dark roots, bleached hair, and a scrawny frame, but I knew it was certainly her mother by the same nasally, Southern twang as she sounded just like RaeLynn. Shit, I hadn't even considered that those two men were related to RaeLynn. I continued to feign sleep and listened to their exchange.

"Doctor said she was at 8 cm, so it ain't gonna be much longer," the woman added, and reached down to take a sip of the older man's coffee.

"Does she want to see me?" The younger man asked in a hopeful voice.

"No, Dwayne, I asked her again, but she is sayin' that the only person she wants to see is that boy, Attie, from Florida."

"Oh, shit," Dwayne leaned his head down and put both hands on the side of his head as though it pained him. Obviously, he cared for RaeLynn, and who was I to stand in the way of his happiness and true love. Hell, even if I were the father, I surmised that the guy couldn't be all bad if he was sitting here all afternoon worried about RaeLynn, and the baby might not even be his. He was still dressed in his AutoZone red button-down shirt, so he had likely left work to come sit with RaeLynn's parents, and they all seemed to be on cordial enough terms. Maybe I could just make a quick exit, head over to the hotel, and leave for

Naples in the morning, and they'd be none the wiser that I had even been here. It wasn't as though I had called and announced I was arriving. Even though RaeLynn had been burning up the phone lines, I had never guaranteed her that I would come to Alabama for the birth, so to these people I was still a complete stranger.

"Well, I better be gettin' myself back to her," Mrs. Yoder said, and took another quick sip of her husband's coffee before she left. "Yuck, it's the worst dang coffee I've ever tasted," she said as we walked away, and I smiled to myself as I doubted Mrs. Yoder was much of a coffee connoisseur.

"You know, Dwayne, you might as well go on home, and I can call you later if RaeLynn be a wantin' to see you."

"Dang it," he said as he stood up and put a 'Bama baseball cap on his head. "Why don't she wanna see me," he said with his voice cracking. 'I love that girl so much, and I don't even care if that baby ain't mine, I'd still love her and that baby until the day I die."

"Dwayne, son, you done messed up when you cheated on her, so I don't know if she'd take you back," Mr. Yoder said. "You know you're like a son to me, but what you did was wrong to shame her in that way."

"I know, yes sir, and I'm regrettin' it every single

day." He said and readjusted his cap. "I'm gonna go on home now, but promise me that you'll call me directly when the baby is born?"

"I will," Mr. Yoder said as he patted Dwayne on the shoulder. "I'm gonna follow you down and go to the cafeteria to get some more coffee."

I looked over at Mr. Yoder as the two of them left, and I was finally in the clear. I could leave if I wanted, and no one would ever know. I hesitated for a few minutes and glanced down at my phone. I had multiple missed calls from RaeLynn that had started early this morning and continued non-stop throughout the day. My voicemail was full, and after listening to two of the messages, I had opted to ignore the rest. She had begged me to come, but I never responded. Maybe that made me a self-centered cad, but I wasn't one to be pushed into something I didn't want to do. After the first message this morning, I had mulled it over and finally decided I would catch a plane out in the afternoon. Yeah, I probably should have returned the call to tell her I was coming, but I knew it would entail a lot of promises that I wasn't sure I was ready to keep.

I got up and rubbed my neck as it had been a long day. It was now or never. Either I stayed and endured having to see, or talk to RaeLynn, and likely feel the wrath from her parents, or else I could just scoot on out. I could go have a few drinks, a nice dinner, and then head back to the hotel for a movie. Based on RaeLynn's dialing history today, I had no doubt she would ring me the minute the baby arrived, and I could return to the hospital for the damned DNA test. If the gods were shinning down on me, then I would get the results in my favor and be out of here in another day. Yep, I had my evening planned out. I was heading out to get a steak and a loaded potato. I deserved it after the day I had been through.

The phone rang at 11 o'clock and I pointed the controller at the television to turn down the volume. I glanced at the phone, and of course, it was RaeLynn's number - again. I hesitated. I hadn't received a call from her in five hours, so it made sense that she had the baby. I picked up the phone and nearly hit the button to answer, but I stopped. I reached over to grab the bottle of Jack Daniels and I took a long swallow. If I was going to talk to RaeLynn, I needed some help as I knew it wasn't going to be pleasant. The liquid warmed my throat, and a feeling of peace came over me. Whatever the outcome, I would deal with it. I lifted the phone and hit the redial button. It rang only two times.

"Attie, it's me, RaeLynn," she said in an excited voice, and at that moment she sounded like the sixteen-year-old that she was. She should have been having a carefree evening laughing along with her teenage girlfriends, but she was in the hospital giving birth to a child.

"I know it's you, RaeLynn," I answered, and couldn't help but roll my eyes.

"We have a baby, Attie," she announced. "We have a beautiful little girl."

I didn't know what to say. True, the baby could be my child, but it could just as easily be Dwayne's child, too, and the likelihood was that it was his. RaeLynn obviously didn't mind my silence and took it as an opportunity to fill me in on the details.

"She was born at 10:23, and Attie, I think it's a sign – a good sign," she said with enthusiasm.

"RaeLynn, I don't understand – a good sign?"

"Silly, boy," she laughed. "We met on Saturday, October 23rd when 'Bama played against Tennessee. Get it 10/23, duh?"

"I get it," I answered directly, and actually found myself laughing along with her, but then I heard a sound – a whimper, a mewling. It sounded like a puppy rather than a baby, but then again, I wasn't around a lot of newborns, so I had no idea what sort of sounds they made. "Is that the baby?" I asked rather reluctantly.

"It sure is, and she's not just the baby, her name is Ellie. I named her after the character on the *Beverly Hillbillies*. I always loved watching it when I was little, plus I love the name Ellie, so she'll be Ellie May," she stated matter-of-factly.

I rolled my eyes, of course, RaeLynn would name the baby after a character from a television show. "How are you doing? How is the baby?" I asked feeling it was only the right and proper thing to do.

"Oh, Attie, you're so sweet," RaeLynn cooed. "I'm doing just fine. Even though it was early, everything went okay with the delivery. Being premature, she's a tiny little thing. She's only 5 lbs., and 4 oz., but she perfectly healthy in every way. The doctor thinks we can both go home in two days!"

"That's great, RaeLynn, it's really great." I repeated.

"Attie, I would really like to see you – can you come over?"

I took another sip from the bottle of Jack Daniels, and suddenly had an urge to see both her and the baby.

"Yeah," I replied before I could stop myself from

backing out. "Yeah, I'll be right over."

Twenty minutes later, I walked back into DCH for the second time that night. I had stopped by Publix to pick up a cheap arrangement of roses. At first, I picked up red ones as I knew Raelynn was partial to the color, but then I set the arrangement back and pick up a dozen pink ones in honor of Ellie. The same nurse was still on duty, and she remembered me.

"Are you here to see Miss Yoder?" She said, and then smiled as she looked at the roses I was carrying. "Aren't you a darling boy to bring those flowers."

"Yes, I'm here to see RaeLynn Yoder."

"Honey, you just go on down the hall and her door is there on the left – it's open," she said pointing.

With each step, I heard my Italian driving shoes squeak on the freshly mopped floor, and I knew each step was bringing me closer and closer to the possibility of my life changing from this point forward.

While the door was partially open, it still didn't illuminate the room; it was dim with only a slight glow coming from the small light above RaeLynn's bed. Several balloons were dancing in the breeze from the A/C vent, but it also circulated the odor of greasy fast food from the Sonic bags on the table. RaeLynn was by herself with the baby which was a relief as I didn't want to face her parents, too. As she halfway reclined on the bed, I could see the small form of a baby nestled in a pink blanket in the crook of her mother's arm.

"You came," RaeLynn smiled, and I could hear the relief in her voice.

"I said I would, and here I am," I answered as I walked over by her bed. I leaned down and placed a chaste kiss on the top of her head. "And, I brought these for you, and for the baby – I mean, Ellie."

"Oh, Attie, they're beautiful," she gushed. "Nobody ever gave me roses before, I love them."

"Well, anyone who just had a baby deserves flowers," I answered, but in all honesty, I was stalling as I had no idea where this conversation might be going. I walked over to the round table and sat down the glass vase with the roses among the balloons and Sonic bags.

"Ellie's asleep right now, but if you come close then you can see her little face," RaeLynn said as she motioned with her free hand for me to come closer.

I glanced down, but it was difficult to see anything.

The baby was tightly wrapped in a pink blanket, and there was a pink and blue stripped knitted cap on top of her head. I could just make out the face, but it was hard to tell what, or rather who, she looked like without seeing her eyes or hair.

"Does she have any hair?"

"Not really, just some light brown fuzz, but Mama says most babies only have a little, plus she's still so young."

"What about her eyes, what color are they?"

"Blue, but Mama also said that most babies' eyes are blue, but they can change," she said and adjusted the blanket where it had opened a bit.

I nodded as I accepted her explanation without question as I had no idea about babies.

"Do you mind if I sit down?" I asked, and she nodded so I pulled a chair from the table and then lifted it up to sit it down by the bed. I was being careful because at least I knew you weren't supposed to ever wake a sleeping baby.

"So, the doctor said the delivery went fine, and the baby is healthy even though she's a tiny little thing, it looks like we can go home in two days."

"That's I great," I said, and I knew I was stalling.

"I hate hospitals, so it will be good to get out of here,"

she stopped and looked up at me. "Will you be picking us up on Sunday?"

"Excuse me?"

"I asked if you would be picking us on Sunday afternoon? And, then how soon are we headed to Naples?" She furthered questioned with a bright smile of those crooked teeth.

"RaeLynn," I said with an exasperated sigh, and leaned closer to whisper so no one else could hear me. "We don't even know that I'm the father of Ellie – hell, Dwayne has been in the waiting room all day, and for all we know, he could be the father, too."

She looked straight into my eyes and pursed her mouth in a pout, but then I glanced down at the baby who was exhibiting an identical pout on her little rosebud of a mouth.

"Attie, I know in my heart that the baby is yours," she stopped and sniffled as she wiped at her eyes. "I just have this feeling deep down, and whenever I've ever gotten these feelings like this deep down, then I know it's the Lord's way of telling me something."

"Well, I'm scheduled for a DNA test tomorrow morning, so we'll know then."

She shrugged her shoulders and still sported the pout.

"Yes, I know. Dwayne is also scheduled for a test, too."

"So, it will be settled tomorrow when we get the results," I said enthusiastically.

"But, Attie, if Ellie is your little girl then won't we make a family and a home for her. I love you, Attie, and I want to be your wife," she pleaded, and I had to admit it was sad listening to her.

"RaeLynn, I do care about you, and if I am Ellie's father, you will never have to worry as I will provide well for both you and the baby. I already gave you $25,000 in January so you know I will provide . . . but we can't get married."

"But, why, Attie?" she whined.

"RaeLynn, it's plain and simple. We don't know each other. We met one-night last October, and we had a fun evening, but it doesn't mean we're getting married. Hell, we don't even know one another."

"But, Attie, I came to Naples at Christmas. I met your family, and we lived together-"

"Wait, RaeLynn stop right there - you stayed at my condo for two weeks, and that does not equate to meaning that we 'lived together' - do you understand me?"

At that moment Ellie whimpered, and then she started moving about in her tightly swaddled blanket.

Within seconds she was squalling with all the intensity that I had no idea a newborn baby was capable of producing.

"See you upset her," RaeLynn surmised with a nod of her head. She adjusted her gown so the baby could latch on and suckle. Obviously, RaeLynn instinctively knew what to do to calm the baby, and Ellie was immediately satisfied.

I walked over to look and saw the baby's eyes for the first time. Ellie's little eyes moved from RaeLynn's face to mine and focused with such an intensity that it was frightening. I had no idea a small baby's eyes could bore into your soul, but I couldn't take my eyes from her dark blue ones; still, I shook myself back to reality.

"RaeLynn, I'm 38 years old, and I vowed I would never marry someone I didn't love," I stated matter-of-factly, and looked at them both. "As I said before, I don't love you. I won't marry you, but rest assured, if Ellie is my child, I will care for her. I will visit her, she will know me as her father, and I will provide everything for her, so you don't have to worry."

RaeLynn looked at the baby as I said those words, but then she turned to look up at me in disbelief. Her eyes were filled with tears, but they were also filled with an intense anger. "Attie Collingsworth, I know your family thinks I'm nothing but white trash, and no, I don't have me no college education like Jennifer or Helen, but I'm not a bad person. I'm a good person. I would have made you a good wife, and I would have loved you until my dying day."

I looked over at her and the baby, but there was nothing more to say. It was nearing midnight, and we both were exhausted. We both needed sleep, and I would be back again in the morning.

"RaeLynn, I'm sorry, but I'm leaving. I'll see you tomorrow," I said and walked out the door. For a moment, I stopped, and considered turning back, but I knew she would read more into it than my concern that she understood my position. I had to remain firm. I shook my head and continued down the desolate hall to the elevators.

CHAPTER 31
Landon

*T*he driver was doing his best to dodge the ruts in the red sand road, but the ride was still jarring my insides. I held tight to the roll bar to steady myself. If I didn't, I would slide into my other companion, another doctor, in the backseat. Without any doors or windows, we were all engulfed in dust on this remote road, but I was told to get used to the dust and dirt as it would now be my way of life here in Botswana. Just before dawn we had set out from Johannesburg, and we were now headed north to the medical camp/mission, New Xade, in a remote area just outside of the Central Kalahari Game Reserve.

Before coming over, I was given a round of

immunizations for protection, but I was not going to be totally protected. This area of Botswana was suffering from one of the highest rates of AIDS/HIV, and a prime reason medical doctors were needed in addition to missionaries. I was briefed by team of missionaries that while the San bushmen had lived untouched by the modern world for thousands of years in the central Kalahari region as hunters and gatherers, they had been pushed out by government police and soldiers in the 1980's due to the discovery of diamonds in the region. Apparently, having these natives continue to occupy their homeland was a threat to those harvesting the diamonds, but there had been no regard by those in power as to how upsetting the displacement had been to the San bushmen's lives and lands where their ancestors had lived for generations. Still, the new President, Festus Mogae, was doing his best with attempts to diversify the economy so it wasn't totally reliant on the diamond industry, and if successful, there was hope the San bushmen could, at some point, return to their ancestral lands. Still, with the resettlement in this area, the psychological toll had affected physical health with malnutrition and disease, and these people were in desperate need of any sort of humanitarian help.

I looked around at the scenery and had to admit it was

a shock to my system. After a cool spring in Atlanta with the lush vegetation of Southern flora, I was met with the starkness of the desert lands. Red dirt and sands as far as the eye could see, and only then could an occasional shrub or tree be viewed. I had no idea how these San bushmen had existed as foragers and hunters in such a desolate area. Sure, there were plenty of wild animals for meat and hides, but I had my doubts if any sort of grains, fruits or vegetables would ever take root in this land.

It was near nightfall by the time we arrived in the village of New Xade with a population normally a little more than a thousand, but the torrential spring rains and flooding in Eastern Botswana had brought widespread flooding so many had migrated west, and now the village had nearly tripled its population. I pulled my bag out of the back of the old Land Cruiser and swung it over my shoulder as the leader of the group organized the others. There had been two other vehicles in our convoy so there were a total of eight new doctors. I took a moment to survey my surroundings. Modest accommodations built from cement blocks with a few windows dominated the central area, and these had obviously been hastily constructed when the bushmen had been forced to leave their native villages in the Kalahari, but traditions were obviously still honored.

There were rounded stick huts with thatched roofs mingled among the more modern buildings, and I saw that the women were cooking over outdoor fire pits made from rocks and stones. I'm not sure if it was the fact that I had barely eaten anything all day, but I had to admit that the aromas of their cooking foods wafted through the air and smelled delicious.

"Dr. Collingsworth, I presume," I heard a voice call out to me with a slight chuckle, and I turned to see the face of a weathered and tanned American man walking towards me. He had a generous smile, and welcoming eyes.

"I'm Ray Morris, a good friend of Reverend Smalls, and so glad to meet you," he said as he reached out and had a firm handshake and then gave me a pat on the back. I felt like I knew Ray as I had heard so much about him in my preparation and studies before coming here, plus we had emailed back and forth quite a bit. Ray was the Director in Charge of Missions & Medicine here in Botswana, and while this was one of three camps he circulated among, he was always was on hand when a new group of recruits came aboard.

"Why don't I show you to your lodgings, and then we're all gathering with 'our friends,' and I would find out that this was the term used by the Americans for the San bushmen. It made the natives smile as they were happy to be known as cordial acquaintances since they had been called far worse by others over the years.

Ray meandered through the maze of small buildings until he finally came to compact structure. I surmised it to be around 1,000 square feet, and it would be the home I shared with two other colleagues for the next eight weeks. I looked in the semi-dark room, and noticed the open windows with screens, but immediately realized I would not have the luxury of air conditioning.

"I know what you're thinking, and it's rough, but trust me you'll be just fine. Sure, it's an adjustment, but the benefits you'll reap while here will far outweigh the minor inconveniences."

I nodded and threw my bag on one of the beds and turned to follow him out.

"We have electric in our rooms, but there's no running water. You will have to go to the central facility for your bathing and other needs," he said as he pointed in the direction of another building that was the only one painted in vivid blue so there was no mistaking it.

"If you're hungry, 'our friends' have prepared a welcome meal for all of you."

"Starved," I said as we walked back over near the

women who were cooking, and I could see an open covered pavilion where tables and chairs were assembled.

"The pavilion is a central meeting place for us. We have our meals there, and we also conduct our religious services there."

I nodded again, and then looked at him. "I'm sorry if I'm not talkative, but I have major jet lag after flying into to Cape Town yesterday, and then making my way up to Johannesburg and the ride today."

"Totally understandable, and I know you'll sleep well tonight," he added with another pat on my back.

With a fire blazing in the distance to provide light, we all sat shoulder to shoulder, Americans and 'our friends,' as we ate and shared fellowship. I would learn that meat was a mainstay of the diet in this land, and tonight was no exception. There was roasted zebra, giraffe, and antelope, which I had to admit it was far more mild tasting than I imagined and tasted like the venison I had from my hunting trips. Another surprise was the mongongo fruit with its velvety, smooth layer of edible flesh beneath the shell, and then the tasty nut that was in the middle. Lastly, the women were kind enough to make sure that they offered some sort of dessert as they knew their American friends loved and missed their sweets so there were fresh melons drizzled with the most delicious honey I had ever tasted.

During the meal, I learned more about the San bushmen's religious beliefs and how the missionaries were attempting to introduce an acceptance of Christian beliefs. Some suggested a syncretic version by blending the natives' beliefs with Christian ones, but the Baptist church had frowned upon this practice, and so sought to do their best to totally immerse 'our friends' into a belief based on Judeo-Christian doctrine alone. Badimo had been the name given to the traditional religion of the land, and it included ancestor worship which continued to be common to many African beliefs. While their beliefs focused on one creator of the world and all that lived in it, they also continued to cling to a belief in a lesser god with power over sickness and death, as well as the power from the eland antelope and its fat as major part of ceremonies.

I found out that women were an integral and respected part of their culture, and children were not required to have any obligations other than playing. While hunting and gathering played prominent roles in their daily lives, they were not exempt from engaging in leisure activities including their music, sacred dances, such as the trance dance, and telling jokes, which the Americans never quite understood, but we still politely laughed along with 'our friends.'

I had to think as I walked back to my room with my two doctor colleagues that I likely learned more in those two hours during the meal about the culture than I had in my entire two weeks of study back home.

We were all ready for sleep, but I had to make my way over to the 'blue' building to wash some of the dirt and grime from my body and brush my teeth. Despite being doctors with awareness of cleanliness, my roommates were exhausted after flying from California, and opted to just go straight to sleep. When I returned, I unpacked my duffle bag and placed my meager clothes and belongings in two drawers of the bureau, and then when I was ready to shove my bag under my bed, I noticed that a letter fell out onto the floor. It was a letter from Jennifer. I could tell it was from her by the way my name was written on the front of the envelope, and I guessed she must have somehow slipped it in just before I left yesterday.

The lights were off, and the room was only dimly light from the large central light in the village on the tall lamp post. So, taking my flashlight, I went over to my bed, lay down, and opened the envelope. It began 'Dear Landon,' and my first thought was a 'Dear John' letter. Maybe I should just put it away and read it when I wasn't so exhausted, but I knew I wouldn't be able to have a restful night's sleep if I didn't know the contents. So, with a heavy heart, I took the letter in hand, and held the flashlight with the other so I could read.

Dear Landon,

I am imagining that you likely won't see this letter until you have unpacked your bag in Africa. It was the way I intended it. I know we barely talked after our breakfast, and I feel badly about creating a distance between us during your time home. I missed you terribly when you were in Atlanta, and I was so looking forward to us returning to normal as a husband and wife, and with our girls. None of this has been easy. It's been difficult, and it's been hell. I have to think that the dawning of a new decade, a new millennium has not been kind to us. It just seems it has been one thing after another wreaking havoc on our lives, and when you confronted me with your plans on dividing your time between Africa and Naples, it really threw me.

I understand that you have been in pain. You have obviously been hurting for some time now, and I only wish you would have opened up to me. I'm your wife, and I would have done everything in my power to help. I will admit that when you did your 'confessions' to me at breakfast, I was pissed. I knew when I married you that you hadn't been a saint as you were 31 years old, but I accepted it, and trusted and believed in your commitment to me. I trusted that moving forward after our marriage, you would be faithful to me. Then, to hear that you had dishonored me by taking other women was something I wasn't prepared to deal with. I was dealing with your addiction, the rehab, the medical malpractice litigation, but then to have our relationship thrown in the gutter was the thing that really sent me reeling. I'm actually glad you're in Africa for the next two months because it will give us both time apart to think and evaluate our relationship. I have no fears that you will cheat on me in the future, which I suppose is a good thing of your new-found religious conversion, but the hurt is still there for me, nevertheless. I hope you understand that this summer, I will be taking time to think about our lives, our marriage, our daughters. Please know that I still love you with all my heart, but I have been hurt, shamed, and embarrassed by your actions. I am asking that you not contact me during this time either by mail, phone or email, but please know you're welcome to make contact with the girls. I will just not engage in a conversation with you until you return as I need time and space to evaluate our future.

Love always, Jessica

I reread the letter a second time, and then a third time when I attempted to see any hidden words or meanings, but nothing came to light. I did notice that Jessica wasn't the young Southern girl from Ole Miss that I married. I'm not sure why, but I had never grasped her intelligence, and had always just assumed she was the typical wife whose only focus was on the home, husband and children. Jennifer had evolved in our marriage, and I hadn't even realized it. I had been so self-involved in my own work, my own addictions, and my own pleasures that I had neglected to see Jennifer other than the young woman I had married. I turned off my flashlight and lay on my back looking at the ceiling. Who would have ever thought six months ago, I would no longer be in the comfort of my million-dollar home on Gulf Shore Boulevard, but in a modest abode at the edge of the Kalahari Desert?

CHAPTER 32
Attie

*M*y phone rang. I opened my eyes. It was pitch black, but then I shook my head and it registered that I wasn't home in my bed in Naples. I was in the hotel room in Tuscaloosa. I glanced at the digital clock on the nightstand and saw that it was 5 o'clock in the morning. Hell, it was likely RaeLynn calling me again. After I left the hospital at midnight, she had called a total of eight times, and I finally turned off the ringer. Still, it didn't make any sense as I couldn't figure out how my phone could be ringing with the ringer turned off, but then I noticed it wasn't my cell phone. The phone on the nightstand was lighting up. I surmised that RaeLynn was pissed that I wouldn't answer my cell phone, so she had resorted to calling the front desk and asking them to put a call through to my room.

Shit, I said, and waited until the ringing stopped and the light went off on the phone. I turned on my side and placed a pillow on my head to block any further noise from reaching my ears. Despite the interruption, I still managed to fall back to sleep, and I awoke with a start as I felt my arm jerk, but then I heard a rapping on the door. Was I ever going to get any sleep tonight? Hell, I hadn't got back from the hospital until after midnight, and then the constant barrage of phone calls. I glanced over at the digital clock again, and now it said 6:30. Whoever was on the other side of the door obviously wasn't going to go away so I got up and made my way to the door. If this was the front desk handing me my check-out statement, I was going to be pissed – why didn't they just slip it under the door and move on?

I twisted the deadbolt and opened the door to find one of the front desk clerks with his hand raised in an attempt to knock yet again.

"Mr. Collingsworth?"

"Yes," I said a little annoyed.

"I have a call from DCH. They have said they have tried your cellular phone several times, and even rang your room, but there was no answer. Sir, I am told it is very urgent that you return the call."

"Oh, fuck," I said, and ran my hand through my hair as I nodded to him before I closed the door. RaeLynn was a real pain in the ass. Hell, she just had a baby, I would think she'd be sleeping all night, but no, she just wanted to call and harass me. I'd be damned if I was going to call her back. I was supposed to be at the hospital at 9 o'clock for the DNA test, and I wasn't planning on going there any sooner. I was going back to sleep for another hour.

After waking at half past seven, I shaved, took a warm shower, and ordered room service of an omelet, grapefruit, biscuits and coffee – I needed a full stomach to deal with everything. It would likely be a long day either way. On the one hand, I would take the damn test, wait for the results and end up flying home later today if negative. On the other hand, if I took the test and it was positive, I would be declared Ellie's father. If the latter were the case, I knew I was stuck here in Tuscaloosa for another week or two to get all the loose ends tied up, but Jack Monroe had assured me that he would get everything worked out. Jack was the top family law attorney in Naples, and while it wasn't going to be pleasant, I had faith that Jack would manage to all the nasty issues.

It was already blistering hot on that June morning, so I had dressed in khaki pants and a lightweight linen shirt. Confident no matter the outcome, I casually sauntered into the hospital, and made my way to the lab where I had been told I would have my blood drawn for the DNA test. While a quiet version of Tom Petty's *American Girl* played in the background, I hummed along as I filled out the paperwork and then presented my driver's license for authentication.

"Thank you, Mr. Collingsworth, if you will just have a seat over there, we'll call you when the lab is ready," the no- nonsense nurse stated, and shooed me on my way.

I sat down on one of the same type of chairs I had sat on in the maternity ward last night, and I waited. Within minutes, I saw my nemesis enter the lab waiting room. In his AutoZone uniform, Dwayne walked over and proceeded to fill-out the same forms that I had done.

When he turned around, he walked over and sat in a chair directly across from me. He looked at me, and then it apparently registered with him as he narrowed his eyes at me. I refused to engage and ignored him. Luckily, I didn't have to endure Dwayne's glower for very long as the nurse called me back, and I gladly made my exit.

Having gone through my adult life without ever being subject to a DNA test, I was shocked to learn from the technician that the results would not be available for at least a week. It meant that I would have to stay in Tuscaloosa longer than I had anticipated, and there was no doubt, I would have to endure wrath from RaeLynn during my stay.

"Shit, shit, shit," I said as I held the cotton ball on my arm and walked back out to the waiting room. I had thought I would likely be heading home either today or tomorrow at the latest, but now I had to hang out at the Capstone Hotel for another week.

I didn't feel like seeing RaeLynn or Ellie this morning even though I had promised to visit. I walked out the front revolving doors and headed to my rental car, but then I felt guilty. I stopped once I got to my car and shook my head. Hell, it wasn't that much. I would just go up to her room, give her a few minutes, and then I would head back to the hotel. Heck, I could just relax by the pool for the rest of the afternoon, and then head down to University Avenue this evening. I might even wander over to Sigma Chi to say, "Hello," as they always loved alumni coming by. So, with a new resolve, I turned around and went back into the hospital. I made my way through the revolving doors and took the elevator up to the third floor.

Tom Petty's song was still on my brain, so I continued as I stepped out of the elevator, but it was then that I saw the yellow crime scene tape in the hall. Why in the hell would there be crime scene tape on a maternity ward? Goodness, I had left just after midnight, and now I glanced at my watch – it was only going on 10 o'clock. I walked over to the nurses' station and inquired if I could see RaeLynn Yoder.

"Well," she hesitated. "The baby is down in the nursery so why don't you go on down there for now," she suggested and pointed the opposite direction of the taped off area.

I shrugged my shoulders, "Yes, ma'am, I replied. I guessed I could go see the baby first, but then I surmised that Raelynn was likely sleeping. God knows, she didn't get much sleep last night as she was calling me most of the time.

I glanced through the glass window of the nursery and spied only three beds occupied with babies. It was easy to tell which was one Ellie as there was a pink ribbon on the end of hers, and the other two sported blue ribbons. A nurse came over to the door and opened it slightly.

"Are you a father? Which baby belongs to you?"

I hesitated to answer her question about being a father, but I pointed at Ellie's bed and nodded.

She motioned me over to the door, "Your name, please, as I just need to check the log?"

I complied and gave my full name.

"Oh yes," she said as she glanced at the white board, and I saw my name listed along with Ray Yoder and Lynn Yoder, but there was no sign of Dwayne's name.

"If you want to just go have a seat over there in one of the rocking chairs, I will get the baby. She's actually due for a feeding."

"But," I hesitated. "I think her Mama is breastfeeding her."

The nurse just looked up, stared at me for a few moments with a puzzled look, and then went to get a baby bottle. When she returned with the bottle, she handed it to me along with a towel, and then proceeded to go over to Ellie's tiny bed.

I held up the bottle and the towel and examined both. The truth was that I had never fed a baby before, so I didn't have a clue. Sure, I'd seen by brothers and their wives do it, but I was dumbfounded.

I sat down on the rocking chair, and I accepted Ellie in my arms. She was just opening her eyes and stared up at me like she had last night. With the bottle in one hand, and the other underneath the baby, I did my best to hold her securely, but I was honestly afraid she might slip out of my arms.

"You don't have to use two arms to hold a baby, you can manage with one, and use your free hand to hold the bottle."

"But, but," hesitated. "I've never done this before."

"Oh, you are poor, poor boy," she said, and her voice cracked as though she might cry.

"Just hold her to your chest like this," she moved my arm up with the baby, and then she directed my hand with the bottle as she helped me bring it near Ellie's lips. I barely had touched the baby's lips, but I was shocked that she instinctively knew where the nipple was and latched on where she began sucking greedily.

"It's very easy, babies just know," she said. "And, every so often you will want to place that little towel on your shoulder and place her there and gently pat her back to burp her."

I nodded to her, but I didn't look up as I was totally fascinated watching the baby.

"I think you're doing just fine, but I need to run and get someone. Will you be okay with her, and I'll be back in a couple of minutes – there's another nurse here if you need anything?"

Again, I nodded, but didn't look up as she made her way out the double doors.

Just as I was getting Ellie into position on my shoulder for her first burping session, the nurse came back in the nursery with two others, a woman and a man, who dressed as a chaplain.

"Mr. Collingsworth, I have one of our administrators and the hospital chaplain who would like to speak with you," she said, and reached over to gently pat Ellie's little head. "If you like, I can take the baby now to finish her feeding, and you are welcome to follow across the hall to Mrs. Timmons office."

"Did I do something wrong?" I said as I handed Ellie over. "I admit I've never fed a baby before, but she seemed to be doing fine."

"No, son," the chaplain said with a gentle voice. "You were doing just fine, just fine," he said as he laid his hand on my shoulder.

The three of us walked across the hall to the small, sterile office that was void of any mementoes that might identify the occupant. Just a plain desk, two chairs in front of it, a dying plant, and a calendar that had yet to be flipped over to July. Mrs. Timmons took the seat behind the desk which left the two chairs in front for the chaplain and me.

"Mr. Collingsworth, we understand that you're Ellie's father?" The woman stated.

I just nodded as I wasn't sure where this was going, and if it had something to do with the DNA test, but I had just been told that it would be a week for the results. Was there another part to the DNA test that wasn't just the physical test of taking blood?

"We have some news, son," the chaplain inched forward in his chair and reached over to touch my shoulder again.

I wasn't sure I was enjoying all this touchy/feely stuff from a complete stranger, but he obviously thought it was part of being a clergyman. Maybe I had to go through some sort of counseling to accept the idea of being a father, or on the other hand, deal with the idea that Ellie belonged to someone else. Either way, I guess I would endure it, and then head back to the hotel and an afternoon at the pool.

"I'm not sure how to phrase it – as it's not easy, but . . ." the chaplain started. "Miss Yoder, Miss Yoder is no longer with us. She passed last night."

"Passed?" I shook my head not totally understanding.

"She died," Miss Timmons stated flatly.

I looked at her, and then I looked at the chaplain.

"But, but I just saw her . . . We just talked. It was only a few hours ago – I left around midnight. She seemed fine . . ." I rambled. "She even told me that the delivery went well, and she was going to be released on Sunday. I don't understand. What happened?"

"She didn't die from complications from the delivery," Mrs. Timmons paused for a second. "Miss Yoder committed suicide last night."

"Suicide," I said the 'word' even though it didn't register with me. Did I actually just say the word, 'suicide.' Suddenly, it became clear, and now made sense. The yellow crime scene tape across the other end of the hall. But, why? Why would she do it? She had talked about leaving with the baby on Sunday, she had talked about us, she had talked about us going back to Naples, about us getting married, and it suddenly hit me. Did RaeLynn do this because I had refused to marry her?

"Mr. Collingsworth, many women have a change and fluctuation in hormones with pregnancy. Many go through post-partum depression, and their emotions are often difficult to understand. They feel overwhelmed, hopeless, and they feel as if they have nowhere to turn."

So, they were attributing RaeLynn's death to post-partum depression, but I doubted it. She seemed fine last night, but just wanted confirmation that she and I were moving forward with a relationship and marriage. Now, I was going to live with the fact that if I had only agreed to marry her then she would still be alive. Would I forever wonder if her death was my fault?

"Mr. Collingsworth, are you okay? I know this is a shock," the chaplain said, and I directed my attention back to him. "Can we do anything? Do you have family here?"

"No, no," I said, and just continued staring at the stupid calendar on the wall that was still showing the month of June. In June, RaeLynn had still been alive, and now she was gone. No, I hadn't wanted to marry her, but never had I thought something like this would have happened. How could she leave Ellie? When I watched her with Ellie last night, there was pure and total love as she looked down on that little girl. It just didn't make any sense that she would end her life because I wouldn't marry her and leave Ellie without a mother.

"Thank you," I looked at the both of them, and stood up. "If you don't mind, I think I will leave now."

"Perfectly understandable, son," the chaplain said. "But, here's my card if you need me, and here's a Bible I would like you to have. It may give you comfort."

I nodded, took the card, placed it inside the Bible,

423

and left. I walked back over to the nursery and looked through the window as the nurse continued with Ellie's feeding. The nurse was intently watching the baby, so she didn't see me looking on, and I was relieved. I didn't want to go back in there, and if she saw me, I had no doubt she would usher me back inside.

I turned and started to walk back down the long corridor to the elevators. Unfortunately, I would have to see the yellow crime scene tape as I waited for the elevator, but there was no way around it. I had no idea the location of the stairwell, but I really didn't have the energy to walk down three flights of steps, plus I felt like I would throw-up my breakfast at any moment.

As I waited for the elevator, all the nurses at the station looked over me as though I was a little lost dog, but I couldn't engage. I turned away from them to wait for the elevator doors to open. I just wanted to get out of here. As soon as I got in the car, I would call Boyd. Boyd would listen, and I knew it would help to just tell him. I suddenly felt as though a weight had lifted as I thought about talking to my brother.

"What in the world are you smiling about?" The words assaulted me as the elevator doors opened, and I came face-to-face with RaeLynn's parents.

"You, wicked, wicked boy, you killed my baby. You killed RaeLynn just as if you walked in that hospital room and took her life with your own hands," Lynn Yoder screamed, but then backed up against the wall where she leaned for a few moments before sinking to her knees. I was sure everyone down the entire hospital corridor could hear her, but the nursing staff seemed to suddenly busy themselves with paperwork.

"Mrs. Yoder, you know I had absolutely nothing to do with RaeLynn's death - "

"Don't you go tellin' me that. You killed her. She was just a baby. She was only 16, but you didn't care. You never cared about her."

Ray Yoder went over to help lift his wife back up, and then turned to stare at me. I had no doubt if he had a gun in his possession, he would have shot me right then and there. I could have declared my innocence and argued that I might not even be the father, but there was no way to talk to these people. Granted, I knew they were distraught, but it didn't give them the right to accuse me of murder. Mrs. Timmons and the chaplain had both said RaeLynn took her own life, and it was well after I had left around midnight so I couldn't be implicated.

The elevator had closed so I didn't intend of waiting

for it. I turned and walked back to the nurses' station,

"Can you please tell me where the stairwell is located?" I asked as I leaned over the counter.

"Are you Mr. Collingsworth?"

"Yes," I answered straight away.

"We just received a call from the lobby that the detectives from the Tuscaloosa Police Department have arrived, and they have requested that you meet them for questioning. They're on their way up."

What the fuck, I thought to myself. Was I in the 'Twilight Zone?'

"We saw what happened by the elevator, and if you like, you're welcome to wait back here with us until they arrive?" The older nurse was obviously in charge and motioned me behind the counter with her hand.

I watched as RaeLynn's parents walked down the corridor, and the security team lifted the yellow tape for them to cross. Obviously, everyone else knew what had happened, but I was still in the dark; I was clueless as to why I was being questioned by the police for something I had no connection. One of the younger nurses must have had pity on me as she brought me over a coffee and cold Danish on a Styrofoam plate. I shook my head 'no.' I had absolutely no appetite; I just wanted to get out of here, but

I also wanted answers. None of this was making any sense. Still, I took the coffee and downed in without even thinking and leaned back against the wall to wait. Within minutes one police officer and two plain-clothed detectives walked up to the nurses station.

"Mr. Collingsworth, can you please follow us," the taller of the two detectives coolly asked and motioned for me to follow, and they led me to the same office where I had just met with Mrs. Timmons and the chaplain. This small, sparsely decorated room had suddenly become my psychological torture chamber. While three of us settled in the chairs, the police officer stood.

"I'm Investigator Gaines," the taller man stated, and then he turned to his smaller, slight companion, and I thought of Barney Fife. "And, this is my partner, Detective Bell - we also have Officer Moore from the Tuscaloosa Police Department."

I nodded to him but didn't utter a word.

"We need to do some routine questions so I trust you don't mind, but we do need to ask if you would like any legal representation present before we begin? You are entitled to have an attorney present," Gaines stated.

I hesitated for a moment – why in the hell would I need an attorney. I didn't do anything wrong. I talked to

RaeLynn ten hours ago, but I didn't contribute to her death. If these clowns thought I was guilty and needed some sort of representation, then things were really crazy. Shit, I had nothing to hide as I did nothing wrong. I didn't need an attorney. I would answer their questions, and then be on my way. Both the hospital administrator and chaplain had stated RaeLynn committed suicide, and I knew others were never implicated if someone caused their own death – heck, I had watched enough television crime dramas to know that, so I simply shook my head.

"Excuse me, we need a verbal answer," the smaller 'Barney' piped up.

"No sir," I do not wish any legal representation. "I am fine to answer any questions you have."

"Okay, shall we start," Gaines began as he pulled out a small recorder and placed it on the desktop, and 'Barney' took out a small pad and pen from his shirt pocket as he was obviously preparing to make notes.

"Please state your full name, birthday, address and occupation."

"My name is William Atticus Collingsworth. I was born April 10, 1962. I live at 450 Gulf Shore Boulevard, Apt. 301, Naples, Florida, and I am self-employed."

"Self-employed – can you elaborate?"

"I dabble as an entrepreneur in many areas. I am financially stable."

All three looked at me, and raised their eyebrows, but they let it go.

"When did you first meet the deceased?"

How morbid, I thought. Why couldn't they simply still call her RaeLynn? She was barely cold, and they had already reduced her to a 'term' rather than by her name, but I shook the thought from my head. If I could just address their questions then I could, hopefully, be on my way.

"I met RaeLynn last October when I came up to a football game at the University. It was October 23rd when we played Tennessee."

"Amazing that you remember all those details?" Moore asked.

"Well, RaeLynn was talking about it last night," I paused as they all looked on for further explanation. "You see, she said that the baby was born at 10:23 last night so she said it was a sign."

"A sign?"

"She thought it was a sign that we were meant to be together as we had met on 10/23 -"

"So, I take it you weren't planning on marrying her?" Gaines asked as he emphasized the word, 'weren't.'

"Well, it's a bit complicated. I only met RaeLynn that one time, and she had a boyfriend, someone named Dwayne, so we don't really know who the father is? I went to have a DNA test this morning, and I saw Dwayne was there, too."

They all nodded, and the two detectives raised their eyebrows.

"We understand from the hospital entrance records that you were here twice yesterday. Please tell us about those two visits?" The 'Barney' look-alike piped up as he clearly liked to just 'keep to the facts.'

"Well, I only got into town late yesterday afternoon. I came by when I got here, but I didn't see RaeLynn. I was told she was in labor, so I left and went to my hotel. She called me after the baby was born, and I came over a little after 11. I wasn't here that long. She had the baby with her, she fed it, and we talked a little."

"We know that you were the last one to see the deceased alive apart from the nurses on duty, and we have already questioned the three of them earlier."

I shrugged, "I guess so, I don't know if anyone else came by after me."

"So, what did you talk about? Did she indicate to you in any manner that she thought about taking her own life? Did y'all argue about anything?" Bell asked anxiously.

"No, no," I responded. "I really wasn't there very long. The baby was asleep when I came in, but then she fed it. She kept on and on about wanting to get married, but I told her that it wasn't going to happen. We only knew each other from that one time . . . "

"Excuse me," Gaines interrupted. "But, I understood from our previous questioning with her parents that the deceased lived with you in Naples."

I rolled my eyes and shook my head. "No, she surprised me. She came to Naples on a Greyhound bus and came to my parents' home on Christmas Eve. She stayed at my condo for a couple of weeks until I sent her back home, and . . ." I hesitated.

"You were ready to say something else," Gaines said.

"Well, she pretty much demanded I give her $25,000 or else she wouldn't leave."

"Interesting," Bell/Barney said.

"So, we have no idea until the DNA results are released whether you're the father, or this other guy – Dwayne? We're questioning him right after you."

"Just another question, did you bring the deceased any flowers."

"Yes sir, a dozen pink roses. I bought them at Publix on the way over here to the hospital last night."

All three of them nodded.

"Why do you ask?"

Gaines hesitated and turned his pen right side up and then upside down over-and-over again. "The roses became part of the evidence as they were part of the crime scene."

I shook my head as I attempted to understand. "The deceased was found in the bathroom. She hanged herself with a twisted bedsheet, and the roses were in her hands when we found the body."

CHAPTER 33

Hollis

*E*ven though it had been a hell of a day, I still gave a cordial wave to Helen as I pulled out of the driveway, but she remained still as a statue with arms folded across her chest. It hadn't been a pleasant morning. Most everyone cleared out of Naples in July as the heat and humidity made it nearly unbearable. While the city was flooded with people in the winter months, it was like a ghost town in the summer. This was a boon for me as the moving company gave me a great deal, but that was as far as my luck had lasted. Helen proved to be difficult. While I could have worked with the movers in a matter of a few hours to clear out my personal belongings, she had wanted to be front and center, and so it had taken double the time. I wasn't sure why? Did she think I would take anything of hers? At least she had relented to my suggestion to let the kids go over to Jennifer's house so they would not have to witness me moving out of the home.

My new house was in Olde Naples just a block away from all the shops and restaurants on Third Street. It was a Key West styled house painted peach and trimmed in white with light green shutters. Stu said it looked like rainbow sherbet. I laughed as I looked at it again, and I had to agree. Bright red geraniums and ivy overflowed from the window boxes, and the white picket fence gave it a storybook air of whimsy. It wasn't something that Helen would have liked as she was always so no-nonsense and streamlined, but Stu and I loved it.

On the drive down to my new home in Olde Naples, I was enjoying the peace. Even though it was the middle of summer, I had the top down in my car and the heat was relaxing me, but suddenly my phone rang. I looked down and saw it was Boyd. It was unusual as Boyd didn't usually call me out of the blue. Sure, we were pleasant to one another when we ran into each other at the brokerage firm, or at family functions, but it wasn't as though we ever went out of our way to just call one another to talk. I really didn't want to engage. I had a rough morning with Helen, and now

I was getting ready to direct the movers to unload everything at the new house. The light went off the phone, and I turned up the radio. Within a few seconds, the phone started ringing for the second time, and I looked over. It was Boyd again. It was Saturday so it was unlikely to be some work-related issue, but even if it were then I knew it could wait until Monday morning, and frankly, anything else could wait, too. In the past, I used to be accommodating with the family and jump at their whims, but I had suddenly become more assertive since I got involved with Stu, and this obviously wasn't setting well with Boyd.

I pulled up in my crushed shell driveway and parked my car as closely to Stu's jaguar as I could so the movers would have room to unload and walk up the pathway to the front door. With my arms loaded with three orchids, I started up the path, but was met with a breathless Stu as he came bursting out of the front door.

"Hollis, thank goodness you're here. I was just getting ready to ring you. Boyd just called. He's been trying you, but no answer," he paused as he came down the steps to relieve me of two of the orchids. "Is your phone charged?"

"Yes," I answered a little annoyed. I just wanted to have a relaxing afternoon and evening after leaving Helen's

435

wrath, and the last thing I wanted to do was deal with any issue with Boyd and work. "I know he called, but I'm sure it can wait. The movers are right behind me. I'll call him back after they leave."

"No, no, no," Stu reprimanded me like a child. "Something is wrong. I could hear it in Boyd's voice – you need to call him right away," he further admonished me as he sat down the two orchids on the table between our two rocking chairs on the front porch and took the last one from my hand before shooing me inside. "Just go on in and call him back. I'll take care of the movers when they get here. I wouldn't think you'll be too long."

I went inside and walked over to the bar, which Stu had more than adequately stocked a few days ago. I pulled out the bottle of Jack Daniels and reached down to the mini fridge to get a coke. I was still reeling from Helen and I needed to relax for a moment before I called. I made my cocktail, and then went over to the new stripped sofa that Stu and I had just purchased.

I untucked my polo shirt and pulled my phone out of my shorts' pocket before I sat down. The dark liquid not only cooled my throat, but I felt the earlier tensions release as the liquid moved throughout my body. I leaned my head back and held my phone up. I flipped it open and dialed.

"Hollis . . ." Boyd answered on the first ring.

"What's going on -" I interrupted before he could say anything.

"Something's happened," he said, and his voice was ragged.

Immediately, I thought it had something to do with Attie. He had left for Alabama yesterday. "Is Attie okay? Did RaeLynn have the baby?"

"It isn't about Attie or RaeLynn, Hollis?"

I was silent, and then my thoughts raced to Landon who had left for Africa a few weeks ago.

"Are you at Helen's, or at your new home?"

"New one," I answered without any feeling as now I was beginning to get scared.

"I'll be right there," he said. I ended the call and drained my glass in one long gulp. I sat there staring at the front window, and at that moment I saw the moving van pull up out front.

Stu walked in from the kitchen, and I could see the concern in his face. "What's going on, Hollis?"

"I have no idea," I said shaking my head. "Boyd has something to tell me, but he wouldn't do it over the phone. I thought it might have to do with Attie or RaeLynn, but he said it didn't – maybe it's Landon?"

"Listen, we don't need the movers in here right now," Stu said as he stood at the door and looked back and forth between me and out front. "I'm going to give them some cash and tell them to walk on over to Ridgeways to have a drink. Something's not right, and the last thing we need is for these movers to be here when Boyd comes over."

"Good idea," I mumbled as I watched him walk out the front door and down the steps to the moving van.

Within minutes of the movers going for their respite, Boyd's Ford truck pulled up out front. He jumped out and headed up our path. Stu let him in, and I could tell something bad had happened from the look on his face. The last time I had seen this look was when we were little, and it was when Landon had his accident at the pool in Tuscaloosa.

"Hollis . . ." he started, but hesitated. "It's Mama."

I shook my head in an attempt to understand where he was going with this, and Stu came over and sat down next to me on the sofa.

"There was an accident -"

"What sort of accident," I barely got the words out.

"A car accident," he said flatly.

Stu reached over and took my hand.

"Is she okay?"

438

Boyd didn't answer but looked down at the floor so I couldn't see his eyes.

"Boyd, you're not answering me," I said as my voice rose higher. "Is Mama okay?"

"She's gone," he said as his voice cut out; he was void of any emotions.

"Oh my God," Stu said as he raised his hand to his mouth.

"When, how, what?" I stammered trying to make sense of it all.

"Not, now," Boyd hesitated. "I think we need to get down to the house. Daddy is there by himself. And, we have to call Landon and Attie."

"Of course, you're right," I stood up, but suddenly felt lost as to which way to turn. Stu took a hold of my shoulders and directed me over to Boyd's side. "You've had a shock, but Boyd's right, you both need to get down to your father's house. I will get the movers to bring everything inside, and just put it here in front – we'll sort through it all later. As soon as they're done, I'll drive down, but y'all call me if you need anything – you hear?"

Both Boyd and I nodded, and we walked in silence together out the front door. I followed Boyd to his truck and got in – we were in a daze.

439

Mama had been out shopping. She had left home after breakfast and headed out on her errands in her little Mercedes convertible. We later found her 'to do' list that she had left behind on the kitchen desk. Her usual stops were all there: the dry cleaners, the Paper Merchant for invitations, Jacobson's at Waterside, Wynn's market, and 5th Avenue Florist. It had been a busy day, but at some point, she had stopped to get a bite to eat. As much as Mama was one of the matriarchs of Port Royal society, she was still a Southern girl at heart who loved the foods from her youth. Mama had pulled into Kentucky Fried Chicken. We were told by the police department who had investigated the accident that instead of going inside, she had opted to go through the drive thru. Mama had ordered two fried chicken legs, a biscuit, and a large Diet Coke. As she was waiting to pull out into traffic on 41, she had started eating a chicken leg, and apparently that's when it happened. She had pulled out in front of another car, and it had been instantaneous. We were told that she may have lived despite the impact, but the cause of death had been determined to be due to choking on the chicken leg.

Boyd, Stu and I sat in the family room of the Port Royal House. The police investigator had just left, and we were all still in disbelief. Daddy had taken a couple of Mama's valiums along with some whiskey and retreated to the bedroom. No one had any appetite, but we were all attempting to numb the shock with a steady flow from Daddy's bar. Both Boyd and I were putting off the inevitable, but we knew we had to telephone our brothers.

"Botswana is six hours ahead of us, do you think we should wake Landon or wait until morning," I asked.

"Well, he's gonna have to get back to the city from his camp, and arrange a flight, I think y'all should go ahead, but that's just my opinion," Stu said as he crossed his legs and nervously shook the ice in his glass.

"Okay, I'll call Landon, if you will call Attie?" I said and looked over at Boyd. "Attie's always been closer to you anyway so it makes sense that you call him."

Even though it was nearing 9 o'clock, the sun still hadn't set, and we all looked out through the glass doors to the back patio as the sun was sinking low over the water of the cove. Just hours ago, Mama had glimpsed this view, and now she was gone. I still couldn't believe it. Mama was only in her early sixties, and it was just so sudden. I had spoken briefly to her over the phone yesterday afternoon about my new house and the movers, and while she still wasn't thrilled about me being so open about moving in with Stu, she had stopped giving me the silent treatment. Who knows how things would have evolved, and I hoped she would have come to accept Stu as my choice for a partner, but I guess I would never know now?

Boyd stood up and smoothed down his shorts. "I'm gonna go out on the patio and call Attie. I feel like I'm hyperventilating in here, and I need some fresh air," he finished and went over to refill his glass before going out.

We both nodded, and I made my way to the kitchen desk to look up Landon's international number. Daddy had said Mama wrote it in the address book. I saw Mama's shopping list again and moved it out of the way. I nearly wadded it up and threw it away but thought better. I took it and carefully slipped in between the pages of her address book; I would tell Daddy later it was there if he ever asked. I flipped through the book several times, but then was relieved to find Landon's contact information was in the front and written on a yellow sticky note on the inside cover.

I sat down at the desk and dialed up the

international number on the land line. After several clicks, I heard an old-fashioned ringing on the other end. No one answered, so I tried again. Granted, Botswana was six hours behind us in time, but it was a medical facility so I couldn't imagine that someone wouldn't be manning the telephones; the second time proved successful.

"Good morning, International Missions and Medicine," said a distinctly British feminine voice.

"Hello, my name is Hollis Collingsworth, and I am trying to get in touch with Dr. Landon Collingsworth – I'm his brother, and it's a family emergency," I found myself talking louder than normal even though our connection sounded as though it was just across town rather than over the Atlantic Ocean.

"Dr. Collingsworth is here, but I'm almost sure he is asleep. I will have to get someone to fetch him for you. It may take a while. Would you like him to return your call?"

"Yes, but please do so as soon as possible. It's a family emergency, and I need to speak with him right away. Please let me him to call Hollis at our parents' home. . . he knows the number."

"Yes, Mr. Collingsworth, I have written down your details, and please expect a call from your brother shortly."

I walked back in the living room from the kitchen

desk, and Stu and I both watched through the glass doors as Boyd paced back and forth on the patio. He had obviously had luck getting right through to Attie, and so we waited.

"I just peeked in on your Daddy, and he was snoring away. It's a good thing he's getting some rest – he's not been the same since he got the news."

I nodded in response, "Thanks, Stu, I appreciate everything."

"No problem, I know you'd do the same for me."

At that point, the landline rang, and I made my way back to the kitchen.

"Hello," I said.

"What's going on Hollis," Landon said over a connection that now had static on the line. The previous connection had been crystal clear, so I wasn't sure what had happened.

"Can you hear me okay?"

"Yeah, go on, but just talk a little louder."

"Landon, it's Mama, she's been in a car accident-"

"How's she's doing?"

"Landon, she's . . . she's gone," I said, and my voice cut-out again.

There was silence on the phone, but I knew he was still there as I could hear the crackling on the line.

"She died," he said flatly.

"Yes."

"Does Jennifer know?" He asked directly.

"It just happened this afternoon. No, we haven't had a chance to call her. Boyd is just now calling Attie – Attie left yesterday for Tuscaloosa as RaeLynn went into labor early."

"Okay, okay, wait a minute . . . no, Hollis," he said, and I could tell he was talking aimlessly as he was thinking and trying to sort all this out. "It will be light soon, so I'll make arrangements to get back to Johannesburg, and I'll get the next flight out. I'll try to make it to Miami by tomorrow night – don't worry about picking me up. I'm sure you've got enough going on there, and just be there for Daddy," he stopped again. "And, Hollis, don't say anything to Jennifer yet as I want to tell her."

"Okay . . . have a safe flight – bye."

Stu came over and put his hand on my shoulder and handed me my drink. "Should we go on out on the patio?"

"Yeah, sure that's a good idea," I mumbled as I continued to mentally go over my brief conversation with Landon.

"You've got to be kidding me, I can't believe it," Boyd said as he sat down hard on one of the lounge chairs.

"When? How?"

Stu and I looked at each other before we made our way down the steps and over to Boyd.

"All day . . . and, you just got out of there this evening? Why in the world are they questioning you if you weren't there when it happened?" He asked as he swatted at a mosquito around his face. "But, you're in the clear right?"

Again, I looked at Stu in total confusion. Granted, we were hearing only one side of the conversation, but it didn't sound right. Something was definitely wrong, and I knew they weren't still talking about Mama's accident; it was something else entirely different.

Boyd continued on for another couple of minutes, and then he switched his phone off before he turned around to look at us. For the second time today, the look on his face was one of mixed emotions – fear, confusion, disbelief and gloom.

He stood completely still, but instead of walking over to us, he turned his back to us and stared out at the water.

"RaeLynn had her baby last night," he stated matter-of-factly.

"Yeah, we knew she was going into labor when Attie left yesterday, but Mama . . ."

"I told him about Mama, and he's coming home, but it will be a few days before he can get here."

"Why? A flight shouldn't be that hard to get – hell, he could just rent a car and drive back. He could be here by tomorrow evening."

"It's not that," Boyd countered, but still didn't turn around to face us.

"What's wrong? What happened?" Stu asked, and even as an outsider, he has an innate sense that it was something beyond simply booking a flight home.

"Is the baby okay? Were there complications?" Hollis started to sound frantic as he was grasping at any explanation to find out the truth of what was going on.

"The baby's okay. It's a little girl," Boyd answered, and suddenly turned around. Tears were in his eyes, and I don't think I could ever recall a time of seeing Boyd cry – he hadn't even cried when he told me about Mama just a few hours ago.

He stood there just staring at us with tears, and I had no idea what to do.

"RaeLynn . . . RaeLynn," he began. "Just a few hours after she gave birth, RaeLynn killed herself."

"What?" Stu screamed, and his hand went to his mouth.

"I don't understand, why would she commit suicide just after giving birth?" I muttered aloud more to myself than Boyd or Stu as I was attempting to make sense of the second tragedy of the day.

"Apparently, Attie told her that he wouldn't marry her, and she got upset . . . She had the baby last night and he left the hotel to go back to see her and the baby just before midnight. They talked, and she was still adamant that she wanted to marry Attie even before the DNA results were revealed. She claimed she loved him . . . and wanted to be together. Well, Attie flat-out told her that he would never marry her because he didn't love her. He assured her that if the baby were his that he would always provide and do his best to be a part of her life, but that he wouldn't marry her."

"For heaven's sake," Stu said, and shook his head.

"Now, Attie has to remain in Tuscaloosa a few more days. He was questioned by the police department for most of today."

"Surely, they don't think he had anything to do with it?" Hollis countered.

"No, he wasn't even there when she hanged herself . . . Attie left around midnight, and it seems she did it shortly after he left." Boyd stopped with that comment because both Hollis and I cringed and shivered at his words.

448

"Still, he was the last person to see her alive, so he has been inundated with questions the entire day, and he has to remain there until the investigation is wrapped up."

"Is he the biological father?"

I shook my head, "They don't know yet. He had the DNA test this morning, but he has to wait for the results so that also complicates him leaving . . . the results could take up to a week."

"Just absolutely unbelievable," Stu uttered. "In the span of 12 hours, a baby is born, and both your Mama and RaeLynn are gone."

CHAPTER 34
Boyd

*T*he massive greenery of the banyan trees cast flickering shadows over the west churchyard. As the late morning sun did its best to penetrate through the twisted limbs and jungle-like canopy, the shadows appeared to mirror the desolate mood of those gathered in the intimate cemetery. Although it wasn't a large turn-out, it was pretty much common knowledge in any small-town that services are not always open to all, and not all would have even been welcomed anyway. It was a funeral which should have never been.

It was a contradiction – plain and simple. The Collingsworth boy was well-known in Naples, and although his family was one of the most wealthy and well-respected, *the actions of the son had not always produced stellar results; the pains he had caused clearly touched many. And, while George Collingsworth had made a name for himself in this Southwest Florida haven for the monied elite with his investment strategies and philanthropic efforts, his four sons had always paved their own way in the world, and it wasn't always the same route as their father.*

Trinity-By-the-Cove Episcopal occupied a central location in Port Royal in Naples. With its roots in the staid and formal Church of England, it seemed an unlikely choice of denominations to be the place of worship for the area named after the wild port city in Jamaica, but when John Glenn Sample began planning the community in the 1950's he was fascinated by the Caribbean city dominated by buccaneers. So, while the idea of foraging one's own way, independence and rebellion against the establishment was a theme that ran deep in the original Port Royal of Jamaica, there was no doubt that the Collingsworth boys were bred with that same spirit pulsating rampantly through their veins.

Although those gathered were observing the end of a life, the spirit of the renewal was abundantly clear on that late spring morning. As the impatiens and bougainvillea erupted in their vibrant displays of pink, crimson and

451

orange against the white stucco of the Church, it seemed a confirmation of another season of rebirth. And, with a gentle breeze originating from the Gulf, a sweet scent of jasmine mingled with the first hints of humidity when the weather starts to grow warmer along the coastal towns. Although several birds answered one another in unison, no one in the group of mourners paid attention to the lively fowl exchange as all eyes were focused on the rector as his words began the eulogy.

"My dear friends we are gathered here today to pay tribute to a life that has departed this world far too soon," he began as he clasped his hands on either side of his worn Bible and bowed his head in a solemn moment.

George and Marion Collingsworth were stoic. The couple were closing in on their retirement years. Their hair was silver and thinning, their movements had clearly slowed considerably, but more so, their expressions were drained. It was true that their age had had an impact as they dealt with the tragedy of the premature death of their son, but it was also the level of stress of associated with all their sons which had affected them over the years, and it was not something which would abate anytime soon.

The three remaining brothers stood side by side. They were dressed in identical dark suits, crisp white shirts and dark ties. It was clear none of them were attempting to win any sort of fashion contest as everyone knew that the Collingsworth boys rarely wore suits. The brothers were far more comfortable in Columbia fishing shirts, ragged khaki shorts and old Sperry topsiders. The brother who stood to the far edge of the group lifted his hand and attempted to adjust his collar on his starched white button-downed shirt; it was clear that he was uncomfortable as he stood facing the final resting place of his brother's remains. To his left, the most serious looking of the brothers managed a sniffle and made an exaggerated wipe to his nose before he clasped his hands back together in front of him. And, the third brother raised his hand to push back his Ray-Ban aviators as he nervously shuffled his feet in an area that was void of grass. The third brother did not appear distressed, in fact, he had the beginnings of a smile creasing his lips while he listened to the service.

"And, yes," the rector raised his voice and lifted his hands to the sky. "Our son was a true child of the Lord, and we commend him to Heaven. He gave life, light, laughter and love to his family, his friends and our town of Naples, and we will forever remember his presence among us."

Although the clergyman continued his words, it

appeared the brothers had shifted into another world apart from the scene unfolding before them. The words were being spoken, but the brothers also knew the words did not begin to describe their sibling, in fact, it was bordering on the ridiculous to raise him to a level of a saint. All three siblings begin to steal glances among themselves, and the slight hints of smiles suddenly gave way to wide grins, but then those grins turned into muffled laughter. As their shoulders began to shake, a coughing fit ensued which concealed their mirth, but the exchange did not miss their mother. Marion Collingsworth looked over at her remaining offspring and raised one of her dark eyebrows in warning. It was a warning like the ones she had given her sons over the years when they were treading on shaky ground, and while it may have frightened them into submission when they were young, it did not appear to phase them at this point. They were grown men, and they were burying the earthy remains of one of their brothers. If they wanted to laugh, then 'the hell with it,' they would laugh.

Their brother was gone, and the way they chose to remember him was not with his ashes being dedicated in this formal area by a Church he rarely ever attended, but rather with a smile on his face and the wind in his hair. As they stared off from the cemetery down the street toward the Gulf of Mexico several memories came to mind, but one of the most vivid ones were those of Saturday afternoons in the summer as he gunned the engine of his Fountain boat and roared it through Gordons Pass as he made his way down to Keewaydin Island. With one hand on the wheel, and the other around the waist of a bikini-clad blonde, he was the epitome of a wild-eyed Southern boy. As the boat radio blasted Southern rock, the brothers felt the spirit of their brother they knew so well. There was no doubt on a day like this, he would be in his element as he would be raising his beer and calling out to them, "Hey, what the hell are you guys doin'? Get out of those monkey suits and come on down to join the party – yee-haw."

"Boyd, what's wrong," I heard Tess' raised voice, and I felt as though my entire world was unstable and moving, but it was just her shaking me.

"What," I mumbled as I attempted to rouse myself to the conscious world, but Morpheus still threatened to pull me back, and I'm not sure why I felt compelled to return as it wasn't pleasant. Hell, it was the death of my brother, and I had been watching his funeral service. Dreams don't get much worse than that.

"Boyd," she repeated.

I opened my eyes. The ceiling fan was circling, but then I focused on Tess' face. God, she was beautiful. How had I ended up so lucky? She was gorgeous, but not just in the physical sense. She was a genuine in every way. I had finally struck gold. I finally found a woman who loved me unconditionally. Never in my life had any woman loved me unconditionally – not my mother, not Libby, and not even my daughter. Tess reached over to stroke my shoulder and then her hand moved up to brush the damp hair off my brow. Her smile was so damned sincere. Those eyes reached to the depths of my soul, and I watched as she closed them and lay her head on my chest.

"Your heart is beating so quickly," she whispered and lifted her heard slightly to press a series of kisses on my chest. "Relax . . . relax . . . sweetheart," she whispered between the short kisses.

I breathed deeply in an attempt to regulate my ragged breath and heart rate, but it was becoming difficult as I was also becoming aroused.

"What's wrong? Is everything okay?" She raised back up on her elbow and I saw the concern in her eyes. "Wait," she abruptly answered her own question. "I'm sorry - that was a ridiculous question. Of course, you're not okay. Who would be? Please know I'll be there with you today, and you can make it through."

I finally felt as though I had fully awakened from the dream, but I just continued to stare at the ceiling and did my best to rid myself of the image of my brother gone.

"I was at a funeral."

"Yes," Tess uttered. "Boyd, you know that we're going to the funeral today – 2:00," she stated very matter-of-factly. "I know it has to be difficult, but you'll make it – you're strong."

"Attie?" I said as I was still pulled back into my dream. Tess shook her head and looked at me with a confused expression. "Attie – you know he'll be there?"

"No, no," I shook my head. "It was Attie. It was Attie. It had happened to Attie?" I continued to question, but Tess was looking at me like I had lost my mind.

There was no doubt that the stress of the past few months had been taking its toll on me. It wasn't just my world. The New Millennium had not been kind to any of the Collingsworth boys. It wasn't that change hadn't been craved or needed; we were all desperate for relief, but that liberation had come at a hefty price for all of us.

I was still having a difficult time coming to grips with the reality. Had it only been a few week ago that we had spoken? Everything had seemed fine, or rather as fine as it normally was, but maybe death is better that way. Time is not wasted on regrets, or false flattery, since you know you will see the person again, and there is the ability to always create more history. Events can be changed, and wrongs can be corrected, but isn't that always the case? We always think we have more time. We always think we have one more day to correct damages we have wrought on one another. But, what would we do if we knew that life was so short? When we have no idea that death is imminent, it doesn't allow for either side to make amends. Is that somehow preferable to being able to put one's affairs in order, and allow one to say 'good-bye?' What if we knew that we might not see that person again? Would we finally treat them with respect, honor, and see the good they have contributed with their lives? Maybe, or maybe not.

My thoughts were racing, but I didn't have time to contemplate 'what if's?' I had to get ready for the funeral.

Epilogue

Boyd

"Hey Boyd," Landon came over and patted my shoulder before giving me an awkward hug. I honestly could not recall ever getting a hug from Landon. I clearly remembered the pushes, shoves and fights, but I don't ever recall Landon embracing me - ever. I assumed it was related to his recent conversion and his love of all mankind, which obviously now included his brothers. "You know God is always with us when we go through trying times, and He will carry you through this time."

I nodded to him, but it was a dismissal. I'm sure Landon could sense I didn't care to further engage with him and listen to him expound on his new-found religion. He nodded and retreated. obviously, to seek another to convert. I turned to place my arm around Tess' waist, and suddenly realized that her tiny waist was beginning to expand; I patted her small bump with my other hand, and then we made our way across the churchyard.

It has been a little over two weeks since Mama had died, and we were all doing our best to comes to grips with her passing. As Mama had wanted to be cremated, we had delayed the memorial service until Attie could return from Alabama. As a result, more had been able to attend and there was an outpouring of friends in addition to our family. I looked around the beautifully manicured lawn where we all gathered at Trinity-By-the-Cove Episcopal.

Hollis was standing awkwardly by a banyan tree with Stu. As much as Hollis and I had been at odds our entire life, I actually felt sorry for him as he appeared beaten and weak by all the recent events of the past few weeks. While he claimed he was relieved and happy to finally be living a life true to his feelings and desires, I could tell he was still having a difficult time with his decision. Helen and the children were in the distance and well-away from Hollis and Stu. I knew their divorce was not going well, and Helen was determined to stay as far away as socially acceptable, but also to keep their children away from Hollis' lover. And, while I had always imagined that Helen leaned toward masculinity, and possibly being a bi-sexual herself, I had it totally wrong. She had obviously needed to take on a more domineering role in her marriage to compensate for Hollis' weaknesses, and this had come across as a woman who was neither delicate nor feminine. I had a new sense of admiration for Helen. Actually, Tess confided to me that Helen had been devastated by Hollis' betrayal of their marriage vows, and now she was doing her best to shoulder the burden of not only raising their children alone, but she had also returned to work full-time as an accountant. Still, I was torn with my loyalties as when Hollis looked at Stu, it was a look of genuine love that I had never observed when he had been married to Helen. It was sad. The fact that Hollis had chosen to leave the family home was one thing, but the friction between Helen and him meant that he was seeing the children far less, and this was reprehensible in my book. You never allowed anyone or anything to keep you from your children. I wasn't a saint, but when I left Libby, I was still doing my best to be there for Carly and Perry. It wasn't easy, but they would never say that I abandoned them when I left the marriage. Children don't forget, and I was sure Hollis would regret his fling at some point once his endorphins had run their course.

"Hey there, Boyd, Tess," Hollis smiled in relief as he appeared thankful Tess and I had finally walked over to talk to him. He reached over to hold Tess' hand and then kissed her on both cheeks as though he was a Frenchman. She returned the sentiments and smiled over at Stu before she leaned over to kiss him in the same manner. God, they were a cordial bunch.

Hollis knew better than to greet me with a kiss, so

he gave an obligatory pat on the shoulder, as did Stu, and I simply reciprocated with a nod.

"Are you doing okay?" I asked.

Hollis shrugged and raised in eyebrows in a return question. In truth, none of us were doing 'okay.' How could we be?

Landon came walking up with Jennifer, and I saw that they were holding hands. Despite, the fact that Landon had stunned Jennifer with his conversion and confessions, it appeared as though his time away in Africa had been a good thing as it had allowed the both of them a period of time to cool down, and reevaluate their marriage. And, from the looks of things, they seemed to have reached a level of mutual respect.

At that point, all six of us turned to look across the way as Attie walked up gently cradling his daughter. The baby girl was adorable, and she was perfect in every way despite all the abuses of alcohol and drugs consumed by her parents. Still, she was obviously a blessing from God in so many ways. After RaeLynn's death, it had been a wake-up call to Attie in more ways than one; he had abruptly stopped all of his vices at the baby's birth. There was no more smoking, no more drinking and no more drugs, and he was due to start working at Daddy's firm once he passed his

Series 7. It didn't take any sort of intervention, or AA meetings; Attie had quit 'cold turkey,' and he was doing great. His eyes were clear, he had put on some much-needed weight in just two weeks, but there was a clarity about him I hadn't seen in years. Yes, it was his doing, but still there was no doubt that the main reason for my brother's transformation was the little girl he held so tightly and so proudly.

"How is Miss Ellie?" Tess cooed as she reached out to touch the small foot enclosed in the delicate pink knitted bootie.

Attie beamed, and I had never seen him look so well. He was finally focused. Now, he had a mission, a goal, and a reason to live. Although RaeLynn had died, it would still take time until all the legalities were worked out, but the bottom line was that the DNA results had proved Attie was most certainly the baby's father; RaeLynn had been correct the entire time despite all of our doubts.

"She's just an angel," Attie boasted as the baby murmured and cooed in return and snuggled her little face into her father's chest.

"Haven't you always wondered what babies are thinking?" Stu asked patting the baby's little knitted cap, and we all glanced up as Daddy walked over to join us.

"You never know, but I've always heard they intuitively recognize the voices of their family," Landon offered after he heard the question.

"She just woke up," Attie added with a proud a smile as he looked down and moved aside the light pink blanket, and then turned the baby's face around from his chest. It was at that moment we all saw Ellie awake for the first time. Her dark eyes took us all in, but those were the eyes of an old soul – not a baby.

Although we had all heard Stu's question and Landon's answer, we remained silent. We were all mesmerized by those dark eyes of Ellie. They were the same eyes that Daddy, Landon, Hollis, Attie and I had seen before. They were the same eyes we had seen our entire lives, and the silence spoke volumes. Marion Collingsworth, was now gone, but it was clear that she lived on in those eyes of her granddaughter.

Special recognition to the songs and lyrics from the following artists: "Green Grass and High Tides Forever" by the Outlaws. Copyright 1975 Hughie Thomasson. "Cotton Fields" by Credence Clearwater Revival. Copyright 1940 Huddie Ledbetter. "Ramblin' Man" by the Allman Brothers. Copyright 1971 Dickey Betts. "Bad Moon Rising" by Credence Clearwater Revival. Copyright 1967 John Fogerty. "Never Been to Spain," by Three Dog Night. Copyright 1971 Hoyt Axton. "Caught Up in You," .38 Special. Copyright 1981 Jeff Carlisi, Don Barnes and Jim Peterik. "I Can See Clearly Now," by Johnny Nash. Copyright 1972 Johnny Nash. "Seminole Wind," by John Anderson. Copyright 1992.

4 North
point.
Trail

M

March 11

chandra A

843 - 592 -
2227

CPSIA information can be obtained
at www.ICGtesting.com
Printed in the USA
FSHW010610310121
78050FS